BLOOD OF THE REAPER

CONSCIOUS NIGHTMARES
BOOK 1

Copyright © Harley Jane Rose

All rights reserved. No part of this book may be reproduced in any form or by any electronic or mechanical means, including information storage and retrieval systems, without permission in writing from the publisher, except by a reviewer, who may quote brief passages in a review.

No portion of this work may be used for training artificial intelligence without written permission from the author.

This is a work of fiction. All characters, organizations, and events are the author's creations or are used fictitiously.

ISBN details:

Ebook: 978-0-6486445-6-9

Paperback: 978-0-6486445-7-6

Hardcover: 978-0-6486445-8-3

Cataloguing-in-Publication Data

Summary: Azariah hungers for life as a Reaper, the elite class of humanity protecting a dying civilization from supernatural threats.

First Edition: October 2025

Cover design © Jaqueline Kropmanns

Editing and Formatting: Chloe Higgins at Booklyst Editing Services

ALSO BY

Tarot Underworld Series
Spells of Tarot & Tragedy (Book 1)
Spells of Revenge & Requiem (Book 2)

For all those sick of feeling powerless? You never were.

Embrace your strength.

One person <u>can</u> change the world.

Author's Note

vii

Please note that this book contains explicit language and scenes, so reader discretion is advised. A content warning is listed at the back of the book for those who want to check them before diving into the story.

PROLOGUE

I've survived the Culling ... Well, almost.

I figured someone, someday, might need my side of the story.

Chapter One
Peace of the Earth

Azariah

The afternoon sun filters through the magick-enhanced skylight at the top of the cave, beaming golden light onto the foliage and soil of the garden bed. The air smells of a beautiful mixture of fresh leaves and a melting pot of warm herbs. With a deep breath, I close my eyes to enjoy a moment of relative silence, hearing only roars and rumblings. It will always remind me that, outside of the Culling, we are not safe. It's up to us to make sure we stay alive if we venture outside. But at least for the day, I am safe and thankful.

I open my eyes, my vision adjusting to the brightness of the underground room, and force myself to focus on the dancing shadow the sunlight and leaves create. Walking further in, I reach my fingers out to the nearest plant. They meet the brittle dryness of a dead leaf. With a sigh, I drop my hand, checking the entryway for others. Thankfully, no one else is around.

The garden bed is beautiful. Each plant is alive and flourishing, except for the singular dead leaf. In this room, among the earth and greenery, it is peaceful. Despite having to leave it all behind in a matter of weeks, I know that no one has ever looked — or will ever look — after this garden better than I have. No one understands the plants the way I do, though not many have wanted or needed to try with me here.

I'm the one who provides the best food and medicinal plants, saving so many in the Culling — some without their knowledge. And now? It's someone else's turn to try. Let's face it, they'll never do it as well as I do.

It hurts to think about too much. The dull ache that began pulsing in my chest early this morning sharpens at the thought of leaving. Even though it's what I've wanted for so long, I feel the need to individually farewell each plant that kept me grounded and sane throughout my time in the Culling.

Footsteps crunch down the dusty walkway behind me, catching rocks in the swing of the stride, the noise echoing toward me as though the tiny pebbles could reach me. I turn, feeling the peace in me disappear before anyone can see it on my face. Rolling my shoulders back, I take a deep breath, inhaling the fresh scents of the earth around me. I already feel my lungs tensing as the tough mask of indifference passes over my face.

The small boy, possibly nine years of age, saunters into view like I don't have better places to be than waiting around for the little shit. I need to teach him the secrets these plants hold for survival so he can take over providing the necessary items for the children in the Culling. I don't know who decided this boy was my successor, but they clearly didn't stress its importance, judging by the way his lazy, naïve eyes amble to meet mine.

"Azariah?" he asks, like my name is odd in his mouth.

I roll my eyes and nod. My lips pull further down, tightening in a scowl. Like I'm not the only one who could be standing here waiting for him to take his time to arrive.

The moment he registers my irritation, fueled by the intensity of my gaze, his brows furrow. His small steps hasten as he moves to stand beside me, his chestnut-brown eyes looking over the vast garden around us. His gaze flickers back and forth between the plants and my face, no doubt clocking what everyone always notices. Surprisingly, he presses his lips shut and says nothing.

"Good," I breathe quietly, hoping the child takes note of what could save his life. I'd hate to waste my words explaining to him why this is important. "Did you request this assignment or were you randomly allocated by the Elders?"

The little boy's eyes scrunch as the tip of his nose turns up. "Why would I request to play with *plants*?"

I run my tongue over the front of my teeth behind my pressed lips, fighting the involuntary reaction that forced its way up my throat. The heat that flushes my head and neck is nearly unbearable.

"*I* did," I say, the flatness in my voice a monotone I can't undo. "What did you request?"

"Meal hunters," the little boy replies, as if it were obvious.

Let's face it, it was. I sighed, aware that meal hunters were the most popular choice when one finally became old enough to pull their weight for the people of the Culling. It had a high mortality rate, sending hunting parties past the safety of the Culling tunnels to kill animals in the forests outside the city. It was also the most appealing option. Every human child in the Culling dreamed of being a Reaper one day, and joining the meal hunters was the most similar you could achieve until after the Crucible.

It's exactly the reason my best friend, Holt, had chosen it so long ago. Now he is a physical force to be reckoned with.

I preferred the more subtle survival arts. Just as vital, if not more, and is hidden from sight.

Maybe this child could realize that.

"Each separate bed keeps plants with a particular purpose together," I start, walking beside the first line of garden beds, enjoying the fresh smell that surrounds me. "All of these are herbs, some with alternate purposes than just simply being seasonings. You see that orange one there? In large doses, it can put a person into a deep sleep, good for certain medical procedures. That one over there," I say, pointing to a particular bushy plant with jagged edges on its leaves, "acts as a settler for the stomach if one is queasy or pregnant."

The young boy's eyes race as I point out plant after plant, focusing intently everywhere I point, before dashing to the next, logging the information. His cheeks flush and his fingers fidget. Not too bad for his first time in the greenhouse cavern. Maybe there's hope for this child, after all.

"There's food and sustenance here as well as down the other corridor, medicinal plants over there, and poisonous plants are sectioned away against that back wall. The notebook in the satchel bag by the entryway has notes from all those who have come before you, including me. It tells you which plants are which, how often each plant needs watering, how to prune, weed, and maintain them, and what happens when they get sick."

He giggles in response, the sound nearly a scoff as it bursts from his lips. "Plants get sick? Like ... like people do?"

I don't laugh. My lips don't move as I watch him ridicule the idea that has caused me so much stress before.

"Yes. Plants are living things, and if not cared for, they get sick. They die and you could die. Understand?"

"Lighten up, okay?" the little boy says, crossing his arms over his chest as he stares up at me. "You're acting like a *pixie* with all your tree-hugger talk."

My stomach plummets, his words slapping me in the face, and heat burns deep in my stomach. The dry rancid taste in my mouth, I'm all too used to, surfaces. The derogatory name isn't new — it's a recurring insult people have branded me with, allying me with fae filth because I'm the only human they've known with jade eyes. I know my similarity to their glowing green irises, but apparently, every person I meet feels the need to remind me, as if I could forget. None of them — including a fucking ignorant child getting my help for free and disrespecting it — take me seriously. But that's their fatal mistake.

I plaster an innocent smile on my pale face, watching his face contort in confusion, his little brown brows furrowing. "What's your name, dear?" I ask, letting my voice twinkle with a sweetness he doesn't seem to realize is laced with poison.

"Caleb." His voice draws the name out slowly, alarm bells finally beginning to make him cautious.

"Well ... *Caleb*." I let the smile slide off my face, hardening as every ounce of my fiery shines through. I step close to him, grabbing his chin tightly, feeling it twitch and resist against my hold, forcing his gaze to mine. "Get this through your thick skull. I'm here teaching you how to *survive* and keep your friends alive. Now, if you want to try and insult me again, I'd be happy to reward your stupidity by shoving some poisonous nightshade down your fucking throat."

As his brown eyes widen and his shaky breathing quickens, I know he's gotten the message.

I release his tiny face, turn on my heel, and call out behind me as I head for the tunnel exit, "What you need is in the book. Good luck making it through the Culling. Next time, don't piss off the person offering to help you."

Chapter Two
The Stench of the Earth

Azariah

There is no manner in which I could fling the privacy curtain in the 'doorway' to my room hard enough to sate the fury in the pit of my stomach. Knowing that the black sheet wouldn't block out my need to scream or be able to lock out anyone wanting to check on me only made it worse. The taste of my interaction with Caleb minutes before is still bitter heat in my mouth.

Crossing the small space in a matter of steps, I sink onto the edge of the single bed that has been pushed just slightly away from the wall. All my prohibited items stay out of view on the other side of it in the gap next to the wall. As I turn and lie back on the bed, I press the heels of my palms into my eyes, as though I can massage the frustration out. I block out the view of my water-damaged wardrobe towering at the foot of the bed, instead trying to breathe deeply and find a sense of calm.

Breathe in, I order myself. *Breathe out.*

Drip.

The sound echoes through my mind, and my body seizes in anticipation, waiting for the sound to repeat. I hope it doesn't. I'm sure I've just imagined it, trying to find another reason to stay angry at the world. The silence stretches around me. Somewhere in the near-distance,

I hear others maneuvering through the labyrinth of caves that only the survivors of the Culling know how to navigate.

You learn or you die.

When I'm finally sure the droplet noise isn't happening again, I sigh. My muscles relax into my bed, at least as much as they can on the ageing straw. I will be glad to be rid of it in a few days. Rumor is that the beds of the Crucible and reaper compound are heavenly compared to these, and I've spent months praying to whoever, or whatever, will listen that it's true.

Drip.

At the return of the noise, I sit up and my head snaps to attention. I scan the room, flipping my wavy black hair from my view as I sweep the ceiling and floor to find any clues about the source of the water. My gaze soon finds the droplets hanging from the ceiling, so close to releasing from the rock. I watch it fall from above me, disappearing down the side of my bed where it's beginning to form a puddle underneath.

Blowing out a frustrated sigh, I roll over and reach down, picking up the potted plant that is nearly overwatered by the unexpected leak. I ignore the unsanctioned weapons I've accumulated over the years, knowing they won't be affected by the water. The steel knives I've pick-pocketed off Others throughout the years are for my own protection outside the Culling tunnels and have served me well over the years.

"Azariah, are you decent?" Holt's familiar husky voice calls from the other side of the curtain, tone flat with boredom.

"Yes," I respond with a sigh, no panic at the thought of being seen holding my prohibited plant. I have no secrets from Holt. Well ... *almost* none.

The curtain pulls back to reveal my sandy blonde, shaggy-haired best friend beaming as he moves into the room. His pale skin is flushed as though he's been exercising or losing himself in laughter. Knowing him, both are viable possibilities.

When he catches sight of me sitting in the center of the bed, nursing the plant that I'm not supposed to have — much less know of its existence — his grin turns to a knowing smirk. He leans against the wall beside the doorway, thick eyebrows raised.

"How did training with the fresh green thumb go?" he asks, reminding me of the absolute shitshow I just lived through.

My mouth flattens into a hard line, scowling, as I try to come up with an apt description.

"That good, huh?" he prompts, spotting my hesitation.

The words spill out candidly before I can stop them. "I threatened to shove deadly nightshade down his throat when he called me a pixie."

There is barely a beat of silence before Holt exhales his understanding in one short breath. "Ah."

I don't want to delve into why he accepts my words so easily, and reliving my interaction with the little shit is only serving to piss me off further. Time for a subject change.

"What about your handover? Lose any children to Others today?"

A slow nod confirms the first mortality of the meal hunter group.

"One of the thirty thought it would be a great idea to play Reaper on the way and tried to fight a hungry dragayastir," he murmurs. An image of a cloaked figure sinking its fangs into a little girl floods my mind. The muscle between my neck and right shoulder tighten, and I reach up quickly to knead my fingers into it.

"How stupid can you be..." I say quietly, although the sentiment is no longer directed at the stranger child and we both know it.

Silence stretches between us. Uncomfortably so.

Until all I want is a new subject to distract me. Again.

I look down at the plant in my lap.

"I still don't know how you think you'll get that out of here without anyone noticing," Holt says softly enough that no passersby could hear.

"Trust me, I'll find a way," I whisper defiantly. He pushes off the wall, his tall, muscular frame overpowering in my small room. It only makes me feel shorter than I already am. I fight the urge to tell him to sit down somewhere and look around for a new, drier hiding place. "I'm not leaving it here for someone to realize what it is."

Despite what it might do to the health of my plant, I know the next best hiding spot for it is inside the decrepit wardrobe. Taking one last look at the thin, scraggly vines and yellow tufts, I cross the short space from the bed to the wardrobe and open the door, placing the plant carefully inside on the floor, grabbing the bag of clothing out of the way. When the door to the wardrobe is closed, encasing my secret, I can't help where my mind wanders.

"Speaking of ... child conception, or lack of, did you hear Perleena is pregnant again?" Looking back at Holt's face, I hug the bundled clothes bag to my chest. His expression remains passive, his light eyebrows raised in curiosity. It's clear the news hasn't surprised him at all. "Surely at this point, she's purposely getting pregnant to avoid the Crucible. There's no way her timing can be that good otherwise."

"I mean ..." Holt shrugs, tone rising in pitch, questioning my statement.

"She's twenty-seven! There's no way!" I fight back. Judging by how his lips tilt up, he's purposely contradicting and arguing with me for the fun of it. *Typical.*

"They did mention there was an underpopulation problem among humans."

My returning scowl should be sufficient enough to shut his argument up, but I can gauge it won't be. I've never been good at staying silent, especially when I know I'm right.

"And she's single-handedly trying to save it?" I scoff, trying to figure out what retort he has under his sleeve.

"Well, someone has to." Holt's blue eyes glance to the wardrobe and the contraceptive plant. To be fair, considering my singular focus on making it into and surviving through the Crucible tests, I haven't had to use it. But there's no harm in having it in case of an emergency. "Clearly you won't!"

My gut twists at the reminder of my circumstances. I roll my eyes, hoping he doesn't push it any further. I'm not keen to delve into the reasons why I keep romance at arm's length. Instead, I keep my attention on the challenges we must soon overcome.

"Some of us are focused on more important things," I retort.

Fates above, I hope he drops it.

"Az—" Holt begins to say, softening in a way I've seen before. And I have no patience for it right now.

"Holt," I interrupt with a sharpness I can't help. "Drop it. I have my reasons, whether you agree with them or not."

His Adam's apple bobs as he swallows slowly, and his lips press into a tight line. In the silence, I move the bag of clothes to my bed, opening the top and searching through the folds of fabric. My mood is instantly lifted by the feel of my heavy and tough dragayastir leather corset and armored padding, designed to protect the soft but strongly woven cotton basics underneath. The true weight of what the outfit signifies begins to settle into my skin. One step closer to what I've always wanted.

"Are you feeling prepared for the Crucible?" he asks, clearing his throat, impeding on my quiet moment with my new outfit.

"Please! I was born ready, and even if I wasn't, this is everything I've trained for my whole life. I wouldn't throw it away for anything. Are you?"

"Not entirely." He sighs quietly. My fingers still as I listen intently to my best friend. I can't bring myself to meet his eyes as my enthusiasm for my situation struggles to fade. "If I'm being honest ... What if I can't pass the academic section of the tests?"

I can't help the hot flash that spreads through me, taking over my mouth before I have any hope of controlling it.

"Maybe if you didn't spend all your time only training the physical set, or trying to get between Elora's legs, you wouldn't be worried about floundering right now."

"You know, sometimes you can be a real bitch," he bites back, hurt seeping into his tone. My gaze lifts to see the downturn on his face, and my annoyance fades. His thick lips push into a thin line, accentuating the sudden anguish twisting his features.

"I just ... I don't want to see you fail. I really don't. But you're suddenly worried about this *now*? I offered to help you study months ago — I *insisted* on it — and you kept blowing me off for Elora. My sympathy is just ..."

Holt's lip curls between his teeth, and his jaw clenches. I can see him fighting the guilt overcoming him, hurt furrowing his brows. My gut twists and the saliva in my mouth sours watching his inner turmoil. It's quickly squashed by flashes of annoyance. This isn't on me. I tried to help him ages ago. But I can't handle the thought of leaving the Crucible without him.

"Hey," I whisper, waving my hand in front of him, intruding upon the silence growing between us. "I'm here now. How about this? Tomorrow, you and I hit the books together. We'll make sure you know your stuff."

"Thanks, Az," Holt says, nodding in agreement.

"What are friends for if not to laugh at you but help you anyway?"

"Who knows?" Holt chuckles softly, shrugging. His light-hearted tone soothes any guilt I had that he'd be upset with me.

Holt stills and I can't help the way my body mirrors his.

"Wait, why not tonight?" His eyebrows furrow.

My body relaxes from its tense position as my lips pull up into a grin, every ounce of mischievousness showing on my face. My eyes drop from Holt's, returning to the newly inherited clothing, excitement building at the prospect of what my night has in store. As I lay each piece of clothing on the bed, I watch the confused thoughts run wild through my best friend's head.

"Do I want to know what you're planning?" he finally asks as I grab the edges of my shirt and yank it up over my head, peeling off layers of clothing until I'm standing in the damp air in just my undergarments.

"We're celebrating in style, of course. Aren't you joining us?" I grin at Holt, waggling my eyebrows as I start to dress myself in the new base clothing. The fabric is softer and better quality than anything I've ever owned before.

"And how dangerous is this going to be?"

"About as risky as my usual ideas," I chuckle. Picking up the dragayastir hide corset, I check the laced up back is loosened and then slip it over my head until it's in position, protecting my ribcage. I turn my back to Holt, showing off the back with an array of undone laces. "Do you mind?"

The corset around my waist and ribcage begins to cinch in gradually.

"I don't know about this ..." Holt says, his voice drawing out the syllables quietly.

"The laces or the celebration?"

"Celebration."

"Come on, Holt. Don't be such a pixie," I retort. My breath is squeezed from me as Holt viciously tugs the laces, letting my ribs loosen the laces slightly as he lets go.

"Az, you know how I feel about that word. I can't believe you're using it now ..."

"Why?" I turn on Holt, the untied corset loosening bit by bit with each word my lungs spit out. "Because that's what they all like to call me? If you can't beat them, join them."

My gaze remains steady as I meet Holt's, determined to prove I'm strong enough to survive the name. I don't care if I'm lying. I refuse to show anyone how the name has battered away at my soul over the years. I'll prove to them all one day just how much they underestimated the one they slurred.

"Real mature," Holt responds, rolling his eyes.

"If the fae didn't want to be known for their inability to face danger or conflict, they could remove the giant ethereal sticks out of their asses and do something about it."

Chapter Three
THE UNEVEN EARTH

AZARIAH

Everything about the streets of Skull's Rest is too loud.

Despite living with the constant echoes of it underground, it's all too much when the muffling rock barriers are removed. Out here, the sounds of explosions, screams, animalistic growls, and roars reach my ears. Every nerve in my body is buzzing with adrenaline. The air feels unnervingly different out here too, and even though I've been above ground before, knowing this will be my new norm somehow makes it all the more obvious.

The air is too dry, a far cry from the dampness that usually clings to every hair on my skin in the tunnels. My body cries for moisture as the hot air continues to blow into me. The notion of changing my home to above ground, after twenty-one long years, makes every muscle in my body tight.

I stand at the entrance to the Culling tunnels, gazing at the chaotic streets of Skull's Rest. The guard didn't blink twice as I sauntered past him in my new reaper training gear and weapons. His job is to protect us from the monsters and creatures trying to get in, not prevent us from getting out. Leaning against the hard rock wall, I let myself absorb the new scents and sounds that would soon be part of my life, or the reason

I find death. For better or worse, in a matter of days, the caves under Skull's Rest will no longer be my home. I will join the terrain above after my Crucible, in whatever capacity the Elders deem me fit for.

Chatter echoes from the depths of the tunnel behind me, and without turning my head, I know who is emerging. Trylan, Holt, Elora, and Hamish are the closest people to me. After our parents left us to the Culling, as the Elders required with human newborns, we quickly became everything to each other — friends, siblings, secret-keepers, confidantes, and protectors. For about twenty years, we had held fast to each other and helped the other survive. Our own pack.

I turn to look at them as they near, my lips pulling up in a welcoming half-smile. My rumination about the future is temporarily forgotten, replaced by the anticipation of the celebratory night ahead.

Trylan, Elora, and Hamish saunter into view first, the glow from the sparsely spaced candles in the tunnel cast dancing flamelight onto their excited faces. Behind them, in the rear of the group, Holt talks animatedly with someone I don't know. Their face seems vaguely familiar; although, anyone our age who has lived in the Culling tunnels their whole life could've been. Looking at his warm, medium-brown eyes as he moves closer, and lean, defined muscles, my teeth grind as I take stock of him. No names come to mind, but the very sight of his familiar features makes me disgusted.

The group stops as they catch up to where I lean against the wall, forming a circle. Crossing my arms, I eye the newcomer, feeling a frown threatening to pull down my lifted expression of excitement. The sight of him feels abhorrent, with how my body instinctively reacts to him. My skin heats uncomfortably under his gaze and my heart thumps unevenly.

"Holt, you've collected a stray," I say flatly, my gaze barely leaving the newcomers face. He doesn't seem to mind though, appearing amused by the whole thing. "I don't remember us talking about you bringing an extra along."

"You jealous, Delstron?" the stranger pipes up with a teasing grin.

My mouth flops open before I can stop it. I want to punch him. I want to rip out the tongue that somehow knows my name and feed it back to him until he chokes on it. Most of all, I want to stab him with the silver and iron knife my hand hovers over in my thigh holster. I don't care if this guy is a stranger to me, his features seem familiar enough to make my stomach twist savagely.

Holt's hands rise in surrender as he moves forward into the circle, ready to step between us if the tension reaches boiling point. All I can do is scowl.

"Azariah, let me introduce Seb Crane. His room is across the hall from mine and he's joining us in the Crucible this year," Holt says, rushing over his explanation.

The urge to stab subsides, although the hot ball of lead in my chest still burns a scowl on my face.

"Huh ... never noticed him before," I find myself saying, the words tumbling out of my mouth into the best version of disgusted indifference I can manage.

As though Seb hasn't noticed the tone in which my words have been delivered, he steps forward with his arm outstretched, ready to grip my wrist in a respectful salute.

"I definitely noticed you, but it's good to officially be introduced," he says gracefully, as though his life goal is to be my friend. All I can do is stare at the gesture I refuse to indulge.

What the fuck is this guy's problem? Is he dim or just incredibly self-confident and thinks he can smooth talk his way into the group?

"For those of us who haven't been told where we're celebrating, mind enlightening us?" Holt says, intruding upon my annoyance and drawing my gaze away from Seb's strong, unflinching hand.

A smirk tugs my lips. "Aw, where's the fun in that?" I tease, looking between Holt and Trylan.

"It's okay, Az, I'm sure it'll still be a great surprise, even if he gets told where we're going. I don't think any of us have been, so it's a new territory regardless," Trylan says. He looks at Holt's curious, jokingly pleading expression.

"You suuuure?" I tease with a grin, wanting to delay the answer, knowing how much of a strain this must be on his already unbeatable impatience levels.

Holt rocks back and forward on his heels, shaking his head when he realizes what I'm up to.

"Come on! Put the poor man out of his misery so he can go back to pining over Elora," Hamish chimes in, making us freeze open-mouthed. It's not really a shock. All of us, including Elora, are aware of how Holt feels about her, and she him. But so far, for whatever reason, neither of them has surrendered to the other. Hamish is always the one willing to joke about what all of us are scared to. In front of the *whole* group, at least.

Elora's cheeks turn pink as her eyes fight to stay down. In her frenzied, flickering glances, she checks the group's reactions and meets my gaze. I collect my jaw and offer a sympathetic smile and a shrug that says none of us judge her. It seems to do the trick, and her small imperceptible nod of thanks tells me I've comforted her enough. Holt is still staring at Hamish with wide eyes and a red face. I know we need to return the conversation to something else before Hamish gets wrestled by Holt and loses spectacularly.

Hilarious, alpha-male dominance shit would just prolong the fun celebratory night ahead.

"Okay, Try, you can tell him." I sigh, making eye gestures at Trylan to break this up before it turns into anything.

He nods at me knowingly.

"We're headed to an underground spot Az found called O Positive," Trylan interrupts Holt's tense, embarrassed stare at Hamish. Holt's features drop at Trylan's words.

"O Positive?" Holt echoes.

"I heard some fae talk about it a few weeks ago when I was testing my language skills. It's supposedly a place where anyone of any species is welcome to drink, party, celebrate, and *mess around*, if that's your thing, free of judgment. The only rule of O Positive is no violence," I spill, noting the approving smile of my friends reflects what I thought when I first heard it. It's a beautiful idea—*in principle*—and I hope the rumors are true.

"Yeah! Let's go fuck some faeries!" Hamish cheers, laughing a little too loudly.

Once again, Hamish's joke takes it too far.

I sigh and skewer him with a stare that tells him he needs to be quiet for a little while. He opens his mouth like he's about to say more, thinks better of it, and shuts it with a nonsensical grumble.

Normally, his jokes are breathtakingly funny. Tonight, I don't have the tolerance for too far, and his jokes haven't hit the mark.

I glance back at Trylan, very aware of how Seb has been silently transfixed with me this entire time in my periphery. His jet-black hair shines with the reflection of the candles, and his dark eyes scream with mischief. He's considering the interaction unfolding in front of him with an air of quiet entertainment.

"You ready to cause some chaos?" Trylan smiles, giving me a reprieve.

"Let's show Skull's Rest exactly what we can be!" I grin, my eyes venturing back toward the city that waits for us. I've been out there before, and the fates knew I'd nearly died out a few times, but with my crew, I feel unstoppable.

Laid before us is the sprawling city. Full of activity, it begs to be explored now that we have the strength in numbers and weapons. From our vantage point of the Culling cave entrance, we can easily oversee the distinctive sections of the city. Though many walks of life move between them, their architecture broadcasts their occupants' preferences. Over to the west, in the dark gray stone area where the spires of sharp towers climb high to the sky in jagged points and the stone buttresses are overseen by carved monsters, O Positive hides. Deep in the dragayastir territory, our planned adventure awaits.

"Do you have the directions?" I ask, glancing at Trylan eagerly. My stomach starts to flutter like excited sprites.

"I've got the directions," Trylan responds with an easy smile.

"Then what are we waiting for?" I urge, determined to be free of any further conversation with Seb, whose gaze is still trained on me.

"Hamish to pixie out!" Trylan jokes under his breath.

Holt's eyes narrow from the corner of my periphery, no doubt wanting to speak up about the use of the slur. But Hamish's open mouth pulls up in a slight grin, and it seems easily forgotten by my best friend. For now.

Hamish's long brown hair whips to us in amused shock. "Hey!" Hamish says, fighting the growing grin pulling his face with mock offense. "I'm the one who retrieved the directions to O Positive, so you can just shut it, Trylan, or I'll make sure you're first on the dragayastir drinks menu."

Despite his words, the grin on Hamish's face lightens the anxiety simmering in all of us at the idea of leaving the Culling and heading into the unknown. Rolling my shoulders back and lifting my chin slightly, I nod to my friends and lead the way into Skull's Rest, flanked by Trylan and Elora.

At the front of the pack, I fall silent, alertness robbing me of any jovial quips I could throw Trylan or Elora's way. Although Elora and I rarely have one-on-one conversations, we have a comfortable rapport between us. A silent language only we know.

I move through the streets of Skull's Rest, feeling the danger that lies in wait, even though we're walking through the human housing section of the city. Rogue predators that feast on human blood and flesh lurk in corners, waiting for their strongest time of day, when the afternoon sun finally sets. The sun's warmth on my side, appearing in between the sandstone rectangular houses, is a mild comfort. Not enough to sate the tension tightening my muscles, but relieving enough to keep me alert and not a scared, shaky mess.

The smell of smoke assaults my nose. It's fresh and new and has a hint of warmth to it that tells me it is no ordinary fire. *Dragayastir fire.*

Despite its alluring scent, the image it preludes is enough to make bile form in the back of my throat.

Somewhere, a dragayastir has changed from its fire-breathing sky form to a hunting humanoid. Some poor human's blood is on the menu. Possibly right now.

A part of me itches to stop it from happening. Another part knows that risking my own safety for someone else, when I'm untrained, can spell death.

I take a deep breath, swallow the bile, and try to forget the image knocking aggressively around my mind.

I force my heels to lift as I walk, determined not to let my thick, black boots click as I move along the uneven stone walkways. The others do the same; subtle turns of my head are the only way to check that they're walking with me. Vigilantly looking down every alleyway and walkway opening we pass, my gaze meets those of many glowing colors and the occasional non-glowing eyes of another human. All of them stop in their tracks when they catch my non-glowing green eyes looking back at them. It isn't until I rip my gaze away that they return to their business in my periphery.

I sense eyes following me as I move, the hair on the back of my neck prickling. I fight the urge to spin in circles, looking for the source.

"Turn left up here," Trylan says quietly, ready and alert but seemingly unfazed by the extra attention I'm receiving. We pass by the last of the plain stone and solid sand houses of the human sector of Skull's Rest and walk out into the central point of town.

Ahead of us, the Spire reaches to the sky, higher than anything else in Skull's Rest, including the jagged dragayastir castles on the mountainside. A cross between a human-made stone pillar and one of the fae's climbing trees, it is solid sand with ornate decorations etched into its walls that glow with green elemental fae magick. Vines hug its height to the top, with some sections more alive and reactive than I have ever seen on a plant. It terrifies and inspires me at the same time.

Around the Spire is a large open area, known to be a place that the Others — non-human creatures — congregate. As we step into the streetlights of the Spire's clearing, the attention of many eyes draw to us. My heart lodges in my throat, and I quickly turn my head to Trylan.

"Your directions took us past the Spire?" I whisper sharply, my throat constricting as bile rises with a vengeance.

"Relax, Az. Why not show the Others exactly what the new Reapers are made of?" he replies lazily as he meets the eyes of the Others around us. It isn't until he turns to meet my panicked, wide eyes that any real confusion scrunches his features. "What's the problem? It's not like any of them would dare do something in a place this public."

I want to shriek at his logic. Or maybe hit him.

Fucking idiot.

"They have before ..." Holt says quietly as he appears over my shoulder, looking at Trylan.

The group stops, this time forming a half circle so we can continue to watch the Others in front of us. My muscles coil tighter, ready to run at the first sign of movement toward us.

Trylan's face shifts at Holt's words, confusion contorting his features, and flashes of fear widening his eyes. "What?" he questions, his gaze darting between me and my best friend.

"I've been here before, Trylan, and that was the day I almost died," I hiss. My friends know the basics of the childhood story, but the details have never seemed important until now. Bringing them up was too painful to address when there never seemed to be any point to reliving it all over again.

"The day you ..." Realization dawns on Trylan's face as the pieces in his mind begin to connect. "The day you got attacked by the rogue dragayastir?" He holds his breath after asking the question, watching me carefully as he waits for a response, hoping I'll say no.

"The very same," I confirm.

The air hisses from his lips in a pained exhale. "Fuck, Az, you never told me *this* was the place. If I'd known, I never would've brought us through here."

The ball of tension in my stomach eases slightly. I won't be able to release the rest of it until we leave this climbing sandstone monstrosity, and the congregating creatures with it, behind us.

"Let's just get out of here, okay? I can feel the Other's creepy eyes on me. And I'd rather not be leered at by a bunch of mongrels," I spit as I catch sight of the hungry, orange glowing eyes of a pack of wolf shifters — luprender — to the right.

Lifting my chin and rolling my shoulders back, I meet the Alpha's eyes confidently. His gaze doesn't bother to hold my stare, drinking up the view of my tight outfit clad with weapons. They narrow as they return to my eyes and their color, a common confusion for humans and Others alike. The hairs on my skin prickle with a warning that I'm being watched. Although it isn't news to me, there is something about the way the current Square occupants shift uncomfortably to a new addition that turns my head. A cloaked figure walks in from our left, moving across the space.

The draping black robe hangs heavy on the newcomer, covering everything and hiding nothing. He doesn't need to show his face; he oozes power. Every Other in the Square shrinks away from his presence. Some clearly don't want to show their submission to him, but I see the way their body language changes as they spot him. On the robe is the embroidered crest of the dragayastir royal ruling class, the Animora family.

I know the moment I look at the figure, and feel his presence, who it was.

My avenging angel.

The dragayastir who saved me here as a child.

"Okay, it's definitely time to leave," Holt says. My group of friends shift, like everyone else who has seen the robed figure.

All except me.

My feet stay rooted to the spot, grounded as I watch him move slowly into the Spire, his hood twisting slightly as he scans the clearing. Despite seeing my friends move closer to the Spire in my periphery, my eyes never leave the Other that saved my life and has watched over me ever since.

In a way I can't explain, I know it's him. I never saw his face or spoke to him, but I know his presence. I'd felt his gaze whenever I left the safety of the Culling caves in the years since he saved me during the attack.

"Azariah, come on!" Holt calls, pulling me from the spell my avenging angel's presence has on me. None of them would understand — it's a secret between him and I. All other witnesses to what happened that day are dead.

I look at my best friend, aware of how far my group has moved away from me, and let my feet hurry after them.

When I steal a glance back at my avenging angel, shivers dance under his powerful gaze. I know he's watching me as I leave.

Chapter Four
Death's Air

Morana

The black-haired fae banshee strode through the streets of Savastral Revon — or Skull's Rest as the human tongue butchered it — with confident steps.

After the day she had, Morana should be tired or drained, at the very least. She'd been called by the curse on her soul to several children's deaths and forced to bear witness as they came to bitter ends before their lives had truly begun.

Human children were idiots, and the parents who abandoned them to those Culling tunnels were even more so. Today had been *the handover* — an annual event where those leaving the Culling and beginning their Crucible testing passed their survival tasks on to those old enough to now assist the human children population.

A human child, not yet ten years of age, had grown confident without cause that they thought they could kill a dragayastir walking by in human form. It would have been comical if it hadn't been so absurdly ridiculous to the banshee who'd had to stand watch, forbidden to help. The blood spilled had been quick, and the group they had been with didn't lift a finger to help them. They all knew the cost of stupidity.

Morana walked slowly toward the north wall of Skull's Rest, past the dragayastir mansions that towered with sharp angles and dark colored stones. Even though the sun hung low on the horizon, not yet set, the night seemed almost eternal in this section of town. The stones of the mansions and buildings were black and shiny, like a pool of darkness surrounded her. She preferred this side of town to venture home through than the other, where the fae frequented.

Morana's skin crawled under the fae gazes when they looked at her with disgust. As though she had any control over what she was. What she was born to do.

She avoided having to relive the rejection of her own kind that occurred too frequently for her liking.

Each step echoed back to her as she moved through the tight, black framed streets. It was relatively quiet, and her muscles tightened, unsure if that was a good or bad thing. It could mean she was lucky, and she had managed to find the perfect time to cross the section of town when no dangers were around.

She was rarely lucky.

As though proving her fortunes to her, a tall, imposing figure stepped out of a side street ahead of her, looking toward her as though he was expecting her arrival. As Morana moved closer, taking in the sight of his twisted horns, adding to his overpowering stature, dark scarlet skin that reminded her of the color of garnet, sharp claws that looked ready for a hunt, and glowing red eyes sunken into his face, she knew exactly what he was.

A daemon.

Despite the skip in her heartbeat, Morana refused to show her fear as she took a deep breath. Her nose turned up as she caught the smell of the daemon's rancid body, the smell of decay strong. *He was old*, she noted. The stronger the smell of decay, the longer they had been alive. No one knew why, but it was something that somehow made the species even more unnerving to Morana.

She didn't slow in her steps as she kept walking toward the daemon, her chin lifted. Her steps didn't stop until he purposely moved into her path, making it clear without a shred of doubt that he intended her to be his target.

Morana halted and reached deep into her cursed soul for the only magick she had on hand. A strain that had saved her many times before and was a last resort.

"Get out of my way, daemon," Morana said, feeling the black veins under her eyes darken against her pale skin. She met his gaze unflinchingly. The place between her shoulder blades pinched as she pushed her shoulders back and stood tall, letting her power fuel a confidence that made her feel cold.

"I don't think so," his rough voice grumbled as he smiled menacingly.

"I'll save you the trouble of figuring it out on your own. You don't want to cross me."

"Why not? I'm hungry and I can smell the earthy meat on you from miles away." His glowing red eyes flashed as he spoke of his hunger.

Morana swallowed, her stomach clenched in warning. She needed to keep moving and not let the daemon attack first, or she just might lose before she could harness her magick.

"You don't want to try it, daemon. It'll be your death." Morana knew the rumors around banshees that Savastral Revon had made up. They were complete lies, but they served to make sure that no one dared approach or attack her if they knew what she was. To attack or kill a banshee, cursed you to die, too.

Clearly, this daemon hadn't realized yet what he was dealing with.

It was time to act or else Morana risked injury and death. Tapping into her death magick, she let the tendrils of darkness spill from her like extended veins from her bloodstream. Sentient black veins with strength she couldn't begin to possess.

They picked the daemon up like he was weightless and pressed him harshly into the wall, restraining him against the shiny black stone of a mansion. His grunt of discomfort blew more rancid air her way, making an acrid taste build in the back of her throat.

As though the tendrils were aware of her subconscious thoughts before she conjured them, one of them tightened across the daemon's throat, cutting off *most* of his air supply.

"Banshees aren't for eating," Morana growled as she stepped closer to his restrained body. She knew he wasn't going anywhere until she willed it so.

His eyes widened for a moment as realization dawned on his face. He glanced frantically to the tendrils of darkness holding him. As quickly as it appeared, though, his mask of fear was covered with an angry bravado that didn't reflect in his eyes.

Morana could tell he was full of shit.

"I didn't think there were any of you fuckers left," he spat at her. Clearly, he also didn't understand the power she had over his fate right now. Curse or not, she had the power to kill him if she chose, and that much he hadn't noticed.

"You thought wrong."

"Evidently. My mistake," the daemon said tightly. The tendrils tightened for a moment before releasing slightly across his neck to allow him to breathe. "Will you let me go?"

"Don't make the same mistake again. I'm the witness to death, remember? Next time it'll be yours," Morana said, keeping her voice as even and strong as she could manage.

Taking a step back, Morana did the one thing she'd always been taught not to do in a fight and turned her back on the daemon. She wanted to present the true power that came with proving she didn't need to watch her opponent, because they didn't pose a threat, and kept walking through the dragayastir quarter.

The tendrils released the daemon behind her, but she let them trail as a warning along the street with her, dancing along the stones like children playing with skipping stones.

The daemon didn't follow her, moving away in search of its next meal that Morana was sure she'd witness later. After all, there were very few, if any, of her kind left.

Chapter Five
The Foreign Fire

Azariah

We walk through the stone streets of the dragayastir sector in silence. I can tell Holt, who walks ahead at the front of the group with Trylan, Hamish, and Elora, is annoyed with me. The moment we'd left the Spire town square and entered the streets between the sharp buildings, hurt and anger clouded his features. He knew I'd held back information from him when he saw my reaction to the hooded dragayastir royal.

The taste of my guilt at the back of my throat is hard to ignore—it's sour and strong.

I stare up at the gruesome figures looming on the edge of the building, casting their judgment on the walkway below. On me. I want to disappear and melt into the black stone walls that have probably seen so much bloodshed. I'm not ashamed of my avenging angel. Honestly, I find his supervision comforting. It's the acidic feeling burning in my mouth and stomach that I've been found out for hiding things from my friends, especially Holt, that is making me feel like shit. We always said we had no secrets from each other, and I know he's finally discovered my lie. I'm not sure if he'll ever forgive me for it.

I want to throw up, and the rising sensation in my throat proves my body might willingly comply.

"You seem familiar with the streets of Skull's Rest," Seb says, breaking the silence of the group with his transparent attempt to pull information from me.

I don't bother looking at him as I walk, letting annoyed flares of heat steal my focus. It's a much nicer feeling than the urge to vomit. "That seems like a poor attempt at making conversation." My eyes scan the walkway opening we pass, checking for threats he doesn't seem to care about. He's too focused on watching me.

"Is it? You're conversing, so it seems to have worked nicely."

I scoff at Seb's words, still refusing to look at him.

I watch Elora and Holt share a glance ahead of me, communicating with raised eyebrows — a message only they can follow — and I'm not enjoying a second of it. I've been gossiped about before, and my gut heats at the prospect of being a topic of it ever again.

There is nothing going on here with Seb. Whatever they think is happening, they are wrong.

"You're not going to get much more out of me on that topic. Given what you've already heard and seen, there's nothing more I'm willing to tell *you*."

I know Holt is eavesdropping and I hope he hears the secret message in the words I don't say, that I'd be willing to talk to him.

"Not even how you knew the Royal that stepped into the Square?" Seb asks.

I see the shift in my group of friends ahead of us. A bristling energy as they wait for my response.

I grit my teeth. "I don't."

"We all know that's a lie. We saw the reaction from both of you."

I stop walking and turn the full attention of my body to focus on Seb. He isn't going to believe any lies, so I have to pivot his attention or else I'll never escape his questions.

"And *you* care *why*?" I snap.

The group slows to wait for us. Seb tries not to show his surprise, but I see it flash across his face as he attempts to cover it with a shrug and an eye roll, continuing his pace.

I start walking again, returning my eyes to the path ahead.

"Just striking up conversation," he says in a quiet voice.

I don't buy it for a second.

"Whatever you're trying to do here, I'd give up now. I'm not interested in whatever you want here. If I haven't told my friends, I'm sure as shit not telling you." I see the muscles between Holt's shoulders tighten at my words, and guilt sours my gut again. My lips want to twist harshly at the feeling, but I force my face to stay as blank as possible.

"I'm just trying to get to know you," Seb replies innocently, to which I stay silent. There are only so many times I can tell him he is getting nowhere. "What is it you think I'm after?"

I turn my head, catching his gaze. His dark eyebrows sit high on his face, climbing toward his short dark brown hair. His knowing smile only makes the blue in his eyes gleam. He stays silent though, his smile affirming my suspicions but seemingly waiting for me to say the words.

He's testing me. He is trying to see if I'll back out of saying it. But I'm no coward. I'm not a *pixie*.

"To get your dick wet."

Holt covers his laugh with a cough up. Hamish stands frozen to the spot for a moment. Elora trips over her own feet, barely saving herself from colliding with the pavement. My attention turns to her as her usual pale, freckled skin flushes pink, and she mumbles her apologies. Once the eavesdroppers have stopped reacting, falling over, hiding their surprised laugh or standing frozen, I return my attention to Seb, hoping that has finally shut his arrogant mouth up.

No such luck.

Instead, Seb's face is scrunched slightly in thought as he watches me, barely glancing around for any oncoming dangers like the rest of us do. Like *I* do.

"You've got some teeth, haven't you, little monster?" he says, the edges of his lips turning up in amusement. Everything in me boils at the audacity this man thinks he has to give me a *nickname*. I almost wish I could breathe the sort of fire the dragayastir's sky forms possess and burn him where he stands.

"Keep calling me that and I'll show you just how monstrous I can be," I hiss, the heat in my body boiling the venom in my voice.

He ignores my tone, instead continuing his questioning. "Sex isn't something you're interested in?"

"I knew that's what you were after!"

"Not at all! But your assumption is very telling of the low opinion you have of others."

My mouth flops open as the insinuation of his words hits me.

It takes a moment of reeling in silence and stillness, my footsteps stopped. I'm not going to win this battle. And I am really sick of trying to.

Snapping my gaze away from Seb to my friends, I power my feet into action and move to join Trylan and Hamish at the front of the pack with a huffy sigh.

"Trylan," I call as I move beside him. "How much further?"

"We are ... here ..." he says slowly, as he leads the way into an alley between buildings. We come face-to-face with an impressively large, deep purple metal door. We halt, observing from a few meters away, and regroup for a moment, preparing for what lies ahead.

"Finally," I sigh as the tension leaves my muscles, and I step forward. A hand clasps around my wrist, and I turn my head to see Seb leaning in close. I want to tilt away but something in the way he looks, as though he has a secret, tells me to wait. The smell of musk invades my nose as he leans close enough for his breath to tickle my face.

"What's so repulsive about being like everyone else our age and having a physical relationship with someone?" he asks. The muscles in my body stiffen like wood planks when I realize there is no secret.

"Because that's not me," I whisper, my tone clipped as heat invades every nerve of my body.

"Because you're special?"

"No, because I'm dedicated to becoming a Reaper above all else and I'll be damned if I let anything, or *anyone*, stop me."

I yank my wrist from his fingers, ignoring the heat I feel under the skin he touched. I move toward the door before anyone can stop me again and, using my anger as driving fuel for my body, I bang my fist against the purple metal. The rattle echoes through the door. A panel slides back almost instantly in response and the purple eyes within stare at me warily.

"Paying entry together or separately?" the husky feminine voice asks, pupils scanning me up and down, only glancing at the others for a brief moment.

"Together," I respond without hesitation. There's an uncomfortable shifting of my friends behind me, no doubt unprepared for my decision.

I know that we'd all brought something of value to trade, but I have an option that would save our prized possessions. One that humans rarely consider.

"Az ..." Holt says from his place behind me. His tone is low in warning as his hand touches the back of my shoulder. "It's fine, we can pay for our own entry."

I don't turn to look at him, instead watching the purple glowing eyes drift to my companions before returning to me, dark eyebrows raising in question. "Together," I repeat with a nod, unwavering in my decision.

"In what form will the payment be made?" the woman asks, ignoring the disapproving noises from my friends.

A small piece of me revels at the power in my answer, a smirk pulling my lips up ever so slightly. "Blood."

A collective gasp sounds behind me. I watch the shifter, strong in my resolve, enjoy the surprise that crosses what I can see of her face. Another panel slides open in the door at the height of my waist and the shifter's scaled and clawed humanoid hand reaches out, her palm facing up. Despite the sight of the claws that make my heart pound in response, she holds it delicately and open as though there is no danger at all. With a deep breath, and moving quickly before any of my friends can try to stop me, I give her my non-dominant hand. She pulls it into the darkness beyond the door, out of sight. Sharp pain cuts through my palm, making me fight to hold back the hiss of air through my teeth or yank my hand back. The shifter's eyes lift to mine from where she's been staring down at our hands. As I meet her gaze, the grip on my hands tighten, guiding it to rotate at the wrist until my palm faces the floor in the dark.

I wait, breathing deeply as the initial sharpness of pain gives way to a dull ache and the feeling of warm wet slips along my skin. The captor of my hand watches me intently, eyes twitching narrower as we wait for an acceptable amount of my blood to drain. I feel like a mystery to be studied as her eyes never leave mine. I'm almost scared to look away, worried about what they might signify to her kind — if anything — if I do.

My friends stay silent and still behind me. For all we know, the woman will take my hand off if we anger her.

The grip on my hand releases entirely, and as I catch the shifter nod slightly, I pull my hand back and study it. A long, shallow gash bleeds steadily as I turn my palm up. The same clawed hand reaches out, a clean bandage offered to me. I take it without another thought and a half-smile of thanks graces my lips before I focus on tidying my hand. I press the center of the bandage on to the wound, feeling the bite at the pressure, before twisting the tails of the bandage around and around to keep it tightly covered.

Without needing to be asked, Holt steps forward, his hands reaching out and tying the bandage for me. I try not to look at Holt's face as I turn toward him, allowing his assistance. Disapproval emanates from him in waves, his muscles tight and brows furrowed. As his gaze finally lifts to mine, no longer having a bandage to busy himself with, I shrug. I want him to think it isn't a big deal, but I fear he can see right through the act.

He opens his mouth, about to address what has just happened, when the shifter speaks.

"Your payment has been accepted. You will receive six entrants passes and fifteen drinks for your trade."

The words have my neck nearly cracking with the speed in which I turn to the shifter. I shiver with a cold I can't place. I'm sure I heard wrong as I glance at the group behind me, just as wide-eyed and still with shock.

"*Fifteen* drinks?" I repeat, but the shifter doesn't bother indulging my need for validation that I heard her correctly. With a bang that echoes through the hall beyond, the door is opened. The scaled shifter stands in front of me in all her curvy glory, and I know as I take in the rest of her body that it is, without a doubt, she's a succubus shifter.

As she steps out of the doorway to let us through, she lifts her free hand toward me. I bring mine up in return, my non-injured palm open as she drops fifteen metal tokens in my hand, all varying in color.

I lead the way past the shifter and down the entrance corridor into O Positive, feeling the thrum of the oncoming music begin to rattle my bones. "Well, I guess drinks are on me! Let's celebrate!" I call to my friends.

Chapter Six
The Lottery of Fire
Azariah

The moment I step through the doorway to the corridor, I know my life will never be the same. O Positive is like an entirely different world I never knew existed and the idea of returning to my old drab one seems disappointing.

An enormous room stretches before me, the outside world hidden from it. Large, heavy curtains hide what I assume are the walls and windows in deep and rich shades of purple and red. The plush furry material is unlike anything I've seen before, especially in the human sector of Skull's Rest.

When your species fight for survival, there's no point in pretty without purpose.

Lounges, booths, and tables are scattered around the edge of the room, and in them sit species of Others I can't identify. In one glance around the room, I spot such a diversity, all co-mingling peacefully, that I lose count. In the center of the room are a throng of bodies, gyrating and dancing to the drum-heavy music played by the musicians against the back wall.

Every nerve in my body is overwhelmed by the sensory chaos. From the heavy scent of sweat, sex, and sweet elixirs, to the heat that emanates from bodies, to a cool and heavy indoor wind attempting to balance the temperature. It's electrifying.

The music is hypnotizing and unlike anything my body has felt before. Each beat of the drum shakes my bones and calls my body to sway and swerve to the rhythm. I feel the presence of my friends shift past where I've stopped to watch, no doubt on their way to the bar on the left that I spotted on the way in. I can't find a way to tear my gaze away long enough to follow them.

The bodies dance, writhing so close to each other that it holds an aura of eroticism. I never expected to encounter it, let alone in such a public place.

Someone stands beside me and I know before he opens his mouth who it is.

"I would've thought this would be repulsive to you, little monster," Seb says, his voice barely audible to anyone but me over the volume of music.

I fight the urge to roll my eyes at his words, unsuccessfully, and reply through gritted teeth, "And why is that?"

"Doesn't the very idea of sex repulse you?" he answers with an air of innocence that I know is mockery. My cheeks grow hot, and I know they flush pink. I'm not even sure, in that moment, if the rage that floods me is at his attempt to embarrass me, or if it's simply the audacity of this dickhead to talk to me when I've made it very clear I don't like him around me.

I turn on him. "I'm not *repulsed* by sex. I am, however, repulsed by the idea of getting pregnant when my reaper dream is so close. I refuse to let anyone, or their *overinflated egos*, get in the way of me achieving that," I say, tone clipped, hoping with everything in me that he'll finally shut up about sex.

He leans closer and my body betrays me, flushing with heat. His face moves toward my ear, his breath dancing along my cheek. I suppress the shiver that travels down my spine and hope he can't see the goosebumps along my bare arms.

"You know ... there are ways to stop yourself from getting pregnant. Herbs that would protect you from all the fun you could have," his low voice growls in my ear. Everything in me tightens into a hot ball in my lower stomach, and I'm thankful he can't see the way my mouth parts, exhaling at his words.

"That's illegal."

"Funny," he responds quickly, leaning back to look at me. He looks anything but amused, instead, seeming thoughtful and contemplative. My stomach tightens painfully for an entirely different reason.

"What?"

"You weren't surprised by the option."

The color leeches from my face as my body goes cold.

Fuck.

I know exactly what I've just admitted to him and it's dangerous. While I'm confident none of the Others, even with their improved hearing, are likely to hear us, the information I've given Seb is something I definitely hadn't meant to reveal.

Faltering, I stammer out the first insult I can think of to try and distract him. "Wouldn't matter either way because the idea of sex with you *is* repulsive."

"Lash out all you want, little monster, but I know you now."

My mouth flops open before I can contain it. I rein in the shriek growing in my throat. "You know nothing," I say, turning on my heel and heading for my friends waiting at the bar.

Stepping up beside Holt, I pull the metal tokens out from where I've stashed them in a holster and put six on the bar. Holt smirks as his gaze darts between myself and Seb, who has followed me and now stands on my other side, making his point silently. I make my response clear by rolling my eyes. I don't care what Holt thinks he's seeing.

"Spirit water?" Holt asks as he points to each of us, waiting for the nod of confirmation. He signals to the fae woman behind the bar that we are ready to order with a dashing smile and a wave.

"Six spirit waters, please!" he says loudly, making sure he can be heard over the hypnotizing drumbeat. The fae woman moves to the collection of containers and bottles behind her in search of our order.

Tapping my fingers on the bar as we wait, the butterflies in my stomach jump about excitedly. I almost don't notice the orange-eyed luprender in my periphery. From the side of the room, he leers unapologetically at me, even as I notice his gaze and don't bother to hide my disgust. Instead of giving up his watching, he pushes off the wall he leans against and comes to stand behind me, waiting his turn at the bar. Rather than cave my courage to a mongrel I've never met, I turn to face him, mouth pressed into a hard line as I wait for him to say what he wants to.

At that point, the fae woman returns with our drinks, passing me my spirit water — a bubbly, glistening liquid that changes color from different viewing angles. I would have spent a few moments indulging in the delightful tricks of vision, but I have bigger issues to focus on ... Like the mammoth of a man that tries to stand over me, leering like I'm a piece of meat.

"Can I help you?" I spit, not bothering to hide my disdain. The smell of wet dog overwhelms me as he closes in.

"I'm surprised you reaper cadets can handle any of that," he responds, his low voice hard to hear against the bass of the drums. His eyes glance at my drink and back to my face multiple times, as though waiting for me to prove it by drinking it in front of him.

"This isn't my first adventure with the fae spirit magick, *pup*." I plaster a smile on my face, raising my glass up in a silent toast but not drinking any of it, merely on principle.

A sneer pulls his lips up for a moment before it morphs into an ingenuine cocky grin. I feel a buzz, knowing that I've gotten to the creep.

Still, he doesn't leave.

"Is that all?" I push, rolling a finger in the air as though I can make him spit out the words. "You seem like you came over here to say something."

Beside me, both Holt and Seb have turned around to face the stranger as well, giving me a sense of security to say what I need to and be backed up by my group.

The luprender's eyes follow the movements, noting the other two in my pack. His cocky smile fades. "No, that was all. Just surprised to see your kind here at all."

"We're celebrating," I say flatly as I fight to make it clear how unwanted he is near me. Then I walk, not daring to look back as I shoulder my way past him, thankful when I sense Seb and Holt following me again.

With a sigh of relief, I take up residence in a booth by the far wall. The seat is plush and red, welcoming me into its depths with a softness that makes me never want to leave. As the rest of my friends filter into it with me, Elora on my right and Trylan on my left, I sink in relief with a heavy, breathy sigh.

"Having fun with your outing?" Elora's melodious voice drawls slowly. A knowing smile pulls her lips as she refers to what has definitely been a night of more than originally planned.

"I didn't expect this much attention, that's for sure."

"Don't worry too much. Extraordinary people will always be harder to hide." She smiles, and the unexpected warmth hits me like a physical jarring blow I don't know how to regroup from.

Mouth growing slack for a moment, I sit speechless.

"Thanks, El," I whisper, hoping she can hear how much her words mean to me.

"You're welcome. You can find some way to properly thank me when we all survive the Crucible and make it to the other side."

The idea of the Crucible and how we will soon have to fight to survive in a whole new way makes my stomach scrunch and leaden tight enough that I'm sure it will drop through me with all its tiny weight. Not that the tightness in my body has ever really gone away. It's always been there in some capacity, keeping me alert, and alive. When it comes to the Crucible, the rate of survival is low. Too low to think about without it becoming physically painful.

What if my pack doesn't survive the Crucible?

What if I don't?

I push the thoughts and stresses of the future aside for a moment, knowing that if I don't, I'll be sick.

Lifting my glass, I look around at each of my friends who quieten when they see the gesture. "To beating the Crucible and becoming the best reapers Skull's Rest has ever seen." I salute, watching as they all lift their glasses in response. Each of their faces house a wide grin I can't help but share. The lack of doubt puts my stomach tightness slightly at ease.

Collectively, we drop our glasses from the toast and bring them to our lips. The first sip of spirit water is always the one that hits the system the hardest, and this was so much stronger than any I've had before. I want to melt as the comfortable warmth spreads through my veins. As my body sinks further into the seat, relaxing in a way I didn't think that I could in public, I feel the lightheadedness grab my mind more fiercely than I expected.

Looking around the room, the colors in my vision brighten. I drop my gaze to my hands, only to see the bandage, reminding me why the drink has more kick in my body. I spot Elora following my focus to the damage on my hand.

"Be careful with that blood loss and the elixirs, all right?" she says. Though her smile is soft and teasing, I hear the edge of worry in her voice. "I don't feel like making the boys carry you home."

"Don't worry, I plan on celebrating, not losing my senses tonight," I reply, giving her a warm smile that seems to soothe her tension.

She giggles. "Not even a little bit?"

"No," I say.

Holt as he stands and downs the rest of his spirit water. He looks nervous, his big hands fidgeting as his whole body bounces on his toes. He rolls his shoulders back, takes a deep breath, and lets the spirit water take effect, his nerves seeming to disappear. He walks around the front of the booth in full view of us, stopping in front of where Elora sits on the edge. With wide, confused eyes, she stares up at him as he stands over her. It isn't until he extends his hand for her to take and asks her to dance that the confusion disappears, replaced by the brightest smile I've ever seen on her face. She takes his hand eagerly and the two hurry off to join the dance floor.

I can't help smiling after them as they disappear into the throng of bodies, my chest warming.

The room holds mesmerizing and contagious energy of celebration and fun that it's hard to believe the other patrons aren't here for us. Trylan scoots closer to me in the booth, observing the way the room interacts with as much awe as I am. Finally looking at him, the spirit water making me warm with nostalgia, I give my longest friend a genuine full smile — a rarity for me. But here, with no attention on me other than that of my friends, I can bring down the hard exterior just a little.

Trylan returns the smile briefly before it straightens out into a concerned frown. "Sorry about earlier. I really wouldn't have gone past the Spire if I'd known. I just figured it would be an interesting excursion and safer if all of us went to see it," he explains, the words tumbling out fast. He checks my reaction intently, searching for any sign of lingering anger.

"It's fine, Try. Really! I know what you thought."

"It's not fine, Azariah. I saw how scared you got."

Dropping my gaze from his for a moment, I sigh, cursing myself for showing my emotions so clearly in the moment. "Trylan," I hush. Taking a deep breath, I force myself to meet his intense gaze. "It's okay now. Really. The incident was terrifying, yes, but I've dealt with that. I'm stronger now. I was just blindsided today, that's all. If I was that scared of the Others, I'd never leave the Culling or be celebrating here of all places. We're okay. *I'm* okay. I promise."

I'm not sure if I'm saying it to reassure him or myself, but it seems to work for both.

He searches the details of my face as though he can read the truth written in my features. He nods, his face returning to a smile. "Okay, if you're sure. Can you believe we've made it?"

"Not really, but I'm glad we did," I respond as he bumps his elbow against mine playfully.

"Who would have thought that the scrawniest children would be the favorites to become Reapers in the Crucible?"

I can't help the breathy scoff that passes my lips as I think back on the bony boy I'd grown up with, who'd spent his life fighting for everything he had, same as me. The one who'd had my back as people continuously underestimated me because of my size, my eye color or my sex. He never had. We banded together since the day we'd met and defended each other through it all.

"We showed them, and we will continue to," I reply, bumping my elbow into him in response.

"We will," Trylan says, nodding. He smiles with a strong resolve that contagiously solidifies in my chest as he speaks. "Are you dancing?"

The question stops me in my tracks. All other thoughts are quietened by the idea of allowing myself such oversexualized fun. Glancing over at where Seb sits deep in conversation with Hamish, I try to gauge if he would leave me alone for a moment if I chose to indulge myself in dancing. I don't bother trying to hide the reason for my wariness from Trylan.

Biting my bottom lip nervously, I answer quietly in case anyone else nearby is listening, "I'm considering it. I'm just worried about *certain people* getting the wrong idea."

"Come dance," Trylan says without hesitation. "I promise if he tries anything, I'll punch him for you."

With a grin, I push myself out of the booth with my drink in hand and head for the dance floor.

The world around me fades away as I dance. The room past the dance floor melts into a blur of color and light that only serve to excite my senses. Bodies around me move to the music, somehow showing their individuality and unison all at once. Sweat mixed with a hint of sweetness surrounds me as I join them in their dance. I should find the scent disgusting, but I don't. The sweet and spicy aroma is unlike anything I've ever smelled. Bodies press against me, but their glancing touches feel accidental and innocent as I sway with them.

I attempt to roll my hips to the music, copying how others maneuver their bodies and find the rhythm my muscles fall into. I smile to myself, leaning my head back to the ceiling for a moment and letting myself feel it all. A cool breeze rushes over me, offering some relief for the heat burning my skin, and the drumbeat pulses through me so viciously it's as though it has begun guiding the rhythm of my heart. My inner thighs heat as the eroticism seeps into my skin. Looking around, my friends are now out on the floor with me. While the rest of us dance, occasionally capturing the gaze of each other in the crowd, Elora and Holt are enraptured by each other. I'm not sure they even know we followed them to the dance floor.

Their arms wrap around each other tightly, hers around his neck, his around her waist, and their foreheads rest together. The closeness with which their bodies press against each other makes me simultaneously happy for them and disgusted by the affection. While I've been waiting for the two of them to admit their feelings, I feel like I'm intruding whenever I glance at them.

Trylan makes good on his promise, giving Seb pointed warning looks every time he tries to shuffle closer to me. I'm relaxed and at peace, or as much as I'm ever going to be outside the Culling tunnels. That is until a tall, overpowering body comes up behind me and pulls me by my shoulders until I'm flush against them.

My muscles freeze. The heat of defined chest muscles press against my back, and I reel for what I should do. Seb and my friends are in front of me, and as I quickly eliminate any possibility that this is someone I know trying to be funny, a warm breath brushes against my ear.

"We don't want your dirty halfling kind here," the low male voice growls, just loud enough that only I can hear. I struggle against his grip on my upper arms, trying to shake his hands loose. They dig deeper into my arm, claws threatening to pierce the skin through my padded outfit.

"Excuse me?" I vociferate, drawing the eyes of Trylan and Seb who have become aware of the newcomer's presence. Their stances change as the dance leave their bodies, and they assess the level of threat that stands behind me.

I reach into my holster, grab a small knife, and swipe at the fingers on one of my arms. The stranger's grip retracts, and I take the opportunity to launch myself toward Seb and Trylan.

With clawed hands and glowing eyes, the daemon towers over most Others on the dance floor. His skin complements his eyes — a deep, dark red that looks nearly black in the lighting. His features are sunken into his face like a human skull. Atop his head are sharp, twisting horns that add to his height. I wonder whether he could impale someone with them.

I don't have time to marvel at the fact that I'm face-to-face with my first daemon because he's watching me, narrow-eyed, as though he is coming to step on me. A space appears around us on the dance floor, the Others wanting nothing to do with the confrontation unfolding.

"Halfling pixies aren't welcome here. They are meals, not guests," he sneers in a low tone that rumbles through his body. He leans forward, his sharp teeth glinting in the flickering dim light.

My blood boils at the use of the name, removing any hesitance and igniting the need to fight. He stinks of death — the smell takes over the space — and I want to vomit.

"I'm no fucking halfling!" I holler, uncaring of those around me. "I'm a human! So how about you fuck off!"

"There's no mistaking the green eyes or the smell. That's fae for certain. No humans have green eyes."

"Well, I *do*! And call me a fae one more time and I'll show you how dangerous this *human* can be," I hiss, letting my eyes show the true level of heat that sears inside me.

It is at that moment a bulky dragayastir walks over from his place at the side of the room. By the crest emblazoned on his chest, I realize he is a peacekeeper in O Positive. He looks between myself and the daemon, waiting for one of us to speak. I barely glance at him though, focused more on the Other that can impale me with his head alone.

"Is there a problem?" the peacekeeper asks.

"No, no problems here," the daemon answers, his eyes not leaving mine.

"Reaper?" the peacekeeper prods, his attention turning to me.

"There won't be a problem if he goes back to minding his own business instead of spreading lies and trying to intimidate me into leaving or threatening to eat me," I respond.

The daemon's lips curl as I speak. The peacekeeper's head snaps toward my intimidator, and he points toward the entrance.

"Xerxes, you know the law of O Positive. Get out or be removed by force!" The peacekeeper speaks loud and clear, not bothering to hide his distaste.

The daemon's lips turn up as though he wants to argue. He doesn't. Instead, his glare toward me only grows darker as he moves past. I half-expect a collision, for his shoulder to smash against me on his way out. But he just rumbles with a low growl as he makes his way toward the exit. The peacekeeper nods to me before returning to his place by the entrance wall.

With a deep breath of relief, the tension eases from my shoulders. My heart rate continues to smash through my ribs, and I know it won't calm down any time soon. I'm sure the spirit water is nearly purged from my veins by the sheer amount of adrenaline that burns through them. But it hasn't yet.

A hand touches me lightly on the shoulder, resting there. Instinct takes over, and I move into action. I barrel away and turn to view my second possible attacker. Seb stands, hands raised in surrender, an apologetic smile on his face. I try to relax from a fresh jolt of adrenaline.

"Hey, I was just going to see if you were okay," he says by way of apology. I'm not keen on the idea.

"Can people not leave me to enjoy myself for a few minutes?" I ask rhetorically, letting the exacerbated sigh reinforce my point. I don't care about the fact that he has retracted his hand like it's been burned when he realizes. Or that the sentiment wasn't playful or sexual in nature, instead showing worry and care.

I'm furious.

I've had visions of what my first night reveling would look like — a great celebration with my closest friends in a supposedly welcoming all-species venue, being able to relax as we drank and joked. Instead, I've had to deal with a crasher in our group, who seems intent on ridiculing me for the personal rules I've set myself. I had to walk through a courtyard full of Others who stared at me as though I was the oddest thing, and I was hate-speech intimidated by a daemon.

It's fucking ridiculous.

All the events of the evening not going my way is one thing, but having people purposely come for me without relenting only serves to anger me. I need some quiet. The idea that there is no moment of peace boils my blood.

I turn and stride off the dance floor before I do something I'll regret, sheathing the small knife I hadn't realized I'm still holding. I don't bother engaging Seb in conversation and hearing why he gives a shit about my well-being. It's useless.

"Where are you going?" he calls after me, missing the way my eyes instinctively roll in my skull.

"I'm going to find some fresh air," I say, tone clipped through gritted teeth. Turning to look back at him, I let the fury in my body heat my gaze. "*Alone.*"

I cross the dance floor toward the bar and wait until the fae woman behind it moves over to speak to me. With how many corridors are off the main room, I have no illusions that I'll be able to find space to myself on my own.

"Do you have a back door where I can have a second to myself?" I yell over the music.

She jerks her head toward a doorway behind her without a word and I force a half-smile of thanks.

Pushing open the back door, I'm surprised by how much the air has cooled down after sunset. I step out into the alleyway, using the provided cement block to prop the door open a fraction. I glance up and down the gray stone, thankful for how alone I am and how quiet the street feels in comparison to O Positive. I embrace the smell of smoke, stone, and river water that normally makes me turn my nose up and my stomach tumbling in the streets of Skull's Rest.

Sinking against the cold stone wall, I lean my head back and close my eyes. My breathing evens out slowly as my body relaxes. *Finally.* A moment to just breathe and reflect that I've survived up to now. It's a feat. Not to mention that I am now a favorite to join the elite human selection known as Reapers.

Being a small and thin child with green eyes meant the odds had been stacked against me since my introduction to the Culling, but finding a way to get an advantage and thicker skin out of it was something I couldn't help feeling proud of. It was comforting in a way, to know I'd done that.

A gust of wind blows past me and the loud slam next to me jolts me out of my comfort. All the nerves in my body vibrate into action as I try to make sense of what is happening. Looking to my right, the door has escaped its blocker and blown shut. Grabbing the handle, the frustration that has slowly been simmering in my body overwhelms me.

My heart rate begins to climb again. Swear words hiss through my teeth, and no matter how many times I strain my shoulder pulling the door handle, the locked door doesn't budge.

As I step back, I try to search for any sign of why it slammed shut when I made sure to block it open, or even how to unlock it from this side, and find nothing. Shivers speed up my spine and my stomach drops lower in my body than I thought possible.

A low growl sounds behind me, and I whip around to find the source of my problem. Glowing red eyes stare at me, moving closer from the open end of the alley.

A daemon.

The air around drops in temperature and goosebumps dance along my skin. The blood pumps quicker through my veins, but doesn't seem to warm anything in me. With the opening behind it and the sealed door locked tightly behind me, I know I'm going to have to fight my way out of here or hope someone comes looking for me. My odds against a daemon on my own aren't good.

"I could smell you from a mile away, halfling," the daemon rumbles, and as he moves closer, I see it's the same daemon who was just kicked out of O Positive.

Fuck, Azariah, you're an idiot.

Air struggles down my throat.

Pulling the knife from my thigh sheath, I move into a fighting stance. I hope my face isn't showing how my body has started to panic. Every nerve in my limbs are buzzing with a weakness I haven't felt in years, and it's taking everything in me to not give in to it. Adrenaline pumps through my veins faster than my body knows what to do with it, and I feel unsteady and alert.

I work hard to keep my breathing even, giving my brain enough oxygen to help me think a way out of this mess. The deeper I force myself to breathe, the less I notice the shaking vibrating my body.

"You know, smelling people is a bit creepy, Xerxes," I say, thankful my voice sounds more confident and badass than I feel. "Also, I'm *not* a halfling."

"I can smell your power from here." He takes a step closer, and I fight the urge to step back and press my back against the door. I'm already too close to it. My mouth dries rapidly, and my hand tightens painfully on the knife.

Weak points on a daemon ... Come on. Think ... Eyes. Neck. Waist. Back of the knees.

Lifting my knife slightly, I coil my muscles, preparing to spring into action when I hear footsteps. Before I can rejoice at possible assistance, they walk into the alley. Four more pairs of glowing, red-eyed daemons join Xerxes.

He grins. "We all can."

Chapter Seven
THE ATTACKING FLAME

AZARIAH

A fist collides with my face.

I don't see the daemon who threw it before another impact comes, my cheek colliding with the stone ground. I cry out before I'm aware that I have. Something hard pounds into my stomach, and as the pain explodes, all my breath disappears.

I can't scream. Can't cry out. Can't get up.

Fuck. I'm going to die here.

I curl into a ball, the only thing I can manage, and wrap an arm around my face. I can't think of much else to do through the pain. The hard bone in my arm serves as a protector for the top of my face and skull. My other arm curves around my stomach.

It doesn't help me much.

The blows continue. Again and again. My shielding arm is little protection against the superiority of sheer daemon strength.

I want to scream.

I want the pain to stop.

I want to die already.

I hear a crack, and the arm protecting my head shatters in explosive pain. Shards of bone break the skin. Pinpricks radiate pain along my head and face, where my bones scratch the skin as they puncture. A blood-curdling scream leaves my throat and I'm sure I've shredded vocal cords.

The ability to breath becomes harder.

Another hit to my broken hand makes my screams silent, and my vision begins to tunnel.

"We can't eat her in human form. That's just wrong!" an unfamiliar daemon grumbles and kicks my stomach. My other arm snaps and the pain has me nearly passing out again as I scream without breath. Their voices are the only thing pulling me into consciousness. "Why isn't she changing?"

The blows stop and I feel their beady eyes on me. I writhe in breathless pain, radiating harshly despite the stopped onslaught of punches. I move and shuffle my limbs, hoping to find a position I can fall into that will alleviate even a fraction of the pain.

No success.

Finally, the silence and stillness of the daemons is broken by Xerxes. "She just needs a *helping hand*."

A pinprick in my neck makes me flinch, the movement making the burning needles worse. I realize too late what he has done when pressure pushes its way into the veins of my neck. It's hot like liquid fire and lights up my body as it spreads.

The scream returns to my throat.

The unconscious black that has been swimming in my vision is long gone. I writhe on the ground, squirming as the pain of the broken bones pale in comparison to the fire seeping throughout my body. I twist my body at angles, hoping for some relief — desperate. It doesn't get any worse, but no matter how I curl in on myself or stretch out, the liquid fire continues to engulf me.

Nothing helps.

I feel it move — a tingling, searing sensation. It reaches my heart and eyes at the same time. It's so hot that it leaves my eyes in the form of light. I point my gaze toward my attackers, hoping to do some damage to them, too.

They back up.

"Xerxes, what the ...? You said she was a halfling!" one of them barks loudly, all amusement gone as he stares wide-eyed at me.

"I was sure she was! I can smell the fae on her. You do, too!"

His reasoning doesn't seem to convince his arguing companion.

"That's like no fae I've seen!" He backs away another step.

I want to take the opportunity to get up and run. The pain, burning and continuously raw, keeps me writhing though, unable to find a strong enough resolve to do it. A glimmer of hope warms me that maybe they've realized their error and will leave me here to be found injured but alive.

All hopes are dashed when Xerxes speaks again. "Then help me get rid of the body before the reapers realize what I've done. They won't take kindly to this if they find her and she outs us."

"Us? You're the one that sanctioned this!"

A low growl sounds from Xerxes that silences all arguments. His doubtful companions halt in their retreat. I watch their resolve set in, helpless to do anything as their intentions shift. The amusement and hunger fades from their eyes. Mine feel like they are going to sear out of my skull.

Movement behind the group catches my eye. A dark shadow looms. Even though the group of daemons advance on me with lethal intent pulling their faces tight, I can't take my eyes from the newcomer. I can't see his face beneath the hooded robe, but my heart leaps as I realize it's my savior. *My avenging angel.*

The pain, while burning and excruciating, seems bearable knowing I'm not about to die. I'm not alone.

My savior reaches the back of the group of daemons, and I know it is all over for them. Despite the daemons' unawareness to the newcomer, it's too late. A pale hand reaches out from the heavy black cloak and an ornate knife whips into view, a glinting sharp edge slice across the throat of the first daemon. It gurgles as black blood flows from the deep cut across the neck. His mouth floods with it too as he struggles to cry out. The others turn to face their new attacker as their comrade collapses to the ground.

Xerxes and his second retreat toward me, covering my view for a moment before they go past to the locked door. A dead end.

Their fear doesn't deter my avenging angel — the mysterious dragayastir royal oozes power and danger. Just not dangerous *to me.* I strain against my tense muscles and fight to stay still, gritting my teeth as I watch the scene unfold.

He works quickly, leaning over the first daemon on the ground. Using one hand and his heavy leather lace-up boot, he cracks a horn off the body. There is no hesitation, and a breath barely sounds before he uses the horn as a throwing dagger, launching it at the daemon beside Xerxes.

There's no time to run as the makeshift weapon tunnels through the daemon's eye. The weight of it throws him back into the wall, and as consciousness leaves him, his limp body stays upright, skewered in place.

Taking on the next closest daemon before he can fight or run away, my savior grips it by the horns. Pulling up viciously, white-knuckled and twisting at the same time, a wet ripping sound reaches my ears before I register that my face is being splashed by decapitated daemon blood.

Only Xerxes and one other daemon remain. Even though they are angered by the loss of their friends and emboldened to fight, a warm sense of safety washes over me. Everything aches with the pain of broken bones and pulses where bruises are already beginning to appear. The need to wriggle from the burning has died down, replaced by cramping and tense muscles as the aftermath of the 'helping hand' settles into my body, fading in its intensity. Taking deep, shaky breaths, I keep both remaining daemons in sight, just in case they turn their anger on me.

The other daemon rushes my dragayastir savior, winding his fist back and powering forward as he moves. The flying fist is caught inches from the face hidden by the hood with a flat palm. My avenger's hand curls around the scrunched fist and pulls his body closer, past him. The daemon stumbles to the side in response. Quicker than the daemon can fathom, my protector grabs his head and twists quickly. A satisfying *crack* breaks through the quiet of the alleyway.

The distant thudding of drumbeats is the only sound that any other population exists outside of this space.

Finally, Xerxes is alone.

"Y ... Your M-Majesty? I don't understand," he stutters, his voice trembling.

As I glance over my shoulder, I'm not sure that Xerxes can move any closer to the alley wall without pressing himself into it. Only my body lying on the ground blocks my protector's direct path to him. Nothing else is slowing Xerxes demise.

"What did you do to her?" the deep, velvety voice growls from beneath the hood.

My body stills.

Despite our history — and I know this is the same person who saved me as a child — I've never heard his voice. I tried to imagine what it might sound like, whether it would be rough and hoarse like I imagined all dragayastir were, or regal and articulate like a Royal. In my mind, it ought to be. It's somehow all of it at once — rough and velvety, and full of protective punch. Nothing seems to do it justice.

"The halfling?" Xerxes asks, his red eyes narrowing as they drop to me. "Nothing! I had no idea you'd claimed her."

"She is no halfling," he replies darkly.

"I ... I swear I didn't know."

"I tried ... to tell you ... twighead," I chime in, the effort of spitting out the words reigniting the pain in my stomach and ribs. I curl in on myself with a groan.

"What did you *do*?" my protector roars, the bass of his voice wet with guttural anger. I'm almost sure the ground shakes with his words.

Xerxes takes the final step and presses his back against the wall, eyes wide and unmoving from where my protector stands on the other side of me. I inhale deeply, the anticipation of what is about to happen making me hold my breath.

The burning in my eyes flare in response. I close them, squeezing tightly as though that will calm the searing heat. It doesn't. A whimper works its way from my throat as I fight to keep my vision from turning black.

"Helping hand," Xerxes admits quietly between my noises.

The rumble in the earth grows with an angry vibration, a gush of breeze and a quick gurgle. I know Xerxes is dead.

Sadly, his death doesn't alleviate the pain strangling my body. A shadow blocks the little remaining light behind my eyelids as a hand touches my broken arm softly. I hiss, knowing it is merely an examination and he doesn't mean to hurt me.

"Azariah, look at me ... Open your eyes," my protector says quietly, his hand lightly touching my cheekbone, trying to entice me to comply. I worry the pain in my eyes will be worse, and though I try to open them a little bit again and again, I struggle.

"Please," he begs. The soft plea has my eyes opening in one quick movement. The pain doesn't worsen. In fact, it lessens. The biggest distractor to my pain is the face no longer hidden under the hood.

His skin is paler than mine, which is a surprise considering I have lived my life in a cave. His eyes glow luminescent scarlet and soften as they met my gaze. His hair is dark brown, and his long shoulder-length strands are tossed about in the light breeze I hadn't noticed still surrounded us. The smell of something rich and spiced floods my nose, and my mouth waters.

His eyes barely hold mine for a moment when words fall from his tightened jaw. "I'm sorry. This will be hard for you to hide, and I can't undo what they've done."

My heart kicks up to an unnatural speed as I push myself up against the anguished complaints of broken ribs to see what in Skull's Rest he is referring to. Besides injuries I don't care about hiding, I can't see the answer on my body. The attempts at movement though have me lying back, hissing air through my teeth and groaning.

"What? What do I need to hide?" I ask breathily as the corners of my vision darken again. His face, framed by a tunnel of black, closes in by the second. My breathing slows as unconsciousness threatens to claim me.

He moves over me, producing a vial of glowing light blue liquid from his robe. Uncorking it, he tilts it to my lips. I press them together tightly, keeping the unfamiliar substance out.

"It's for healing," he explains quickly, his eyes not faltering from mine.

I surrender, pursing my lips and feeling the surprisingly cool liquid roll back into my throat. Like the temperature of the concoction, the taste feels ... cold. It consumes my mouth with a flavor that's sharp, strong, and somehow spicy. Its taste amplifies the cold temperature, making it hard to bear. His hand slides under the back of my head and despite his gentle touches as he lifts it slightly, I know it's already bruised.

The position makes it easier to swallow, and though the action causes me pain with my broken ribs, the drink starts to take effect immediately. The pain begins to soften, and the burn lingers but with less intensity.

Unconsciousness still closes in, a heaviness on my mind and limbs.

"When you need answers, come and find me at the Animora Castle. This necklace will grant you energy and help you hide in the meantime." Something cold slips into my palm, the chain looped around my fingers. Before the darkness finally claims me, he whispers in my ear, "Ask for Ezekiel."

Chapter Eight
THE FIRE IN DARKNESS

AZARIAH

The pine scent is relaxing, but an intrusion upon my sleep. I become aware of the soft, fluffy ground beneath me as I open my eyes. Blinking rapidly, eyes adjusting to the light, my fingers explore the surface. I know without looking that the cool leafy feel is a bed of grass, and though I drop my gaze from the moonlit sky, I already know what I will find beneath my fingers.

What shocks me more, stiffening my limbs, is the setting. An unfamiliar forest surrounds me, unlike anywhere I've ever before. Dense, thick and overgrown in a way that places in Skull's Rest aren't.

I pull myself to my feet quickly, only for my heart to ratchet up its speed as more foreign things reveal themselves. I'm barefoot, which is entirely unlike me, especially in a forest away from home. I'm standing in a moonlit, dense pine forest in only a sleeveless white flowing dress, one that seems more reminiscent of a sprite faerie than a Reaper.

This is a cruel joke, right?

Someone surely thought it would be funny to play a joke on me when I was unconscious.

Unconscious ...

The thought touches a memory, reminding me of the pain I've endured. I look down to survey the state of my injuries, only to discover there are none. I distinctively remember the splinters of bone through one arm, the clean break on the other, the bruising all over my body, and the injection mark on my neck, which I feel for with my fingers to no success.

Nothing. My body is clear of any indication that there was ever an altercation.

Ezekiel.

What the fuck did he give me?

Also, where am I?

I look around, ignoring my bare feet and dress, to try and see if there is anyone or anything around me that might give me a clue as to what is going on. Nothing presents itself.

The close pine trees surround me, the forest floor coated in soft, plushy beds of grass. Moss and flowers grow in little sprigs all around. It's a wild forest, and besides the sound of the wind breezing through the trees, it is quiet. All of this is decently visible due to the full moon above, filtering its light to the forest floor.

Standing here and waiting for answers or someone to come find me seems irresponsible especially if, for whatever reason, no one I know is here. Heading out in search of answers with no weapons or protection seems equally reckless.

I take the first step. My gut tells me I should turn and head right, even though nothing seems different. As I turn and begin to walk through the forest, something feels right, like an invisible string on my soul tugs me in that direction. Step after step rustles through ears, the smell of flowers and pine keeping my breathing calm and steady, despite my heightened confusion. Finally, after walking in silence for long enough, about to question my instincts, the answer reveals itself.

The tree line halts, opening to a grassy clearing. In the center is a scene with so much happening that it takes me a moment to piece it together. Movement on my left draws my attention before I can study it further. Where the almost circular tree line begins on my left is a woman. She walks away from me, and all I can see of her is the white dress she wears, nearly identical to mine, and her black hair that hangs deathly straight. She moves with a grace that is inhuman, and I know from the sight of her, floating away bare foot, that she's an Other. Probably a fae of some kind, given the setting.

Under my gaze, she stops. Her body freezes for a moment, sensing my sight, before she slowly turns to face me.

The first thing that strikes me is her eyes. While they glow an emerald green, shining and captivating as they meet mine, they are framed by black veins in the space under her eyes. As though she has seen so much darkness that it has entered her bloodstream. The intensity in the way she looks at me, her face surprised and widening at my presence, makes me feel as though she can see into my soul. I can't identify her species even if I tried. The sheer amount of fae subspecies is hard to distinguish without reaper training. As my gaze breaks from her, traveling down her body and assessing the similar outfit to mine, I catch the stark sight of fresh red blood on her pale hands. It's human. It must be. As far as I know, humans are the only species living in Skull's Rest that bleed red.

My breath hitches, and the calm I've tried to keep in my body vanishes. My heart kicks up its speed as my body readies itself to run. My gaze quickly darts to the center of the clearing where the bodies lay, and as my eyes leave her, she darts off into the tree line.

She's gone.

Shivers crawl over my buzzing skin as I hurry toward the mess she has left behind in the clearing. Five bodies lay facing away from me, no blood visible as I inch closer. They lay on their sides, facing away from me. I glimpse the markings on the ground surrounding them, and my blood runs cold, sending a chill down my spine. White mushrooms with a blueish tinge create a ring — chaos contained in a faerie circle.

Before I can cross the natural ring line indicated on the ground, I stop. Everything in my body turns frantic except for my movement. My heart is thundering, threatening to crack my ribs if I don't get myself away from this precarious predicament. My breath can't be slowed as I gulp down air in short, shallow gasps. The adrenaline speeding through my veins is like a drug awakening my mind. My muscles are still frozen in place. My feet press into the soft grass on the outside of the mushroom circle.

Among the five bodies is one that differs — taller, leaner, dressed in different clothing. While most of the bodies scream 'human' because they are dressed in the fitted black protective gear of the reapers, this body is not. He is in green and gold clothing, only made of natural fibers with no added padding and armor built or woven into the outfit. He's an Other. He's also the only one facing me, eyes open and unseeing. They probably once glowed green, but the luminescence has faded with his life. His stomach is clutched in both hands and green blood, starting to dry now, stains his hands. A blood-coated reaper knife also lies on the grass between him and the other bodies.

As my gaze drags to his attackers, somehow all dead, I notice the person lying directly in front of me. The back of his head and body is recognizable, familiar even, and my body stills for a moment before moving again. Despite the warm air, my body feels cold.

I fight the urge to step toward the recognizable Reaper in front of me and walk around the circle slowly to confirm what I'm seeing.

"Seb?" I call, hoping maybe he's not dead. Maybe the fae earlier hadn't collected the blood on her hands from here. He frustrates me immensely, but I don't wish him dead. Certainly not here and not like this.

I move around the circle, careful to stay on the outside. When his face comes into view, there's no holding back the sharp gasp. His face is nearly unrecognizable. Blood, now drying, leaks from every orifice unrelentingly. I've never seen anything like it. I stare into his bloody eyes, vacant and open. It's not Seb, but I do know who it is. I'm not upset by my discovery though, and I try not to sigh too loudly with my relief.

As I look around at the other bodies, their faces — now visible — leaking in the same way, a heavy pit weighs down my stomach. The lightness and easy breathing I feel that it isn't Seb on the ground is squashed by the rancid taste of guilt in my mouth.

No one deserve to die like this.

There is so much blood pooling in the grass from their faces that it takes every ounce of self-control not to throw up. Suddenly, I'm thankful I can't go any closer to this scene because I don't know what, if anything, I could do to help, and I'd feel obliged to try.

My eyes scan the bodies and catch slow movement beside the head of the familiar Reaper. It's gradual enough that my eyes didn't catch it before and if the hairs on my skin hadn't been prickling up, warning me that something was very, very wrong, I never would've seen it.

The shadow under the semi-familiar face is somehow darkening and expanding. The blackness becomes more and more tangible on the ground as it chews up the space. I back up slowly, unsure what it would do in contact with a live person. The dead bodies look unchanged by the growing, living darkness, but I'm not taking the chance. It reaches the ring of mushrooms and like it has hit an invisible wall of glass, it presses up against it.

Whispers call from the void that has swallowed any view of the grass underneath. They are daemonic in language, and though I can't understand their words, I can tell they're malicious.

Without questioning why this is like this, what has happened or how I got here, I turn and bolt for the trees in the direction of the fleeing fae.

Chapter Nine
THE INITIAL AIR

MORANA

Savastral Revon was a glinting light in the distance for Morana. She stared out the open window of her home, built into the trunk at the top of the tree, glancing over the dense expanse of forest to the bloodbath city she'd spent too many hours in. It was odd for her to spend an entire night in her home, not being awoken or called to its depths by her curse. And yet, despite all that, her body hadn't seemed to get the message about uninterrupted sleep time.

Morana had jolted from her sleep, tossing and turning the entire night, beaded with sweat on her porcelain skin. Her white sleeping gown had felt like a gross shell as it stuck to her skin and drove her from her bed, rather than attempting to return to sleep. In her sleep-starved state, she'd managed to change out of her sleeping gown and wrangled the black mess that was her hair into an acceptable state. Her hair now, thankfully, hung flat, straight and untangled, blending nicely into the clothing she'd changed into. The pants were tight against her skin, as were the sleeves of the light-weight sweater, but at least it was dry. It wasn't typical attire for a fae, more reminiscent of the power-hungry reaper uniform. Then again, Morana had never been a typical fae. She was one of the 'cursed' and that had clearly marked to others that she wasn't worth getting close to. It didn't matter how hard she'd worked to create and maintain rela-tionships with her kind, they only saw her as a curse. Banshees, clearly, were the dirt of the fae.

Lesser.

She stared at the lit dot in the dark, taking deep breaths. The breeze was cool, intruding upon the warm evening, working hard to chill the anger in her blood whenever she thought about the isolation they'd pressed on her since she was a child. Despite the deadly city she could see on the horizon, and the loneliness that struck her in her home, she felt utterly safe nestled in the treetop. The breeze cooling her face had a deep and smoky scent, thanks to the redwood trees that always made her feel calm.

Right as her mind and body had begun to settle, she felt it. Power zapped through her veins, pumping hot energy unlike anything she had ever felt. Her skin tingled from the underlying heat but thankfully not hot enough to burn.

The change didn't scare her. In fact, if she wasn't breathing quickly from the physical shock to her system, she would have breathed a sigh of relief.

Finally, she thought to herself.

Knowing exactly what it meant, she turned away from the window, not waiting for the power to die down before she considered leaving. Emboldened with confidence that her fae elemental power had finally been awakened, she didn't consider changing out of her attire. The new power inside her thrummed to life as she began moving, begging to be unleashed. She didn't dare test her new powers indoors without any equipment though, knowing that regardless of what element she now possessed an affinity for, wielding inside could be destructive. That was assuming it even worked. While she'd lived with her death magick her entire life, she had been waiting for this day for some time.

Morana moved through her bedroom to the stairs that twisted down the trunk of the tree, headed for her living room. As she moved down the many winding steps to the bottom landing, she figured she had a few hours until the sunrise ceremony she would now have to attend. Just enough time to go out early and test her powers her own on the way, rather than wait to find out in front of everyone. The ceremony was nerve-wracking enough without the additional elemental question hanging over her head, too.

She made it to the living area, crossing to her front door without a second thought. Grabbing her keys, she looked down at her chosen outfit, giving herself one last chance to change her mind before she left.

Black outfits were typically a color only worn in Savastral Revon, not what fae wore in the grove. She'd always been different, and Morana knew whether she caved to fae propriety or not, they'd still look down their noses at her. Why bother trying? At least now, despite all her variations from being a 'typical fae,' she would go through the same rite of passage with her awakening sunrise ceremony and be a little less odd. At least she hoped it would bring a semblance of normality to her life.

She knew, no matter how much closer to normal fae she was, the curse would remain. And it was exactly that: *a curse*. Despite never causing the harm that had brought the curse upon her breed of fae, Morana had been born into it. She was pulled on near-daily excursions into Savastral Revon, more often than not, to bear witness to death with no reprieve, but never to interfere. If she tried, she was met with blinding pain shooting through her skull. It had taken a number of occurrences as a child to put together that she wasn't allowed to assist. It was an even longer couple of years learning and training to fight her instinct to try and help. It was not without mistakes or tears. Morana had always had too much empathy for a banshee.

With a quick sigh, sliding the key into her pocket and nodding to herself that her decision had been self-affirmed, she swung open her front entrance and stepped out onto the sturdy branch outside. The lock clicked shut behind her and she smiled. The apprehension of the upcoming event broke through the nerves as she imagined herself finally able to access fae elemental magick.

Glancing over the forest floor below her, she looked for any glowing eyes in the dark. More specifically, red eyes. She wasn't about to let her excitement and eagerness make her complacent. When she was sure no daemons lay in wait on the forest floor, she bent her knees and sprung out over the air to the vine that waited for her. Even as her body jumped away from the safety of the branch, the fall to the forest floor 200 feet below, she wasn't scared. The rush of adrenaline and the air whooshing past her was freeing.

Her hands clasped the vine rope she knew she could trust, remembering its dimensions after so many years. As her body swung out, her knees and bare feet finding the vine with ease, she let her muscles stop her fall and the vine rope settle in its swing before she moved again. With trust and memory, she scaled the rope to the ground, falling easily into her routine. Her muscles worked, tensing and doing as they were supposed to, years past ever complaining about her house exit strategy.

Her toes left the rope behind as her upper body lowered to the forest floor. She'd chopped it to her head height years ago to ensure it wasn't too obvious to those looking. Besides the 200-foot climb, they'd need the ability to lift themselves onto the rope, something common daemons were not skilled at.

The grass beneath her toes was cool compared to the warm air. Morana let herself revel in the sensation as she glanced around again her. Confident she was still alone and that no one had spied her exit from her house, she let the adrenaline drive her through the forest. The air collected her hair as she powered forward with her arms and legs, enjoying the freedom it brought. Enjoying how freeing it was just to be in the moment among the trees of the grove and not be pulled along and controlled by fate to witness.

Tonight, Morana was in control of herself, and fate could bend to her will for a change.

The training grounds were entirely empty when Morana arrived. The expansive clearing with monumental stone structures designed to test and train fae magick waited for her. The shrill beat of her heart was powered by the adrenaline of her excitement. It took all her energy not to skip over to the first structure and begin testing.

She looked around at her four options bathed in full moonlight and was thankful she was alone to find her answer with no interruptions or obstacles. She wasn't sure if she could be patient and wait for someone to finish practicing their element if it was the same as hers.

Now it was time to figure out what element was hers.

She knew that the element one manifested an affinity for most closely matched the energy signature of one's soul. Morana wasn't sure which element was most like her soul. She had some ideas but was glad there were no crowds around to witness in case she was wrong. Most fae had enough quiet in their lives prior to their awakening to get a self-reflection of what their element was. Morana had not been so lucky. If her soul had an element, she supposed it would be darkness like her current death magick powers, and that was only because she hadn't had a quiet moment that wasn't surrounded by death since she was eight years old. At the age of thirty, a late bloomer to her elemental powers by fae standards, she still had no idea which order of magick she belonged to — earth, air, fire or water.

Taking a stab in the dark, she headed over to the section of grounds designated for training earth wielders. In the center was a flat stone circle with a large gray boulder in a divet. In a spiral around the human-sized rock wound dark green ivy vines, close enough that they were nearly touching. She could tell the point of the exercise was to use them to lift or move the boulder, so she stood in front and kept her eyes on them in her periphery.

Morana squared her shoulders, holding her arms and feeling the magick in her veins buzz excitedly in response. Her toes sunk into the grass outside the stone circle, hip-width apart as though grounding herself could help with the onset of her wielding. And then she tucked her chin and willed the ivy to move the rock.

Silence followed.

It didn't matter how close her brows scrunched together or how intensely she watched the vines around the rock, nothing happened. The magick in her shook the cells in her body, like at any second they would burst forth from her in a flood of power. But they didn't.

The longer it dragged on, the more she chewed her lip. She'd been hoping her element had been earth, that she was grounded and sturdy and unmoving like the boulder in front of her. But that wasn't the case.

Too much time had passed with no luck moving the boulder. Morana lifted her eyes to the other three options and tried to consider what her soul was called to. Considering that she could be destructive and overpowering, she moved over to the fire section to her right. The eternal flame burned in the pit with kindling suspended above the flames. Again, she could tell what the point of the exercise was and how she would need to manipulate the element.

When she raised her hands and focused on growing the fire to reach the kindling, she knew it wasn't going to work. She was living magick without a connector and the more impatient her magick became, the more it did the same to her. She was wasting the time she had on finding her element instead of training her magick like she wanted to. It was more than just the fire in front of her heating her skin as she pushed her lips into a thin line. No matter the amount of concentration she dedicated to the element, the flames stayed the same height. It danced with the breeze, playing coy in a waltz as her magick refused to influence the fire.

Her eyes raised, resigned to the other two training areas remaining — water and air. Even though she felt the awakened power strengthen and ready her body, as though a battle were imminent and it was eager to fight, she had a momentary chill. The thought occurred, for a mere moment, that maybe she wasn't gifted with the power of an element like every other fae.

Another reason for the 'regular' fae to push her away.

As quickly as the fear stilled her, Morana forced herself, step by step, toward the water training exercise. A small rock shard protruded from the ground, and in it was carved a halfpipe zigzagging across it like a mini river moving up to its peak. A pool of water waited at its base, as though it had already used the slide and enjoyed being at the bottom.

It seemed almost unfair that she could envision exactly what her magick needed to do before she ever connected with her element. Yet so far, her understanding of the exercise didn't seem to help make it happen. As her hands raised, she tensed with the physical manifestation of her concentration.

This time though, she knew barely a breath after she had begun that this was not her element.

With a growl, she heaved a sigh. Turning on her heel, she headed for the final element.

"*Cavrasa!*" she cursed in her native tongue. "It had to be *air!*"

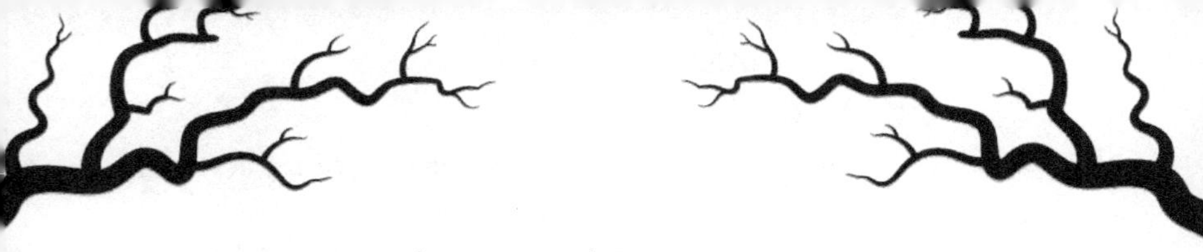

Chapter Ten
The Binding Waters

Morana

Morana was going to be late for the sunrise ceremony.

Of course she was.

The first time she'd been given control without being dragged to death for a whole day and she had spent too long playing with her element.

She'd been thankful when her magick connected with air. Eager to test out her abilities with it, she'd stopped keeping track of time. She knew she was going to struggle to make it to the ceremony on time when the sky had lightened enough that it was sure to be cresting over the mountain any minute now, when the ceremony was due to start.

Morana sprinted through the forest, not looking down as she powered as hard as her legs could carry her. She didn't have the ability to breathe a sigh of relief with every minute that ticked by without sunrays blinding her eyes. It needed to hold out a little longer.

Breaking through the trees, Morana found the group gathered for the ceremony. Forty other Seelie fae, of varying species, queued in the clearing, all waiting behind the large stone bowl that sat near the cliff's edge. Two of the Elders stood on either side, their backs to the fall behind them, unbothered by the steep drop to the barren land. Kenrick — one of the fae Elders — glanced up at her arrival, pointedly peering at the sun as it rose behind him.

The ceremony had begun, and Morana had made it just in time.

While Kenrick was not overtly friendly with Morana, he was the closest she had to an acquaintance. With long and flowing silver hair, high cheekbones, and an aged wisdom starting to show in the creases of his skin, she was sure he didn't feel the friendship with her. The other Elder fae — the King — was personally unknown to her.

Ignoring the side-eyed glances from the other fae in line, she joined the back of the queue and kept her eyes focused forward on the ceremony unfolding before her. The King began speaking loud and clear, his voice carried further by his manipulation of the wind. Thankfully, any murmurings that had begun in her appearance quieted.

"Welcome to your awakening into the greater Seelie Court. You will have made your way here today because your powers are now awake." He spoke proudly in the fae native tongue, and Morana worked hard not to cringe at his words. For all the fae talk of peace and the beauty of the Seelie Court, the fae had a very elitist attitude toward those not of the norm. It's exactly why she'd always favored the human tongue. Despite the fact humans feared other species, they didn't look at her like she was dirt on their shoes. She couldn't imagine that being awakened into the greater Seelie Court would change anything about the way the fae saw or treated her.

"This is where you finally join the ranks of the fae, announce your element, be assigned your position of service, and be introduced to your soulmate," Kenrick continued, rehearsed in his delivery. "The fates have engineered for you both to be awakened today."

The fae standing a few paces down in the line looked over their shoulder with wide eyes. The details beyond attendance were always kept secret, and clearly all the fae felt as blindsided as Morana. A couple of male elves ahead of her looked back at Morana, their lips pulling back into a sneer as they noted her species. Like they hoped she'd be driven away by their looks and then none of them would have to be stuck with her.

"We will begin. Each of you will notify us of your element, complete the pledge of service to the greater Seelie Court, be notified of your service area, and finally, your blood will bind this into a covenant. As a reward for pledge of service, the fates will guide you to your soulmate. Once they make the pledge also, you will be free to leave," Kenrick announced and waited for any questions in silence.

No one said a word, the resounding silence speaking volumes of either the anticipation to begin or the fear of admitting they didn't understand. Morana hoped it was the former as her eyes trailed person by person down the queue ahead of her. Her heart fluttered as she stretched out her tense hands at her sides. Each person in the line didn't look at all like her soulmate; fae generally didn't like her presence, let alone want to spend an eternity with it.

Morana considered for a moment if this was a trick by the fates and she'd find out she was the only one without a soulmate at the ceremony. Swallowing against the dry sensation of fear in her mouth, she focused solely on the first ceremony ahead of her, hoping it would distract her.

The first in line, a small green sprite, flew at face height to the area where the King and Kenrick waited. At five inches tall, she had a soft smile, green skin, wore a yellow dress, and her colorless translucent wings shimmered in the growing sunshine.

She spoke to the two, probably announcing her element, but her voice didn't carry down the queue. The King nodded and spoke softly to her in return, and she seemed to agree, her smile brightening in response. From his pocket, Kenrick retrieved a pin and waited while the bright sprite turned and submitted her hand. With a quickness Morana almost didn't catch, he stuck the pin into her tiny hand and guided it over the stone bowl on the cliff. Tipping it slightly, all fae in the queue watched in open-eyed fascination as water bubbled in response. It splashed over, the activity in the bowl growing into a ball of light, lifting from its center. The water calmed as the light ball left the surface behind and traveled down the side of the queue. Halfway down, it stopped beside another female sprite with green skin. It moved closer, shrinking until it was smaller than her and then disappeared in the skin of her right wrist.

She lifted her wrist in open-mouthed awe as everyone else turned to her expectantly, waiting to see what would happen next. Even from her place at the back of the queue, Morana could see the new marking that had magickally inked itself to the inside of the sprite's wrist. The banshee fought the urge to walk up and inspect the marking herself, swallowing her impatience. The sprite chosen by the light looked up at the bowl and other of her kind, mouth wide and open eyes as the meaning seemed to dawn on her. Kenrick extended his arm and calmly beckoned her forward as though he had all the time in the world to wait.

Maybe he did?

Morana had no idea how long this ceremony would take or if she'd leave sooner or later. How long would it take to make it to the end of the queue?

The unpledged sprite's wings beat quickly as her hand dropped to her side and moved toward the bowl. The smile on her face was mirrored by her newly discovered soulmate's face. Neither displayed a trace of doubt or reservation about what the universe had revealed to them.

The other sprite spoke to the King and Kenrick quietly, the same way her soulmate had, returning a verbal agreement to what they said to her, and flinched as her blood was submitted to the stone bowl. The water in the bowl stayed still this time and without any further ceremony, the two left the cliff edge together, disappearing into the trees.

One by one, fae of various types submitted their covenant to the bowl and without fail, the ball of light uncovered their soulmate in the waiting crowd. Some had even been standing together in line without realizing.

As each person stepped up to the front and began, Morana felt her stomach squeeze tighter and tighter. Each time another couple left the area, Morana surveyed the remaining and became more certain.

Her soulmate wasn't a banshee.

There were none here like her. Sweat dotted her skin as her racing mind overworked her frantic heart. Her experience with other fae were all the same and she couldn't imagine anyone other than her own cursed kind being okay with a banshee soulmate. But there wasn't one here. Either someone was about to be annoyed at whatever their universe had chosen for them, or her soulmate was running very late.

Morana was so deeply focused on her panicked mental ramblings, she didn't notice the ball of light until it stopped beside her. Her mind went silent as she glanced at its brightness. She almost needed to squint before it began to shrink and lower until it pressed into the skin of her wrist. Her arm flooded with a comforting warmth, like a soothing bath of magick. As she lifted her inner wrist up to look at it, she could see the detail she'd been eager to before.

Two lines overlapped as they traced like a continuous infinite symbol up her wrist — one filled, one not. At the place where her hand met her arm, the lines curved to meet in a circle and in the center of the topmost circle was what looked like the points of a compass. As she turned herself back and forth, the compass moved, always pointing in the same direction.

It was at that point Morana looked up at the male elf waiting for her by the cliff edge, curiosity opening his features. She stepped forward, knowing what to do before Kenrick indicated, but her eyes didn't leave her soulmate's. She searched for any sign of disgust, any disdain that scrunched his eyes as he spotted the black veins underneath hers, signaling her cursed breed to the world. She didn't find any, and with each step she took, she felt lighter.

As she finally stepped beside him, facing the bowl, ready to proclaim her element to her Elders, a hand broke through her view. She looked over and met his glowing green eyes that matched hers, staring at his outwardly friendly demeanor in shock. The lines around his mouth were creased in a way that made her think he smiled often. His almond shaped eyes watched her with a softness as if they'd never been narrowed in judgment before, and his silver-blue hair left slightly shaggy was such an unusual striking color for an elf — all she wanted to do was run her fingers through it to see if it was real.

She took his outstretched arm, gripping his inner forearm. His hand was warm and comforting as it closed around hers.

"I'm Morana." She smiled slightly, still wary of his reaction.

His lips widened as he met her gaze unwaveringly. "I'm Alva."

Chapter Eleven
The Nightmare of Fire

Azariah

Drip. Drip.

I lie on my back with my eyes closed, wishing I could silence that infernal dripping noise. I'm all too eager and excited to finally be done with my room in the tunnels of the Culling.

My room ...

The thought is like ice cold water on my sleepy state, and I sit up in a rush, eyes wide open. It takes them a moment to adjust to the dim light in my room, the candles on the wall unlit. Even as I squint to see in the lighting, my gaze darts around as though it can provide an explanation. I remember the forest and the woman in white with black veins under her eyes who'd fled from the dead reapers, but not how I got out of the forest.

Or how I made it into the forest for that matter.

Before that, I'd been ... *wounded in the alley.*

My mouth goes dry as flashes of heat pulse through my veins. The crunching of bones, the pain exploding behind my eyes, and the overwhelming urge to make it all stop, even for just a second. And then ... my savior came. Same as when I was a child, he'd been there to save me, watching over me.

I look over my skin, noting I am in my loose sleep shirt and shorts. I lift my eyes and note the yellowish marks where the broken bones through my skin should be, and my heart beats wildly. I'm thankful for the fact that my bones clearly aren't broken anymore, but how long have I been asleep to explain them healing and my skin losing what would have been aggressive black bruises?

When you need answers, come and find me at the Animora Castle. This necklace should help you hide in the meantime. Ask for Ezekiel.

Ezekiel.

As his words return to me, I hold on to the name. My savior was Ezekiel. After all these years, I finally have a name. And a face. Bits and pieces of the night appear clearer the longer sleep stays away from my mind.

The metal in my fingers when I fell unconscious haunts me like a bad dream I can't quite grasp. I can't shake the memory, feeling the weight of its importance but not knowing why.

Following my instincts, I immediately pull back the covers and stand on the cold stone floor. The lack of soreness in my body as I move makes me panic more, fueling my speed. Flipping between the gray blankets, I look for a glimmer or hint of the jewelry but find nothing. I hope it made it back with me and wasn't discarded where I'd been found. Then again, I'm not sure how I made it home and what this gifted item looks like.

Almost in answer to my recurring question, the curtain across my doorway flips back and Seb walks into the room. He smiles as he sees me, his face smoothing out worry lines that have become etched into his face.

"Hey, you're awake!" he says loudly, drawing my full attention. The panic and speed driving my body fuels my annoyance at whatever he is doing here. As my eyes meet his and he catches the fire burning in me, he stops in his tracks. His hands raise in surrender as he rocks back on his heels, eyeing the scowl pulling at my lips. "Whoa!"

"What happened?" I demand, eyes searching his face. "And don't bullshit me."

"I carried you ... with Holt's help," Seb admits sheepishly. The way his eyes refuse to leave mine, mesmerized, irks me. I try and ignore it because I don't have the time or patience right now.

"Is Holt here? Can I talk to him instead?"

"He has gone back to his room to rest. You can talk to him a little later when you're feeling better ..."

"I feel fine," I interject, my impatience pushing me into action. I feel better than I expected to, after what happened in the alley. I step toward the doorway, hot spikes of anger heating my glare when Seb steps in my way, blocking my exit. "What are you doing?"

"Just take a breath before you go out there."

I cross my arms over my chest and sink into my hip. "Why?" Seb's jaw opens and closes for a moment as he struggles for words. "Spit it out," I order.

"Um ... we might need to figure out ... how to explain this to your friends," he whispers the words like it's a secret that needs to be kept hidden. Besides Ezekiel's presence, there's nothing wrong with what happened.

"What do you mean? What the fuck did you tell them?" I grind my teeth, waiting for whatever absurdity is about to spill out of his mouth.

"The truth? That horned bastard from O Positive came after you in the alley after you got him kicked out, and I arrived just in time to get you out of there," he explains in a tone that has my brows furrowing and my stomach clenching. His volume suggests this isn't the secret.

I ignore the fact that he conveniently left Ezekiel out of the description. He helped me, but I'm not going to thank him. "So then what's there to explain?"

He freezes again. "Ummm …"

I growl. "What are you doing here?" I'm not sure why he thought I would be happy to see him here when I woke up, knowing my disinterest in him last night.

"I'm the one who found you. That bloodsucker might have saved you from the daemons, but *I* brought you back here."

My cheeks flush as furious heat rise up my neck and my teeth click shut. "What did you fucking call him?"

Seb's eyes widen with fear, but I can't find it in myself to care why he is suddenly so afraid of me.

"Sorry. The *dragayastir* that saved you handed your body to me when I came out into the alley," he explains, and despite my question on how I'd made it home being answered, I still wish it hadn't been him.

"How long was I asleep?" I force out through gritted teeth. As I drop my eyes and think about what other answers I need, all I want is him out of my room and sight. I don't like him or want him around, but I know I must get answers first.

"Two days." His answer only serves to create more questions as to how all my shattered bones healed in such a short time. What had Ezekiel given me for healing? It was unlike anything I knew existed. "But there's something I should probably tell —"

"The necklace!" The words spew from my mouth before I can contain them as my thoughts return to what I'd been searching for.

"What?" Seb's spine straightens as his face scrunches in confusion.

"When you found me, was I holding a necklace?" I continue, breathing a bit easier when he reaches into his pants pocket for something. He produces a long chain with a chunky pendant. Before I can control myself, I snatch it from his opening palm. He flinches, tensing as I come close.

This time I notice.

I back up slowly, watching his body calm as I take a step. The hairs on my arms begin to prickle. Something is *very* wrong. The panic that takes over his face for a moment as he looks at *me* makes my stomach twist.

When my eyes drop to the necklace, it's temporarily forgotten. The chain is plain and a dull silver, but the pendant is breathtaking. It's oval, with purple gemstone shards sprinkled like stars in the silver. On it are foreign runic etchings. The amount of detail in the whole piece is mesmerizing. I can't tear my eyes away, bringing it closer to my face so I can see every tiny detail clearly. Like soothing rain washing over me, my impatience, anger, and frenzied emotions quell and lose their heat. I cup the precious necklace closely. I will never let it go.

"Did he give you that?" Seb asks, voice tight and forced, as though the notion is abhorrent.

Just like that, the necklace's spell is broken, and my eyes snap to his. Both my hands fall to my sides in fists, the necklace from Ezekiel securely in my right hand.

"And what if he did?" I stand straight and tighten my arms across my chest. My breath tightens as my mouth pushes into a scowl. I'm not sure why he suddenly thinks we are friends or that I owe him an explanation after one day of knowing me, but he needs to take a hint.

"Then I'd need to know what sort of relationship you two really have."

My mouth drops open as far as my jaw bone will allow. I can almost hear the click of it hitting its limits as my body freezes. *How fucking dare he!*

"*Excuse* me?" I know my voice is getting loud, and I fight to keep my volume at a level that won't make people aware that we're fighting and try eavesdropping.

The corners of Seb's lips scrunch, eyes locking with mine. His body tenses, shoulders rolling back as if it'll help ease the frustration seeping into his features. Gone is the fear that was etched into his features moments ago, now replaced with simmering anger.

"He had a perfectly good reason to!" I say quickly, remembering the way Ezekiel had justified it. He had a reason even if I'm not sure what it is yet.

"And that is?" Seb counters, his hand gesturing as though the answer is a physical thing I could offer to prove him wrong. Something in my gut twists in warning as I open my mouth to respond, but I shut it quickly, reconsidering what I should tell him.

"I ... I can't tell you. I-It's private," I stutter. My stomach tightens, the sensation telling me Ezekiel's words were meant for me. I want our secret to be just that, but he involved Seb the moment he handed me over to him. I find myself wishing it had been Holt, because *that* I could handle.

Seb's eyes widen like he's uncovered the greatest secret in history as he rocks back on his heels and crosses his arms, mirroring my stance. "Because you two are together? Or because you don't trust me?"

I fight the urge to vehemently deny the first claim, knowing the more I do, the worse it will seem. There's no evidence to support the claim except his own jealousy.

"Trust you? I barely know you!"

"You can trust me. I helped save your life. Why would I do that if you couldn't trust me?"

I scowl and divert my focus back to the necklace, dropping my arms to play with it. "I'll be the judge of who I can trust." The clasp is fiddly and despite my fingers being small and nimble, it really isn't easy to maneuver.

"Here, let me help," Seb says, reaching out. He crosses the distance between us in a few easy steps.

I pull the necklace away before he can reach it, determined to open it myself. The more my fingers desperately try to open the clasp, the more it slips over the pads of my fingers. "I can do it myself." The tight words slip out as a whisper. I know they aren't true the moment I say them, but he waits, hands at the ready, just in case.

The frustration isn't worth it. I surrender the necklace to him, if only to be entertained by him struggling with the same thing.

But he doesn't.

Of course he fucking doesn't.

His fingers slip over the clasp, undoing it with ease. He opens the chains to fit around my neck, and moves behind me. I grab my hair, still pulled back in its style from the past two days — albeit messily now — and wait patiently. The chain is cool against my neck, but where Seb's skin grazes mine is on fire. My heart pounds loudly and fast in response, seemingly trying to catch his attention. I hope it doesn't. I don't want him to know how much my body enjoys the touch. The shivers that dance excitedly under my skin are intoxicating. I don't know why my body is reacting this way to a man I don't know, but I don't have time to question it. I don't want to tell him that I don't want it to stop.

I don't need to.

The clasp comes together, and calm settles over me ... Well, it's more like a sense of clarity. I feel more *me*, though I can't quite pinpoint what has changed. Seb's fingers trail the back of my neck and down my spine, over my clothing, as though making sure the necklace is still in place.

I fight to keep my heavy breaths from making it too obvious that my body revels in his touch. Heat flares up and down my spine along the skin where his fingers press. I close my eyes and find myself leaning into his touch, fighting to swallow the extra moisture pooling in my mouth. I know pink has crept into my cheeks but I don't care, even as he moves around in front of me. Only now, his fingers rest on my neck, his touch so gentle I'm not sure I can hide the way my body twitches in response, especially when his eyes are fixated on mine.

Seb's eyes never drop to my flushed cheeks. They meet mine — mesmerized and surprised. So much so that I feel the weight pull my stomach down uncomfortably.

"Whoa!" he breathes quietly, his hand falling from my neck.

I fight the urge to feel rejected as confusion takes over. It doesn't seem like he can make up his mind on his own feelings. Is he scared, turned on, annoyed or trying to be platonic? The way he's been back and forth at the outing and today is starting to give me a headache.

I step back, crossing my arms again and meeting his stare as intensely as I can. "What?"

"Your eyes ..." he whispers. His lack of information only serves to make me want to punch him. Clenching my hands into fists, I plant my feet into the cool stone, hoping it will quell the furious burn in my system.

"What about them? Because in case you hadn't noticed prior to today, yes, they are green. They have always been that way, and no, I'm not a fae." I don't hide the venom as it leaks into my tone, annoyed that once again my fucking eye color has created a barrier between myself and almost everyone else.

"There's something else I should probably tell you," he says slowly, his palms lifting slightly like he was calming a cornered animal.

He is one minute away from being slapped.

"Out. With. *It.*"

"Since the attack, your eyes have been glowing green like a fae."

"What? No! There's no way!" I move quickly, ignoring that he looks like he wants to say more. Crossing to the wardrobe that has seen better days — thanks to the eternal moisture from my room's leaks — I yank the door open. Inside it is a mirror. I check my eyes in it, dreading what I'll find. The solid weight in my stomach disappears.

My eyes are normal. Well ... normal for me. They are the same un-glowing jade green they've always been.

"What are you talking about? My eyes are normally like this." I scowl at Seb, not sure what kind of dumb joke he is playing. He isn't smiling, though. His mouth pops open and closes several times like he can swallow the words from the air.

Still, I wait, watching him fumble silently until he eventually speaks.

"The necklace ... when you put it on, they dulled back to normal. I know your eyes are green. I've known since long before you knew I existed. But when I found you in the alley, the blood—*dragayastir* warned me and they were as he said. They were *glowing green.*" It wasn't a perfect explanation, but it was enough to make me realize.

My head snaps to my reflection as my fingers fly up to the necklace. Ice chills my veins as Ezekiel's words finally make sense.

This necklace should help you hide in the meantime.

I have something to hide.

The necklace pendant is cool against my fingers, even in the places where the pendant has been resting against my warm skin. Every hair on my body stands up as I chew my lip.

"Let me see …" I whisper, as though I can make the glow present itself just by willing it. I feel Seb's movements in my periphery before I see him slowly move behind me. His fingers graze the back of my neck again as he moves to updo the chain, but I barely feel it.

I know the moment the clasp is undone. The calm that has blanketed my nervous system, dulling my emotions, lifts and everything becomes heightened. My eyes brighten with a glow I've only ever seen in my nightmares.

The world, the floor, doesn't feel stable anymore and my empty stomach threatens to throw up its contents. Seb's hands grip my upper arms near my shoulders as I fall back into him, holding me upright. My gaze finally drifts to him in the mirror as he steadies me by my upper arms, the necklace dangling and knocking my elbow. He watches me, his face creased slightly.

"You're not going to call me little monster?" I ask quietly, swallowing the break as my voice catches.

He frowns in response as though I've told an offensive joke, his fingers squeezing me reassuringly. His breath tickles my ear as he whispers, serving to distract me, "You're not a monster."

"I feel like one," I whisper.

I see him fighting the urge to disagree with me, his mouth opening and closing like he's trying to find the right words. A moment of heavy silence passes between us. More than I'd ever thought silence could.

I'm cold.

Despite the warm humidity of the room, I'm trembling. None of the heat reaches me. His hands, hot against my cooler skin, are the only reminder that warmth exists. I drop my eyes from the mirror, unable to look at myself. I can't look at the pity etched on his face a moment longer.

But I don't want to feel alone anymore.

"Seb?"

"Hmm?"

"I'm scared." The admission lightens me more than I ever imagined.

Chapter Twelve
Darkness in the Air
Morana

Morana moved through the forest, step by reluctant step, following the call of death. It had been a number of days since she'd been subjected to witness, and she was thankful to the fates for that.

She'd been lucky enough to spend her last two days inundated by questions from Alva. Not that she minded. It was weird but surprisingly nice to have someone care about who she was and how she got there.

That was until the call of death had yanked her by the soul out of her conversation with Alva, and she had to heed it. She promised to return soon and made her way out of his treehouse home, surprised when her trail took her out and away from the city of Savastral Revon. Normally, she'd gone there to witness a death of a human or something else that had fallen prey to a daemon's hunting games. None of the true predators strayed far into the grove. Occasionally, a daemon would get brave and hunt outside the city, but they never liked staying for long, and most fae were too much hassle for the chase.

It was a surprise to Morana as her wary but obedient steps took her further from the main city.

She finally took note of how late it was. She hadn't realized when she'd been with Alva how long they'd been talking. It was dark out, meaning it was the middle of the night. While the sun wouldn't be rising for many hours, she'd never been someone to spend late nights with ... anyone. It felt good though, and she'd barely noticed the change to her routine. Although, she wasn't sure she had a routine anymore with Alva in her life.

Morana smiled to herself and kept moving, undeterred by the tug on her soul like she usually felt. For once, the distraction of thinking about Alva helped keep her mind from the fact she was walking toward scenes of death. For the first time, she felt just a little less cursed.

As she reached the outer edge of the grove, her smile fell from her face. Her heart skipped beats as her mind raced and her stomach sank. She looked at the barren lands. Fae don't go out to the barren lands and no amount of tugging would take her out past the treeline, her feet stopping where the grass ended in a neat, straight line.

Nothing grew past the line.

Nothing tried.

The barren land was a dusty wasteland that stretched out for miles. Morana wasn't sure how far it went. No one had made it to the other side and returned. Or if they'd made it, they hadn't wanted to return. Dust storms, blazing heat, and a lack of water and vegetation made it inhospitable to everyone.

Well ... almost everyone.

The witches somehow thrived on this land. No one was sure but they were a secretive bunch, and no one got close to them. Not even their own species seemed to trust their magickal race. Witches were the humans that had given up their souls to darkness for immense power, though how much, Morana wasn't sure. Their eyes were devoid of color, the entire eyeball consumed by the blackness to which they had succumbed.

Morana breathed a sigh of relief as the pull against her soul subsided, letting her know she had reached the place of witness. She stared down at where the ground changed just in front of her toes, and her stomach twisted at the notion of taking a step further. The idea of witnessing a death here wasn't particularly appealing either.

Looking around, Morana struggled to find the person whose death she should witness. It had happened on occasion that she would appear before the victim, but rare. Usually, it gave her a chance to hide before the death occurred, so that she could keep herself safe from whatever attacker was in the area.

Without hesitation, she turned to the nearest tree and reached for the lowest branch, just above her head height. Hoisting herself up, she hooked her legs around the branch and shuffled on top of it, moving to the next secure branch she could find and making quick work of the climb. It wasn't until she was nestled among its pine leaves, looking down through a gap in the foliage, that she let her body relax slightly. This was where she was thankful for her choices in all-black outfits. Only her green glowing eyes gave her away, but she knew there was no way to hide that. She had to hope the danger in this death scene never looked up.

She settled in and waited, her senses on high alert in the silence. Her heart hammered aggressively in her ribs as she sunk into the scent of oak. It was strikingly quiet out in the barren lands, only the wind moving dust or leaves making any sound. There were no animals, or other creatures rustling out this far from the city and the nothingness outside of the forest.

Time passed and her heart slowed, but it wasn't until her body had calmed completely that the movement around her began. Dread dropped like a heavy boulder in her stomach as the rustling of multiple bodies below her came closer.

One by one, cloaked figures moved into her view — four in total moved to sit in a circle facing in toward each other, no words among them. They sat in silence, their movements ceasing. The rustling and crunching reached Morana's ears. Two more cloaked figures approached, both tugging on a rope behind them. The leashed creature — a dryad — came into view, and Morana's throat constricted. His eyes glowed brighter than Morana's with skin that was dark and textured, perfect for blending into the trunks of trees. Their camouflage was enviable in the forests, and they were typically the quickest among the fae.

The cloaked figures removed their hoods, and Morana finally saw the lack of color or glow in their eyes. Solid black eyeballs glistened back in the moonlight like the onyx stones she sometimes saw when swimming in the shallows of the crater lake.

Witches.

Morana sank closer to the trunk of the tree carefully, her body cold at the thought that if witches had managed to catch a dryad, she had no chance of escape if they looked up and spotted her. Not many knew the powers of the witch, what the limit or capabilities of their powers were, so she had no idea whether they would be able to see her. She hoped their eyesight were like humans and not magickly enhanced at all, so that she only needed to close her eyes to hide.

She didn't want to put it to the test to find out.

Witches had been in hiding most of her lifetime. Everyone knew about them because of the danger they had posed to the fragile peace in the past, but she'd never actually seen one, let alone a whole coven of them. They'd disappeared after their leader had been locked away for conspiring to end all races.

The two with the rope dragged the dryad to the center of the seated witches circle, not being gentle as they shoved him backward to the ground until he was lying on his back. The bindings made it hard for him to attempt to get up, everything except his feet bound close to his small body. Dryads measured to half the height of an average human, so he was powerless against them, even with his fae strength. The two standing witches in the center of the circle took hold of the dryad, holding his body against the ground as they disregarded the rope. The witches around them lifted their hands in unison and whispered to the air. The wind stole the words before Morana could hear them, but the lilting tone suggested an incantation of some kind.

Even at the thought of attempting to help the poor, defenseless fae, a splitting headache threatened Morana to stay put. Pressing a finger to her temple, she waited until the thought passed and the headache with it. She grimaced as she settled in to witness.

Black thorns burst from the ground. Morana fought to keep her quickening breath quiet as she watched the scene unfold, open-mouthed. She had witnessed plenty of gruesome deaths previously, but this was ritualistic and unlike anything Morana had seen in her time being one of the cursed.

The hands of the center witches fell away as the thorns took over the role as restraint, and they slid back to sit between their sisters, their hands and words falling into perfect sync with the ritual. The magick in the air was cold, despite it being a warm night, and the hair along Morana's arms stood up as though electrified. The thorns moved with a life of their own, tightening against the dryad's skin until Morana was sure she was about to see him pop. He screamed into his gag, his muffled horror making Morana breathless like a physical punch to the gut.

She wasn't sure death would ever get easier to witness.

Clapping her hand over her mouth to hold back any stray noise that might escape, she pulled her knees into her chest and watched as the thorns dragged the dryad into the ground, green fae blood bubbling where he'd disappeared. A pool formed in the circle, more and more liquid flowing out until Morana was sure it would reach the witches seated nearby and soak their cloaks.

It didn't.

Like it hit an invisible barrier, the blood splashed and stopped just short of the witches. None of them flinched as the liquid came strikingly close. Morana was fascinated by its edges, waiting for something to spill just a little closer. The surface shimmered to life with the vision of a grotesque elderly witch's face with solid black eyes and more wrinkles than scrunched parchment. Despite the fact that Morana's soul had lifted its weight, that she had been witness to what was been meant to, she stayed, unable to move.

"Sister..." the elderly witch's vision said, her quiet voice echoing across the pool, hoarse and snakelike.

A witch rocked forward slightly and moved her face over the pool, speaking clearly, with a sense of admiration for the witch in the reflection, "We are your humble servants."

"Good. It is nice to see that my family still respects me."

Chills skated across Morana's skin as she listened, her stomach twisting aggressively.

"We don't have long and we ask for your guidance," the first witch spoke up again, her head bowed to the woman in the reflection.

"Then my guidance shall be yours, my dears."

The witches leaned over the pool of blood, their bodies blocking Morana's view of the reflection. She saw the mouth moving on the woman in the pool but lost the words in the wind before they could reach. She fought the urge to lean forward on the branch for any scrap of knowledge, knowing it would risk too much. So she stayed, waiting even as the face shimmered away from the surface of the lake.

The witches lifted their hoods ceremoniously and stood, leaving the pool of green fae blood on the ground. Morana watched it carefully, half-expecting the blood to disappear as quickly as it had appeared, but it stayed, slowly drying at the edges.

Morana was curled up in the tree, feeling comforted by the silence. For a time, she sifted through the information of what she'd seen. Fate had wanted her to see that. The idea of witch activity growing was something that made her feel sick to her stomach and kept her rooted to the trunk. She barely moved from her place for hours, even as the sun began to rise somewhere behind her. She stared down at the green blood seeping into the dirt and felt the weight of his death so much more than she'd expected.

A rustle below startled her.

Her eyes scanned the forest floor below, frenzied. When she caught the flash of familiar silver hair below her, she simultaneously relaxed and panicked. Alva's kind face climbed into view, and Morana couldn't help pulling him close in an embrace as he reached her branch.

"What are you doing? You shouldn't be here," she rushed out quietly, in case any others lingered around. She didn't bother to ask how he'd found her. The mark on their wrists would forever be a compass to finding each other, thanks to the activated magick that flowed through their veins.

"I'm not here to interfere. I know what you said about that. I just want to learn more about your world," he said just as quietly. Morana's eyes widened as she watched him.

"Then ask me about, silly." Morana flicked her hand lightly against his arm in a mock slap. "It's really dangerous near some of these deaths. You can't just appear to see what I see. You could get the timing wrong, or accidentally give away the location, or interfere when I'm not supposed to ... I—"

She was hyperventilating, her pulse racing at the thought that the male she'd found could be taken from her so soon. It was unbearable.

"It's okay. I won't do it again, I promise. You were gone for a while, and I figured you might need some food." From his pocket, Alva produced a piece of fruit and held it toward her.

A smile pulled her face up as she took it. "Thank you!"

Morana found herself smiling a lot lately.

Chapter Thirteen
A Trip Through the Fire
Azariah

"Do I have to get Holt to talk some sense into you?" Seb pushes, tone hushed and voice grating.

Despite the fact I have made up my mind and he has no say over what I do, he still thinks he is entitled to tell me what to do and where I can go.

"Do you want me to trust you or not? You can't go threatening to tell Holt every time you disagree with me," I shoot back, turning on him as I try to put my armored wrist cuffs on in peace.

"What you're planning to do is stupid. At least bring me as a backup."

I stare at him for a moment, the scowl on my face evidence of how I hate his insinuation that he is my savior.

"No, because I need someone to cover for me here while I'm gone. That's what I'm *trusting* you with. Can you handle it or not?" My voice is quiet but clear as I hold his gaze. I need to make sure he holds up his end of the bargain, whether he likes it or not. I know he wants to be the big strong man to save the day, but he isn't the one with the answers, and for all he knows, I'm more dangerous.

I need to know the truth, so I have to do this.

"I can handle a few people asking where you are," he says, lip curling up in disgust at my questioning his masculinity. "What I can't handle is you going on your own as the favorite food into a literal dragayastir den, all for answers from someone you've met in person maybe twice in your life because he gave you a necklace."

"Well, I'll find a way because I can handle myself." I drop my gaze to the task at hand, doing up the ties on the back of my wrist cuffs before moving to the other.

Seb scoffs. I try not to sigh heavily at yet more disagreement. "Not from what I've seen. Are you forgetting that a matter of days ago, you were lying in an alley dying and only survived because you had help? *My* help."

I roll my eyes. "Yes, I remember that *Ezekiel* saved me. Which is why I know I can trust him. He wouldn't ask me to visit if it was going to endanger my life, I know that."

Seb's jaw tightens, trying not to react to my comment that Ezekiel saved me and not him. He can pretend to be the hero all he wants, but we both know the truth.

"How can you know that for sure? He has saved you twice in your life, but what about all the other times?"

"Because he's been my avenging protective guardian my entire life!" I spit the words in a whisper as I round on him, covering my mouth the second the words are free. I can't believe I said that. I have never told anyone that before.

Seb's eyes widen, and I know there is no taking back the words. "You conveniently forgot to mention that part!" he hisses, but I can only gape at him, lips parted.

"I ..."

I can't believe I just told him that. Fuck, I'm an idiot.

"What do you mean? Trust goes both ways, Azariah, and you need to tell me or I'm not going to let you go alone."

I sigh.

"My entire life, well ... since the first time I was saved by him as a child, I've known I was being watched. I could feel it. Conveniently, anyone who has ever come up against me or threatened me in the world outside the Culling tunnels has ended up dead or maimed enough that they never bothered me again," I admit, voice dropping low enough that no one else can hear.

Seb listens quietly, not meeting my eyes as he absorbs the information, head nodding.

Silence drags. I wait for him to say something — *anything* — to let me know he understands that even outside these walls, I'm hardly in danger.

He says nothing.

"So, can I go without you fighting me on it?" I push, and finally he lifts his eyes to mine.

"Yes, but please be careful. And don't take the necklace off unless you absolutely have to. I don't have to tell you that there are clearly enough daemons who could mistake you for fae and try to take a bite out of you if you do."

I want to remind him that even in human form there are enough dragayastir who want to take a bit out of me too, but I know that would be counterproductive.

I lift my fingers and touch the necklace, reminding myself it's still there. As though becoming aware of it makes me attuned of the magick, I feel the calming presence it carries. It's still cold against my breastbone.

For a fleeting moment, I could get lost in fiddling with it again, but I have something I need to do.

Pulling my focus back to the present, I check over my armored clothing pieces, making sure they are all secure, before placing the knife and dagger sheaths all over my body, ensuring they are hidden. And finally, I retrieve the heavy black cloak from my wardrobe, rolling it up and shoving it under my arm until I am away from the tunnels.

Wearing it here would draw too much attention.

"I'll walk you out," Seb offers.

I fight the urge to say no. I don't want to cause an argument that might convince him he has to come with me.

Just keep him agreeable, I remind myself.

We venture out of my curtained doorway and into the dark tunneled walls, taking all the turns needed to climb to the surface and the entrance to Skull's Rest. Most of the other children in the tunnels are already relaxing in their rooms or getting up to their own mischief. Not many wander the tunnels at this hour.

"Just promise me you'll be careful," Seb whispers as we walk through an empty section of the Culling.

I roll my eyes. "Honestly, why do you even care?"

"Why wouldn't I?"

"Because I've given you no reason to," I say with an exasperated sigh. "Because we're not close and we don't know each other well at all. And no matter how much you want to *get to know me*,' I'm never sleeping with you. Got it?"

"Got it," he says quickly, and when I check his face, he doesn't seem surprised.

Acceptance, really? This guy is so confusing, and I can't get a handle on his motivations.

"Okay, so why are you still here?"

"Do you assume that every guy that wants to get to know you wants to sleep with you?" he asks, genuinely curious as his stupid eyebrows knit together.

"I ..." How the hell does this guy have such an ability to make me flounder for words? I've always been sure in my confidence and able to defend myself verbally around others. But when I'm with him ...

"Honestly?" Seb murmurs. "I've seen you around and even though you have been quite abrasive to me the last few days, I admire you. You work harder than anyone I've seen, are fiercely loyal and protective of your friends, and ... honest."

"Honest?" My brow arches, confused.

"You're the tough-love kind of honest that a lot of people don't understand. But you give people the truth they don't want to necessarily hear because you care."

My steps stop as I take in what he was saying. No one has ever described me like that. No one has seen that part of me. I'm not denying it exists, but I haven't necessarily wanted anyone to know. It wasn't a secret, but it ... kind of was.

I chew my lip as he slows in front of me, realizing I'm no longer beside him. Seb watches me attentively, as though he is worried I'm about to bolt. I'm just ... speechless.

Again.

Come on, say something.

"Thanks," I say, my steps starting up again. I move past him, the speed now increased. "I guess."

I walk in silence, speed-walking as fast as my legs will carry me. He doesn't say anything and the more he catches up with me, the more I find myself increasing my pace to keep ahead of him. My lip grates between my teeth as I think about what he said. What he has seen in a short time around me. Watching me.

I don't need any more friends. I don't need anyone else in my life. I have plenty and any more would be a distraction from my goal of becoming a true Reaper. It could possibly even spell out my death.

I keep moving, not bothering to say goodbye as I reach the opening to the city.

I swing my cloak on from under my arm, desperate to get answers. I'm thankful the afternoon sun is still out as I power walk from the entrance to the Culling tunnels. It's only a matter of time before the darkness of the night creeps in and the risk of being outside alone grows immensely. For now, the Others that I worry about, the dragayastir and the daemons, are staying out of the light. It's not a weakness but they have a discomfort that keeps them away during the day. I have an hour or two before that all changes, so I will have to act quickly.

The large hood of my heavy cloak works well to hide my face in its depths. No one looks my way long enough to see beyond the heavy shadow and material over my eyes, and for that, I'm thankful.

I turn west, heading toward a section of town I've done well to avoid my entire life, only feeling mildly comforted by the sunlight as I head for the dragayastir quarter of Skull's Rest. In the distance, I hear screams, roars, and growls that do nothing to sate the buzzing building in my veins. I want to run, to make sure I can get to the Animora Castle before the sun sets, but I know that could risk drawing even more attention.

I have to look like I ooze power, like being any individual in the street couldn't bother me. Actions of fear will get me killed.

I walk briskly, making sure they're long strides and not hurried steps, and work to keep my shoulders back, ensuring my hood is over my face but not impeding my vision. The city of Skull's Rest smells of stone, ash, and river water. My nose is already complaining at the dry air again. I have to get used to it all before I move out of the tunnels.

It takes me longer than I would have liked to reach the change in architecture that signals the dragayastir housing quarter, and finally, the castle. It isn't hard to find, considering the way it towers above Skull's Rest skyline, its black towers reaching toward the sky. It's monstrously higher than anything else within view.

As I reach the beginning of the footbridge with very minimal Others around me, my chin tilts up toward the sky as I follow its height. I don't care that my hood lifts with it — no one is close enough to see my face as it meets the light — but I am in complete awe of how truly massive the castle is up close. From afar, it has always been large, but it is a whole different thing seeing it up close.

The entire castle is black stone; I'm not sure if it has been built that way or charred from dragayastir fire. All its edges, despite being ornately carved, are sharp and look a bit like a death trap to anything that can fly. I'm not the one to ask that. The irony isn't lost on me. I keep expecting to see the giant flying bodies of dragayastir with expansive, scaled wings and large bodies able to swoop down on its prey.

The castle is secluded from everything else, a deep crevasse in the stone around it serving as a steep-drop moat. It adds to the isolation of the castle from the rest of the quarters, and makes it look like it resides on a floating island. As I look over the bridge, the drop disappears into the dark, the afternoon sun not reaching the bottom to see what lurks beneath. That is if you survive the drop.

At the beginning of the bridge, there are pillars with miniaturized dragayastir gargoyles in their flying reptilian forms watching over the pathway. Many of these statues are placed along the long, winding bridge that makes my heart ratchet up in its beat. It's the only way in or out of the castle for those that can't fly, so I take a deep breath and begin my journey up the bridge.

Among the black stone, as the sun finally begins to set, yellow lights come alive from the windows. They glisten like stars against the dark building, almost mesmerizing with how many there are. The closer I get to the end of the bridge, and the sharp dark gray wrought-iron gates, the more my body wants to run in the opposite direction. My muscles tighten, ready to retreat, and my heart rate spikes. I force my lungs to take deep, calming breaths.

Reaching the gate, I pull back my hood as I meet the glowing red eyes of a guard waiting outside. I'm surprised to see him out in the daytime, even if the light is quickly disappearing, but I know they aren't injured by sunlight. The dragayastir can still kill me without breaking a sweat when they are weakened, but it gives me a small amount of solace that I stand a better chance in the light. The guard's eyebrows scrunch together as he looks me up and down, before they catch and stop at my chest. I drop my eyes and follow his line of sight to the necklace, just below where the cloak connects at the hollow of my throat.

I lift the pendant, showing it off as I speak clearly, trying to avoid letting my anxieties shake my voice, "I'm here to see Ezekiel. He's expecting me."

The guard doesn't ask for more information, he just nods, turns to open the gate, and steps aside. I move past him and come face to face with another guard on the other side of the gate, who has clearly heard our interaction but is good at hiding. He doesn't speak to me either, simply indicating with a hand gesture to follow him.

We move through the front receiving area of the castle, a sprawling space of black sand with small gardens of thriving black and dark purple flowers. The sand we walk on is just as black as the stone on the castle, and I can't help feeling like the darkness is so much heavier here with the lack of color. Even the human quarters in Skull's Rest are a mix of dark browns and grays, and they are nothing compared to the way this makes me feel. Like darkness thrives all around me.

The sun is entirely gone by the time we scale the wide, deep steps leading to the castle doors. There are too many, in my opinion, and each step causes my legs to stride further than is comfortable.

The inside of the castle is just as dark and imposing as the outside, except the level of affluence I have never seen before. The furniture, walls and every item in sight looks extravagant, clean, and new. Giant struc-tures house hundreds of candles suspended above the ceiling, perfectly dusted and glistening despite the black shining surface. The candles, despite melting down in various heights, leak no wax on the structure that holds it. It's dark and yet ... pristine. Perfect. Luxurious.

My heart squeezes, wondering if the reapers will ever get to experience anything this phenomenal. From what I've seen of the humans, cleanli-ness and extravagance isn't a priority, survival is.

It hasn't occurred to me that I have stopped moving to stare around the receiving hall until a voice clears in front of me. Drawing my gaze, I open my eyes wide as I mumble an apology and continue to follow the dragayastir guard through the room and into the next.

Each room is more beautiful than the last, and I can't help but feel my steps slow more and more. The guard doesn't say anything, but I do notice him slowing his steps as we move, and eventually he stops. The room we make it to is one I can't name. The closest I've seen is our social space or academics library in the Culling tunnels we use to catch up with each other and study. This is nothing compared to that. Lavish cushioned benches face each other, and the walls are framed by tall floor-to-ceiling shelves that are packed with books. The black hardwood floor clicks under my boots, and I fight the urge to check if my dirty shoes have left behind marks.

The guard says nothing else as I stand in the center of the room, before his steps retreat. I turn to see him shutting the door behind him, leaving me alone in the space. Taking a deep breath, I try not to panic when the lock clicks in the door.

It's probably nothing. They just don't want you wandering.

I try to keep my mind under control so that I don't freak out, and instead walk over to the bookshelves. I scan the titles, finding dozens relating to different kinds of magick, some of which I've never heard of. I'm sure I'll learn about it all once I make it into the reaper training grounds, but some part of me questions if the elder reapers even know about all of these books.

How much do we actually know about the world outside of our human scope?

Before I can delve too much into questioning my own species, the door clicks and opens again. I turn my head to see Ezekiel striding into the room, swinging the door shut behind him.My feet want to move closer to him, but I stay rooted to the spot. I'm not sure what I should be doing here — what we are to each other when I'm not being followed out on the streets of Skull's Rest. Judging by the way his steps halt abruptly as he catches my blank face, he is thinking the same.

Chapter Fourteen
The Promise of Fire
Azariah

Silence falls between Ezekiel and I, neither of us wanting to speak first.

The only sounds between us, besides my heavy breathing, is my heart bashing against my ribs and the heavy ornate clock ticking away in the corner of the room.

Tick. Tick.

The smell of old books and leather do nothing to calm the way my mind races for what to say to Ezekiel. I pick at my cuticles, feeling the sharp pain as I pull up more skin than I should have.

He's known me nearly my entire life, and yet somehow, I'm not sure what to say to him. What are we to each other? Does he even like me or am I just entertaining to keep alive and protect for now? Is there a reason he chose me? Why? Do I want him to care?

What if he cares in a way I don't want him to? What if he wants me to do things I'm uncomfortable with? Have I royally fucked up by coming here? What if he has been protecting me to lure me into a situation like this to become his personal blood bag?

I open my lips, same as him, silence thick between us.

Speechless, until …

"Hi," I whisper before I can register I've spoken.

Like the tension has been let out of the room, Ezekiel's shoulders relax. His muscles and jaw lose their tension and he takes a step closer. All I can focus on beyond his shoulder-length untamed dark brown hair is his mesmerizing, glowing red eyes. Any panicked thoughts I had about the situation I've put myself in fade away.

I'm not used to seeing his face. Watching how his strong, handsome features pull and move in response to … *me*. It's striking. The sharp bones of his chin look like they're etched in porcelain, and the way his gaze meets mine makes my chest and stomach tighten.

"Good evening, my Belladonna," he responds. His deep, velvety voice sends chills skating up my spine. My stomach clenches tightly, robbing me of the ability to breathe deeply.

"Your what?" I ask breathlessly.

"Belladonna." His voice lilts over the name like a foreign language I can't speak.

"Like the flower?"

"I had a feeling you'd know the reference," he whispers.

"That's where the understanding stops," I say. Despite trying to halt any intentions there with clipped words, my voice comes out softer and less harsh than I mean it to. I can't bring myself to be my usual vicious self to the man who has protected me for the majority of my life. "My name is Azariah."

"I know. But just like the flower, you are beautiful and deadly to those who get too close."

My stomach clenches tighter as shivers dance up and down my arms. Crossing them, I try not to show how much his words affect me or the way his assessing gaze raking over me makes my organs twist like they want to escape my body and pull me to him. I swallow hard, making sure every bit of dry weakness in my tone is gone before I reply.

"I guess so ... or you see they are getting too close to me. A danger to me," I say, trying to keep a modicum of emotional distance between us. I am eternally thankful for the protection he has given me, but I'm skeptical that he might ask for something in return one day.

"You have a powerful ally in me," he says, stepping forward again.

I watch him carefully as he strides slowly into the room, closer to me. He waves his hand out, indicating to the cushioned bench chair as he sits in the opposite one. I follow his gesture, taking a seat. My body sinks into the cushions. It's hard to stay alert when this new comfort draws my body in. Like a welcoming hug, my muscles relax in the seat's hold, despite how much I want to stay attentive. The full weight of how tired I am melts into the soft furniture.

"I do," I start, knowing no matter how tired I feel or how comfortable Ezekiel's furniture makes me, I need the answers I came for. "As my powerful ally, I need answers about what happened. Something is wrong with me, and I need to stop or undo it."

"You're wearing the necklace, that's a good start." Ezekiel nods, his eyes dropping to the pendant just as the guard's had. Only with his eyes on my body, I feel naked. I'm hyper aware of how my cleavage presses up in the corset and where the necklace falls, bringing attention to it. I try not to reveal how I feel under his gaze, forcing myself to breathe evenly as though I don't notice.

It doesn't seem like he cares or notices it, though.

"It hides my *glowing green eyes.* Of course I'm wearing it."

"You've seen them, then."

I stare at him for a moment, my lips parted. His eyes don't leave the necklace. Does he really think I wouldn't have seen the way my eyes glowed?

The memory of Seb breaking the news intrudes upon me, and I know there was every possibility that I would have left my room in search of my friends and created trouble for myself before I discovered the new eyes that could get me killed.

"I need to know how to rid myself of them. If anyone but Seb sees me like this, they'll kill me." A Reaper, even a novice that wasn't my friend, wouldn't think twice about putting a knife through my heart if they saw it. My non-glowing green eyes have given me enough grief. Looking like a fae in the tunnels would be a sure-fire way to my death.

"You are safe here." Ezekiel leans forward, his elbows resting on his knees as his red eyes lift to mine, holding steady. The clenching in my stomach alleviates as I return his gaze, scared to look away.

"But what about back at the Culling? What happens if the necklace falls off?"

Ezekiel's brows furrow and his head tilts slightly. He stays silent for a moment. His behavior and confusion signal alarm bells in my head, and though my muscles don't pull me from the couch, they tense as though they are ready to run for the door.

"Why would you return to the tunnels?"

I sit up straight, my spine electrified. "Because it's my home? Because I need to study for my Crucible! All I've ever wanted is to be a Reaper and I plan on seeing that through." The volume of my voice rises, but it doesn't seem to bother him as he watches me with a frown and tense jaw.

"You can't. The reapers will kill you."

"Then tell me how to get rid of the glow."

"You can't."

Ice floods my veins as the weight of his words settles on my shoulders. Every muscle freezes but the erratic beating of my heart. My mouth opens, wanting to fight him with a quick retort but nothing appears. Pity swims in the depths of his eyes; he didn't want to have to break the news to me. The weight on my shoulders presses down, making it harder to focus on my breathing.

"Why not?" I finally ask, voice quiet.

"How much do you know of banshees?" he drawls.

All I can do is turn my lip up in disgust as I think of the cursed creatures I've heard venturing around Skull's Rest. "I know they're creepy looking fae who are cursed to watch us all die. If you see one near you when you're hunting, likelihood is you're done for," I say matter-of-factly, reciting what I've started learning for my Crucible tests.

Ezekiel nods in response, rolling his tongue over his teeth behind his closed lips. For a moment, he looks at the ground, before he says, "There are a race of fae cursed to watch the deaths of others, yes. But do you know how they were made?"

"*Made*? I thought it was a bloodline ..."

"It does affect a bloodline. Some banshees, a number of them these days, are fae born into their curse. However, it began somewhere earlier in their lineage when one of their ancestors encountered a witch who cursed them."

"Ahh, okay. What does this have to do with me?"

"Typically, the banshees are cursed elves, only because that is the race that has historically had the most exposure to the witches."

"So, you're saying that banshees can be any species?"

Ezekiel nods. "I am."

"And are you trying to imply that I'm a ..."

"Yes."

My stomach drops so hard and fast that it disappears through the bottom of my body, creating a cavernous hole through the couch with its weight. The breath from my lungs is knocked out of me as though the single word was a punch to my gut.

"No," I whisper so breathlessly I wonder if he heard it. "No, that's not possible."

"Unfortunately, like the fae, you were born into this. It's highly uncommon and I don't think I've heard of it happening to a human for many hundreds of years prior. But it can happen."

"No."

"Azariah ..."

"No!" I finally find my voice, standing abruptly. I refuse to let my muscles enjoy the comfort of the seat any longer. I don't want to be here listening to these lies because there is no way it is true. I would *know* if I were a banshee.

I'm a human. Always have been, always would be.

He knows nothing.

"I know it's hard to hear, but ..." Ezekiel tries, his voice soft in an attempt to soothe me. He stays seated on the couch, looking up at me. I don't move, but I don't sit either. I stay standing, letting my small stature tower over him.

"I haven't pissed off any witches. I've never even seen one! I wasn't born a banshee. I'm human. Just because I was born with green eyes means nothing. They didn't glow *ever* until that daemon attacked me!"

"You hadn't been awakened yet. The powers typically don't appear until you are thirty years of age. Assuming the curse isn't broken," he explains.

"Then why are my eyes glowing *now*? I'm only twenty-one!"

"What the daemon gave you is called 'helping hand.' It's designed to force a halfling or a shifter to transition to their Other form, but for you, it brought forward your curse."

"This is ridiculous! I can't be ..." I hate the fact that a part of me believes him. I've always been different, I know that. The fact that my blood is a greater trade than any of us ever expected at O Positive is another clue that seems to bolster Ezekiel's information.

I hate it.

I want to close my eyes and find out this is all a hideous dream. Each time I blink, though, I'm in the grand library sitting room of Ezekiel's castle, talking to the unreasonably attractive protector who has looked after me my entire life as he tries to convince me I'm a *banshee*.

Fuck.

"How do I undo it?"

Ezekiel leans forward, his unruly dark brown hair shifting as he tilts his head quizzically again. "You can't. You need to get away from the humans for your own good. They'll kill you when they find out what you are."

"And where am I supposed to go? Here? In case you hadn't realized, I'm also in danger of being killed here, too." I scoff, shaking my head.

"I wouldn't let anything happen to you," he growls. The roughness in his tone makes him sound dangerous again, in a way that makes the hair on the back of my neck stand up uncomfortably.

I ignore his protective guardian act, knowing it doesn't matter. I'm not taking him up on his offer. I won't even consider it.

"All I've ever wanted is to be a Reaper. And now you're telling me I can't because I've been cursed since birth? How the *fuck* do you know this?"

"I was there," he utters, leaning back in his chair, seeming confident that his words will be reason enough for me to stay and continue this conversation.

My mouth dries out as I stumble backward, my calves knocking against the structure of the seat. I refuse to drop though, watching wide-eyed as Ezekiel's porcelain face darkens with an emotion I can't pinpoint. "What?"

"I was out in Skull's Rest many, *many* years ago when a Reaper crossed my path. It was in the time before the Shadow and Unseelie Courts were locked away. She was on a mission to find information on Baba Vada."

"Baba Vada?"

"What you need to know is that Baba Vada was the leader of the witches and a very dangerous creature who had to be stopped. The witches, however, were never going to give her up without a fight. The Reaper who crossed my path was your mother."

My face falls, the color rushing from my skin. His voice is hoarse with a vulnerability I've never seen a person give. My body slides onto the seat, perching itself on the edge. I press my lips shut.

"I don't think she knew she was pregnant at the time, but I could smell it on her. She went after a witch, Baba Vada's second-in-command, with the intention of torturing the information out of her. When she went to capture her, she was cursed instead."

My eyes tear up as the image plays in my mind of a woman who looks like me trying to do her job and being cursed for it by a horrid, untrustworthy witch. My chest tightens, and though I can hear Ezekiel's words, I barely register them. I'm too caught up in the mental image that will haunt me for the rest of my life.

"She knew that she could never return to the reapers with what she had become and so she retreated into the forest. I lost track of her for months when she'd left Skull's Rest. I'm not sure what she did in that time, but she returned after she had given birth to you and crossed my path once again. I found her sneaking through the city one night toward the Culling tunnels with a baby in her arms. *You.*"

I blink free the tears, feeling them slide down my cheeks as I look at Ezekiel. He hasn't looked away from me, but I know he sees the water trails down my cheeks, watching with a frown and clenched hands.

"I wondered what happened to the girl with green eyes who'd been dropped off at the entrance to the tunnels to be raised like all the other humans, when fate rewarded my curiosity. The night you were attacked by my own kind, I found you again and couldn't stand the thought of not knowing what you would become. I saw the fire in you to fight; the strength of an eight-year-old girl who thought she could take on any Other that came her way. I stepped in to save you that day."

"You knew what I was this whole time? What I would become, and you never tried to warn me?" I ask, so many questions and thoughts rising to the surface like a bubbling pot about to spill over. "You've been protective of me for years knowing I was cursed and would be killed as the one thing I wanted to be more than anything else."

"I knew you wouldn't awaken till you were thirty, and by that time, you would have achieved your dream of being a Reaper and spent time living it. I figured once the curse triggered, that you would be able to maturely step away and keep yourself protected from the human society."

Something about the way he speaks to me lights a fire of rage in my chest. Like I'm a child that needs to be protected. My dreams of being a Reaper isn't some flight of fancy that will be sated by one day on the job. The fact that he doesn't know that, or respect it, proves that while he's been watching over me, he hasn't fucking paid attention.

"And what? Now that I'm triggered early, you expect me to walk away and live out my days trapped in your castle like a child that needs to be protected?" I shout, every word clipped. My hands ball up into fists at my sides, nails biting into my palms.

"You can't return to your humankind. There's a limit to how long you can hide this before they realize what you are."

"No! You're wrong. If this necklace hides my eyes, then that's what I'll do."

"You won't be able to hide this for long," Ezekiel presses, tone firm. "This curse will take its toll on you, even if you manage to hide it from your humans. You should abandon your cause to be human and break your curse."

"I can break my curse?" I question.

He nods. "By transforming into an Other."

My mind screams at me to run. There is no way I am being transformed into a dragayastir or a luprender.

No fucking way.

"And that's the only way?"

"It is. The only way to break the curse is to change your soul's power."

"Then I guess I will be a banshee hiding in plain sight forever," I say defiantly, wiping the tears from my cheeks and standing slowly. I lift my chin and stand straight so he knows I'm not going to back down. "I won't abandon my dream."

"You'll get yourself killed," he whispers, his voice low with a dangerous warning I refuse to heed.

"Well, then you've been relieved of your protective duties, haven't you?"

"You don't mean that."

Ice floods my veins as I look at him. It's clear he isn't just a protective guardian, but someone who views me as a child. I try not to question whether it's because of his view of me as the little child he's been watching over for years or because I'm from a *weaker* species.

I'm not weak.

"I do mean it. I'm not some weakling child that needs to be protected anymore. I'm a Reaper — always have been, always will be. I can look after myself."

Without another word or checking to see that he got the message, I turn on my heels and walk out the way I came, anger burning through my veins like a power I have yet to tap into.

Chapter Fifteen
THE CRIES ON THE WIND

MORANA

The treehouse Morana had resided in for years had never looked so full. Maybe it was the fact that she had a full stash of food waiting on the kitchen counter or boxes of personal belongings covering the front room's floor.

A coo from outside pulled Morana to the branch outside her front door, where a rope had been slung over the overhead branch. She took the end that conveniently hung within reach and held it taut as activity happened on the end. It twitched and yanked beneath her fingers as the last box was secured at the forest floor. She took deep breaths as she waited.

She'd been surprised that after a mere few weeks, Morana had gathered the courage to ask Alva if he'd move in with her. After all, they were soulmates and she knew by fae standards, she was slow to embrace the change to her life, but this was special for her. She'd never truly had a friend in her life, let alone a partner, and while Alva had been nothing but supportive and patient, she knew the only reason she hadn't embraced him was fear.

Fear that he would turn and bolt the other way the second he had enough of her. Fear that even though he was her soulmate, he'd live with her and find her death calls inconvenient and offensive.

She was scared that the one person who was supposed to end up loving her wouldn't.

Another noise from below, akin to clicking, sounded. Morana began hoisting the rope toward her in response. With each strong pull, she made quick work of the box from the ground, thankful this one was not as heavy as some of the previous. In no time at all, it had reached her eye height, and Morana put the rope she'd been pulling under her bare feet, as she reached forward to grab the box. Once she was sure she had the weight of it in her hands, she undid the intricate knot and setup of ropes Alva had placed it in and walked back into her house. Plopping it on the floor, she took a second to look around at all the boxes Alva had brought with him. Her throat tightened as she stared at it, aware of how much of her heart she was risking by letting him into her home. But she was also sick of being alone.

She heard movement behind her. Alva heaved himself up the vine rope she'd always used to get to her front door and knew she needed to pull herself together. This was supposed to be a gloriously happy day, and her insecurities were surely going to ruin it.

With a deep breath, she turned to Alva as the front door branch creaked. He stepped into the home that now belonged to both of them. "Most people have a ladder to their door at least," he said, out of breath. He pushed his hair back off his face, flustered by something she could nearly do in her sleep. It made her smile.

"Most people live closer to the central grove where there's safety in numbers. Here, I'm just using it as another measure to keep the daemons at bay. If you're having trouble climbing it, imagine how a daemon would go," she said as she moved over to put away some of the extra food Alva had brought with his belongings.

"We have numbers now. We're both here," he said, his breathing evening out as he moved toward her. She knew what he was angling at and couldn't help but smile at how domestic it felt that he was convincing her to change things about the house.

"I know. And maybe with a little time I'll feel comfortable enough to put a ladder in. Until then, imagine how good you'll get at climbing!"

Alva nodded, his eyes narrowed in faux annoyance as he moved to help her with the fresh food sitting out waiting to be put away. When the final pieces were away in the cupboard, Morana and Alva turned to look at the number of items to be unpacked into their now-joint home. Her throat threatened to tighten again as she fought to swallow the feeling down.

Alva never missed changes in her emotion though, and like he was perfectly in tune with her, he turned to her carefully. Moving toward Morana, he stood in front of her view of the boxes on the floor, tilting her chin up with a finger to meet his eyes. "You're still happy with your decision, right?"

"I am. I know the fates put us together, and honestly, I've been happier with you than I think I've ever been before. More seen, more heard, more understood. It's still a change my mind is trying to get used to ... Sharing my space, I mean." She knew she was babbling, but his soft smile didn't fade as we watched her carefully, searching her face for any changes in her features. Tracking every word through her lips as he held her chin delicately.

His other arm circled her waist lightly where she leaned back against the kitchen bench. "I get that. And I am happiest with you also, Morana.

If this is something you are still glad to share with me, then I am here wholeheartedly to keep it your safe space."

The wideness of the smile that lit up Morana's face was unlike anything she'd ever embraced. The utter warmth radiating from him staved off the cold of the outside world, making her feel like they were the only two alive. Tears welled in her eyes. Happy tears. She leaned into his touch, pressing her face into his shoulder and wrapping her arms around him in return.

"You really make me feel a little less cursed," she said against his shoulder, hoping he heard and understood her despite the way she'd squished herself against his body. His other arm that had been under her chin moved to wrap around her also. She felt him squeeze her tightly before he relaxed into the embrace. Alva helped her breathing steady just by being there.

"I'm so glad," he said quietly, chin rested against the top of her head.

When she pulled back to gauge his face, she saw glistening in his own eyes that said her words had made him just as emotional. Staring up into his eyes, she felt the pull to him like they were never going to be close enough. Her stomach did flips when his lips met hers softly, pressing in as though she were so fragile she would disappear if they embraced too harshly. She loved it though, feeling precious enough to be touched so delicately but knew she needed more. They'd kissed before, and though each time she could feel her self-consciousness and doubt creep in, that feeling was slowly being smothered by how much she cared for him. How much she *craved* him.

Lifting up on her tiptoes, she leaned into him again, pressing her lips harder against his as she tried to get as close as their bodies would let them. His tongue traced the inside of her lip, and she opened her mouth to him. Morana's stomach was alighted with a fire she worried she wouldn't be able to control. The heat traveled lower, surprising her as her entire body was set alight by Alva's touch.

His fingers traced circles at the bottom of her spine and shivers danced in response that made her want to moan against his lips. Before she could surrender, Morana pulled back from the kiss, needing to breathe air that wasn't theirs. Undeterred by her abrupt break of the kiss, Alva leaned back to survey her face, still holding her waist with a tender fire that made Morana want to lean back in and get lost in him.

Looking past his shoulder, she eyed the boxes that they needed to un-pack at some point. "Let's get you moved in," Morana said breathlessly. She tried to focus on anything other than feeling Alva trace his hands over every inch of her body. She knew her cheeks were flushed, but she wasn't sure she wanted to do that with Alva before he'd properly moved in. There was something so finite about giving herself over to him — the first one who'd cared for her — that made everything about their soulmate status so concrete to her.

Alva let her slip through his fingers as she moved for one of the boxes on the ground, checking the label nailed to the hardwood box. *Clothing*. With a nod, she picked it up and smiled at Alva before leading the way up the stairs. She heard him collect a crate of his own and follow her up to the bedroom, his steps heavy on the wood behind her as they moved in silence. She collected her breath as she walked, keeping Alva out of her view for a moment to recenter herself.

Putting it down on the bed, she began to open the top of the box. Alva moved around her, putting a crate down on the bed beside her, standing in her view as he opened the crate. She tried not to notice his bare arms flexing in her periphery, but it was hard to ignore the defined muscles that begged to be gripped.

Focus, she ordered herself.

Looking inside the open crate, she moved over to the wardrobe to find room for the new items that needed to be housed. When she returned to the bed, Alva had already begun unpacking the items on to it, refolding any that seemed out of alignment and discarding the empty crate in the corner of the room. Rather than focus on the task of finding a home in her decently full closet, she followed Alva's lead, pulling item after item from the crate and refolding what needed the attention.

The silence was comfortable between them, and Morana knew she had nothing to fear with her and Alva — they were perfectly suited. True soulmates. Any fear she had disappeared the longer they spent enjoying the quiet together.

"I have some news I forgot to share as well," Alva said, breaking the silence with a smile.

"Oh?" Morana challenged, as she placed the empty box on the floor and readied herself to face the piles of clothing on the bed.

"I have been given my assignment with the guard. I did request it some time ago, but I'm truly honored they listened to me."

"The central circle assignment?"

"It was a high goal to have for my first posting, but I did it."

"You're going to be the protector of the *central* circle?" Morana's voice squeaked as the excitement rose. She was worried when Alva told her of his ambitions, that his association with her would hold him back. That her status as a cursed one would be a stain upon him simply because fate had chained him to her.

She was excited that it hadn't been the case.

"That's amazing, Alva! I'm so happy for you!" she gasped excitedly, jumping to him and swinging her arms around his shoulders. His laugh vibrated against her as his arms wrapped around her in return, leaning back to keep her feet off the ground. Without a thought, she lifted her legs and wrapped them around his waist, unabashed that she could climb him as easily as a tree.

As she looked up into his face, Morana was sure her smile had never been wider.

"I'll have the posting of my dreams and the female, too. What more could I ever ask for?" he asked rhetorically, his face softening in a way that only seemed to happen when he looked at her.

Morana knew no matter what happened, she was done for. She was irrevocably Alva's, and it didn't matter how much she tried to shield herself now, it was never going to change that.

Morana's heart fluttered as she stared deeply in Alva's eyes, feeling loved for the first time in her life. Morana was thankful for the person the fates had tied her to.

Without hesitation, her lips smashed into Alva's, claiming his mouth with a frenzy she hadn't allowed herself to give in to. They both knew the only reason they weren't consistently tied up in each other's bodies had been Morana's fear of rejection, but she felt how deeply entrenched Alva's feelings were in this relationship. They were both set to ruin each other if this didn't work. But it had to. They were soulmates brought together by the fates and they both knew they would never need anyone else.

Like Alva could sense the change in Morana's resolve, like he could taste the desire on her tongue, he moved them onto the bed. It didn't matter that they were on the piles of clothing, they were enraptured by each other. The kiss didn't break as Alva moved them so he was on top of her, their bodies pressing against each other suffocatingly as though they couldn't be close enough.

His lips traveled down to her neck, her gasps of pleasure the encouragement he needed to push him to indulge in more of her. Her fingernails scraped through his silver hair, pressing into his scalp as his fingers curled up under her shirt. Lifting her slightly, he shimmied her top over her head and barely a moment passed without his lips against her skin before his teeth claimed the ready bud of her nipple.

She moaned loudly, her back arching off the bed as his fingers skated across her bare chest and sides, trailing goosebumps in their wake as they danced over her skin. She couldn't find a place her hands were content to be, moving unfocusedly between Alva's hair and skin and the mattress. She fought to bring him back to her lips.

Alva had other plans that Morana couldn't argue with. His fingers teased the waistband of her pants, and he looked up at her from where he'd shifted to between her legs on the floor, as though he were waiting for her to deny him the pleasure. She pushed her head up and watched as he slowly and teasingly slid her pants to the floor, bearing herself to him. Her hands danced once again as he kissed between her thighs. She didn't know where to caress or grab, trying to gauge the place that made him feel the best and convey the pleasure he was making her drown in.

Alva's hands gently took a wrist in each and pressed them into the bed at her sides. Before she could argue with how to please him as much as he was her, his tongue found the place between her thighs. Her chest tightened as his tongue feasted on the gathering wetness. Urged on by her moans and screams, Alva guided her hands, pressing them together against her bare stomach as only one of his hands held them both now.

With his other, he pumped inside her, pressing in places Morana hadn't known could illicit such a reaction.

The world exploded around her, her eyes closing as stars danced in her vision. Her back arched so harshly off the bed she was sure her muscles would complain tomorrow. She cried Alva's name and expected that to be it. But he didn't move, chasing wave after wave of her pleasure, and settled between her legs with all the time in the world for his soulmate.

Chapter Sixteen
Refinding the Earth

Azariah

I didn't see the elbow coming until it swung out and wrapped around my neck. Before I have a chance to react, I'm pulled back by the coat hanger elbow and pressed against a heavy block of muscle behind me. I automatically reach up to the arm, attempting to rip it away, my fingers gripping the skin. No matter how hard I pull at it, though, it stays in place. Sweat and musk assault my nose as I struggle.

"Come on, little monster. You can do better than that," Seb says quietly into my ear.

Despite the adrenaline powering through my veins, cold shivers dance up and down my spine as his breath tickles the side of my neck. My lip wants to pull back in a sneer, but I fight to keep my face neutral.

I lift my foot quickly, intending to stamp down on Seb's foot, when Holt moves toward us with speed. His foot is like lightning, lifting and flashing out faster than I can comprehend, and then the whole side of my body explodes in pain. I feel the weight of Seb pressing against me as Holt's kick to my side threatens to buckle my knees. Pain radiates through my muscles. He hasn't broken any bones, my armored bodice would make sure, but the initial jolt to my system was enough to wind me. Dragayastir scaled armor is strong enough to protect against human attacks, and even some Others, but it doesn't completely remove sensation.

Before I can question my earlier choices, I slam my boot down on Seb's toes. The moment his arm loosens around me in surprise, I seize my chance and drop to a squat. Launching forward, I roll out and away, past where Holt stands prepared for another attack, and come to stand on the other side of them, keeping my distance.

"This is hardly fair. I didn't go nearly this hard on either of you," I say breathlessly as I take a moment to regain my composure and even out my breathing. The jarring shock to my ribs is beginning to fade and thankfully is not replaced with much of an ache. The damage, if any, will be minimal.

It has been a long half-day of sparring in the padded area of the caves we call our training grounds. It's a large open cavern with practice weapons mounted on the walls and enough floor that is sufficiently padded for the knockdowns that occur. It's up to us if we choose to use it, and what we learn in order to prove ourselves. Some were Culled over the years, believing themselves too untouchable to bother training and met their end when they ventured out into the word. I refuse to be one of those people.

"And that was your choice," Seb says with a grin as he looks at my sweat-soaked appearance.

Holt bounces on his toes, ready to keep the onslaught going. "We're not taking it easy on you because we care, Az."

Holt advances on me. Seb stays noticeably absent from the fight. Fists fly at a speed I'm not ready for, and I barely manage to block each time — the couple close calls near my face make my heart rate jump.

High block. Low block. High block. Side block. Low block

My mind quiets of all thoughts except looking for an opening to punch back. Finally, a gap in time presents itself and I launch a jab for Holt's smirking face. He lives for the fight. So much so that he clearly saw the move coming.

Before I can pull my hand back from Holt's block of my punch, he twists and grabs my wrist in his hand. Yanking me closer, he pulls my body weight onto a heavy punch to my gut. I keel over his fist with a wheezing breath as the air leaves my lungs in a rush. Holt lets go of my wrist and I surrender to the exhaustion and ache in my body.

"Yup ... I can really ... feel the love," I push through gritted teeth and heavy breaths. My hands brace on my knees as my eyes drop, and finally, I sink down to the ground on my knees, tapping my palm against the cushioned ground.

"Dragayastir, shifters, none of them will take it easy on you. Learning to fight against multiple opponents is a skill that could save your life," Seb says. Neither of them advance on my weakened positioning.

I try to ignore the not-so-subtle reminder that I almost died to multiple opponents recently. We both know I couldn't have fought my way out.

I have exhausted my body and mind after the severe number of hours we've been sparring. I'm not sure why I'm the last of the three of us to go in the two-on-one sparring matches, and why neither of them wants to give me the same small mercy I granted them, but it has fried my fitness fast.

"I don't think being beaten up by multiple people is very beneficial to learning how not to get beaten up," I say quietly, staring at the cushioned floor thoughtfully.

The number of knockouts this mat must have seen over the years is astounding to think about. The stories it could tell …

"I think that's probably enough for today," Holt says from above me, a hand lightly touching my shoulder for a moment before it disappears. "I'll meet you outside when we're all done bathing and we'll go study, okay?"

I nod, my neck complaining at the idea of holding up my skull any longer. My chin dips to my chest as my head hangs. I lean forward onto my aching hands until my body hovers over the floor.

I feel defeated.

I'm fucking sore.

I close my eyes and breathe in deeply, letting the tiredness take over my limbs as the adrenaline leaves it. Getting to the bathing chamber seems like an exhaustive feat unto itself. But I know I have to make it soon or I won't at all.

I hear Holt walk off, leaving me to my self-pity sore defeat. For a moment, I had forgotten I was alone. Then the other person's footsteps walk toward me.

"Whatever you're about to say, I'm not sure I want to hear it." I breathe deeply, lifting my eyes because I know I want to keep an eye on where he is and what he is doing. Despite our new status with him keeping my biggest secret, I still feel like there should be some ulterior motive at play.

Seb saunters over, running a hand through his sweaty hair which seems to be the only indication that he has exercised. His recovery from the fight, in terms of his breathing and tiredness, has returned to normal by the looks of it. He approaches me with a deep frown. His lips are flattened into a straight line, mirroring the curve of his eyebrows. I try not to think about his apparent concern for me and why he cares. That only seems to confuse me when I do.

"I was going to say you need to lean into your fighting strengths more," he says, offering a hand in a gesture to help me up. I think about refusing it for a moment, but instead, I push back onto my knees and take the assistance, letting him pull me up off the ground. The sheer strength behind his tug on my hand has me nearly airborne. "Even when you're fighting multiple opponents."

I struggle to right myself, with little muscle control left to stop the swaying in my muscles. "My strengths?" I blink, looking up at meet his gaze, locking my knees to ensure I don't fall to the ground. I don't feel very strong right now.

"You're fast when you want to be. With multiple opponents, your ability to dodge *should* be unmatched *if* you focused on it. You let Holt dictate the game. Your quick kicks are deadly when you land them, so don't sit there trading blocks and punches if that's not your strength. You don't have to be the best at everything, just use what you're good at. Be quick and deliberate and take them down faster than you tire." He nods to my appearance, obviously tired and feeling it in every fiber of my being.

I look down at myself, disappointed that my body has betrayed me and tired quicker than I'd expected. My training gear clings to my body in patches where the sweat seals it to my skin. I'm sure I look like a drowned creature from the black crater lake near the center of Skull's Rest. If I expect to keep up as a Reaper and be the best of the group in the tests, I need to make sure I have an edge and keep it that way. Taking another deep breath through my nose and blowing it out heavily through my mouth, I nod.

Reluctantly, I must admit, Seb is proving helpful. And thankfully, not asking for anything in return. We've been studying and sparring in preparation for the upcoming trials, and while I consider myself improving, I'm impatient because it doesn't feel fast enough. The help from the two of them is required, though, and if they hadn't given it, I probably wouldn't be where I want to be ahead of the testing day.

My fingers return to fiddling with the necklace pendant once again, grimacing as I think about what my life would've been if I hadn't agreed to their assistance in exchange for my help with their study and information finding. I start walking toward the back of the chamber that leads to the bathing areas, picking up my water cannister on the way and downing the remains of it.

"Have you told him about what you are yet?" Seb asks quietly. I look over at him, and he nods toward my necklace.

"No, I haven't. Holt's been ... distant. The closer we get to the trials, the more he seems like his mind is somewhere else." I lower my voice, somehow worried he'd overhear us talking about him even though I'm fairly certain he has his head completely submerged under the bathing waters by now. "I've never seen him this stressed, and the more I try to help, the more he shoves himself away. Telling him comes second and even if it wasn't, I can't seem to find a time to catch him alone."

"He'll be okay. This is all taking a toll on each of us, but we'll all get there, and he'll see. Until then, you just need to stay on your guard and keep the necklace on."

The idea of another thing to focus on — on top of already making sure I become a Reaper — is painful enough.

All I want is to be normal.

I've told Seb exactly what I am, what Ezekiel has said and suggested, and he seems almost ... relieved that I chose to stay with the humans. Despite the fact he is still very certain I'm not safe here either. And these days, given all the conversations we've had on it, I'm not sure I will ever be safe again.

"I know what to do. Doesn't make it easy all the time though," I say, surrendering the truth to him, the weight lifting off my shoulders.

We finally reach the split in the hallway that leads to separate bathing chambers. This is where we part for now.

"Well, I guess I'll see you when we're done." I sigh, turning to head down to the left.

"Not keen on helping me wash my strong, sweaty muscles?" Seb says, a teasing edge pulling his tone up. If I turn around, his lips will be twisted up in a half-smile, but I keep my gaze forward, feeling the pull of temptation to say yes.

The thought of him massaging my muscles that are beginning to ache is enough to make me moan, but I have to keep my focus on the end goal, I know that. But I will never trust him *like that*.

No distractions, I remind myself.

"In your dreams ..." I say, chuckling under my breath as I walk away before I can break my own rules, knowing I have a secret contraceptive plant weapon in my room that has been growing like crazy lately in the ideal temperature. I haven't even begun to address or figure out if human banshees can get pregnant.

I have to remind myself I'm not testing that theory *any* time soon ....

"Oh, it definitely is," I hear him whisper to the air behind me, leaving goosebumps dancing along my skin in response. His steps disappear down the other corridor.

Chapter Seventeen
THE FIRE IN HESITATION

AZARIAH

"Hey, can we chat for a second?" I say with a sigh to Holt's back as I walk out of the bathing chambers, enjoying the feeling of being clean and warm. He turns around at the sound of my words, curiosity scrunching his beaming face.

I'd coached myself while cleaning up after the session, convinced that now is the right time to talk to Holt before our world is thrown into chaos with the Crucible testing, reaper training, and everything else that comes with it.

"Of course, Az. What's on your mind?" he asks.

I take a slow, steady breath. Plastering a smile on my face, I try to ignore the way my gut churns and an uncomfortable lump forms in the back of my throat.

"In private?" I ask tightly, glancing around us as others pass by. A small smile tilts up on both our lips, a perfect mirror, a reminder of the lack of privacy available in a tunnel system with no doors. "Your room, maybe?"

"You don't want to wait for Seb before we go to the room to study?" he asks, an eyebrow cocked as his grin widens. He knows something is up. Hopefully, when I explain the situation, he'll understand that it's not what it looks like. I roll my eyes with an entertained grimace as I start walking and leading the way.

"He'll find us eventually." *Let him panic when he steps out of the shower, thinking he has me drooling over him and his muscles and discover my absence.* The image makes me smile while Holt and I walk in comfortable silence to his room.

My steps are quick despite the fact I consider slowing down to draw out the journey until I have to tell Holt about what I am.

I'm not sure how he'll react.

I don't doubt he'll keep my secret, he wouldn't condemn me to death by telling anyone, but whether he'll still talk to me after this, I don't know. I'm close enough to an Other we all despise for him to be at war with himself about staying friends with me. We all know those friends who change species are lost to us after the Crucible, so why would it not be the same for him in the Culling?

I push the unhelpful thoughts aside, knowing if I dwell on them too long and let the churning in my gut grow, I will pixie out and not tell him. My skin buzzes as if bugs are crawling under my skin, mixing with my steps bouncing off the charcoal tunnel walls. I force myself to take deep breaths. The air is damp and smells of stagnancy from hiding within these walls. I sometimes wish I could do that since I don't know what the future holds for me as a cursed one.

Turning left, I flip open the curtain to Holt's room without hesitation, hearing him behind me. I need to tell him. I can't handle the idea of Seb being my only secret keeper anymore. It just feels *weird*. It should've always been Holt there to go through this chaos with me and be my shoulder to lean on.

The first thing I'm always aware of in Holt's room is how much drier it is than mine. It still has enough moisture in the air to not make my lungs complain, like they do in Skull's Rest, but a strong enough reminder that my room constantly leaks. It's closer to the entrance, and his furniture has lasted a lot longer without the insane moisture levels. It's also not subject to the weird echo effect that comes into my room from the depths of the tunnels. I would question why he got the better room when we arrived at about the same time, but I already know the answer. The older kids had hoped I'd get lost early and die in the depths of the tunnels.

"Come on, Azariah, spit it out." He smiles, unaware of the chaotic revelation to come.

My throat seizes at his waiting face. "I, uh ... just wanted to see how you were going preparing for the Crucible?"

His smile falters. Running a hand through his shaggy blonde hair, I watch him falter, the same way my insides shudder at the idea of talking to him about being a banshee. "Honestly, it's hard. I'm glad that we're studying together. And thanks for your notes on those plants for me to use for my Crucible. I think it'll give me an interesting edge."

My chest squeezes at his words, giving me discomfort as punishment for choosing Holt's least favorite subject to distract us from what I really came to say.

"I'm glad. And I know you're going to get through this. One day you'll look back at this time and laugh, wondering how you ever doubted yourself. We just need to push for a little bit longer."

He nods, the tension in his shoulders relaxing. I'm glad he believes my words and can take comfort from them.

"The idea of not being a Reaper, I ..."

"I know," I say, making sure he knows I understand. That it's okay.

"I'd rather be dead," he says bluntly, his clipped words freezing every muscle in my body. I'm not sure how my limbs can be this still, and yet, my heart keeps thrashing against my rib cage.

"You don't mean that, Holt. There are a couple of options that you could get picked for that wouldn't make you want to *die*, right?"

"No, anything that isn't a Reaper ... I'd rather be dead. Surely you're the same?"

"I mean, I ..." He isn't wrong about the statement. The person I was before the incident at O Positive would have wholeheartedly agreed, but now I don't know what I feel toward the other options. I still want to be a Reaper with everything I have, but being one could also spell death, given the fact that I'm a banshee.

"Can you imagine being an Other? I can't! I know I hate it when you use the slurs, but I don't want to be a luprender or a dragasyastir or anything else. I even hate the thought of just being a servant to the reapers! And working with the fae? Eegh." His fake gagging rattles through me like a physical blow.

I feel all the color fade from my face as the words I've been anxious to say, waiting in my thoughts, sink lower and lower in my body until I know they are never leaving my mouth.

"You okay? Is that all you wanted to talk about?" he questions.

"Ahh ... yeah. That and thanks for last week. You and Seb saved my ass." I try smiling, even though the gesture feels foreign on my face.

"No problem. Seb did most of the work; I just helped him get you home," he says with a shrug before his smile softens. "I'm glad you're okay and that you weren't hurt. I don't know what I'd do if I lost you, Az."

"Me neither, Holt."

Chapter Eighteen
THE AIR OF CATASTROPHE

MORANA

It was the middle of the night when Morana was pulled from her bed by the tugging feeling in her chest.

She'd fallen asleep in Alva's arms in the bed they now shared after a long night of deep conversation. It was a cool night that had combatted the heat of their skin pressed against each other and made sleeping curled up in each other's arms bearable. It made escaping the embrace difficult though, when Morana's eyes snapped open at the familiar feeling of her curse. She knew it was time to go.

Painstakingly, feeling her soul complain at being made to wait, she peeled Alva's arms away from her body and slid out of the bed, careful not to jostle him out of his deep sleep. Throwing on the clothing she left prepared by the side of her bed, she readied herself in her usual black attire and quickly hurried out of the house. She checked below her before she shimmied down the vine, still feeling unsure about Alva's suggestion of a rope ladder, but she had promised to consider it. For now, though, she made her way down the vine like she had hundreds of times before and followed the call of death toward Savastral Revon.

Morana jogged, feeling the weight on her soul lighten the quicker she moved toward her fated role of spectator. She knew the sooner she got to the scene she would have to witness, the easier it would be to keep herself safe from danger.

In no time at all, she made it to the outer wall, and rather than dealing with the reaper guards at the gate and explaining her passage like she had to do when she entered the city often, she climbed a tree nearby the barrier and used it to leap onto the high concrete wall. She'd had too many instances where she mentioned she was in the city for her curse and here to witness death, only for them to decide it must be their job to prevent it. Their actual job was to prevent the endangerment of human life, and most of the time they were the victims. Some of the humans thought that meant it was an easy way to save someone and get the credit with their commanders for it. They didn't care about the pain it caused Morana when they attempted to intervene. The balance would usually find a way to restore itself later and they would also die alongside the person they had been working to save.

To avoid endangering innocent lives or intervention by others, she dropped herself down on the other side of the wall without going through the gate or making a sound. Feeling the need to stay hidden from humans and Others now that she was in the city, Morana used a drainage pipe on the side of a nearby house to scale the side of the building until she had pulled herself up on to the top of the structure. With the ease that would make most humans — and even some Others — jealous, Morana bounded across the top of the roofs with grace, stealth and silence as she followed the direction her soul was pulling her toward.

In her black outfit against the dark moonless night, Morana would appear as nothing more than a dark shadow over the tops of the dim street lamps below, her glowing green eyes the only thing that could give her position away to the world below — if they looked up. In Morana's experience, despite the fact that there were creatures that could fly, people rarely glanced up without reason to. For that, she was thankful.

She finally slowed her journey over the tops of the houses and streets as the tugging in her chest lessened, until she stopped and felt only the slightest pull. She looked below as she stood on the edge of a two storey building, spotting a group of black clothed humans. They walked together in a formation, their hands hovering over their weapons. Morana slowly moved behind, following as fate had planned for her to; she knew they were reapers.

The team of men moved with an ease that screamed they were seasoned in their role as the human protectors within the city. They ensured no Others were attacking their own kind — a military presence to keep wayward Others in line. They knew how to kill anything that wasn't human and would not hesitate to do so, sometimes even when the evidence was biased. They had a tendency toward being violent before uncovering all the facts. Still, unless Morana gave them reason to go after her, she knew that they wouldn't do so.

She followed calmly, waiting for one of them to eventually die. Her guess was a daemon or potentially a hungry, rebel dragayastir, as was typical when humans were the ones to die.

Morana's stomach twisted savagely when a shifter with glowing purple eyes stepped out into their path. She crouched to make herself smaller in case the female succubus looked up and spotted her. The reapers' hands gripped the hilts of their chosen weapons as they watched her, their steps slowing to a complete stop. They didn't attack, though. The succubus, while an Other, had given them no indication at this stage that she was going to injure or kill a human.

Succubus and purple-eyed shifters of any kind were extremely rare as a threat to humans. While they fed off soul-power and could do it to humans, they never took enough to kill the person. Soul-power feeding was one that could easily be healed from over time. There hadn't been a case of a human death by a succubs in tens of years.

All the men's hands slid off their knives as they took her appearance in, trailing down the long, blonde softly curled hair that did nothing to cover the barely clothed body in front of them. Her purple dress dipped low in a V to her navel, only a thin piece of fabric covering her hard nipples. The fabric from her navel hung in two thin sheets covering the front and back of her, leaving little to the imagination and displaying her long legs all the way up to the tops of her thighs. Morana saw the change overcome the men as they finally looked at the succubus properly and fell under her spell of illusion. Not a single one of them was unattracted to her and as such, they were hers to do with as she pleased.

If a person were attracted, they were the succubus' to command or use until they saw fit to dispose of you. Usually, it was just to feed from humans and then they moved on, but something about the fearlessness with which she approached an entire group of reapers, instead of just going to somewhere like O Positive, didn't sit right with Morana.

The succubus crooked a finger at the men, beckoning them to follow her. As they did, the call of death pulled Morana with them. She hoped the death was merely due to the distraction of the succubus and not the Other herself. Maybe being caught under the spell would get them killed due to lack of preparation for a daemon. At least she hoped that was the case, because the alternative seemed more sinister and cause for alarm.

Morana had too many instances lately that had put her hair on edge and soured her stomach, more so than witnessing deaths all the time already did.

The group with Morana in tow on the roofs above, arrived at the edge of the black crater lake in the center area of the city. Morana stayed on the rooftop closest to the group, lying her body along the surface so that only her face looked out over to the ground in view. The light of dawn had started to creep in, and though she was in black and very rarely seen when above, she didn't want to take any chances. Her stomach was trying to warn her that something was wrong, and though she couldn't leave, she would heed its alarm.

They reached the lake, the succubus's dress swaying as she moved, made Morana surprised and somewhat impressed she hadn't managed to flash any of her parts. And then the top of the lake rippled as five heads broke the surface of the water. Each had their eyes trained on a different member of the team. Morana's stomach felt like it was weighing her to the rooftop she lay on, so heavy that she was unable to move an inch. It felt hard to breathe, even though her lungs weren't restricted by anything but the dread overtaking her body.

The reapers heads turned to the movement and for a second, Morana sighed a breath of relief thinking that the spell would be broken long enough for them to realize what was wrong.

It didn't.

The eyes in the lake, the glowing purple of the sirens, were clearly just as mesmerizing as the ones they'd seen previous. None of them twitched toward their weapons.

Sirens were more dangerous to humans when water was involved, and the fear of drowning was exactly why humans typically avoided the area.

But just like the succubi, sirens typically fed and moved on from their victims without killing. None were vindictive enough to risk the wrath of the reapers by killing humans, much less the species' guardians.

But here they were.

Morana was forced to watch as the men waded their way into the lake toward the sirens, who slowly lifted out of the water to reveal their shapely alluring bodies. One by one, they disappeared into the depths, the water moving as they dropped below the surface and began to instinctually thrash against the feeling of dying. The longer they fought, the lighter the weight on Morana's soul felt, but the dread in her stomach twisted tighter and tighter.

Her mouth dried out as the water went still. The succubus stood on the shore of the lake, arms crossed, leaning into one hip, and watched the entire scene like she was already bored. Her foot tapped with an impatience that made Morana sick to her stomach. Before the crater lake had even stilled and the sirens had disappeared, she turned on her heel and strode away, her shoes audibly clicking on the cobble stone street.

Morana felt the rancid acid in her gut putrefy, and even though fate had removed her need to witness, Morana pushed up to her feet and followed the succubus before she could question herself. She wasn't sure why she felt the need to follow her on the rooftops, but the sheer dread and confusion as to why she had just witnessed what she had made her follow.

She wanted answers. She needed them.

Not once since she was a kid had she ever witnessed a purple-eyed shifter kill a human, hadn't even *heard* of one *injuring* a human, and yet a group of them had just conspired to murder a group of reapers in cold blood.

Something was seriously wrong.

Morana had a feeling that following the succubus would give her the answers she needed.

It wasn't hard to sneak behind the succubus. She walked loudly and carelessly, her hips swinging with every step and her shoes echoing through the street, that she thought she was invincible. Still, Morana made sure that every step was careful but quick, and for extra measure, pulled her hood up onto her head, letting her eyes be shadowed by her black outfit. She stayed on the rooftops as far as the city would let her and registered the journey they were taking was toward the gate out of the city.

Without another thought, Morana disembarked from her rooftop hopping and scaled the wall to drop down into the forest area outside of the gate. She stayed there in the shadow of the wall, watching as the succubus woman charmed her way past the guards, not a single question about where she'd been or what she'd been doing. Although they never really questioned those exiting, merely entering. They should have been, considering what she'd just witnessed. Morana was amazed to see the power a succubus could have when they wanted to. Clearly the humans had never been wary of something like this happening.

How times had changed.

Morana already felt herself becoming cynical of the world around her and it only soured further when she caught sight of another figure stepping out from the darkness to meet her stalkee. As the succubus left the city behind, a witch dressed in a black heavy cloaks walked toward her, meeting her feet from the citadel. The banshee could see the side-eye some of the reaper guards at the gate gave the witch when they spotted her, but as the succubus met her and the pair walked off, they seemed to abandon their revolted scrutiny.

Morana wanted to scream at them for their stupidity and acceptance just because it wasn't in their city. She also wanted to follow the two women, to hear what they exchanged. Something inside Morana's heart told her it was a problem everyone in Savastral Revon and the grove should fear.

She also knew she wouldn't be able to get close enough to hear what they were saying without endangering herself. With a sigh, Morana squatted in the grass by the wall and dropped her head into her hands.

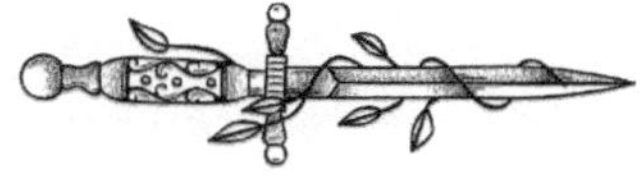

She walked through the front door of the treehouse quietly, trying to swallow the lump of dread in the back of her throat that hadn't disappeared since she'd left the city. She was still trying to wrap her mind around what she'd seen, and even more so the circling thoughts that had begun to plague her at the trend of events lately.

A storm was forming, and it had to do with the movement of witches. The problem was Morana wasn't sure what it all meant. She also wasn't sure if she should report it to the fae Elders or if she was making something out of nothing and would be dismissed for her concerns.

As she entered her dark kitchen, a figure sitting at the table downstairs sent her heart rate speeding forward. She stopped in her tracks until her eyes adjusted to the dimness of the kitchen and the figure stood from the table. As they moved, Morana caught a glimpse of silver hair in the darkness and felt her body relax, a tiredness sinking in as relief washed over her.

Her large exhale of breath was an audible signal to Alva, who pulled her in without question, hugging her to his chest. She wrapped her arms around him and embraced the feeling of safety he always brought to her with his presence.

She stood there in silence for a while, holding onto her safe harbor, unsure if she should voice her concerns. Convinced that maybe she was blowing this up in her head, she wasn't sure how to confide in someone. She'd never had the option before. Her breathing quickened as she fought an internal battle, panicking about everything she'd begun to witness.

What if it gets worse and I never told anyone?

At that moment, Alva pulled back to look at her in the darkness her eyes had finally begun to adjust to. Morning would break soon but the darkness seemed to follow her for the moment, hiding the true fear that marked her face.

"What happened?" Alva whispered, setting her heart spiking again as she thought about how to explain it.

For a moment, her mouth opened, and no sound spilled out. Alva waited patiently, his eyes piercing and glowing as he watched her. She knew he could see the wideness of her glowing green eyes, too. She sifted through everything for the right thing to say, to voice her feelings without catastrophizing what she'd seen.

"Shifters ... ahh ... *purple-eyed shifters* ... killed a whole squad of reapers," she whispered. Alva's breathing ceased for a second as it caught, and the silence between them built with a tension that thickened in the air. "And that's not all."

He stilled beneath her touch, his arms holding her stiffly as he listened intently.

"A few weeks ago, when you visited me at the site of a death, there were witches. I hadn't seen them before then. *Ever.* But I saw them sacrifice a dryad in some sort of ritual to speak to someone, and tonight ... a whole squadron of reapers died when a succubus led them into the hands of sirens. They drowned them all. I followed the succubus when she left — before you say anything about my safety, I *had* to — and she met up with a witch. I know this might be unrelated or that I'm making something bigger out of something small, but my gut is telling me there's *something here.* And it scares me."

"We need to tell the Elders then. We have to report it," Alva responded quickly, making the weight in her feel less painful as she realized that she wasn't crazy or making something out of nothing. "If you think there's something in this, then we need to at least tell them."

Morana nodded and sighed in relief, knowing whatever storm lay ahead with the witches, she could weather it with Alva.

Chapter Nineteen
The Fire of Determination

Azariah

The words on the pages were embedded in my brain like they will be tattooed there forever. The sheer amount of information on all the Others is astounding, and yet I have a sneaking suspicion that I've barely scratched the surface. I'm not sure if there are particular things I should be remembering in preparation for the Crucible testing. No one knows. They want to see what knowledge we accumulate and what we think is the information to be valued as we enter the world outside the Culling tunnels.

My quill scratches on the parchment, filling the silence of the study session with myself and Seb. Neither of us have talked since Holt stormed out of the room, mumbling about exercising to clear his mind. And I've tried not to let his decisions make me worry for him.

Once again, Holt has ignored the help I'm offering and chosen to follow what he finds comfort in, despite how close the Crucible tests are to beginning. The last few weeks, I've seen a shift in him that scares me. The fear of the future has begun to show on his face, etched in a way I've never seen before. We are all worried about what our place is going to be in the future, frenzied to action by the idea of being turned into an Other as part of the treaty if we fail certain parts of the testing.

But here we were studying, just like so many others.

It seems that Holt has run away from his weakest points and chosen to bolster what he is already strong at. *Again*. I don't agree with it, but there is no way to tell him what he has already heard from me a hundred times before.

I've done well for the last hour at ignoring my worries for my best friend, instead learning about the different physical weaknesses and vulnerabilities of dragayastir, in particular, ways a human could kill them. I'm sure that knowledge of how to hunt them will be useful in the testing, given the purpose of a Reaper is to be a protector.

My anxiety decides now is the time to creep back into my mind and take over the space in my brain. My studying focus is degrading rapidly. Putting my nail into my mouth, I can't help clicking it between my teeth, feeling the urge to chew them down until I can't anymore. My stomach is tumbling over itself uncomfortably in time to my swirling thoughts.

"You don't look okay," Seb says slowly, his eyes narrowing in a way I've become used to. It's one that says he thinks I might explode if he approaches with the wrong words.

I sigh, not in the mood to bite his head off for being too observant. I'm kind of sick of him always being around. But he is also the only one who knows my secret, so it's hard not to feel lonely when he isn't around.

"I'm just ... worried about Holt," I say, feeling his lack of presence like a physical hole in my gut. The fact that he isn't here studying with us anymore and has opted to go back to the safety of working out makes me anxious that he might not get picked to be a Reaper. The other alternatives for his future make me want to vomit.

"This might be completely unwarranted, but you two ... are you ... I didn't think you were but ..." he starts, drawing me out of my mental stewing. I grimace at him as he stumbles over his words.

He can't be asking what I think he is. *Surely?*

"Spit it out," I say curtly, uncaring if I sound mean.

"Are you together? Or were you?" he asks. I can't help the way my mouth parts slightly and my top lip turns up. I know I probably look unattractive with my face pulling weird expressions, but what he is asking is seriously ludicrous.

As silence ticks by between us, and I realize he is serious, I scoff a laugh. "Are you seriously asking me that?" I put my lip between my teeth to bite back laughter at the absurdity.

"I know I've seen him fawning over Elora, but you two have always been so close. I wasn't sure if maybe there were feelings from *your* side."

"No! There isn't! We're best friends, that's it. He's been part of my pack since I was a child. He gets me in a way that someone like *you* can only dream of. And if there had ever been feelings from my side, I'd never tell you. It's none of your business." My lips press into a line.

He leans back in his chair and crosses his arms over his chest, all trace of the nervousness gone as he seems to take offence with my words. "Surely by now you've realized."

"What?"

"I'm interested in you. And no, I don't mean just bedding you as you so eloquently put it before, although I wouldn't ever say no to you, but I admire you. I want to be *with* you."

The world around me mutes and every cell in my body screams at me to run.

I won't fall for this shit.

"It's not going to happen," I say quietly, but I know as the words leave my mouth there is a tone that contradicts my statement. It's clear to him too by the way his lip tilts up.

Fuck.

"I don't know if you really mean it," Seb says, as though he is waiting for me to convince him that I do. I know whatever I say, he'll hold onto. He's stubborn like that.

I give up the fight for now, hoping one day he'll realize I won't indulge his fantasies. It could get me killed.

I run my tongue over my teeth beneath my lips, composing my words carefully. "If the idea of being with me is what you need to make it through the Crucible testing and to the reaper compound, then by all means allow me to be your light at the end of the tunnel. But that's as far as it goes. I can just as easily break your heart once we're safely past the Crucible and you realize that this isn't something I'm going to give into." My tone is harsh and blunt.

His face loses the amusement it held moments ago as he leans forward. His fighting spirit burns behind his eyes, and something about the way he looks at me has my heart thrashing to jump up my throat and into his hands.

"Why are you so abrasive?" he questions, tone rising.

I check behind me at the curtain as though I can see passersby through it, stopping to eavesdrop. "You've seen the world we live in, right?" I ask, my voice pointedly dropping to a low volume in case anyone outside the room tries to listen in. "I have to be independent and hard-skinned, or else I die. We *all* do if we can't look after ourselves."

"Hard-skinned and independent, sure. But you have a special hatred or something for me, I can tell. It's more than what you give off to others."

My jaw tenses as he points it all out.

The thing I've done so well to ignore until now.

Someone else's eyes and face stare back at me through his. They are all too familiar and my gut tenses when I think about it. It's exactly what I try to forget. I drop my eyes and try to think of *anything else* but the person he reminds me of. All I feel is sick when I think of it, and at this moment, all I want is for him to disappear without me having to explain why.

Helpless screams faintly echo in my own memory.

I can't bring myself to walk away from this conversation and look weak. I'm not weak and I never will be again.

"Just drop it," I say through gritted teeth.

"No."

"Please?"

"Why should I? I deserve to know why you've written me off before getting to know me."

"You don't."

"Why not?"

"Just fucking abandon it, okay?" I explode, the volume at a level that makes me cringe as my hands bang on the table. He grows silent. The hot rage bubbling my blood has control of my mouth before I can stop it. "Your family is good at that."

I curse myself the second the words find air.

"What the fuck did you just say?" Seb asks.

I still like a statue, knowing I've spilled what never should have left my mouth. Something about the anger I possess when I'm around him and the way he keeps prodding has me losing all sense over my words and spilling secrets I never tell anyone.

I run my teeth harshly over my tongue, wondering if I should bite it off and stop myself now or put him out of his misery and tell him why we'll never be together. Why I've always hated him.

"You are related to Jayden Crane, aren't you?" I sigh heavily, looking up at him. The color leaves his face. "That's the real reason you know me so well, isn't it?"

"I told you. I know you so well because I live across the hall from Holt. You guys aren't good at being quiet when you talk and I heard you two over the years. I never meant to but that's it," he says quietly, looking as though he's taking deep breaths to keep his tone cool and under control. "How do you know my older brother?"

"You're not trying to finish what he started?" I ask, not letting his detached tone and stillness fool me into thinking he has no idea.

Seb's eyes widen as he looks at my face, but it's as though he's unseeing, staring past me into a memory I can't join. My stomach drops as I realize he's clueless and I've revealed way too much.

But I also know there's no going back now.

"What did ... he do?" Seb whispers through gritted teeth. For the first time since I've met him, he looks ... scary. He's angry in a way I've never seen, but I can tell it's not directed at me. He's stiff, containing a vibrating rage not meant for me. There's no amusement in his eyes or face anymore, even as he meets my gaze. My mouth goes dry at the sight.

He hates his brother just as much as I do.

"I was eight. I thought he was the best at the time. Despite having my own friends, I wanted to be his. Call it my first childhood infatuation, but he was expected to become one of the most powerful reapers at the time and I was convinced that one day we'd be … together. He could tell that I was a stupid kid with an admiration for him, and he led me on. He convinced me that one day, when we were both older, we'd be the most powerful reaper couple Skull's Rest had ever seen."

Seb's chin tightens but he says nothing. I let the story out so quietly no one outside would ever be able to catch a word.

Good.

I've never told this to anyone, and I never will again.

Not even Holt.

"He convinced me to sneak out with him one night, telling me he was going to kill his first dragayastir and prove himself way before his Crucible. He told me I'd be safe. I wanted to witness his feat that would put him in the history books like he said, and so I went."

I take deep breaths, collecting myself as I relive the worst night of my life. The space between my neck and shoulder aches and I knead my fingers into it.

It's harder and harder to breathe the further I get through the story, but I push through, feeling the weight of it become more physical for me, and hope that once I finish, I can abandon it like a heavy rucksack I don't need to carry anymore. *I hope.*

"We made it out to the Square and …" My voice catches and I fight to swallow as I pick at the cuticles on my hand with the other. Seb's hands cover it lightly, comforting. The gesture doesn't reach his eyes, though. He sits there, stewing in whatever hatred he possesses for his family.

Recoiling from his touch, I pull my hand off the table and into my lap, fighting to finish the story and get myself out of this emotional anguished hole I've put us both into. The smell of spiced smoke floods my memory — a scent that haunts me and makes rancid bile rise up my throat like I'm still there.

"He tied me to the Spire in the Square and cut into my skin again and again," I say, feeling my limbs tense with the living memory of the metal slicing through my skin. My eyes water as my throat tightens. The rustic scent of my blood joining the smell of dragayastir smoke makes me wish I could cover my nose from the memory. "All I could do was scream and cry and beg him to stop. I couldn't understand why he'd hurt someone he'd *claimed* to care about. Then he just ... left. He walked away and left me screeching till my throat hurt more than the cuts."

The cuts Jayden had left that day were nothing compared to the wounds he'd carved deep inside me. Holes in my heart that made me feel cold at the thought of ever giving it to someone new again.

I look at Seb, whose anger is still there, but there's a sadness in his eyes. As I continue, I fight against the way my voice threatens to break. I refuse to let him pity me.

"He cut shallow enough I was never going to bleed out, but it attracted a dragayastir, which is what he clearly wanted. He wanted to find one to kill and he did. A whole swarm showed up which he hadn't accounted for. He got knocked and I got bit. Again and again. That's when Ezekiel arrived, or maybe he'd been there the whole time in hiding, but that's when he stepped in to save me the first time. He walked into the Square and they all listened to him when he told them to leave. I fell unconscious and woke up on the doorstep to the Culling tunnels, surprised I had survived."

The space between us falls quiet, and each second that ticks by only serves to make me more anxious. So, I keep talking, hoping at some point Seb will stop me by saying something — anything — because I can't sit in these traumatizing memories a moment longer.

"After that, all I wanted was for him to leave me alone. I thought he would now that I knew the truth about what he'd done. But he was fascinated, confused by how I'd made it home on my own and gotten away when he hadn't. For years afterward, he kept trying to convince me that he'd never meant to hurt me and that I was always going to be safe but things had gotten out of control which he hadn't planned for. The older I got, the more he was convinced I was special and the more adamant he got. He wanted me to sleep with him, I could tell. By the time I was sixteen and he was about to disappear for his Crucible tests, he was trying to persuade me that we would make a child that would be the greatest Reaper this world had ever known. And then he disappeared again ... and all his nagging finally went with him. I could breathe again. I could be myself and not have someone banging down the door for my secrets. Not be a constant reminder of the crap I'd fallen for. And now here *you* are, just as stubborn, just as adamant that *I'm* the one you want. Well, *fuck you.*"

I know I'm babbling and that I have given up restraining the words that flow out of me, but there is hope that he will finally leave me in peace. I don't listen to that small part of me that doesn't want him to, that wants him to be different than what I've experienced before.

I don't wait for a response, though.

The silence that keeps Seb still as a statue hasn't resolved itself to let him speak. I get up and leave with my books and parchment under my arm, wishing the curtain could slam with my exit.

Chapter Twenty
The Fire of the Crucible

Azariah

"You may enter," the loud voice booms through the hall on the other side of the doors.

The reaper facility, and in particular the area dedicated to Crucible testing and housing, is completely different to the world we've left behind in the Culling tunnels. I said goodbye to what once was my world a mere couple of hours ago and packed my small number of possessions into a bag, leaving behind my mouldy, damp room forever. My potted forbidden plant is not going to like being kept in a rucksack for a few days but there is no other way to transport it without it being found.

Regardless of what happens in my Crucible testing, I will never return to the life I've led until now. From here on, there are many future possibilities I can take but only one I want.

Reaper.

As I push through the great big wooden doors into a great sparring hall, I keep my mind focused on one goal. I lead the line of entrants for the Crucible testing into the grand sparring hall, my feet sinking into the padded flooring as we all disperse upon entry. The group spreads out, heading to the front of the room where the assessors wait, and line up across the opposite wall. The sheer noise of over two thousand boots on the padded floor is overwhelming and I fight to keep my eyes forward to stop from looking at all their faces.

Two thousand out of the forty thousand-ish that live in the Culling caves under the city are here to prove themselves worthy of becoming a Reaper, and only a quarter of them ever will. The other three quarters will be split up and divvied into factions based on their strengths or weaknesses and sent to either bolster populations in the luprender shifter packs, dragayastir, or become a servant of the human race and join teachers, butchers, and other ranks that live only to populate the human race again and serve the reapers' needs. Anything but Reaper to me is as good as death, regardless of the curse I live with.

Rolling my shoulders back, I stop a few feet from the line of assessors at the front of the room. An odd sense of calm washes over my body as I take in the people that stand in front of me. Elders and leaders of the reapers wait patiently for us all to enter and take our places in the room. People shuffle forward behind me, still adjusting, but the reapers ahead stand still. Their arms are held behind their backs, their feet in a wide stance. The reaper blacks, while uniform in color and content are individual in style and all vary slightly from person to person, each suit their bodies. It's a uniform and yet ... refreshing to see.

Finally, silence falls.

We all wait with bated breath for information on what needs to happen next. None of us knew what to prepare for — this Crucible was a well-kept secret among the human race because of its ability to decide the fate of hundreds if anyone had an advantage. So here we are, waiting for someone who is running this to finally speak.

"Welcome to the Crucible," the man in the middle speaks loudly.

The roar of cheers sounds from behind me like a wave. Goosebumps dance up my arms as I soak in the moment. The test we've all spent our entire lives training for, surviving to get to, is finally here.

Let's fucking do this, my mind screams excitedly as I cheer with my peers, ready to take on whatever they are going to throw at us.

"I am Axton Gates, your Reaper Elder and the leader of the facility that you all hope to enter. As you well know, only a quarter of you will make it to the elite group of protectors who keep the human race safe. The rest will ensure we have what we need to be the best protectors we can be, or you will be sent to replenish numbers of the Others and be part of our delivery to keep peace in the treaty."

Even though none of us speak, the mood is echoed in the heavy frowns that pull our excited smiles down at the mention of becoming Others. The reminder of what is at stake weighs on the frantic heart in my chest more prominently than ever before. No one wants to lose who they are to dragayastir or shifters.

Don't fuck this up, I tell myself as I take deliberate deep breaths and ensure my mind stays on task. I don't look around at my friends, not wanting to be distracted by their emotions or panic, and keep my eyes squarely on Axton. He is tall, older than most humans I've ever seen, at maybe fifty years old. Years of responsibility have weathered his face. His eyes are sunken sightly, and wrinkles crease his skin in places where it is evident he's been focused and happy. He stands though, stronger than any of us probably look. Without testing my theory, I know his years of experience could put any one of us into an early grave if he wanted it to, even without weapons involved. Axton is a legend among reapers and has a wealth of experience I can only dream of having one day. And I do dream of it.

"For the next hour you, will be in constant sparring matches with a rotation of opponents. There is to be no serious injury. If the opponent risks it by staying in the move they must tap out. Know your limits and what your body can take," Axton continues, his weathered face frowning sharply before lifting in a smile. "Show us what you've got."

Cheers erupt around me and I join in, feeling empowered by the idea of proving myself in this hall. The other assessors begin to call out names and we break off into pairs. I've inadvertently ended up with someone whose face is slightly recognizable, but ultimately, I've never really spoken to her before.

Rolling my shoulders back, I settle into my fighting stance, readying to spar with her. The moment the assessors call to begin, I don't wait for the other girl to make the first move. With a flurry of action, I kick out and chase her down, watching as her quick feet try to retreat and her upper body works to block the kicks to her head. She gets the first couple, both her arms lifting to shield her head as she curls into herself and falls backward. I change my placement at the last moment and land a kick to her side, feeling the impact across my shin as I knock the side of her ribs. The breath whooshes out of her as she keels over and I launch my attack.

I move behind her while her eyes drop to the floor, and she tries to regain her composure. I wrap my elbow around her throat, lifting her back up. As I hold on tightly, waiting for her inevitable tap out, I survey the room. Others are involved in their own sparring matches, a mess of limbs moving quickly and going all over the place, fills my view. In among them, assessors walk between, taking notes based on the numbers that have been marked on our shirts in multiple places. I was lucky enough to get number one.

An assessor walks up to us from another match as the girl I've been sparring finally taps out on my arm. I release her, seeing the nod of approval from the reaper assessor walking by. Losing sight of the woman I've released, who coughs and drops herself to the mat, I look around at the matches around me. I hope to see my next opponent, but they are all caught up in their fights, none looking close to starting a new match.

"Are we supposed to go again?" I ask the assessor.

He lifts the feather of his quill and points over my shoulder. I turn to see Hamish standing over his downed opponent, trying to figure out where to go next.

With a grimace at the idea of us being assessed against each other, I walk over to him and ready myself again to fight and win.

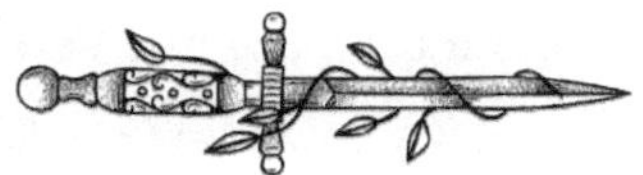

I step into my individual assessment room that I've been instructed to go to, aware that in the thousands of tiny rooms around me, others are doing the same. All of us are competing against each other. All of us are fighting for the quarter that would become reapers.

I steady myself, breathing deeply as I move inside the room and shut the door behind me. It's a small desk loaded with parchment, a quill, and a pot of ink. Against the opposite wall is a large window that overlooks the city from its place in the tower of the reaper complex. The sheer size of this building is outstanding enough without the unnerving knowledge that not only am I not underground, but I'm also high above it in a tower.

Slow, deep breaths, I urge myself as I step up to the desk and take in the person that stares out at the world beyond the window. His back is to me, but he looks older, weathered, and it isn't until my assessor turns around to face me that my entire body hardens to attention.

Axton. Fucking. Gates.

The head of the reaper compound stands in front of me, and suddenly, all the anxiety and panic I've been trying to hold back from feeling is a physical weight on my body I can't shake. All I can do is stand there in wide-eyed silence, hoping he can't see how much his presence shakes me.

"Miss Delstron, welcome to the final test of your Crucible," he says, his deep, heavy voice calm and level as he moves away from the window toward me.

I rock back on my heels and flounder, speechless for a moment, before kicking myself into action. I must make sure I do this well or else I can kiss being a Reaper goodbye. My entire body feels stiff. I worry I might snap if I move too much.

"Thank you, sir. I'm honored to have you as my assessor for this task," I say, pulling my shoulders inch by inch. I clasp my hands behind my back, the way I've seen the other reapers doing, hoping he approves.

"Glad to hear it," he says, his mouth tilting up as he nods his approval. My chest loosens its vice on my lungs enough to let me breathe. Then it tightens again when he says, "You understand your task prior to this Crucible was to learn and bring knowledge to us that you believe would be valuable as a Reaper?"

"I do."

"And what do you believe is the valuable knowledge that you have learned prior to joining us in the reaper ranks?" he asks.

I force myself not to focus on the way it is worded, as though we are all going to make it to being reapers. Instead, I form a mental list of everything I've focused my studying on and recite it, item by item.

"To be frank, sir, any piece of information we bring to this group can be valuable. It merely depends on the use you want it for. However, the information I have chosen is on the various species located in and around Skull's Rest, the history of the city, the treaty information based on records as far back as I could find, uses for plants for frontline medicinal purposes, and the language of the fae and dragayastir."

His head cocks to the side as he watches me for a moment. "Explain the value of these please before I get you to write your knowledge out for us to assess on each topic we deem worthy."

"Well ... the various species knowledge is valuable as a protector of the city to know the weaknesses, strengths, limitations, and physicality of each of the species we have records on. It assists us in ensuring we can effectively defend against them. The point of history is something we learn to ensure the evolution of our race. If we don't know our past mistakes and triumphs, we can't expect to grow and develop from them. Otherwise, we will always be in a loop of the same events circling again and again. I've been the garden caretaker in the Culling and learned fast and efficient uses for medicinal plants that would assist with injuries in the field, and some unsavory combinations that could be used covertly on enemies. I chose to learn the two languages, other than the human tongue, because I believe in order to keep peace between species, it's imperative we make as much of an effort in their language as they have in ours."

"I will admit, learning the old tongues of the Others is one that not many participants have chosen as a point of study, if any. Are you so sure that it's necessary given almost all who deal with our kind know the common tongue?" Axton questions.

Don't be intimidated by the questions.

I take a deep breath before I reply, "As someone who has spent time outside the Culling tunnels, sir, it could be a great source of intel and reconnaissance to understand what is being said when they think we're not listening. Not many humans ever bother to learn the Others languages, but I think that it would give us a powerful advantage."

"Interesting prospect. One that would be underestimated by a number of assessors."

"I find that being underestimated leaves room for real strengths to hide in plain sight."

Axton's eyes narrow in a way that I can't quite place what he is thinking. There is no animosity, but I'm not sure what it is. My hands behind my back vibrate nervously.

"Insightful. Your rare choices have been noted. As we don't have someone to test your skills with this language currently, I'll ask that you summarize the histories you have learned, the species information in notes, and the plant information. Once we have read over these for your Crucible assessment, you will be allowed to take those notes into the reaper compound as extra study."

I nod and keep my eyes focused on him, avoiding the urge to look at the desk and see how many pages they've given me. "How much time do I have to complete the written, sir?" I ask, waiting patiently as he pointedly looks over his shoulder at Skull's Rest through the window. It is bathed in sunlight, appearing strikingly different from above.

"Until the sun drops past the horizon," he answers before walking toward the door I stepped through. "Take the time you need. You will not be allowed to leave unless you have finished your writings, so if you need to relieve yourself, I suggest following my colleague now before you begin."

Chapter Twenty-One
The Fire of Waiting

Azariah

I lay back on the bunk, glad to feel something soft beneath my aching, tired body. The metal of the bed above me is almost mesmerizing with how tired my brain is. I can barely bring myself to move my gaze from staring directly at the base, tracing the way the metal twists and twines in it's structural pattern is more beautiful than most things humans make for themselves. I hear the exhales of those around me as they, too, surrender themselves to the mercy of the mattresses that are leagues above what we've had in the Culling tunnels.

The lack of dampness in the air is unnerving, as I breathe in air that is far too dry. It doesn't matter that I fight to remind myself continuously that this is my new norm, my body's equilibrium is disturbed by it.

The bed above me creaks as Seb climbs onto it. I wait, hopeful that he will leave me to my moment of peace after a very long day.

I'm not scared of my results from my Crucible tests. The interaction with Axton gave me a rare amount of confidence in what I've chosen that I'm not sure others can say about theirs. I'd been lucky in terms of my opponents for sparring matches, too. Something I wasn't sure others could say about theirs, either. Unfortunately for Hamish, I made quick work of him, which I hadn't expected.

The nervous whispers around me pick up as more and more people arrive in the long room, one of many stacked with fifty bunk beds. At least for this part we'd gotten to pick our room and see our friends for one night before tomorrow has the power to change our lives forever.

I'd gone looking for the room with those I knew and found Hamish and Elora already saving space for the six of us in the end of the third room I'd checked. I'd moved down and as I sunk into one of the beds they'd saved, I saw Seb stride in behind me confidently, taking the bed above mine. I fought the urge to roll my eyes because it seemed, of late, that he'd been my closest friend. My shadow.

With slow, deep breaths, I fight the urge to fall asleep in the comfort of the bunk bed, sad that these beds lay empty most of the year while we slept on the lumpy things they call beds in the Culling tunnels for the rest of it.

But this was clearly the perk of the last night before your new life began, I guess ...

In my periphery, I catch sight of Holt walking up beside my bed on his way to the next one. My desire to lay down and ignore the world for the rest of the night disappears. I sit up as he moves past, catching how he makes eye contact with no one until he reaches the bed next to the wall.

"Hey ..." I call out, loud enough for him to hear but quiet enough not to collect the attention of anyone else.

He looks up for barely a moment and tries to smile before taking a seat on the bed and dropping his head into his hands. His skin is much paler than I've ever seen it before, and the anxiety that has been slowly and quietly chewing at me for weeks becomes impossible to ignore at the sight of him.

Something is really wrong, or at least, he thinks it is. I move to get up, but Elora lifts her hand from where she sits across diagonally from me, physically closer to him than I am. She gets up and heads over to where he sits. I know what it means, though I hate it.

She has this. She's been the one to console whatever fear and anxiety rages in him, and I have to sit back and wait. It only makes the feeling in my gut, that gnaws away the remains of the food I ate from the provided lunch, worse.

My lips twists as I watch her move to sit beside him on the bed, sliding her hand up and down his back. My mouth dries as I watch him, somehow feeling further away from him emotionally than I ever have before, and I hate it. We've always been the number one person to each other, the call for help, the closest friend — everything.

A sour taste curdles in my mouth at the thought that our closeness is fading from reach.

The bed moves beside me as someone sits down. I turn to Trylan, who clearly entered while I was distracted.

"How worried about him are we?" Trylan asks as he looks past my face to where I've been focused on. I follow his eyes to where Holt pulls Elora into a hug, burying his face in her shoulder, and try not to let the hurt in me show.

"Very. I can see him pulling away from us. Well, some of us."

"Do I sense some jealousy?" Trylan asks, his eyebrows raising beneath his hair.

"Not like that. More ... a grief that I feel like I'm losing him. And annoyed that Elora seems to be the only one who can get through to him," I say, my eyes leaving the image of Elora and Holt to look at my fingers. I can't bring myself to look at them anymore, for fear of finally letting all the emotion get to me. "Trylan, what if not all of us make it through?"

"Unfortunately, we all know it to be a possibility." I look up and see his twisted frown. He looks at all of us until his gaze settles on Hamish in the bottom bunk across from mine. Hamish's face is twisted in anger as he glares daggers at me, but I try not to meet his eyes. "But we can't let whatever happens break our friendship."

Trylan says the words loud enough for Hamish to hear too. The response is a deeper frown from Hamish as he looks me up and down, then lies back on his bunk and rolls over to face away from us. My stomach squeezes at how many friends the Crucible has taken from me.

Despite the fact I've been waiting for this, I'd never accounted for this part of the process.

"What happened there?" Trylan whispers as he leans in closer to me, knocking his shoulder against mine.

"I kicked his ass in the physical ... quickly." I add the last part because I know the speed with which I'd taken Hamish down could have ruined his chances of becoming a Reaper. I hope not. But if I'd given him the chance, he would have done the same to me.

In the Crucible, it was do it or have it done to you and possibly lose your dream. I couldn't afford that. We are all here to become reapers, so surely he knew that.

I hope Hamish's other fights had proven to the assessors that he is worthy of being a Reaper.

Trylan's face wears a ghost of a smile as he looks at me. "You surprise me sometimes."

"I live to do that," I say, mirroring his soft smile. "Holt and Seb have been helping me over the last few weeks, and I've been trying to help them. Although ... Holt grew less and less inclined to take it."

"Because he was getting the swing of it?"

"No, because he went back to what he knew he was good at. Now I'm scared for how it all went for him."

"I can tell you he at least aced his fights. We were close to each other in the sparring, and I narrowly avoided being paired with him. He was a force to be reckoned with, and I think he nearly broke someones leg with that kick of his. He's a formidable opponent. Here's to hoping he managed okay in the written and didn't get into his head."

"Here's to hoping ..." I agree, although the nagging feeling that I'm wrong pulls my stomach lower, lower, lower with each moment of silence in our conversation.

"What about you? How do you think you went?" he asks, nudging my shoulder as the hopeful look fades from my expression. Anxiety pulls my body in so many directions that I can't make sense of all the sensations.

I can tell Trylan is trying to keep my mind and possibly his busy, and for that, I am super thankful. Even though I'm sure it's a wasted effort. Holt has been part of my pack for as long as I can remember and my closest friend in that time. I've never not worried when the prospect of his entire future hangs in the balance.

"I definitely surprised them," I say carefully. Trylan's hand gestures for me to explain further. "I had Axton for the written."

"And you kept a level head? Congratulations! I wouldn't have been able to do that." He smirks, and I can't help the way my insides warm slightly at his words.

I'm a little bit proud of how I'd handled myself, too.

I feel the bunk shift as Seb lifts his head over the edge, his ears probably perked in curiosity. I ignore him as I continue talking with Trylan.

"I did. He was really impressed with the topics I chose, even though they couldn't necessarily assess me on all of them."

"Why's that?"

"I chose to learn the languages of dragayastir and fae ... but they don't really have someone who could check my work."

His jaw drops open as though it loses all strength as he stares back at me. For a moment, I'm not sure whether to beam in pride or feel that I've made a mistake. I wait for him to collect himself to tell me whether his surprise is a positive or not.

The answer never comes.

A loud, single clap sounds through the room from the doorway, drawing the attention of the entire room and silencing any conversation. Axton stands at the door, dropping his hands to stand with them held strongly behind his back.

"Congratulations! You were all invited here today because you were deemed worthy of your Crucible. After years of surviving and finding your independence and teamwork in the Culling tunnels, you have made it here. We were astounded by the show of physical and mental acuity in all of you and will be excited to share the results of your trials tomorrow. For now, ensure you rest. Please note, you will not be allowed to leave these quarters — we don't want anyone with a poor showing today attempting to violate the treaty and escaping or heading out to celebrate and ruining your hard work with your death. It is for your own safety and for the peace of Skull's Rest," Axton says, loud enough for everyone to hear, ignoring the anxious murmurs at the mention of not being allowed to leave. "Lights out will be in five minutes time, so prepare as required." He turns on his heel. The door shuts and locks behind him.

Something about the way the door silences all the anxious murmuring is like ice in my veins.

This is it. Everything about our day feels so much more real knowing they are keeping us here until we move to our new futures. Some could be worse than death. Some would leave behind being human altogether.

With one shaky breath, I look down at the bag of belongings at my feet, seeing my whole life trapped in one spot.

Fuck, please don't let this be the end of the line. I will the fates to listen, hoping if I'm not already headed to my Reaper dream to make sure I do.

"Well, I suppose I better get ready to sleep then," I say quietly, but I'm not sure Trylan is listening anymore. All of us are strangely quiet as we head back to our beds, faced with the same prospect that some of us might not make it through this. And we are stuck on that path now.

Lying back on the bed, I take deep, shaky breaths and shut my eyes as I wait for the lights to go out. I'm not sure how I'm ever going to sleep now, and yet, at the same time, my body aches for it.

By the time the lights go out, majority of the people in the room are already asleep, exhausted from the day. I feel Seb tossing and turning above me as he fights to find a comfortable position to sleep in, and even though it's distracting, I know there is no way my body wants to sleep either.

An ache in my chest begins.

It's a pulling feeling that starts gentle at first, yanking me toward the door as though I can leave at my own free will. As minutes and minutes stretch on, it becomes painful and insistent. The room grows with the sounds of snoring and heavy sleeping breaths.

I fight to stay quiet.

The pain worsens, radiating from my chest sharply, attempting to pull me out of bed.

My breath quickens and I fight to keep from whimpering. *What is going on?* The necklace hidden under my clothing feels like ice, searing into my skin. I begin to sweat as my body vibrates with pain. I'm shaking, I know that, but I can't control it. I press my lips close together to stop myself from crying out.

So much fucking *pain*.

Movement above me barely distracts me as I press my eyes and mouth shut as tight as possible. Whimpers fight to free themselves as blinding pain skewers my skull.

"Hey ..." a soft voice whispers in my ear, hands touching me gently. It's comforting despite the sheer pain that radiates from within me. "What's going on?"

"I ... I don't know ..." I whisper, gasping. I'm fighting to stay quiet and not alert anyone else to what is happening. All I know is it isn't normal, and I can't afford questions that would have people poking around my current state. I need to keep the knowledge of my curse hidden as long as possible. "It hurts. *Fuck*, Seb, it hurts."

"It's okay," he whispers as though he's confident it will be. As though he can understand my pain as he wraps his arms around me. I curl up in a ball on my side, hoping it will ease the pain. Seb holds me together, his arms pressing in around me as I fight to keep quiet.

Tears fall from my eyes as the pain sears into every inch of my body. "It wants me to move. I think it's the curse."

"Sssh, I know. It's okay. We can't go anywhere so you're just going to have to ride it out."

"I don't think I can," I whimper through clenched teeth.

"You can. I know you can. You're the strongest person I know. Just hold on a little longer."

We lay like that for what feels like an eternity. My teeth grit together until I'm sure they will snap at any second. My lips form a thin line as every inch of my body vibrates with silent sobs.

Through it all, Seb holds on, determined to make sure I ride out the call of death that tears at my soul for not moving. We both know that they'll never let me out the door, even if I tried. In order to survive to become a Reaper, I must make sure no one else knows my true identity. It's the only way.

Chapter Twenty-Two
Etched into the Earth

Azariah

Here we go.

The final decision is here, and though I've looked forward to this my entire life, I'm not sure I'm ready for it.

All of the Crucible initiates wait in lines, standing as straight as our bodies will allow, despite the soreness and tiredness that pull at our muscles. We've been able to pick our lines, able to choose who we stand with for one last time before it changes forever. Holt stands to my left and Seb on my right, with the rest of our group on either side of them. We all watch the stage in front of us. Waiting.

Just in case this all goes badly, our group have said our goodbyes before we entered the announcement hall, which is just the sparring hall from yesterday reshuffled to create a large space for us to stand and a stage.

There's been friction between our group, and I know Hamish has not forgiven me for beating him in sparring the day before. He said goodbye reluctantly, nonetheless, believing what he was saying more than the others. There was a fragile sort of confidence among us, reassuring each other that we didn't need to say goodbye because in no time at all, we'd all be entering the reaper barracks together.

But we all know the statistics of how likely that will be for every single one of us.

I didn't say goodbye to Seb, mainly so that I wouldn't have to address the obvious topic between us. I wanted to keep hating him and not remember how I'd caved last night and let him hold me. It had been a momentary, *very stupid,* lapse in judgment that would never be repeated. I also couldn't put up with him if he was going to be smug about it today of all days.

I needed to focus.

Click. Click.

I flick the retractable knife in my palm out and back to its resting position, fidgeting as my nerves buzz beneath my skin. I watch the Elders of Skull's Rest, one for each species in the main treaty, climb the stairs into view on the stage. Seeing Others, even if they are Elders, at the ceremony that spells out my future is unnerving. My stomach, which is very empty — thanks to my lack of appetite at breakfast this morning — twists jarringly and steals my ability to breathe.

I feel like I'm trying to breathe through a tiny pipe covered in gunk. It's a chore to get enough air for my body to stay standing.

Click. Click.

"You're going to be fine," Seb whispers from his place beside me. His eyes glance down to look at the weapon I've decided is the answer to my anxiety.

My eyes look at Seb, but I barely see him beyond the rampant thoughts in my mind, consumed by the all possible outcomes of what the Elders will announce.

Returning my attention to the stage, I take in the sight of each one of the Elders as they sit in large throne-like chairs, unsure which will be my new leader. I hope with everything I have that it's Axton. While not all the species have been represented here with the four Elders, they are the most essential to the peace treaty in Skull's Rest and the only ones that have agreed to it officially. Notable species absences from the treaty include purple-eyed shifters — who generally keep to themselves and cause no real trouble with humans or Others in society, daemons — who are ruled by the dragayastir royalty but refuse to broker peace with humans directly, and witches — who no species can trust due to their decision to trade their own souls for power. That is assuming witches still exist today. They have been a myth no one has seen for as long as I have been alive. Even if they are still around, they reside too far north-west of the grove, in the barren land, for any human without power to venture near.

The first to seat themselves on the far left side of the stage is the fae elder, Kenrick Dubois. He's taller than the other Elders and somehow despite looking wise, he almost looks ... timeless. His long silver hair flows down to his waist. His eyes pan over the crowd with an expression that seems almost apathetic. His brother had been the King of the Seelie Court before the prince had married and taken over as the new King of Tisanra, the fae realm residing on a plane separate from ours where most of the fae resided. I'd heard stories that the grove over the wall of Skull's Rests resembled that realm, but I hadn't seen enough of the world outside the walls to know. I imagined it was beautiful though — the fae always seemed at peace.

Kenrick's glowing green eyes meet mine for a second, squinting as his extraordinary sight probably catches the color of my eyes. I move my gaze onto the next Elder, trying to ignore his stare.

The dragayastir Elder, Vladimir Basescu, takes the seat beside him. His entire being oozes a powerful aura unlike anything I've seen on the streets. I imagine I've never seen the oldest living vampire in existence walking through the streets of Skull's Rest. His posture is so stiff it seems like if he moves, he'd snap in half, but it doesn't look like you could move him even if he didn't want to. The 2000-year-old has skin that appears ageless, and yet has creases around his eyes and a stare that says he has seen so much of this world that I can't even begin to imagine. How many of these ceremonies has his salt and pepper hair been through? He looks around at the crowd like he's seen thousands of us before.

With a grimace at Vladimir, the luprender Elder, Huxley Darch, takes the seat beside him. Even with a peace treaty in place, it can't make them like each other. Huxley looks like the youngest of the four Elders on the stage, despite being near 500. He has dark black hair that is relatively untamed, abundant on his head and skull, joining into a heavy black beard and moustache. He isn't as poised as the others and looks less comfortable in his human form than I imagine the Alpha of the wolf shifter pack looks in his animal form. He sits down and watches Axton rather than the students who might join his pack.

Axton Gates is the final one to scale the stairs of the stage. Instead of taking a seat in a chair, he strides to the podium at the front. He looks out at the crowd, meeting as many eyes as he can. "You all participated in the Crucible yesterday, and while I'm sure many of you thought you could have performed better than you did, this was a test to show us how you perform under pressure. We saw who takes the time to adequately prepare themselves for the pressures ahead. "

The group of us exchange glances with shifting eyes as my muscles stiffen nervously.

"As you all know, we have decided your futures in accordance with the four sections of the treaty. Those of you who failed or were in the bottom sectors of the physical and the mental, will be joining the dragayastir. They require none of these traits for their purposes. In order to replenish their numbers, you will be serving the human race by joining them." Axton's words ring through as my mouth goes dry at the thought of joining the hard-scaled winged creatures that shift with blood magick into fanged humans that feed on our kind. The thought of drinking any humans blood makes me want to die.

"Those of you that were in the top sectors of the physical but not the mental will be joining the pack of the wolf shifters. Strength is required for the luprender, but you do not need to be the most mentally agile. I hope you find your home with the pack and feel supported in your new futures." Axton's face is serious but calm as he delivers his message, all the more chilling as I notice how much Holt and Hamish tremble at his words.

"Those with mental agility but not a physical prowess to back it up will be working closely with the fae or serving the human race to keep this wonderful civilization of ours running. Kenrick will specify your role in this more broadly once you are escorted to your new future."

I take a long deep breath in and push my shoulders back a little further as I try to focus on Axton and not on the way my friends shift nervously around me. If I have to be picked for *something* other than a Reaper, this would be the only option that wouldn't make me want to die.

I push the thought from my brain the moment it appears. I will not die. I will not get anything other than Reaper. I have to believe it.

"And for those of you adept enough at sparring and also had the foresight and know-how to do well in the written, you will be joining myself and generations of reapers at the facility to begin the next stage of your training."

At those words, I feel the collective breath of the Crucible attendees, all sighing in unison at the dream. The one thing all of us have ever wanted.

"When I call your name, you will congregate beside the stage and be taken to your new future. There will be no time for goodbyes. I wish you all luck and hope you enjoy what the fates have in store for you." Axton says, his lips twisting into a ghost of a smile for a moment. It disappears as he begins.

I hear the collective breath of everyone around me inhale, and I'm fairly certain some are even held. I force myself to take deep breaths in the hope it will alleviate the need to pass out. It barely does.

Click. Click.

I can't contain the urge to flick the knife in and out, even as the room falls deathly quiet around me. I catch Seb glancing at me in my periphery, his features twisted with worry. I don't care; it's the only thing I can control in that moment.

The first list begins, and as each name is called, a person starts their hesitant trek toward the side of the stage where a group of reapers waits. They move into a barrier around the group, stopping any friends from coming to the rescue and halting them from making an escape if they don't like the result of their future allocation.

None of my friends are called and our line remains. Worry sparks in my chest before Axton tells us what their destiny is.

"As part of the treaty, you are our dragayastir sacrifice. I wish you luck in your future endeavors," Axton says, his eyes no longer looking at the group as the cries and screams echo from their corner.

A few gasps sound around me from those I assume were friends with the chosen. I can't find it in myself to care about their lives in that moment. I'm so damn thankful that I haven't lost my friends, that it hadn't been me on that list. One less bad option is on the table for my future. I breathe a little easier and stare at the floor, collecting the semblance of calm in my body.

The group is ushered out and Vladimir stands from his seat to follow them. A new group of reapers replace the departed ones, ready to be there to restrain any Crucible initiates, should they require it. Axton has barely waited a few moments for the group to disappear, their screams and fighting still sounding in the room outside, before he continues.

Click. Click.

The muscle in Seb's jaw tighten in my periphery as his head turns toward me, glancing at the knife in my hand like he might rip it from my grasp to silence the noise. I don't care. Let him try.

Axton prattles through a list of names alphabetically by first name again, encouraging those called to go to the side of stage. With each name, a renewed wariness ripples through the room. None of them know what awaits, except that it isn't with the dragayastir. Elora's name joins the group assigned to this particular future, and like we've all been jarred with a blow to the lower spine, we stiffen. *Oh, no.* She steps to the side of stage, weaving between those remaining.

Holt looks ready to run after her, to try and save her from whatever fate she is due to find. A part of me panics as people walk up, that maybe this is the list of reapers. He stiffens and his body leans forward, as though this is the moment to chase after her. Before I can think about it, I reach my hand out and take his lightly. His head snaps my way in surprise, eyes wild.

"Don't. It won't stop it. I'm sorry." The words leave my mouth in a whisper, knowing that if this is the Reaper list, we still haven't reached where his name might be. Making a scene could ruin any of his chances.

If I couldn't be a Reaper, and this was it, I hoped at least that Holt and Seb would.

Hamish's name is called. Some rational part of my brain knows then that this isn't the Reaper list. I'd beaten him fair and square in the challenge, and therefore, even if I'd placed low in the physical, I'd be placed above him.

My racing heart eases as I look at those walking to the group at the side of the stage, the knowledge that I hadn't missed out on becoming a Reaper not yet hitting me. The types of people called up are ones who have a similar look — those who had failed the physical but are generally very intelligent people. It paints a picture of what this group is. Before they've even called the title for this prospective group, Kenrick stands from his place and confirms my suspicions.

"Kenrick will welcome you and give you your assignments in the peaceful arts. Thank you for the work you will do to better and continue our civilization for years to come," Axton says. The group is ushered out of the room. There are less shouts this time. We all know that even though they are to help out the fae or humans in teaching, building and medicine for Skull's Rest, they aren't being subjected to becoming an Other.

Still, I feel Holt shaking beneath my hands, his body vibrating as he watches Elora slip out the door with a sad glance at him over her shoulder.

My heart squeezes, knowing it must have been hard for Holt to say goodbye to her when they've only just gotten together after so long admiring each other from afar. I let go of his hand, not feeling that my touch will help him at all.

The moment they are out of view, the next group of reapers step up, and Axton begins his list again with no explanation of what future awaits them. I look around at the remaining friends lined up with us, my heart thundering as our group shrinks. We knew this was always a possibility, but I think a part of me had thought, somehow, we'd defy the odds and all make it to the Reaper list.

Click. Click.

I flick the knife out and back again, hoping it will soothe the buzzing anxiety low in my gut as the alphabetical list races past my name.

My muscles freeze when Holt's name is called, and ice floods my veins like a tsunami. My eyes catch his as my heart drops into my stomach. The panic in my chest is mirrored on his face as we realize this is where we separate and lose each other.

I'm not sure if I should cry for him or me, or scream out as he blanches white and steps toward the side of the stage as many before him have done. Trylan's name is read out too, and it's like a bomb of harsh reality has been dropped on my life.

Either Seb and I are fucked, or Holt and Trylan are.

This is it.

There are two remaining lists to be called, either those doomed to become wolf shifters, luprender, or reapers. With two on either side of the reaper bodyguards, there is no avoiding our fates anymore.

No matter which way the coin flips, I have lost my best friend.

I barely register that I'm crying until I struggle to see through the water swimming in my vision, impeding my view of my friends waiting to leave me. Trylan and Holt in one hit. Of our group, they are the closest to me.

They are my pack, and now one of our couples will have a new pack and I'm not sure who.

"I'd like to extend my thanks for your sacrifice as part of the treaty. You will be joining Huxley Darch and the luprender in keeping the peace," Axton says, and the knife I've been playing with clatters to the floor.

I don't care about the noise, or hurry to pick it up. I meet Holt's eyes across the room, my skin as pale as his. I feel my feet move as I prepare to go to him. I know it's useless, but I'm no longer in control of my body anymore. I want to tell them that they've made a mistake, how Trylan and Holt are the reason I can even become a Reaper, and that they deserve to join the ranks just as much as those of us standing in line still.

A hand grabs mine, stopping me mid-step. My head snaps to Seb and even through the tears in my eyes, I see the pity pulling his face into an odd expression I've never seen on him before.

"You can't stop this. I'm sorry," he whispers, repeating my words to Holt back to me as his fingers squeeze mine.

A part of my soul cracks as his words ring in my eardrums over and over.

The group is ushered out, with Huxley walking behind, and I know before the door even shuts that it will be the last time I see my best friend.

"Congratulations!" Axton's voice rings out through a room that feels severely empty, even though there are still a quarter of us left. I glance at the others left behind, and all of them look as gutted by this whole thing as I feel. No amount of wishing to be here prepared us for the feeling of losing those close to you. "You are the newest Reapers to join a large group of protectors making this city and the human race safer for all. You will follow us to your new home where you will finally be welcomed into a whole new world you have all worked so hard to achieve. It will be a luxury you aren't used to and a place where we will teach you the best of our survival tips. You are not alone anymore. You are Reapers."

As we step toward the door that the others have exited from, following Axton who hasn't even bothered to read our names out, I struggle to wrap my head around the whole event.

I've got what I've always wanted ... so why do I feel more alone than ever?

Chapter Twenty-Three
LOVE IN THE AIR

MORANA

Morana glanced down at the inside of her wrist, her thoughts focused on Alva and watched the way the compass responded to her movement as she moved through the sunlit grove. She didn't care that she'd just left another call of death for the day, unable to recall in that moment the sheer amount of blood spilled. She simply breathed deeply and calmly as she walked to Alva's location.

She knew he would be on duty at the ring just like he had been every day this week, and the thought of seeing him erased the sadness in her body like darkness under a ray of light.

He was her ray of light and had become that so easily. It was just like breathing.

She knew this was what soulmates were supposed to do. Sometimes, though, she had a hard time believing he was real and hers. Not a nice dream she'd wake up from and realize was only her imagination playing tricks on her in her sleep.

The sweet smell of the grove greeted her nose like an old friend that soothed her soul. As she quickened her pace, nearly skipping on her way to the fae ring she knew all too well, she marveled at how much she'd changed — in the best way. She felt lighter, less cursed, and less alone. It was a feeling she wanted to hold on to forever.

As Morana finally reached the edge of the treeline where the old oak trees broke away and formed a clearing bathed in direct sunlit, she pulled herself behind a thick trunk. Alva stood on one side of the ring, talking to a small, winged pixie. While his face was pulled in his serious expression he reserved for his guard duty, he didn't look upset with his conversational partner. The small pixie was barely visible in the sunshine, merely a glistening dot reflecting the sunlight off her wings from the distance she stood at. They spoke for a while, and Morana watched from her place. Even once she'd cleared off and Alva returned to the readied position in the quiet grove clearing, guarding one of the most important fae rings, she didn't emerge from her hiding place.

She liked watching him in his element, seeing his calm, protective demeanor when she wasn't around. It was a reminder that the kind elf she knew wasn't an act. It set her soul at ease that this wasn't a ruse, and he really was *her* soulmate.

Her lips pulled into a soft smile as she knelt against the roots of the tree, peering around at him, thankful he didn't look over at her. She stayed that way for a number of hours, watching as he never faltered, keeping his professionalism and strong position the whole time. A couple of fae moved past, saluting him on their way through the area. He gave them a nod of kind courtesy in response, dedicated to his position.

The first time Morana saw him break from his position was to glance down at his tattooed wrist, looking at the mark he wore that signaled his soulmate. As though he were thinking of her, he glanced in the direction it pointed, and she knew he hadn't meant to catch her gaze when his eyes widened upon meeting hers. She hadn't had time to hide, and by that point, she hadn't wanted to. She'd become accustomed to watching.

"How long have you been there?" Alva called out, trying to hide the smile that tugged at his lips. He wasn't mad but she could see the confusion pulling his face as she lifted herself from her kneeling position behind the tree and stepped out into the sunlight in her dark, forest green dress. She'd expanded her wardrobe since meeting Alva and had begun to wear more colors, feeling more welcomed into the fae society she'd spent her whole life shunned by. It draped off her like scraps, showing skin in provocative ways that she knew drove Alva wild. It was flowing and flattering in style, the type Alva was always tracing delicately with his eyes.

Morana saw Alva fighting the urge to trial his eyes down her tempting dress she wore only for him.

"I've been here for a few hours," Morana admitted with a sheepish grin.

His features softened into a confused expression. "Well, that's not good that a guard like me didn't notice you there that long," he said slowly as she neared. She saw the hint of harshness at his own failings.

She hated that look on his face.

"It's okay," she replied, voice gentle as she moved closer to him, touching him softly on the shoulder. "I have insider secrets, so it doesn't count."

He looked up past her, as if glancing for any Others that might be around. Once he was certain that they were alone, he reached out, his hand tracing the exposed patch at the top of her hip, where the dress provocatively opened in a high slit over her thigh. She saw him take a deep breath as his hand raised and pulled her body to his by the waist. "Oh?"

"It's only fair I visit you at work to distract you when you've done it to me so many times." She looked up at him with an innocent grin, her gaze flicking between his eyes and lips.

"I guess you're forgiven this time," he whispered, as the doubt in himself disappeared, replaced by a playfulness she could see him trying to hide beneath the surface. He was at war with his bodyguard self. She could see in his eyes how much her exposed skin made him want to abandon his post, even though she'd never let him.

"Forgiven?"

"It should be an offence to distract an officer at his post," he explained, tone teasing. The way he only smiled for her made her stomach flip-flop. Her mouth fell open in mock horror.

"Excuse me?" she quipped, waiting to see where he was taking this.

His pretense dropped though, and he didn't take it further as his fingers traced circles through the thin dress fabric. "You know I'm kidding."

"Do I?" Morana said with a taunting challenge in her smile.

"You do ..." And as quiet fell between them for a moment, Alva slid the hair framing her face on one side, behind her ear. Morana hated having her hair tucked behind her ear, but loved the way his fingers grazed her cheek as he did so, leaning into his touch. "Hey ..."

"Hmm?" she said, opening her eyes slowly after they'd closed, enjoying his touch.

"I love you. I want to make sure you know that you are loved, Morana."

"I love you too, Alva," she said as she looked up at him, wide-eyed with a tight throat. The sheer emotion in his expression tightened her chest, spreading warmth to every inch of her body.

It was ecstasy. It was bliss. And she wanted to cry with the sheer amount of unfamiliar happy emotions that flooded her. She wasn't sure she could contain it.

"I know sometimes you think you're not worthy of love, but you have always been enough. You are worthy of all the love in this world, Morana. I'm so glad fate put us together so I can show you that."

"I'm so glad for that, too," she whispered, unsure her voice could stand speaking any longer with the way it cracked.

Pulling herself up on her toes, Morana kissed Alva with all the love she knew how to express, not sure it would ever be enough.

Chapter Twenty-Four
THE FIRE OF DEATH

AZARIAH

I woke from my deep sleep to a sharp pain in my chest. A pulling sensation I'd only felt once before tore from near my heart and a pained scream sounded before I stop it. It echoed around the room, almost deafening. Before I can panic about raising undue alarm among the reapers, I spy the solid hunk of wood I'm desperately not used to having in my room. A door.

Even though my chest pulls at me to get out of bed, it takes me a moment to remember where I am. The room is three times the size of the one I'd had in the Culling tunnels. It's strikingly quiet and free of any noises to fill the silence — so much so I almost miss the dripping sound — and most of all, it's private and mine.

Flipping the soft covers back, I sit up and swing my feet over the edge of the mattress. Taking a deep breath through the tightening pain in my chest that insistently tugs me to move quicker, I plan to follow it. I know I can't survive through the pain of not listening to it again, not when I know I can finally give in to it. I grab my reaper blacks from the chair in the corner and start changing, breathing through the burn searing through my chest.

Knock, knock.

I nearly jump out of my skin at the noise on my locked door. Cursing under my breath, I secure the armored bodice around my middle and move to the door. Pulling it open, I let out a sigh of frustration and relief when I see Seb, dressed and ready for an outing, on the other side.

"When I agreed to let you request the room next to mine, this is not what I envisioned you'd do with it," I say, rolling my eyes as I step aside and let him into the room. Shutting the door behind him to avoid behind overheard by anyone in the hall, I then turn on Seb with crossed arms.

"And what did you envision I'd do with it?" Seb responds quickly. He walks around, looking at the limited possessions I've decorated my room with. I glimpse the taunting and suggestive smile that pulls his lips up.

"Ugh ... Not *that*. Can you focus on anything other than sex?" I sigh heavily as I move to leave him in my room, desperate to follow the call of death on my own, rather than put up with him.

I almost make it to the door without him when I notice his steps halt abruptly. I turn and follow his gaze to the forbidden plant I keep tucked beside my bed. It's out of sight from the doorway when opened but isn't as hidden as it had once been in the Culling tunnels. The reapers have less tendencies to monitor their recruits now that we are in the facility.

I drop my jaw, intending to explain, unsure of what to say exactly. My argument about keeping my thoughts away from sex has gone out the window with the discovery I know he's recognized.

"Clearly I'm not the only one who thinks about it," he says with a surprised grin, his eyes traveling back to me.

"It doesn't matter if I think about it or not, Seb. It's not happening with *us*. Not tonight. Not ever. Now, I need you to leave because I have places to be." I don't care how defensive changing the subject makes me look, I'm not standing here and explaining my reasons for having the plant to him. Especially since at this point, I know he can at least keep a secret. Of what he already knows about me, a problematic plant I'm not supposed to have doesn't even top the list of information he could spill and ruin me.

"I can see that and that's why I'm here."

"What?"

"The walls are thick, but not that much. I heard your cry and figured a certain curse might be grabbing at your soul again. So I came as quick as I could. Where are we headed?"

"*We* are not headed anywhere. *I'm* going to see what this is all about," I say, using my hand to circle my heart and general chest area where the pulling takes hold of my soul with a vice grip.

I grimace before I can contain my expression, and I know he catches it.

"You might technically be a Reaper now, and allowed out of the facility, but you're not invincible. I'm coming with you, if only to help as backup in case something goes wrong."

"Nothing's going to go wrong and I can handle myself," I retort with an eye roll.

"We've both seen that help can be beneficial. Considering the last time you were around creatures that wanted to kill you, you didn't fare so well. Extra weapons and preparedness now or not, you don't want to be looking over your shoulder for predators on your own the first time you follow the call of death."

I scowl, listening to his words and hating he's right, but there is no one else I can tell. That feeling of loneliness outside of Seb stings more than the call of death does. I force myself not to focus on it.

Grabbing my weapons and putting them in their holsters on my outfit, I sigh in resignation. "Fine."

No one questioned us when we left in the middle of the night. The guards stationed at the exit doors and gates that surrounded the compound merely asked for our names so they knew who would be returning later that night. It was an eerie feeling that somehow made my stomach chew itself even more, knowing that we were trusted not to do anything wrong. And here I was hiding my real identity from them, something that they would not accept under the rules of the Reaper guidelines. If you were an Other, you were out, and I was pretty sure being cursed in a magickal way constituted for that.

The darkened streets somehow feel more threatening than ever before now that I know what I smell like. Now that I know what I hide but not how to harness the powers for myself, it somehow makes everything I do more careful, quiet steps echoing off the buildings louder to my own ears. It doesn't matter that I still wear the suppressing necklace around my throat, or that I have more weapons than ever before since joining the Reapers. I still feel like the target on my back has gotten bigger.

It should be smaller, shouldn't it?

Seb stays a few steps behind me, watching my back and following quietly, his quippy remarks gone the moment we stepped outside the safety of the gate. Somehow, I miss it. I kind of wish he'd take it less seriously so I can tell myself it's all in my head and I'm being crazy. His silence and the concentration coming off him in waves makes my gut clench tighter. I take deep breaths to keep my brain calm, focusing on the scent of smoke, river water, and stone that always perforates the air. I'm still not used to the dryness in it, but my body is slowly acclimatizing.

The tugging eventually stops over in the dragayastir part of town. I catch sight of the glowing red eyes ahead of me, stalking a human child who has clearly gone on their own exploration adventure for the evening. I pull myself and Seb into an alley, my throat tight. I know the whole point of letting us leave the Culling as we wanted growing up had been to weed out those not strong enough or smart enough to survive, but it doesn't stop the sour taste in my mouth at the thought of a child dying for dumb mistakes.

I know I'm here to see a child die.

The moment I even consider running to their rescue, and taking on the dragayastir myself, my head explodes with blinding pain. Keeling over in the alley and forcing my teeth together to stop from crying out, I understand the message from my curse loud and clear.

You cannot interfere.

You must watch.

Seb's hand touches my shoulder from where he is behind me. He's fighting his own urge to jump in. The way he looks at me when I turn to meet his gaze, full of pity and sadness, makes the pounding in my head worse. Without saying a word, I take his hand, squeezing it tightly as I force myself to stay rooted to the spot and watch as the dragayastir walks silently behind the unsuspecting child, who can't be more than twelve years old.

The dragayastir moves silently, his mouth opening as long, protruding fangs are ready for its next meal. In the blink of an eye, he launches on the small frame of the little girl. I stiffen where I stand, looking out from the alley, unable to think about helping as the dragayastir's fangs in human form stab into the muscle between her neck and shoulder. My throat tightens as the rusty smell of her blood reaches my nose.

Right as I'm about to fight against the curse and go after the Other, his head is separated from his body and rolls along the floor, leaving trails of blood in its wake. The body of the dragayastir spurts black blood from the clean-cut stump of a neck that has been exposed by his decapitation. It takes a moment to register what has really happened.

The little girl screams as she is freed from the fangs of the creature, but I can already tell her blood loss is severe, the puncture in her body too great for her to survive on her own without assistance I can't provide. Still, she tries to run away.

Every inch of my skin buzzes at what I find standing behind the corpse and where the girl had been a moment ago. A Reaper, clad in black, stands over the body of the dragayastir, brandishing a scythe with a wicked smile as he looks down at the destruction he created. I know this is part of the Reaper job, to dispatch Others that are breaking from the treaty and save human lives, but I can already tell this is no ordinary mission. This person isn't on duty and is enjoying the life he's taken too much to be doing this out of concern for the dying little girl he let run off without another word.

This was for the thrill of killing Others.

Well, some of them.

As his eyes lift, sensing my gaze, another woman catches up with his position and comes into view with glowing purple eyes. Her dress hangs and dips in ways that show off skin, coming strikingly close to exposing private parts that I wouldn't have dared try to show in public. I can't help the way my lip curls back in ill-tasting disgust as she reaches the Reaper in front of me and drags her hand down his chest, diving toward the middle of his pants, unaware of my presence.

But his eyes never leave mine.

"Azariah," he breathes, paying no attention to the female succubus that now cups him between the legs, massaging where her hand rests. She stills at his words, turning her head sharply to meet my gaze.

Behind me, Seb's hand rests on the small of my back, trying to act as a comfort as he tenses as well, stepping out from the alley and into view of his older brother.

Jayden.

The sight of him standing there pummels me in the gut, robbing me of breath. It's like a walking nightmare I can't stand to be a part of and yet can't escape. My eyes flicker between him and the succubus, making a show of touching him suggestively.

The taste in my mouth is dry and rancid, no matter how many times I swallow.

Jayden's eyes glance over my shoulder and I see the way his features physically tighten at the presence. The balled-up fist tightening against the back of my shirt indicates Seb feels the same.

"Seb," Jayden says through gritted teeth.

"Jayden," Seb mirrors, his tone eerily as tight.

Fuck, they even sound the same right now.

"Still a weakling, little brother?" Jayden retorts, malicious teasing lilting his tone.

"Still a psychotic dickhead?"

"Aww, you're not still mad about that, are you? It was all to make you stronger."

Seb stays silent as his brother prods. My curiosity peaks but I fight to glance back at him and request answers right now. Jayden doesn't give anyone details. His gaze returns to mine as the succubus' hand rubs him in a bid for attention again.

"Reaper blacks look good on you," Jayden drawls, his eyes tracking up and down my body, leering. The woman beside him massages what has very obviously gone hard.

Fucking disgusting.

I don't bother to thank him for the compliment — the idea of doing so makes me want to throw up. Instead, I turn and walk away, feeling the pull of death no longer yanking on my soul.

I don't wait to see if Jayden and Seb communicate any further, refusing to stay back if Seb wants to fight with his older brother. I push my legs as fast as they can take me out of there without looking like I'm running away.

Chapter Twenty-Five
Weapons Forged in Fire

Azariah

The harsh wood of my chair is ridiculously straight and in no position is it comfortable. No amount of sitting straight seems to appease the chair or push my body to cooperate. The lecture hall is large, and thankfully, everyone looks deterred by the posture the chairs force us to sit in. Yet despite all the shifting in seats for the past hour, no one has made a comment. I can imagine the grunting noises Holt would have made trying to maneuver his large bulky body in these chairs, and almost like alternate life I'm glimpsing, my face ghosts with a smile.

The reality of the situation, and the grief, punches through me hard a moment later. It robs me of breath, squeezing my chest. It take all my focus to bring my attention back to the class at hand and ignore the niggling feeling that Holt should be here.

We have all been glued to the bottom of our tiered seating by Axton, holding on to every word he projects out to the group. It is nearly magick. But it isn't. It's the first information session for new Reapers on Others. Axton has talked us through a particular species residing in Skull's Rest, how to identify it, its capabilities, weaknesses, and how to overcome and kill it without powers if required. While some of this information are items that I have studied for my Crucible, I take feverous notes, nonetheless. Axton uses the information sessions as a way of filling the knowledge gap, in case cadets who made it through hadn't collected all the correct information. It also ensures we all have the best methods and up-to-date information to protect humankind and Skull's Rest.

This week's focus is dragayastir. I try not to think about Ezekiel and the fact that I'm learning how to kill him as my hand seizes with cramps after too long with my scrupulous notes.

"Can anyone tell me why the dragayastir are supplied humans as part of the treaty?" Axton continues without reprieve. Those around me have tired after being seated for an extended time, at attention and forced to stay focused. The novelty of my first information session is keeping me excited enough to stay interested.

From his seat beside me, Seb shifts for the tenth time in the last hour, each movement making me hyper aware of where his body warmth is.

"To use them as food ..." Seb jokes under his breath for only us to hear. However, in the silence of the room, even his small murmur makes it clear to Axton that there was some sort of response nearby. Axton's slightly sunken eyes zero in on us. I try not to smile at Seb's comment. I know Axton sees it.

"What was that, Mr. Crane?" I can tell by the challenging glint in Axton's eyes that even though he probably didn't hear what Seb said, he knows it was an unofficial answer. It was derivative and it's obvious. Axton doesn't tolerate disrespect for other species in his lecture hall.

Without thinking, I speak up, hoping I can convince him that Seb wasn't being rude. If he gets punished, it's just as likely I might as well. "He was just reminding me, sir, that the dragayastir can't breed so they need our help to boost numbers."

"That is the correct answer, Miss Delstron. However, I would appreciate it if you let *Mr. Crane* learn from his own mistakes," Axton says, nodding at me in a way that tells me I'm not in trouble and won't be punished, but Seb might be in the future. A warning of how things can be if I'm not careful. "While the common *misconception* about dragayastir is that humans become 'blood bags' and food for the predators of Skull's Rest, I'm here to tell you this is very wrong."

The look that he levels beside me at Seb has him shuffling uncomfortably in his seat as Axton makes it very clear he didn't have to hear what was said ... he knew.

"The dragayastir don't need any help finding prey or food. Many years prior to the treaty being put in place, they hunted from the skies in their monstrous forms. You would only be able to spot one by its large winged scaled bodies above you before it dove down and shifted to bite you. Outrunning a dragayastir in the old times would have been impossible. We are lucky we have found ways to benefit both species to keep the peace. Blood is donated by humans from all walks of life, including Reapers at certain times of the year, and those who are due to become dragayastir themselves. As Reapers after the installation of the treaty, we now only dispatch and kill those who break the treaty and go rogue, harming humans or threatening the protection that this city and the treaty provide. You are under no circumstances to just kill a dragayastir because of *what* they are. Understood?"

Axton's eyes lock on to each one of us for a tiny moment before moving to the next, ensuring his intense, unblinking gaze touches each of us to make his point very clear.

"Yes, sir," the reaper initiates in the room echo in near perfect unison.

"Okay, make sure you study your notes from this session thoroughly and pair it well with your group sparring practice later today. You'll be expected to revise this yourself. You need to stay up to date on all materials and techniques in your own time rather than relying on us to reteach you. It will keep you alive. Dismissed."

Axton turns on his heel and disappears from the room before most of the new Reapers are standing, probably because we are all so stiff from sitting pin-straight for so long. Flexing my hand and dropping the quill into my lap, I wait for the remainder of my ink to dry and then pack my things into my satchel at my feet. Standing is a slow process, but it feels good. Stretching out, I feel the groan work its way up my throat from somewhere in my lower back that has tightened up with the lack of movement. I'm not the only one — chatter and relieved moans of stretching fill the room as we all begin the journey out of the lecture space and toward the meal hall.

I don't rush. I collect my things and let my brain focus on having to absorb dense information. We hadn't even had the sparring session yet and I already feel exhaustion weighing on me.

Seb waits for me, packing himself up and preparing to go well before me. I move for the door in silence. I don't entirely mind him hanging around me lately. The first few days with him around as we began all our information sessions and sparring, I had found it tedious and borderline annoying, but now I know if he wasn't with me, verbally challenging me and distracting me, I'd only be consumed by the hole I'm missing in my life. The space that can't be filled by one person. Where my friend group, and Holt, had once been is a void in my life I'm not sure I'll ever fill. But I would have been feeling it a lot more if he hadn't been there to keep me company.

"I can tell you're in your head thinking too hard. What's the matter?" Seb asks when we are finally out in the hallway and the group has begun to thin.

"I'm just ... thinking about that dragayastir from the other day," I say, giving as little information as possible, in case others might be listening. It's enough for him to realize the weight of what we'd witnessed together when I was out listening to my call of death.

"Be careful about saying too much in a public space," he says, his voice lowering as he walks a little closer to me.

"I know. I just keep thinking about what would have happened if *someone* hadn't intercepted ..."

Seb's body presses against me. Turning to him, my back connects with the wall. The thud echoes through my spine, though it doesn't hurt. The bag from my shoulder slips to the ground, knocking against my feet and Seb's, as his body presses in close to mine. He doesn't seem to care. He is so close, the warmth of his body mere inches from mine as his hand palms the wall beside my head.

To anyone else passing, it looks like a couple driven to passion in the corridor, wrapped up in each other, but I can tell by the frenzy in his eyes that his actions were driven by panic at the depths of my words.

"Say too much and you could be putting yourself, or them, into an inquisition," he says so low he is nearly whispering against my lips. His breath dances over my skin, raising the hairs along my body. Shivers race across my spine in response, like they love the closeness. No one will overhear them now.

I'm not dumb. I know I have to be careful with my words, and even though he is warning me, I can tell he is enjoying the play too much.

As the people in the hallway around us clear away, the panic in his eyes disappears, replaced by a glint of mischievousness.

I press my hands against his chest and shove him, but he only retreats one step. It makes the mischievousness reach his lips, pulling one side of them up in a wicked half-smile. It reminds me of his brother, and my gut twists sharply at the sight. He doesn't seem to notice my discomfort, though, moving back and closing the one-step gap between us again.

"Did I tickle a nerve, little monster?" he whispers as he brings his lips close to mine again. A part of me waits in anticipation and stillness to see if he will actually do it. But the feral part of me wins out when he playfully pokes me in the stomach.

"No, you just seem to misunderstand the concept of personal space," I spit through gritted teeth, no longer whispering.

"Getting turned on by the feel of my body on yours?" The breath from his words dances along my skin again. I hope the heat in my face isn't showing in the color of my cheeks.

He is fucking frustrating. Who is he to tell me how I feel and what I want?

His fingers poking me disappear as his hand touches my waist lightly, as though it's going to rest there and hold me. Before my body can give away how much I like the feeling, how my body flushes with heat in response, I slap his hand to his side. It stays there barely a moment, though. It returns to poking me, harder this time. I try to escape his touch, writhing against the wall to stop his hand each time it moves to antagonize my body.

His body closes in on me with every poke he manages to land through the sparring flurry of limbs. "I know if you really wanted me to stop, you could take me down easily. Do you want me to go away? Or are you trying to hide that secret heart of yours, little monster?"

A growl of frustration escapes my lips as I try uselessly to get away from his poking hand, knocking it away. Eventually, though, I tire of the game he's playing, and as I try to collect his hands, he switches and collects both of my wrists in his grip, pinning them above my head and pressing his body against mine.

My body is stuck between the wall and him, his warmth meeting mine. I know he can feel the way my body has been responding to his touch, and I hate it. There's no room to move, a path to escape, or a way to kick out far enough to create an impact. I'm stuck, and he knows it. It's what he wants.

His face is far enough from mine, searching my expression as though he's studying the way my body reacts to him, but if he's looking for longing, he'll never find it. I've spent years of my life mastering my features, and while he can make my body heat and dance for him, my brain and logic know better than to fall for whatever trick he is trying to sell.

I wait, knowing I have one possible way to get away if I want to, but curious to see what he'll do if I stop fighting. If I just wait for him to release me. Would he do the honorable thing?

The corridor around us has gone silent as Reapers dive into their food in the meal hall, where we should be right now if Seb wasn't trying to make some point that he thinks he has control over me.

"Gonna try and steal a kiss, are you?" I say, hearing the sharpness in my voice as it leeches into the air between us. Somehow, despite secretly hoping it might close the distance between our lips, to push him to move away, it has the opposite effect.

As his face moves back, I see the mischief in his eyes, and his face has grown more serious ... and for a second, I think I might have pushed him too far.

My stomach feels like it's being heated by a fire I can't contain, and I fight the urge to bite my lip as my tongue runs over the back of my clenched teeth. I meet Seb's gaze unwaveringly as he attentively watches every twitch in my expression. I swallow hard, kicking myself when I see him clock the movement. His free hand moves to tilt my chin slowly, his other hand holding my wrist tensing.

"I don't need to steal it from you, little monster. I just have to wait. You can pretend for now, but I can see how much you want it." His lips are so close to mine as he leans into whisper that they briefly touch with some words, setting my skin on fire when it does.

My breath becomes shaky for a moment before I regain control and swallow the weakness that will leak through in my voice otherwise. "I don't know what you're talking about. You're delusional."

I ignore the way my mouth waters at the thought of him closing the gap between our lips, or the way the apex of my thighs heat at the feel of his hand strongly holding my wrists above my head.

"You like the power of being pursued. I can see it. You enjoy when I push more than everyone else who you've pushed away when they got too close."

"I take it back. Not delusional. You've lost your fucking mind." I pull lightly against his hands, testing his grip. It tightens in response. My stomach tumbles over itself excitedly. It's a physical effort not to show on my face that I enjoy the sensation.

"Okay. I guess I'll be waiting for you to kiss me for a long time then."

I blanch at his words. "Me *to kiss* you?"

"I'm happy to wait. I don't need to steal anything. Eventually you'll kiss me and that will be worth the wait."

My stomach sinks as I realize he is taunting me. Teasing me into begging or making the first move. The excitement that has warmed me is squashed like a sprite underfoot, and with it, all my patience.

"Keep dreaming," I spit, hearing the venom and edge in my tone. I lift my knee quickly as though I am about to kick him between his legs. He flinches, letting go of my hands to fend off the attack, but I stop myself a mere breadth from his privates. The halt just shy of the impact is enough of a message and still gives me the satisfaction of seeing him flinch.

I can screw with him just as much as he is screwing with me. If he wants to play with me until I break, instead of being brave and making the move himself, he is going to learn the hard way.

Donning the cruel smile I have practiced all too well, I zip out from between Seb and the wall, grabbing my bag from the floor, and strutting down the corridor toward the meal hall, refusing to look back at him.

Chapter Twenty-Six
Jealousy's Fire

Azariah

The mess hall is a large room that seats thousands, and is the home to many sights and smells, making my body just want to curl up and hide. It's overwhelming and unlike anything I've experienced before, but it is also something I know I will have to grin and bear until I get used to it.

There are many different food smells assaulting my nose that it's hard to make out what they are. My stomach alerts me with an alarming aggression that it's hungry by vibrating harshly until I feel like I could keel over from the painful sensation. I know it's counterproductive to the goal my body wants me to achieve, so I press my lips together and push through the feeling as I walk to my usual table in hopes of leaving my bag with my new friends.

The booth against the wall where my new friends are sat is loud and animated, just like every other person in this room. It only adds to the echoing cacophony of voices that fill the room to a near deafening level. I walk over to the booth, rewarding Seraphina with a half-smile when she slides further into the booth to give me room to place my bag on my future seat. She doesn't stop the conversation though. I look around at the new cadets Seb and I have surrounded ourselves with, happy with my choices for friendship. But they could never come close to the pack I'd created in the Culling tunnels. I'm not sure I'll ever find that level of friendship and camaraderie again. It took so many years making the deep relationships I had with my Culling pack and the idea of making that with others who might die on patrol at any time is hard to commit to.

Seraphina, the closest to me, is a short petite girl with cropped black hair and pale ivory skin, whose presence here is deceptive. I can see why so many underestimated her in the sparring section of the Crucible. She is dangerously quick. I've seen her when I've been at the gym, and she is feisty and cunning. It's no wonder she made it into the reaper group with the way I've seen her move. When she fights, there is no empathy for anyone else. No remorse. You have to put her down quickly or get put down. When she speaks off the mat though, she is hilarious. Some of the things that come out of her mouth shock me so much that all I can do is laugh.

To her left is Darian, a large, heavy built guy who looks like he should be the dumbest person. His face has a stoic appearance to it. He has to put in effort to show emotion, and he always absorbs information before the words or expressions show themselves. I've developed a pattern of collecting friends who aren't what they originally appear to be. They are a mystery to solve. Darian is probably the most intelligent of the group, though he hardly ever shows it. I've caught glimpses of the brains he hides behind his silent muscles. He is also secretly the most empathetic person I've ever met, and despite looking like a human wall of muscle, he looks after us in ways he thinks we need. I still remember the first day after training when I tried to hide the way an old injury reclaimed me, and without alerting anyone else, snuck me a heat pad.

Next to him are the inseparable two of our group. Ivan and Vadik have known each other since they were children and have grown from best friends to lovers. Ivan is the hardest working man I've met. It doesn't feel like he is ever not trying to improve himself. He is lean but not bulky, and average in height. He'd shaved his hair off when we arrived at the reaper compound, convinced it would give him an edge in battle and sparring because no one could grab onto it. I don't think it mattered but he is welcome to think so. I wasn't going to argue with him over it.

Vadik seemed to mind that his partner had cut off his hair, although he's given up on discussing it ... at least in front of us. While Vadik is similar in looks and build to his other half, he has his full dark hair to compliment his darker skin and eyes. Vadik is the calm to Ivan's storm, even though they were both just as capable.

Somehow, this group has come together after our first day in the facility and built the foundation of a friendship since. It is even nicer that none of them pry into what is going on between Seb and me.

I plonk my bag on the seat of the booth, feeling the tingle of being watched prickle the back of my neck. Without turning around, I can tell Seb finally caught up with me, but I don't want to deal with him. I'm still fuming that he teased and played with me, hoping I'd make the first move.

No fucking way.

"Good food choices today?" I ask Ivan and Vadik, who are already tucking into their heaped plates of food, clearly too hungry to wait for all of us to arrive. Ivan doesn't swallow his food to reply, he merely nods vehemently between large mouthfuls as though he must eat quickly and get back to work. Both Darian and Seraphina glance at movement behind me, and climb out of the booth, confirming my suspicions that the last of our group have arrived and it is time to collect food.

The four of us walk toward the opposite wall where plates are piled up on one side and food options laid out for easy view and serving. Seraphina moves ahead of Darian and I. Seb glances over his shoulder at me before joining her. I fight the urge to roll my eyes and make a rude gesture at him.

Seb and Sera squeezes between a gap of two tables and as I step in front of Darian to do the same, a chair pushes out from a table. With the space closed, I wait impatiently as the group of Reapers gets up from their table to leave. I step back as the exiting person closest to me turns and moves my way. When my eyes lift to his face, my muscles tense.

Jayden meets my gaze, his eyebrows raising in recognition as his lips twist into the half-smile that looks too similar to Seb's. Another Reaper on the other side of him stands too, noticing the way Jayden has stopped in his tracks.

"Jay, you know this fresh blood?" his friend asks, breaking the stillness spell my presence has put over Jayden. He turns and glances back at the speaker, the half-smile growing cruel as it redirects back to me.

He scoffs a laugh. "Oh yes! Just some little sprite that used to want me back in the Culling." His words are like tiny knives slashing through wounds I thought had healed long ago. I hate it. I'm better than this, and yet somehow Jayden has this horrid power to make me feel like I'm a betrayed kid all over again.

To remind me of every word he'd uttered to me that was nothing but a lie.

Heat stings my skin as I fight to keep the expression from my face. I refuse to let him win and make me look like a fool.

Never again.

Darian steps up behind me, his hand touching the small of my back to remind me I'm not alone. I know he is comforting me in his silent way, proving our new friendship means something, but all I can see is the way Jayden's jaw tenses, nostrils flaring as he watches Darian's movement.

A deep-seated feeling of elated triumph dances about in my chest. I can jab him back as well.

"I think you're remembering it the wrong way around, Jayden," I say, working to keep my voice as calm as possible with an innocent smile on my face. I hear the little twinkle in my tone that probably sounds like nothing has fazed me, even though it's exciting me to make him squirm and panic the way he made me.

Stay calm. I know if I get emotional then everyone here will think he has some hold over me and I refuse to let him win ever again.

Over Jayden's shoulder, on the other side of the table, Seb has turned to investigate the commotion. He looks tense and nearly as solid as stone. His eyes dart back and forth between me, Jayden, and Darian. The rage I see burning in his eyes when he looks at Jayden is immense enough to make my mouth sour with guilt.

Fuck, I hated having an audience for this sort of thing.

My eyes drift back to Jayden, expecting to see him rattled by my words, but the tilt in his smile and the glint in his eyes tells me he's enjoying the verbal sparring I've supplied him with.

"You sure you're not just upset that I left you all alone in those tunnels?" he asks as though it's an innocent question. As though I'm still a child that needs protection.

The words out of his lips gets a snicker from his friends, and the heat in my chest feels like fire. I wish I could breathe on him like the dragayastir can. The fact that he knows the right buttons to press that almost instinctively make me want to launch down his throat with curse words should make me worried. Until I glimpse his nearly invisible gaze flickering at Darian again.

All I see in the 'so quick I nearly miss them' moments are that Jayden doesn't like Darian standing so close or touching me in that way. I couldn't care less if he's jealous, but it's a way to stab him in return.

I don't care if I'm being petty or spiteful. I'm going in for the kill.

Stepping in closer to Darian's hand on the small of my back, I bring my body into the gap between his arm and his side, glad when Darian follows along. His hand slides into view on the opposite side of my waist, his arm wrapping around me exactly the way I planned for it to be. Jayden's chin tilts up as he watches, his eyes ever-so-slightly twitching uncomfortably. His friend standing beside him can't see the expression hardening Jayden's face, but I can. Petty jealousy looks so much better on Jayden than I ever thought it would.

"I wasn't alone." I smile, trying to keep my face as innocent as possible. I ignore the way Seb tenses over Jayden's shoulder and focus on the task at hand: to get Jayden to lose his nerve and back off.

"So this is a consolation?" Jayden scoffs, trying to play it off as amused shock.

"*A consolation?*" I echo in mock horror as my hand presses against my breastbone for dramatic effect. "Oh no, Jayden. I've learned there's much better out there than you."

Everyone listening to our conversation, including Jayden's friends, huff an obvious exhale at the insult I've dealt him. I smile, pretending to be unaware. The venom in the back of my tone gives away that I know what I'm doing. I don't care.

Sugar coating the insult even more, I turn my head to Darian, my eyes pleading with him to go along with this as I press my body into his tighter. His hand grips my waist, squeezing in response — a silent signal that he's here to help. I push myself on my tiptoes and take in the sight of Darian's full lips. I really hope I haven't overplayed my hand.

With a deep swallow, I lift my lips to Darian's, thankful he gets the message and doesn't hesitate. Darian's lips, surprisingly soft, crush mine as though he needs to taste me. It's addictive the way he kisses, and I almost want to forget that this is all for show. His touch is like a magick drink I can't get enough of, and the fake romance is so real, I'm almost convinced. His tongue traces the bottom of my lip as ours move in perfect unison, and it takes everything in me not to moan against his mouth. His hand tightens on my waist, and I press my body harder against his for a split second more.

Darian breaks the kiss, both of us breathing unevenly. For a second, I'm lost as to where I am, the kiss robbing me of awareness. I haven't been kissed or touched like that in a long time, not since ...

"Well, I'm glad to see someone has been filling the hole I left behind," Jayden snickers, intruding upon the spell of Darian's touch.

My head snaps to Jayden's smug expression, the only hint that I've bothered him visible in the tightness of his face. His amusement is only for show. I know I've gotten under his skin.

"You're disgusting, Jayden," I spit, staying wrapped in Darian's arms.

"Az ..." Darian whispers in my ear. I know he's warning me not to push my luck challenging a higher-level Reaper in a public place. But I'm not going to let Jayden win this. He's already robbed me of too much. He can't take my public dignity, too. Not here.

"Now, why don't you get your filthy fucking mouth out of here before I show your friends how quickly this *fresh blood* can kick your ass." The shocked exhales from our audience, including Jayden's friends, rings in my ears. By the way he nose scrunches, I've finally pushed him to emotion. The only question that has my stomach churning anxiously is: Have I pushed him *too far*?

I slowly let go of Darian, stepping forward and rolling my shoulders back. Crossing my arms, I watch him carefully in the strongest stance I can manage. Jayden steps closer in an effort to clear the corner of the table on his way out.

On principle, I don't move. Once he's past and about to walk away, I feel my organs relaxing and my heart attempts to slow its rhythm.

He turns his head as he moves and speaks only to me, so low I know even Darian can't hear him. My body dances with the shivers of a physical memory my body can't forget. "I remember how much you used to love my filthy mouth." He catches the drop in my expression that I can't mask and grins. Walking further away, his voice lifts in volume to make sure everyone around him can hear the rest of his exit. "I remember what your filthy mouth can do, too."

His friend catches up with him, snickering over his shoulder at me. Cold shivers dance across my skin in a way that somehow makes me both nervous and disgusted at the same time. My body clearly remembers the feel of his mouth on me and what I did in return. Even though there's a mix of pleasure and sensation, resentment and regret rears their ugly heads.

Heat from my gut builds, driving me to want to follow them and stab them with the knife in my holster. That won't do me any favors in the middle of the meal hall when all I want is to be a Reaper.

Darian grips my shoulder with one hand, reminding my body to stay put when it seems like it almost doesn't want to listen to common sense.

"What the fuck?" Seb breathes into the air, drawing my attention away from his retreating brother, celebrating his vocal victory with his friends.

The look on his face removes any emotion from me, other than a hollow feeling punching through my chest. My mind is black and empty as I look at the distraught realization on his face.

"Seb, I—" I start, but realize once I do that, I have no end to the sentence that will justify what he now knows about me. No words can justify what my younger self did. Something I regret to this day. And now the Reapers linger in the mess hall know my secret, their image of me forever changed over a stupid mistake.

"You fucking *slept* with him?" he hisses. I know that I have no right to tell him to shut up as the weight of my own stupid teenage decisions catches up with me. The adult decision not to tell him the whole truth is biting me in the ass now. I know by the heat leaving my face that my paleness has given him the confirmation he needs. "I can't right now. I just ... Fuck this."

Seb starts walking to a separate exit than the one his brother just disappeared through, not slowing for any possible interruptions to his hasty departure.

"Seb!" I try calling after him, but by the way his head is dropped low between his shoulder blades, it doesn't matter what I say. He won't stop.

Not that I have words to voice right now, my throat tight.

"Fuck," I curse quietly as I kick the leg of the table with the toe of my shoe, feeling the shockwave through my leg. I'm thankful I barely escaped breaking my toe in my frustration.

Maybe I should have, as it would hurt less than the pain tearing through my chest.

Chapter Twenty-Seven
The Darkness in the Fire
Azariah

I know before I open my eyes that the scratchy material under my cheek isn't my bed. The smell, as I come into my waking awareness, is sweet and moist and smells of the garden back in the Culling tunnels. When I open my eyes, I'm not sure what I expect to find, but it isn't me on a forest floor again.

It's still night as I lift my head off the bed of dried dying leaves. Either I hadn't slept that long, or I'd slept long enough to make it to the next night. I'm hoping it's the former. A chill dances up my spine as the cool wind brushes my bare arms.

Looking down at what I'm wearing, any hope I require about how long I've slept isn't necessary. I wear a white dress that I've only ever seen before once, in the dream of the forest I'd had a while ago. I know this isn't real.

But it feels real. The ground between my toes and the air pushing away my loose hair feels so vivid that I could have sworn I was really here in the forest, that looks like how I imagine the fae grove surrounding Skull's Rest.

The forest has changed since the last time I've been here. With the seasonal shift, it has grown colder and some of the leaves have fallen and died on the ground. The mossy earth is now harsher beneath my feet, but I can't escape the feeling that there is a reason I'm here, in a place I could not have imagined, in such explicit detail.

Running, I head for the clearing I have seen before, feeling goosebumps dance over my entire body. I'm a bit more careful as I move in the darkness, but still step with a confidence to where I know I'm supposed to be, feeling the soft tugging in my chest reinforce my sense of direction.

When I break past the treeline and stop on the edge of the grass clearing, bathed in soft moonlight, I expect to find the same carnage from before.

I don't.

A group of Reapers stand in front of an elf in the center of the space. One of them, Jayden, faces inside the mushroom circle that lines the ground, his body poised for a fight. The elf, with silver hair that catches the light — appearing luminous — remains calm. He talks in a soft voice with Jayden. I can't hear the conversation, but the gentle tone seems to be attempting to diffuse Jayden's aggression.

They are alive.

Glancing over at the edge of the clearing where the girl had been last time, I see her standing, watching curiously. She isn't covered in blood this time, but she does seem ... scared. The black veins under her eyes are evident against her pale skin, same as last time, and she watches the confrontation as though she is unable to move from the place she is rooted, her eyes tracking Jayden's movements.

Her eyes flash wide and she starts running toward the center of the circle, her scream of horror threatening to haunt my soul forever.

I turn back to see what has gripped her.

Oh, fuck.

Jayden presses his body into the elf, who is curled forward over something. For a moment, I think maybe he has just punched the fae in the gut, but when he retracts a knife savagely and lets the blood loose from the wound with it, I know that isn't the case. I can't move as so many things happen at once that it feels like time slows just to show me it all.

The fae banshee bolts for Jayden, her scream given force as it reaches a higher octave. With each step, she closes of the distance, her screams having more of an effect. Jayden and all the other Reapers bend over, their hands clapping over their ears as pained moans escape their mouths. It's loud but it's like I'm immune to whatever is happening in the clearing. Maybe because it's my dream.

I want to step closer, to try to get a better look in the dim light at what is happening, but it's like I have no control over my body anymore.

I'm just here to watch from afar.

Jayden and the other's pained cries grow louder as the banshee nearly reaches them. I see dark blood dripping from between the fingers of their hands, sliding down their necks to the grass. One by one they drop, and though some of them face away, I know what I'll find when I look at them later, blood leaking from every orifice.

I know before they've even stilled that this is their end and I'm here to watch. Even in my dreams I can't escape death, even if I'm less upset at the notion of Jayden dying a painful death. It's still hard to watch anyone be subjected to such a severe pain — blood spilling from their eyes like bloody tears, from their ears as though their very mind is leaking, and out of their nose even though no punches have been thrown.

The banshee fae woman throws herself down on the body of the elf who has lost all light from his eyes. The wound in his stomach has turned into a gaping hole by Jayden's exit strategy with the knife. It's clear that it killed him quickly. The elf might have been lucky; it could have been relatively painless after the initial attack. I don't know, and trying to imagine what the feeling was like is too much for my brain to comprehend right now.

All of this is too much to follow right now. Whatever this means to my life needs to be more conspicuous and obvious because I hate trying to sort through riddling images.

I watch her for a moment, seeing the absolute heartbreak written over her face as she cradles his face and pulls his head into her lap carefully. It's as though she is afraid to wake him too suddenly, even though we both know he is well past gone. She cries quietly, all the bodies around her still and cold.

She never looked up to notice me. Although, for that, I am thankful.

I want to turn and leave. I consider it. But something about the whole scene and what I've just witnessed tells me I need to stay. It isn't until something about the earth where the bodies lay shifts that I understand why.

The mushroom circle, which had been alive and thriving, shrinks in on itself, decaying in accelerated death. The grass inside the circle dies near instantly, turning brown and losing all color. Even in the dim moonlight, I see it change. And from the grass seeps a darkness blacker than the night.

The banshee in mourning doesn't notice the shadows take over the ground, lying in wait for when they are alone.

A loud warning bell sounds in my head, telling me that something is very, *very* wrong.

Chapter Twenty-Eight
Fire's Desire

Azariah

I sit up in my bed, gasping. The amount of adrenaline jolting me awake is so severe that it's nearly painful. I feel like jumping onto the ground and bouncing around with the nervous buzz speeding through my system.

What I managed, though, is breathing hard through an adrenaline-soaked sweat as I try to process what I've just seen in my dream and why. Maybe after my lunch in the mess hall, I wanted to see Jayden and his friends killed, but that doesn't explain why I'd seen it after I'd been given the 'helping hand.'

Was it real? Have I seen something that is going to happen? Something that has already happened?

A cold chill seeps into my spine at the thought. I consider if I should tell someone about my suspicions. The problem is if I told people, I'd have to tell them why I think it's real. I would have to explain my curse and that's a risk that I can't take without being sure that what I've seen isn't just my imagination playing with me.

The only person I can tell had chosen to spend the entire day ignoring me.

Seb.

I know why and it makes sense, but I'm not sure I should tell him my suspicions when it involves his brother. I'm not sure how he'd react, and if it results in him outing me to try and save his brother ... I can't risk it. It's my life against Jayden's, and he won't get any salvation from me, if that's the price.

My chest is tight, every bit of my anxiety squeezing it like I'm still wearing a bodice.

I need to get my mind away from the dream that keeps replaying in my head. The fact that it isn't leaving, even in my conscious state, adds to the racing of my heart and the way my rib cage threatens to silence me forever by squeezing too hard.

Flipping back the mess of blankets tangled around me, I slide out of bed and change into plain clothing I can exercise in. I already know the idea of going back to sleep is impossible and sitting around spiraling about what I've seen helps no one, including myself. I need to feel like I'm doing *something*. Even if that is beating the crap out of a sandbag until I feel bruised and every muscle in my body is aching.

Ducking out into the dark, quiet hallway, I walk toward the gym. For a brief moment, I glance at Seb's door, considering if I should knock and tell him about my dream. But I imagine him on the other side of the door, fast asleep, interrupted by a dream I'm not even sure is true when I've already ruined his day with earlier revelations about how much of myself I'd given to his brother. He deserves to have a restful night's sleep if he can get it, without me intruding upon it.

Before I can question it, I keep walking, leaving my doubts behind me. The walk turns into a run the moment I hit the training area. The soft mats cushion my bare feet as I begin running laps around the sparring mats, warming my body. I push myself into a sprint until my legs start to complain from the sudden strain, and my body heats to the point sweat beads on my skin.

That's when I take the anxious energy to the sandbag that hangs from a frame in the corner of the room.

Punch. Punch. Combo kick, punch. Block.

It doesn't matter that no attacks are thrown back at me, or that my limbs complain at the full weight I'm using them for, I need this. I let all my anger at myself, the world, and the fates. Its swells inside me as though it's been waiting to be unleashed for a very long time.

I hadn't realized how many things there were to be mad about until every single one of them swirled through my head in the quiet of the room.

My pointed breathing and impacts on the sandbag are the only things breaking through the silence. Even though I had foolishly believed that this would distract me from the war raging in my thoughts, I was wrong.

I'm going to drown in my own thoughts with no one around to witness.

Another punch, and another. I can't punch hard enough to satisfy the heat in my stomach or the urge to scream at the sandbag for the ways it has wronged me. For the ways I have wronged everyone. For the ways that the Crucible could've gone better and how we all could have ended up here together as Reapers. I'm fairly certain I'm fucking everything up.

I've been cursed enough. Aside from my supernatural ailment, I've been cursed to lose my friends, and now the closest thing I have to one. And on top of that, I have to deal with fucking Jayden. Why can't *anything* be simple?

How am I so good at fucking it all up?

I don't notice I'm crying until my vision swims with the salty water of my tears bubbling to the surface. I feel the hot tracks down my cheeks and the very thought that I'm feeling weak enough to cry has me battering the sandbag hard enough it begins to swing on impact.

I don't care.

A final heavyweight kick sends the sandbag swinging away as my eyes drown in tears. I don't see the bag swing back toward me until it collides with my body. The air leaves my lungs as I'm knocked backward, past where my feet can collect underneath me. The collision with the ground blows out the last of the air in my body. I wait for a moment, trying to navigate through the emotional pain if I've injured my back, refusing to move. Nothing flares up other than humiliation that a punching bag has defeated me.

Surrendering to the soft floor, I fold my arms over my face and close my eyes, crying silently as though I can hide the tears from myself.

Steps walk over from the doorway, stilling my silent sob as all my nerves snap to attention.

I'm not alone.

I wait, listening intently, considering whether to remove my hands and give away that I've been crying. My eyes are no doubt still swamped with the glassiness of my tears. Even if I find a way to get rid of the water before they see, I can't imagine I've escaped the red rings that usually accompany my weakness.

"I think the sandbags had enough of your abuse," a low, familiar voice says.

Of all the people to witness that, it had to be *him*, didn't it? But would I have wanted anyone else in this compound to see my weakness?

"Don't you dare come near me right now, Seb," I say through gritted teeth. His steps thankfully halt in response. I don't care if I hurt him earlier, I'm not letting him see me like this. "Do it and I guarantee I'll knock you on your ass."

Shuffling of his feet and clothing draw my attention. He isn't approaching but he also isn't retreating. My curiosity piques. Carefully lifting one arm and turning my head from where I lay, I watch as Seb removes his jacket and loose sleep shirt until he stands bare-chested and barefoot in the middle of the sparring mat. Heat rushes to places I don't want to deal with right now.

I sit up quickly, dropping both arms from my face as I turn to Seb on the mat. "What are you doing?" I snipe.

Seb shrugs nonchalantly, as though he was preparing to walk me back to my room. "I'm getting ready to get knocked on my ass."

"In what world does that include taking your shirt off?"

"I can't get all my shirts soaked with our sweat or I'll have nothing to sleep in. Now get up and spar with me, if you think you can knock me on my ass." His eyes meet mine as he speaks, and it's almost a breath of relief when he doesn't react at all to what he sees. I'm sure my face is a mess, but he doesn't waver in his easy, casual demeanor as he settles his feet into a fighting stance.

I lift myself to my feet and in nothing but a tank top and shorts I typically use for fitness, I move into a fighting stance. Neither of us call to begin. We start in sync, our muscles twitching a signal to the other. I strike first with a direct punch, annoyed when he blocks it. But I brush it off. I have something to prove. I'm not weak and none of my threats are empty. I need to know that I made the right choice risking my life to be here as a Reaper. I fight the urge to fiddle with the cold weight of the pendant around my neck.

Using an onslaught flurry of attacks, I try to keep him on the defense, not letting him launch any of his own physical replies. Each time our skin connects, heat flushes, and it only serves to drive my frustration. My determination. Seb doesn't seem to mind or get flustered by it, though. He blocks my attacks consistently.

Sweat forms on both of us, and the sound of our heavy breathing grows in the space. I try not to take too much notice of the bare chest glistening in the dim lighting of the training hall. The way my neck and thighs flush hotter than the sweat on my skin tells me it's going to be a harder struggle than I thought. Seb smiles, his lips tilting up in a teasing grin that makes me stumble. The expression makes him look so much like Jayden.

He presses the accidental advantage I've given him. Moving forward, close enough that there is no real room to wind up a punch or space to kick out, he collects me in his arms, tackling me to the ground. We roll, and every time I think I've taken the opportunity and will end up top, he bucks me off. When we finally stop, he has all my limbs pinned under his bodyweight. It's impossible as I roll my eyes, realizing this might be worth more energy that I have remaining.

"You kissed Darian," he says as I struggle to find a way to free myself and continue the fight. *Fuck.* Of course he'd use this as a way to question me when I can't get away. "If you had to use someone for your ploy, why not me?" he continues, and I feel heat creep into my cheeks. I try not to show my guilt or embarrassment in my expression, but there is no escaping his gaze on every inch of my face, assessing from mere inches away.

"Because he was right next to me. I gave you your chance to take your kiss, but you played with me."

"Played with you?" he questions, lip tilting up in amusement and his eyebrows shooting up to his forehead. I'm more than willing to enlighten him on the ways he's messed up.

"I'm not begging for anyone's affection ever again," I say, enunciating every syllable like it's an important detail not to be missed. His amusement drops as he leans his face closer, as though he were about to play with me again, out of spite.

"Did you beg for my brother's affection?" His words are a warning, a challenge for truth.

Even though I know he won't like the answer, I refuse to back down.

"I did, and when Jayden gave it to me, he also broke me. Never again." I grit my teeth at the memory before focusing in on the breadth of space between us. "You want me to prove it? I won't ask for you to kiss me. I want you to show me how much you want it and take it."

"And how do I know *you* want it?" he whispers as his lips draw closer until I could have sworn they grazed mine when he spoke. My lips part. "Considering you just had my brother's name on your lips."

"You brought it up."

"You gonna answer the question? Do. You. Want. Me?" He releases each word into my parted lips, letting the burst of breath dance in my mouth. He leans back slightly, studying my face, and my body instantly lurches at the growing pace.

My muscles tense without hesitation and I know I'm ruined before the words spill out. "I want you," I whisper quietly, watching as his tongue dances across his lips. I almost lift my head and break the distance between us to prove it. I wait though, wanting to see him prove it to me.

He takes the chance, his lips crushing mine and his body readjusting to release the lock. My legs fall apart as his knees touch the ground between them. I feel how hard he is pressed against me as I wrap my legs around his waist.

I kiss him back like I'm starving, because for years I have been. He's been the only person to ever admire me before truly knowing me and then push me harder until I realized he is here to stay.

His mouth meets mine, his tongue dancing between my lips, a feeling I can't get enough of. As his hips begin to grind his hardness against my thighs, I groan against his lips and almost cry out when his mouth moves off mine. His mouth traces along my cheek, peppering kisses at first until he reaches my throat. He presses himself harder between my thighs, his dick finding the right spot to pull the breathy groan from me again, even through the layers of clothing. He smiles as he sucks and kisses my neck. With each movement, I grip his hair harder.

I can't take it anymore.

I pull his head up by his hair until his lips meet mine again, moaning into his mouth as my hands trail down the muscles of his arms. Every taste of him is intoxicating, every touch like an addictive flame under my skin, and I can't get enough. His hands explore too, squeezing my breasts.

"Tell me what you want, and I'll do it to you," he murmurs against my lips.

"I want you to make my body forget the memory of anyone else," I reply, letting my instincts speak my truth.

I move my body in unison, rolling in the movements with him as we explore every way our bodies can meet on the sparring room floor.

Chapter Twenty-Nine
The Memory of Water

Morana

The body under Morana's cheek had now grown cold and stiff that it was no longer a comfort. She fought every wayward thought with everything she had when it strayed to what the corpse under her really meant. Her eyes stayed squeezed shut as she clutched the fabric of the shirt between her fists. Something wet had soaked her hair and dress, but she refused to think of what. It didn't matter what noise sounded in the dark, Morana refused to move. She knew she had been there for hours, but she couldn't bring herself to move. Even when a strong hand gripped her shoulder.

"Morana, it's time to let him go," a low, soft male voice said as another hand took hold of her other shoulder and tried to pull her upper half from where it rested on the body. She held on tighter, shaking at the thought of removing herself from holding her soulmate. She couldn't handle the reality of facing the world without him. She refused.

"Please, Morana. He's gone," the man pleaded with her as the pulling on her body softened. "We need to do the ceremony or he won't make it to the next world."

The words broke through to her and ripped the beginnings of the scab anew in her. Morana embraced Alva's body, the blood drying and staining both of them. The pain of losing her soulmate was raw, reminding her of her situation.

"Let me go with him," she whispered to the universe, hoping it would listen. The only person who seemed to hear it was the elf standing over her, and she knew he was making a point not to acknowledge her plea for death.

"Morana, let me say goodbye to my brother," he said quietly.

The words rocked her from the inside out. Morana's hands loosened from Alva's shirt, and she stopped resisting the pull on her shoulders. She still felt unsteady as she was pulled into a seated position, but she knew it was the first necessary step. Opening her eyes and catching the sheer amount of blood that stained the white dress she'd decided to wear today, Morana was sure at any second she'd begin vomiting. That was if she had anything in her stomach to expel.

It had been hours since she'd come to meet Alva at the end of his guard duty for the day so that they could go and eat together. That was when she'd stumbled upon him in a tense interaction with Reapers who were in the grove for some unknown reason. She hadn't been bound by the call of death and all she could taste was rotten acid in her mouth at the reminder that she had stood by and done nothing while her soulmate had been murdered. It didn't matter that she'd killed the humans afterward, weaponized her voice in a way she'd never done before. It was never going to bring Alva back.

Morana turned eyes to the lifeless, pale body she'd been curled up against just before, punishing herself with the painful view. The breath punched out of her like a hole had been punctured through her lungs, just as large and messy as the one in Alva's abdomen. A hole she couldn't mend, no matter how long she stared at it.

Pulling her eyes away, she looked up at Alva's brother, Elijah, who'd removed his hands from her shoulders and instead offered them to help her up. His face had strong features, so similar to Alva's that it made what little remained of her heart squeeze in agony. Elijah's hair wasn't quite the same shade of silver, and he was considerably taller than his brother had been. Morana couldn't decide if the resemblance was comfortable or painful, or both.

She took Elijah's offered help and was pulled to her feet. She wasn't sure if she could stay standing very long, given how weak and shaky her legs felt beneath her. She nodded her readiness to cooperate with Elijah's request and held her breath as air stirred quickly around her. Elijah's hand flexed and commanded the air around them with solemn confidence.

Alva's body lifted from the ground until it hovered at waist height. Without a word, Morana focused her energy on the spaces between realms, on the fae realm she tried often to avoid, and felt her power rush like water released down a hill to meet it. The warm power inside her, jolting through her system, should have been like a welcome friend, energizing her with their presence. Instead, it merely made her alert of her already-depleted energy and how close her body was to just buckling under the weight of her own body.

A portal responded to her rush of magic — a shimmering vertical lake of transport clouding the space a few feet in front of her. It was almost a relief to feel like she could do something right. Almost.

Morana looked around at the clearing and carnage she was leaving behind when her eye caught a movement in the shadows. A witch, her eyes black and consumed by the darkness, stepped toward Morana, away from the treeline. Their gazes met, each watching the other carefully as though at any moment it would turn into a second confrontation in the clearing tonight. Morana realized that while she had no love for witches, she didn't care anymore. So long as Alva was out of the picture, they could desiccate the bodies in this clearing as much as they wanted.

Morana stepped through the water-like surface of the door between realms before she could question herself. A weight lifted off her shoulders as she glanced around at the destination around her. The heavy forest was somehow thick and more luscious than the grove she'd left behind, enhanced by the magic that grew in every root, vine, and speck of the realm. The leaves on the trees had glistening veins of silver, shining like stars in the canopy and reflecting onto the surface of the body of water that lay ahead of her in the dark.

Alva's body came through the doorway behind her, Elijah's magic finding no interruption as he followed with a distracted sorrow consuming his face. His eyeline was on his brother's body but his gaze was far away and unseeing. Morana was sure the body could've risen from death to dance a jig and Elijah wouldn't have noticed.

Every breath Morana sucked in as she looked at Alva's unmoving body felt like shards of glass scraping down her throat. She hated to look at him like this — lifeless, pale, and expressionless — but she also knew she wanted to see Alva in the next world and that required urgent action. All fae had been told the horror stories of what was missed out on if you waited too long to hand the body over or if you couldn't recover the remains. Alva's soul waited, like all fae recently deceased, in the space between worlds. When his body was returned to him, he would be able to move on and head to the other world. One day, when Morana died, she knew she'd see him again in the plane. That knowledge was the only thing stopping her from crumbling where she stood.

With each step toward the body of water that extended in front of her, she felt a little more at ease with the loss she'd suffered. Morana would see Alva again in the next world, she just knew it would be hard on her own without him until then. She'd lived on her own before, but that was before she'd known anything different. Now his absence would be an obvious void in her life, reminding her how she should have had longer.

The water was cool around Morana's toes as she stepped into the shallows and stopped. Alva's body floated to her side, still under Elijah's control for a little while longer. He waited on the dry ground, silently letting her have her moment to say goodbye.

Taking a deep breath, she tried to steady herself and focus on the soft surface beneath her toes as she waded further in. The deeper the water got, the closer Alva's body skimmed the surface until it rested on the water. Morana slipped her hand into Alva's and progressed until the water was chest height and it began to stir around her.

A head appeared in her path, rising slowly from the water, its eye trained on her, unblinkingly. Water cascaded in rivers down the sides of the newcomer's beautiful face. With dark wet hair clinging to her skin, the lady of the lake moved gracefully toward Morana and Alva. The woman's expression remained flat. Her lips dripped water, unmoving as she reached the pair.

Morana watched as the woman placed her hands on the body softly and began to guide Alva's stiffening corpse back the way she had emerged from. Morana's throat tightened as she watched her soulmate drift from her, and took a moment to squeeze his hand before letting go.

As Alva's body moved further from her, pulled under the surface by the lady of the lake, Morana's wrist felt cold. It was sharp like someone had held ice to the spot where her magickal tattoo was. Morana looked down at it, her chest pinched painfully at the sight. Where the compass usually sat inside the weaving lines with infinite possibility was now empty.

The compass and her way of finding Alva on this plane was gone, just like him.

Her eyes teared up as she looked back at the place where his body had disappeared, only seeing ripples where he and the lady of the lake had been.

Chapter Thirty
DEATH BY FIRE

AZARIAH

I knew something was wrong when classes were cancelled for the day. We'd all sauntered to the usual lecture hall to discover that notes had been pasted on the walls declaring that not only were our information sessions not taking place, neither were our sparring lessons. Despite the note's light-hearted suggestion to revise current information and 'rest up,' I couldn't stop the heaviness in my stomach that weighed me down.

Every Reapers' reaction — new and existing — was strikingly different, and I wasn't sure what to make of it all. Some were living it up and using the time to laze about, and others were in a nervous frenzy asking everyone they could to find out what they'd heard as to the reasons behind the cancellation. I knew, however, that my dream last night was too much of a coincidence not to make my mouth dry and limbs tremble. I had managed to make it to the mess hall for lunch with my weak-kneed shakes and racing heart, but the number of times I'd stopped myself from going to Axton with my suspicions was exhausting.

I'm not sure why I'm even considering it without any other proof, when trying to explain why I had these suspicions would end up with me possibly being kicked out, imprisoned or killed.

"Hey ..." Seb whispers, clicking his fingers next to my ear, snapping me out of the mental spiral I'd fallen into again. "What's wrong?"

I glance up from where my fingers fiddle nervously in my lap, spotting Darian and Seraphina talking excitedly on the other side of the booth, paying us no notice. I glance at Seb, noting the furrow of his brows, heavy with worry.

"It's nothing," I try to reassure him but the crack in my quiet voice gives me away. His eyes widen and I know he's heard it.

Fuck, good luck getting him to drop the subject now.

"There's something or you wouldn't be shaking like a scared sprite."

My lips tug up in disgust at the image that I'm at all like a sprite, but I know how quiet and nervous I've been all day. It'd be idiotic to think he hadn't noticed it when he's been by my side all morning.

"I—I can't," I whisper, glancing at our friends sitting at the table. All I can hope is he drops it and intends to come back to it later when we're alone.

He doesn't.

Glancing over at our friends, he smiles widely to indicate he's intruding on the private conversation they seem to be having too. "Hey, Darian, I think they are putting second helpings of that vegetable mixture you like out," he says excitedly, nodding to the wall of food on the opposite end of the mess hall from our booth.

"Really?" he responds, lifting his head as though he could see over the crowds of people moving between him and the food.

Seb smiles enthusiastically. "Really."

Darian needs no more encouragement. He stands and takes his empty plate with him in the hunt for seconds. Sera moves quickly, smiling at us as she follows him. I try to echo her happiness, but I already know it's a pathetic attempt. But just like that, the table is empty except for us, and I have no excuse to hide behind anymore as Seb turns to me.

"What is with you today?" His voice quiet and soft as the worry once again scrunches and consumes his expression.

"There's something I didn't tell you last night," I start, unsure how to explain my dream or suspicions to him in a somewhat delicate way. I know I have a tendency to be blunt, but I don't want to be a callous punch through his heart if some part of him does still care about his older brother. He rocks back in the booth slightly, his eyes wide. I can tell he's trying to figure out where I am going with this before I spill it.

"Please don't tell me you regret fucking me. I might just get up and walk away if you do," he says slowly, his expression guarded in a way that reveals he expects me to backtrack on last night's decision to let him into my life.

My cheeks heat at the memory of how good it had felt letting him take me on the sparring mat, how much my adrenaline spiked at every other noise knowing at any moment someone could have walked in and seen us. And yet we couldn't stop.

"It's not that. I really enjoyed that … *a lot*," I spit out quickly in a whisper, watching his shoulders relax slightly. I still see a wariness about him as I try to broach the issue again. "I should've told you what pushed me to the gym though and why I was so upset."

Seb's jaw clenches in a way I've only ever seen around, or at the mention of, Jayden. I know where his mind has run to and the horrid feeling in my mouth only worsens at what he could be imagining.

"I take it back, I'm not sure I want to know …" he says through gritted teeth. It gives me an escape from the conversation I've been wanting to stop but now I'm not sure I can leave him with whatever torturous thoughts are causing destruction in his mind.

"I had a weird dream last night that felt so vivid ... I'm scared that it's real. I also knew if I told anyone else, they'd ask why I was worried about it being true." I know I'm babbling. I can't help it. For some reason, I desperately need to fill the gap in his knowledge with the truth.

"The curse ..." he whispers in understanding. The tension in his jaw disappears and his eyes go round.

"Exactly."

"What did you see?" I can tell by the sharpness in his quiet voice that there is no doubt in his mind. He believes me and that somehow makes my terror at the situation chew harder through my heavy stomach.

"Um ... I don't know how to tell you this. I was in the grove, I think, and Jayden was there with his squad. They killed an elven guard—"

"What?" His voice breaks through loudly, drawing a couple of gazes from nearby tables before he realizes his mistake. Giving me an apologetic smile, he lets me continue, leaning in close so he can whisper, "And ...?"

"I don't know why or what might have made him do it, but a fae banshee was there and she killed them all for what they'd done. I think the elf was her mate."

I'd read the research on fae soulmates, that their links to old fae earth magick meant they were able to sense the soul fate had destined as the most compatible. That when their powers officially manifested, they were introduced and that was it, but it was hard to imagine.

Seb stops moving, absorbing the new information with a stillness that was almost eerie.

"I'm so sorry," I whisper, unsure what else I can say to ease the war he seems to be having in his mind. Of course that is the moment Darian and Seraphina decide to return. Their steps falter and slow as they catch sight of Seb's stillness.

"Are we interrupting?" Darian asks, his eyes flicking between myself and Seb. I steal a glance at Seb, who has finally broken from his dazed stare but still seems understandably speechless. I improvise.

"A little bit but it's okay. We're done now and I'm able to tell you." I ignore the way Seb's head snaps to look at me as Darian and Sera rejoin us in the booth. "Seb and I are together ... officially."

"About fucking time," Darian chuckles, his face breaking into a wide smile as he looks between us. Seb's gaze doesn't leave my face even as his body relaxes. I know he's going through a rollercoaster of emotions right now, but I know I've gotten another secret message across in my announcement: I have no regret about last night and I'm finally letting him in.

The mess hall around us hushes into an eerie silence before I can reply, stealing the attention of the booth and the entire hall. Axton has walked in, flanked by two other high-ranking Reapers. His face is flat as he strides into the room. He ignores the quiet around him and keeps his steps even, his eyes on our table.

Fuck.

My body goes cold as it becomes increasingly obvious they are headed toward us. I keep my hands below the table, squeezing them tightly and funneling all my nervous energy there while I school my features into calm surprise. Axton stops at our table, and I straighten in my seat, feigning confusion at his presence.

"Sir?" I say, glad my voice comes through strong as terrifying thoughts of what he might know tighten my throat.

"Miss Delstron, Mr. Crane, I require your attendance now for a private meeting."

I want to pepper him with questions but fear the answers in public. Asking for both of us is unusual, but maybe it has nothing to do with Jayden. Perhaps someone had seen us in the sparring hall last night? Is that any better? Honestly, I'm not sure if there are any rules against it. Although, it probably isn't something he wants to bother himself with.

"Yes, sir," I say before anything else can fall from my lips. Seb echoes my sentiment and follows my lead. Every person's gaze in the mess hall is trained on us, and it's like they are all holding their breath in anticipation with me.

Chapter Thirty-One
TRUTH OF THE EARTH

AZARIAH

Axton's office is messier than I expected. I'm trying to focus on that rather than the possible reasons why both Seb and I have been summoned. Paperwork litters the expansive wooden desk, ignoring the very notion of piles beyond a few pages as they coat its surface. The smell of the room is musty and stale, as if despite the amount of air ventilation throughout the compound, this room is continually closed off from the rest of it. Regardless of Axton's superiority among humans, and even in the greater political landscape of Skull's Rest, the furniture looks old and weathered, and in need of replacement.

How many people have seen the inside of his office?

The thought seems to bring me back to the fact that there is a reason we are here and I'm not sure why. If it had just been Seb, it would have made sense that this was about the content of my dream, or if it had just been me, I had been discovered as a banshee and about to be punished. Or if this is about last night's extra activities in the sparring hall, I'm drawing a blank. Surely that is it — the sparring hall. We'll get a reprimand for allowing ourselves to fornicate in a public training area and that is it.

And yet I can't ignore the sense of dread and tightness in my stomach as Axton speaks to his fellow Reaper leaders outside the door, leaving us to stew with our own panicked thoughts about what is to come.

Seb hasn't said a word to me, probably running through the same confusion and anxiety I am, and processing the death of his brother. I don't bother trying to engage him in conversation. Especially when at any moment, the door can open behind us and expose our secrets to the elder Reaper.

The click of the door opening behind me in the silence makes me jump even though I've been waiting for it. Axton walks around the desk in silence, not addressing or looking at us until he has taken his seat. He sits, leaning forward at his desk, looking between us expectantly, his eyes ringed with bags of tiredness. He hasn't slept, which means this probably isn't about us having sex in the sparring hall. Surely he has many important things to deal with other than someone messing around where they shouldn't have been.

The silence is like a physical thing, growing and consuming all the air as Axton flatly stares at us with his serious, waiting expression.

"Sir, are we in trouble?" I ask quietly, feigning innocence in my voice. I sit straight in my chair and ignore the way my stomach is eating itself viciously under his gaze.

"Not yet," he responds, his voice curt and sharp as he turns his eyes on me. My stomach drops at the word *yet* lingering in the air between us. I know there is something wrong. He knows something and the way he's looking at me with curiosity or prideful expectation is gone. *Fuck.*

My back threatens to curl under his gaze, afraid to be seen. There isn't enough fucking air in this room. I open my mouth, expecting to reply but fall silent. I have no idea what to say without giving away that

I have something to hide. What if this is all a ruse to see if we have done something we shouldn't have or are hiding things?

Axton's gaze holds mine for another moment, seemingly waiting to see if I'll say anything, but as I draw a blank, he turns to Seb, his face softening. "I have some unfortunate news to report. I am still collecting details as to how this occurred or why, but it appears your brother, Jayden, and his team strayed from their planned route last night and ended up in the grove. I'm sorry to report your brother is dead. We are still looking into what drew them to enemy territory, or to a faerie circle in particular, but it appears both the guard of the circle and the entire squadron were brutally murdered."

My skin hums with goosebumps dancing to the surface of my skin as the rest of my body goes cold. I fight the shiver that tries to shake my body as I process what we are actually here for. *Why would we be in danger of being in trouble for last night's incident?* The tightening, horrid feeling in my stomach stills as it becomes a heavy weight holding me in place. My mouth grows dry. *Why am I here if this is what this is about?*

As though Axton can hear the clattering thoughts of my brain and read the confusion on my face, he glances at me. Leaning further forward on the desk, he clenches his fists together in front of him until I can see the strain of his knuckles against the skin. His eyes twitch with a narrowness of inspection and his head tilts to the right.

"What I can't explain is something we found at the scene."

I can't help the way my face scrunches in confusion, feeling as though there is something I am missing. "Sir?" I question, hoping he'll go on and explain.

Thankfully, he obliges.

"Your blood was spilled in the faerie ring and splashed over all the bodies." I hear the accusatory edge in his voice as he meets my gaze harshly, no longer concerned with the bad news he had to deliver Seb.

My body feels frozen, slack at the notion that there is nowhere I can go right now to escape this, or nothing I can say to explain it. My heart shoves its way up my throat as though it wants me to choke on it to escape this. It all feels like a cruel joke — one I'm not in on or know the punchline to.

Oh fuck, I'm going to die for something I didn't even do. Out of everything I've done, this is how I go?

"What?!" Seb says loudly, jumping in for me as he sits forward in his chair, finding his voice again. "Elder Axton, that's *impossible*! Azariah was with me all night. If you're insinuating she had anything to do with this, you're wrong."

Seb's words snap me from immobility as my heart flutters back to my chest. I can breathe a little easier. It still feels like I'm breathing through a tiny hole but at least I can breathe.

"Seb's telling the truth, sir. I was inside the compound all night." I don't care that I sound scared or desperate for him to believe me. I am. For the first time in my life, I'm facing the real possibility that my own kind might imprison or kill me, and it isn't for anything I've done.

Axton doesn't show any surprise at my admission, still watching me intently like I'm being studied. "Our records indicate that. What I need to understand is how your blood ended up there. Have there been any situations where your blood had been collected?"

I take a deep breath as I try to absorb that he knows I'm telling the truth, relief taking the weight off my shoulders a little and making me dizzy in the process.

"What about O Positive?" Seb suggests, looking at me, surprising me with his answer. I glance at him as I reel over why he'd suggest that ...

My attack maybe ... or ... o*h*.

The color drains from my skin as realization dawns on me, and the short-lived relief is replaced with dread.

"O Positive?" Axton echoes, drawing my gaze back to see his eyebrow raised at the recognition of the name. He glances back and forth between us, waiting for one of us to explain why that name has come out in conversation.

"We ... we went to O Positive to celebrate when we found out we'd been selected for the Crucible this year. I paid entry for all of us in blood. I *know* it's not conventional for humans to pay that way usually, but I didn't really think anything of it at the time," I rattle off, leaving out the bigger questions I want to ask: *Why would they spill my blood there? What good did that do them? And who would do that?* I'm scared to lead Axton down a line of questioning that would point him to the things I really want to hide. Panic sits heavy in my chest knowing that he has already been led down this line of questioning, which is why I'm sitting in this chair.

"Mr. Crane, could you please escort yourself out so I can speak to Miss Delstron in private, please? I will provide you updates on the investigation of your brother's death as it becomes available. For now, I ask you to keep this incident between us," Axton says sternly to Seb, although I can see that it's soft enough to be understanding of the news. "If you require anyone further to discuss this loss with, in future, please confide in me."

Seb stands and tension grips my shoulders again. I dread being alone with Axton. Seb hesitates before following orders and leaving. I don't look at him for fear of showing how much I wish he didn't have to go. Putting my hands together in my lap, I look down and begin to pick at the nail beds while Axton watches Seb leave.

When the click of the door sounds softly behind me, I look up at Axton, trying to hide all the anxiety buzzing through my blood.

"Do you have something you need to tell me?" Axton asks, sitting back in his chair like he has nowhere else to be. The silence building between as he waits expectantly is like a punch to my gut, robbing me of all the air in my lungs. My mind starts reeling. What does he know and what can I tell him?

I swallow hard. "Sir?" I question, thankful my voice comes out stronger than I feel right now.

"Funny thing about blood and why it's used as a currency in Skull's Rest is because you can't hide anything in it."

The curiosity and concern that had been pulling his face open in Seb's presence has been wiped clean from his features, replaced with a serious edge that tells me excuses and distractions are useless. He's on a mission to get answers and I'm the target.

I refuse to drop my eyes as I work to keep my face calm. "I don't know what you want me to tell you, sir."

"Let's start with *what* you are."

All possibility I was going to be able to keep the terror off my face disappears at Axton's words. There's no hiding behind half-truths or pretend confusion. He knows *something* and I need to find a way to stay alive.

He waits as I open my mouth to try to form the words, no empathy for the fear I know is turning my face pale and making my expression slack and shaky. My hands have given up picking at my nail beds, too shaky to accomplish anything.

"I'm … cursed," I say, wanting to gauge his reaction, which reveals nothing.

He raises a curious brow at me. "We detected magick in your blood but had nothing to compare it with. Mind explaining what you mean by cursed?"

"I have recently discovered that I'm a *human* banshee."

"Impossible. They don't exist."

"They do. My mother was cursed by a witch, that's how banshees are made, but aside from an uncanny ability to be at the scene of a death or weird dreams, there's nothing special about me," I say slowly and clearly, hoping it will lessen the danger that awaits me for what I've hidden.

"And were you at the scene of the deaths last night? Was Mr. Crane covering for you just now?"

"Seb wasn't covering for me. I really was here with him. I swear I have no idea how my blood ended up there, sir. But I did see the incident in my dream."

At the new information, Axton leans forward, his face softening as he tilts his head slightly. I take a deep breath, unsure what to make of the change, but continue holding his gaze, determined to find a way to save myself. *Somehow.*

"You witnessed the event from here in the facility *in your dreams*?"

"That's correct, sir."

"And you didn't come forward, knowing it was valuable information about your fellow Reaper's lives?"

"With all due respect, sir, I didn't know if I would be imprisoned or killed if I came forward about the magick in my blood. I'm still not sure of my fate."

Finally, his face softens as my eyes glass with tears I refuse to let fall. "Miss Delstron, you are a *human* that has been cursed, as you pointed out. I don't see any reason your status as a Reaper initiate has to change."

In one breath, all the tension left my chest and my airways open. I gulp in breaths of air as though it is the freshest thing I've ever tasted.

"Really?" I breathe, unable to stop my smile tilting up in a hopeful smile.

He nods, keeping the tension at bay. I relax my posture slightly, letting my shoulders sink with each breath.

"You are an invaluable asset to the Reapers. But your curse must remain on a confidential 'need-to-know' only basis. Does anyone else know what you are?"

"Just Seb," I say quickly, not daring to mention Ezekiel. I'm not sure why I don't say anything about my guardian over the years who gave me the answers, but something about our relationship and the way my stomach twists at the idea of telling Axton warns me to keep my mouth shut.

"Good." Axton nods with an approving smile. "Your *gift* will be a valuable tool to get an insight into how we can better protect this city and the happenings we do not see. You'll report them to me, understood?"

"Yes, sir," I say quickly, not willing to argue with it. A new future ahead of me, full of possibilities, appears before my eyes.

Chapter Thirty-Two
Dark Changes in the Air

Morana

Morana was almost thankful when the pull of her soul yanked her from her bed. She had been struggling to sleep in the quiet treehouse all alone. Ever since the loss of Alva, it had been something she'd only ever found when she was exhausted and ready to pass out.

She climbed out of the bed, already in the black clothing she'd retreated to since Alva's death and sourced her shoes from where she'd haphazardly tossed them in the corner when she'd walked up in a daze the night before. She walked slowly down the stairs leading to the front door, feeling as though she were sleepwalking without Alva in her world anymore. It didn't matter to her that she'd see him again — she wanted to curse the fates for allowing them to be introduced in the first place, only for her to lose him so quickly. It was cruel.

There was no hesitation or checking of the grove floor before she slid down the vine rope, letting the friction tear at the skin on her palms just so she would have a physical pain to focus on rather than the ache in her heart.

She let loose a heavy breath as her ankles took the brunt of her impact to the ground. A hiss slipped through her teeth as she straightened, realizing how little she had to soften her fall. But she pushed on, letting the soreness keep her focused on something else for once.

The last two weeks had been hell. In a way, she couldn't describe it to anyone ... because no one seemed to care about her with Alva gone. He had introduced her to a world that had seemed inviting and made her think her race could be kind and welcoming, but as quickly as the knife had lodged in his stomach, her doorway to her own kind was shut and locked.

Morana followed the call of death through the trees toward Savastral Revon, unsurprised by the fact that once again humans were the ones probably in the line of fire. But when the tug on her soul softened at the gates into the city, she climbed the nearest tree and perked up with interest.

She waited and watched, the night quieter than normal, any wildlife in the grove near the edge of the city long since abandoned the place or silent ... waiting ...

A dark shape stalked out of the trees below, and she was thankful she had chosen to climb high enough to be out of its immediate scenting range. The unfamiliar creature moved toward the gates into the opening space between them and the end of the treeline.

The Reaper guards on duty turned toward the creature, their eyes widening in fear as if they were trying to determine the threat the furry black mass of a creature posed. It was larger than any wolf shifter in its animal form and darker than any fur Morana had seen on one. Its eyes glowed red, unlike wolf shifters eyes that glowed an amber orange.

One of the humans manning the gate with a clipboard stepped aside to let the creature pass, writing down its entrance on her sheet, probably hoping it did not mean any harm. Unfortunately, she had no idea of the banshee that sat in the trees, no longer hopeful that the humans would survive this encounter.

It growled. The sound was low, guttural and disturbing, causing the hairs on Morana's arms to stand up under her shirt. She tried not to gasp in surprise. Morana pulled her body as close to the tree as it would allow and observed the creature she'd never seen before with a mixture of terrified awe and alert awareness. She could be next if she wasn't careful. And while she would gladly meet Alva in the next life, she needed her body transported in order to do so.

It launched without provocation, its fanged jaws clamping on the body of the nearest Reaper, shredding through the dragayastir scale armor they all wore like it was little more than parchment. Blood sprayed everywhere, covering the nearby guards who unsheathed all remaining weapons and began their onslaught. They cut and slashed, shot arrows and stabbed, but it barely had any effect. The weapons lodged in its body seemed more like pinpricks to it as it grunted from the action but continued its attack. It didn't eat, merely killing and moving on to the next, leaving the pieces littered along the ground.

The metallic scent of blood reached Morana up in the tree and she almost retched at the combination of it with the vicious visual she was unable to tear her eyes from. The more it thrashed and tore through the humans, the more a story from her childhood stirred of a text she'd read as a child. It reminded her of a terrifying creature that had haunted her nightmares after she'd found it, but it was impossible.

The hellhounds had been locked away, just like everything else in the Shadow Court, and couldn't be in Savastral Revon or anywhere near it. They were in an entirely different realm out of reach of where she sat. Yet there it was below her, chewing through human meat and discarding it for sport — the carnage splashed and strewn along the border of the city and the pavement. Its wide jaw stole Morana's breath.

As it tilted its nose to the sky and let loose a blood-curdling howl, Morana launched herself back from the city through the treetops, hurtling at a ridiculous speed without looking back to see if she'd been followed. She headed for the same clearing she'd watched her soulmate be murdered. She had a suspicion she couldn't shake, and she needed to make sure she was wrong.

When Morana finally stepped into the moonlight-soaked clearing, she knew it would be the opposite. The bodies of the Reapers still lay around the faerie ring, its mushroom line rotted and black in a way she'd never seen before. Other blood that smelled of fae was splashed all over it, and in it, symbols were drawn. She could smell that other humans had been here, no doubt looking at the destruction their people and Morana's had caused, but leaving it undisturbed until they had answers. She hoped they had them or else nothing could prepare them for what was to come.

And like a tear had been ripped in their world, she could taste the darkness in the air. The unconventional shadows that seemed to connect with the darkness in her cursed soul. She knew something was very, very wrong.

She stepped into the scene she'd left behind, the space inside the dead faerie ring where the murdered body of her beloved had laid, before she removed him for the goodbye, and felt cold air around her. Leaning down, she touched the dead grass beneath her feet, unnatural in its browning where it met the faerie ring. Outside the ring remained lush and green. Her heart stuttered as she connected all the information she'd collected so far.

"Oh," she breathed in a whisper as she realized that the gate her soulmate had been guarding had been smashed open. Now the door between the worlds was not only unlocked but wide open.

Noise and movement stirred beside her, on the edge of the circle like someone or something was stepping through the portal between worlds in that moment.

Without hesitation, she bolted for the edge of the treeline as heavy footfalls stepped into the clearing behind her. Crunches sounded, and as Morana glanced over her shoulder, she saw a foot as large as her standing on top of one of the Reaper bodies. She followed her gaze up, turning and continuing her momentum, backing up as she looked at the gargantuan man-like creature that had appeared in the clearing. Its red eyes looked down on her, his head tilted. She knew she couldn't wait around to discover if it was friendly. Her guess was not.

It was time to warn the elders what had been unleashed.

Chapter Thirty-Three
The Earth Shatters

Azariah

I have been awake long enough to soak up the feeling of Seb's hot, naked body curled around me. It's nice in a new kind of way that surprised me. I'd fallen asleep last night and slept deeply for hours, but early this morning, my body had jolted me awake at every tiny movement of him against me. I didn't mind it. I understood why my body panicked over each new sensation, but I still would have liked a little more sleep.

By this point, I resigned myself to the fact that I'm not getting any more sleep. We have to be up for training soon anyway.

I breathe in deep and enjoy the comforting skin-to-skin contact while I can. My room is dark, but my eyes are beginning to adjust to the dimness — a mere sliver of morning light starting to break through the small gap in my curtains. I look at the corner below the window where my little forbidden plant sits, short a few leaves after I used some to make a tea last night. Remembering the way Seb had grabbed my hips, seized my mouth with his and claimed my body, has me biting my bottom lip at the memory.

His hand lies over my waist, his other resting under my neck as we lay on our sides, him asleep and me softly trailing my fingertips over the back of his hand. I can tell he's slowly waking as his body stirs and shifts against mine. While that hadn't been my intention, I don't regret my decision as the length of him twitches against my ass. I gasp breathily, my body heating and eager for him. I know he's sensed it by the content moan that escapes his lips as he pulls my body tighter against his and lets his lips lazily kiss where my spine meets my neck.

The loud knock on my door jolts through my entire body.

I jump up out of bed and grab a nearby towel to cover my nude body. Wrapping it around me, I make sure it's secure, covering everything it needs and ignoring the soft chuckle of Seb behind me. I shoot daggers at him before opening the door a fraction and peering out.

"Hello?" I say quietly as I meet the gaze of an unknown Reaper. I can tell he is high-ranking by the service anniversary insignias on his shirt and the confidence in the way he stands, shoulders rolled back.

"Axton requires your presence at an Elders emergency council." He shows no surprise as his eyes scan quickly down my appearance.

"Now?"

He nods, waiting expectantly for me to follow him.

"Fuck," I mutter under my breath before addressing him. "I'll be right out."

Shutting the door quickly, I turn back to see Seb well and truly awake, looking somewhat amused by the view of me answering the door in a towel, his eyes tracing the skin I'm showing. I scan the ground for where we left the remnants of my clothing, collecting pieces quickly. I drop the towel, uncaring of what Seb sees as I get dressed. I can't have Axton waiting for me. The way Seb is eyeing me in my periphery, making me flush with heat and longing to take the fabric off again. But the thought of the Reaper outside sobers me.

With a heavy sigh, I pick up the armored bodice that I still have to wear with my outfit, even though I'm not going outside into the dangerous streets. Seb ushers me toward him with the wave of his hand. I oblige, watching as he sits up, flexing his defined muscular torso in the process. I try not to look too long, for fear I'll crawl right back into the bed. His fingers adeptly waft over the ties of the bodice, tightening them with ease.

"I need to go. I trust you can show yourself out after I leave?"

He smirks as he looks up at me from where he sits on the bed. He releases my tied bodice and lets me step back toward the door and slip my boots on. "I think that is a fair possibility."

With a final nod of approval, I slip out a small crack in the door to join the Reaper waiting for me, careful not to open it enough to make the man in my bed obvious. I'm not sure if he notices, his face passive as he begins to walk, leading the way down the hall.

I follow behind the Reaper, pulling my shoulders back and waking up more with each step toward the unknown. I know I will need every ounce of alertness to deal with whatever an emergency council entails. Taking deep breaths, I try to prepare myself for whatever I'm about to walk into. But is it possible when I have no idea why they want to see me?

Walking tall, I fight the urge to question my silent leader as we turn down the hallway toward the section of the compound mainly used for the Crucible. Right as I fear my chest will seize up, worried that we are about to walk back into the hall where my future began and my friends were removed from me, the Reaper leads me down the opposite corridor to an area I've never explored.

One door appears at the end of the corridor, bare walls surrounding me. It looks more imposing the closer I moved towards it. I keep my shoulders back, refusing to let the panic weigh down my chest. I'm thankful Seb tightened the armored bodice enough that it is hard to slouch.

The Reaper opens the door, indicating for me to enter ahead of him. As I move into the expansive space, it's hard not to halt in the doorway. Sloped steps are raised up around the circular room, and a congress of people from the species involved in the treaty fill the seats all the way to the top. They stick to their own, not associating between species. I catch sight of Axton on the podium in front of the human section of the auditorium and I hasten my steps to him. I try not to stare anywhere else as I make a beeline for him, the nervousness from everybody in the room seeping into my skin.

"Sir, what is this all for?" I ask as I step beside him, looking out at the loud room.

"An emergency meeting of all high-ranking officials. The fae have called it. Apparently, they have information from the incident that affects all of Skull's Rest," he says under his breath, as though they were all listening. With the Others super hearing, they most definitely had the ability to, but they all seem way too wrapped up in their own panicked conversations to notice ours.

"You don't believe they do?" I whisper, checking for any who might be focused on us.

"I just think forewarning for the human race would be acceptable given our involvement in the situation." I can tell he is being particular with his words, just in case.

I nod as a hush silence falls over the crowd.

Across the room, where the fae congregate, an elf steps up to the podium. His eyes focus on the crowd as he looks around, his presence commanding the room to silence. Other representatives from shifters and dragayastir step up to their own podium, Axton matching them.

I know I'm being watched intently by the way the hairs on my neck prickle. I know who I will see before I turn my head toward the dragayastir section.

Ezekiel.

Just as powerful and confident as the last time I saw him, he stands at the podium at the front of his area, his eyes widening at my presence. My entire face flushes with heated annoyance at the memory of how he made me fear and panic for my life when he had been so wrong. The humans would never abandon me — one of their own — and it had been horrible for him to make me think otherwise.

I lift my chin and turn my attention back to the fae who stands tall, preparing to speak and adjusting his clothing precisely. By the glancing shivers, I can tell Ezekiel is still watching me.

Axton's face scrunches in confusion in my periphery. Stepping slightly closer, I drop my voice to a whisper as the last of the conversational whispering echoes around us. "Who is that? What's wrong?"

"That's the Crown Prince of the Seelie Court."

"Which one is the King?"

"He's not here."

My stomach feels like it's filled with heavy rocks. "Why wouldn't he be at an emergency meeting?"

"I think we're about to discover why," he grumbles, and I know that is him silencing our conversation and my curious questioning.

The Crown Prince of the Seelie Court's voice rises across the room without having to strain. "I have some grave news to share and developments that will affect Savastral Revon. A matter of days ago, our very own faerie circle was attacked by a group of Reapers. We are not sure if they acted alone or under orders." The Prince glances up at Axton, as though he wanted the Reaper Elder to challenge the claims. "A guard of the circle was brutally murdered. A banshee, and the soulmate of this guard, retaliated in kind to the threat but the damage was already done. The realm he guarded until his dying breath was none other than the locked doorway to the imprisoned Shadow and Unseelie Courts. The creatures of which have now found their way to every corner of Savastral Revon and beyond, and in the process, killed our King."

A collective gasp echoes around the room, matching my own. I have no idea what these creatures are. I imagine it is something that has been removed from human public records since they've been locked away, whenever that was.

I look at Ezekiel, whose gaze is fixed on the Prince with widened eyes of ... fear. I didn't think he could be scared. Feeling my eyes on him, he glances up at me and the silent words that pass through the space between us tell me *exactly* how bad this is.

There is definitely a reason they were locked away and all Others in here are scared.

Fuck.

If the dragayastir looks panicked by the notion that these creatures are out, something is very, *very* wrong. I try to contain all my questions from spilling to Axton in such a public space where anyone can hear and humans are being accused of inciting this entire thing. I make a mental note to ask the questions later once we are out of this emergency council.

"Prince Malachai, I—"

"That's King now, thanks to your insolent species actions," he interrupts Axton with fury written in flushing red across his features.

"Are you insinuating that this was *planned* by my people? Because I assure you, we had nothing to do with this grave incident and are investigating the guilty Reapers actions and movements," Axton explains, features passive.

"Your assurances mean little. It will not bring back the dead or undo what has been done."

All I know from my short time seeing the Price of the Fae, or new King, is that I don't like him. He is arrogant and curt, and the way he looks at Axton resembles the way we look at bugs on our shoes. We mean nothing to him, and he has no respect for us.

"Then allow us to assist in the recapture and imprisonment of the Dark Courts as we did all those years ago," Axton says in a diplomatic and calm tone. Calmer than I would have been if I were speaking to the fae spokesperson.

"We need nothing from your weak species that has lived only by the graciousness of Others too long." The new King's eyes glance out across the auditorium, meeting the eyes of the representatives from each species as though he is seeking validation that they are all sick of looking after humans. "We will abide by the peace treaty no longer."

Every person that isn't King Malachai appears to be utter shock, including those who stand behind him. The fae stare at him as though he's decided to stab himself in front of them, and it isn't far from the truth. While the fae are elitist, it seems odd for them to pull out of the treaty. They have always been the most peaceful beings in Skull's Rest.

What the fuck is happening?

Malachai strides off the stage, headed for the door, uncaring if his people follow him as he leaves chaos in his wake. The auditorium erupts with noise — yelling, arguing, panic — as everything I've known my entire life implodes before my eyes at the hands of one Royal fae.

Chapter Thirty-Four
THE FIRES OF WAR

AZARIAH

Seraphina and I sit on either end of her bed, the mattress between us laden with knives, daggers, and arrowheads. Holding my sharpening stone securely, I pick up the first one in front of me and get to honing the edge.

"Thanks for spending time with me. I know we don't normally do this." Seraphina smiles at me from where she sharpens an arrowhead with her own tool.

"Perfectly fine. I don't mind changing that." I look up at her for a moment to smile, feeling slightly lighter.

The last two days since the emergency meeting have felt like the whole world was crumbling down around me, because the world as we know it really is. The walls around the compound are the only things making me feel safe, and sometimes it felt like the new creatures flying could get inside with one ill-timed flight.

"This might be our only chance for a while," Sera says, her voice mimicking the wariness of the future that my mind is swimming with thoughts of.

"I know. I'm not really sure what the future holds for us," I answer, not wanting to be too pessimistic of what I fear the world will become.

The dragayastir had always been the top of the food chain. If they were terrified by what awaited, humans stood no chance. Even the trained ones. I worry that by the end of the year, all humans might be dead and there is nothing we could do to stop it.

"That's big coming from Axton's personal mentee," she says with an attempted grin, trying to lighten the mood. My lips tilt up in response.

Only one more week of being Axton's mentee. The idea is both a relief and terrifying. I've been reporting my dreams to him as required and super thankful to the fates that the call of death hasn't pulled me out into the world that has been swarmed by the creatures of the Dark Courts. For now, the compound offers a safety I know will leave me soon. I'm trying to absorb the comfort of safety while I can.

"Mm-hmm," I agree, thinking about the honor that will be mine for only one week longer. The darkness of what awaits us all is hard to ignore. I look up at Sera's slack features and the arrowhead she is sharpening. "It's going to be bad. Of that, I'm sure."

"You're making me a little nervous, Az."

"I'm not really the person who pulls punches, Seraphina. Surely by now you know that," I say, putting down my own knife and focusing my attention on her. I can't hide the truth from my friends, at least not when it comes to the chaos and pain we are all in for.

"I suppose I do. Okay, how bad are we talking?"

"Well, we were supposed to get years of training before we are to start patroling the streets, but now we're moving out next week with a new guide we're supposed to learn in our own time. Half of this new guide is supposed to be on Others that have been locked away and classified since we were born. Even the Others we've always known seem horrified."

Seraphina's swallow is audible in the quiet of the room as she digests the weight of my words. "And the fae, shifters, and dragayastir really won't help us?" she asks hopefully, but as she glimpses my head shake, I see it fade from her expression.

The way the shifters and dragayastir had backed out so fast after the fae had left the peace treaty was unnerving. I hadn't realized how much the fae had held it all together until it was gone. Even though humans sacrifice the most to the Others, it isn't enough.

I think Axton had been relieved to make the announcement that the Culling was no longer going ahead, and all human children would now be trained as Reapers. While it meant we now had to protect ourselves from every Other now too, not just the dark and rogue creatures, I couldn't help but secretly wish the treaty had fallen apart earlier.

Holt.

Trylan.

Elora.

Hamish.

All the people I'd lost from the Culling felt like a cruel twist I could have narrowly escaped but didn't. And now they are gone, and everything has fallen apart for nothing. Their *sacrifices* meant nothing now that the treaty is over. I begin to worry the amount of people I lose will get too long to remember them all.

"There's every possibility that we all die in this," I whisper, staring down at the sheer number of weapons that could be coated in blood within a week.

"Maybe pull your punches a little," Sera suggestions quietly.

I know she won't like the answer, but hiding the truth of our current world order would only get my own kind killed.

"If you want someone to tell you the painfully honest truth, you ask me. Plain and simple. I don't pull punches, and it hurts. But learning to deal with the brunt of it will keep you alive longer than pretending the danger doesn't exist. I know it's not fun but at least you know how bad it is right now, and we can prepare for the worst."

"And hope for the best?"

"Definitely. We still must prepare for the worst but absolutely be optimistic. Crazier things have happened in Skull's Rest." I force a small smile on my face, knowing I've delivered the bad news. Even though I'm so utterly devoid of confidence that it can get better from here, Sera needs this.

She smiles back, her lips sliding up a lot more naturally than mine. "Having you as our squad leader on the outside will help our chances, too."

My chest warms at her words. "Thank you. I hope I can live up to the faith and trust you have in me."

"You already are."

We sharpen the other tools together in silence and the warm feeling in my chest refuses to disappear. A knock on the door breaks into our little bubble away from the chaos of the world. Seraphina calls to invite entry and we both look up, surprised when Seb's head appears through the small opening.

I raise my eyebrow, ignoring the fact Seraphina is grinning at me in my periphery. His tousled hair is coated in sweat from exercise, and I wait expectantly for him to explain why he's here at Seraphina's room.

"I wanted to stop by and check what time you think you'll be coming back to your room," he says softly.

"Umm, whenever I feel like it. Why?"

"I need to discuss something with you," he responds, smiling at Seraphina as a reminder that we're not currently alone.

"I'm sure you can wait a little longer for sex, Seb," Seraphina butts in, giggling. I smile, too.

His cheeks flush as he flounders, embarrassed, for what to respond with. This time, I choose to save him.

"I'll be an hour or so, and I'll come past your room," I say. He nods, relief seeping into his features before shutting the door behind him.

Chapter Thirty-Five
The Change in the Air
Morana

The breeze whispered across Morana's face, listening to her commands like a well-trained pet. Her fingers twisted and curled on her outstretched hand, and the wind complied, altering direction and stirring against her skin with each tiny change. It was soothing for her to feel so in control.

Morana sat by the edge of the lake where she'd farewelled Alva, staying out of reach on the soft grassy earth, away from the water lapping at the edge. The sound of the dancing shoreline was a comfort as she shut her eyes and tried to focus on her magick. She'd chosen to sit here out of need. While it was a painful reminder of what she'd lost, it was the only place she'd managed to find that made her feel close to her soulmate.

Steps sounded behind Morana, slow and deliberate, making her aware of the person's presence. She opened her eyes and twisted where she sat, preparing her muscles to jump up and move out of the way if someone else was here to farewell the body of a loved one. Instead, she saw Malachai, the new King of the Seelie Court, make his way slowly down the tread-worn path in the grass toward her.

Morana scrambled to stand as he approached, nearly tumbling back to the ground in the process and turning the movement into a curtesy to cover her tracks.

"Can I help you, Your Majesty?" she asked in the human tongue, making a point of separating herself in language from her own kind; they hadn't done much for her lately, anyway.

His head tilted to the side as he observed her, but followed her language lead, submitting to her lingual comfort. "No need for formalities," he said as she lifted herself from the curtesy. "You're the banshee that witnessed the breaking out of the Dark Courts and reported it to Kenrick?"

"I did. Although I wasn't there when the door was fully unlocked. There appeared to be some other ritual, after I'd left to farewell Alva, to fully unlock the door between realms. But I was there when my soulmate was murdered by the Reapers, yes."

He nodded, attentively hanging on to every word. "Thank you for what you did to those humans. Behavior such as theirs should not go unpunished."

His words caused Morana's gut to clench tightly. She fought not to show her reaction on her face. She hated the idea of being thanked for her rage-filled reaction. While she didn't regret killing those Reapers, it had been an emotional response that had served no purpose other than getting even. The meaning she drew in her actions was one that repulsed and made her skin crawl with alarmed warning.

"It didn't bring back Alva and it didn't stop what inevitably happened so I'm not sure why you're thanking me." She found the words spilling from her lips before she could stop them.

"You were brave enough to act in the best interest of the fae. And I'm here to offer you a new position in my Court."

The tightness in Morana's stomach twisted sharply again, gnawing violently as though a small creature were trying to eat its way out of her stomach. "I'm ... I'm flattered?"

"I know you have a unique point of view and are able to see the dangers we are up against, when you follow the call of death."

Morana wanted to leave the conversation behind, but struggled to think of a polite response. All she wanted to tell him was that she hated the offer but the curiosity over his level of derangement made her stay to see this conversation through to its conclusion.

"They have definitely changed recently," she admitted, giving him small nuggets of truth to see what he'd do with them.

"I was hoping, rather than reporting them to elder Kenrick, you would report them directly to me," the King said calmly. Morana swallowed the urge to ask why he wasn't being briefed by his fae representative. Or why he wanted to go over the head of his informational advisor. "I also wanted to request, that if bodies of victims are recoverable, you assist me in collecting them."

Morana felt the moisture in her mouth disappear as she swallowed hard. "You want me to retrieve fae corpses?" she clarified, hoping it was not worse than what she was rationalizing. "To aid in farewell ceremonies?"

"*Any* corpses," he responded. Morana's body stiffened like she was also dead. "Any victim — whether it be human, Dark Court, luprender, or dragayastir, even — would be helpful."

"To what end?"

"The fae have been kept in the dark by the Reapers too long," the King answered. "We are not privy to certain information from the treaty that I think is prudent we understand now."

"What sort of information?" Morana hesitantly prodded, worried for the answer.

"Weaknesses and capabilities of the species mainly. The Reapers had their guides and tools to kill any one of us but never offered the same information."

Despite the warm air that hugged Morana's skin, she shivered against the cold feeling that washed over her. Even though her heart thrashed at an uncomfortable speed, it felt like the only thing capable of moving as realization dawned on her.

Everyone knew that the humans withheld their information on the species in order to even the playing field. They were the species without magick bestowed upon them and physically were weaker, slower, and more vulnerable. To ensure equality and safety, they were the keepers of the knowledge on the species and donated members of their race to the growth of the others. Everyone knew that, which meant if Malachi was trying to discover the information for himself ...

"You really aren't looking to renew the peace treaty ..." Morana whispered aloud as she searched his hardening expression. She wasn't sure if he could see through the questioning due to the growing repulsion underneath it all. She stayed out of arm's reach from him, just in case.

"Humans and the Others in Savastral Revon have taken the fae for granted for far too long, and it is time that ends. If they are willing to come to the bargaining table and establish a new treaty, one that sees fae are given their rightful place leading the lesser, then I will be more than happy to call a ceasefire. Until then, we must protect our own kind in any way we can, wouldn't you agree?"

Morana wasn't sure how to respond in a way that didn't expose her real feelings or make her a liar. Instead, she tried to change the angle of the conversation. "The fae have never looked after me."

"That will all change now, you'll see. If we look after our own and stick together, we'll all survive," the King said, offering a hopeful smile she didn't know how to return.

"And you think me bringing you the corpses of Others will help us look after our own?"

"Yes," he said simply with a smile and nod. "In the west grove is a facility, if you can manage my request, drop them off there. Our researchers will know what to do."

The idea that the capabilities and facility were already prepared and briefed made the dry, ashy taste in her mouth rancid. She feared what would happen by telling her deranged King no, but also didn't want to listen to his rationalization for this cruelty any longer.

"I'll definitely think about it," Morana said slowly, leaving her half-truth for him to excite over. "Now, could I please be left to my grieving, Your Majesty?"

The King's face lit with a triumphant smile as he nodded and bowed to her. Morana fought the sneer that wanted to pull up her lips at the sight of him bent over in respect for her.

"Of course," he said, backing away several steps before turning and striding off, his chest puffed up and his arms swinging jovially.

Chapter Thirty-Six
The New Earth

Azariah

The key slipped into the lock too easy. I almost expected a struggle from the first use of it, some semblance that the house we were about to open hadn't been used in a long time and that it would provide some resistance for its new occupants.

It didn't and I tried not to think about how long it had been since the house had been occupied. Whether its previous owners were recently deceased Reapers or if this house had been waiting many years for us and had just recently been reviewed for use by headquarters. If I thought on it too long, I might think myself into a panic and that would help no one.

Seb follows behind me as I swing the door open and hesitantly tiptoe into the dark front hall of our new house. I'm not surprised that I let Seb talk me into living with him once we were moved out of the facility, but I'm shocked by how quickly I said yes.

The idea of living alone in a home outside of any perceived safety in the Reaper compound of Skull's Rest was too much for me to bear, on top of everything else happening around me. I'd lived around people, in such close quarters, for so long that it felt odd to try and break from that. Even the private room at the compound had been more isolation than I knew what to do with. I couldn't handle being away from the compound, out on real patrol and going home to be completely … alone.

The front room is dark as Seb shuts and locks the door behind us. I pull the light medallion from my pocket and survey the room as it illuminates. It's simple and bare, devoid of markers from previous occupants. The dark, brownish color gives me small comfort, reminding me of the Culling tunnel walls. The air is stale too, and while I know that means it has been some time since anyone has lived here, I find comfort in finally feeling closer to where I'd grown up than I had before, and finding joy in knowing I've made it to where I'd always dreamed of being.

It is way earlier than expected, having our first patrol tonight feel rushed, but I'm officially a Reaper. As I step toward the back of the entry hall and take the stairs down into the earth cautiously, an odd sense of calm washes over my anxiety-ridden body. Being underground, away from the windows, especially given the lack of protection away from the Culling tunnels or the gated Reaper compound is a small solace that stops me from panicking that the dark creatures in the city could reach us well before our first patrol.

The space is simple downstairs, but it's ours and only ours for as long as we are alive and human. A kitchen greets us at the base of the stairs, complete with wall-mounted light stones that glow to life slowly at our presence. I watch Seb place the full and heavy rucksack from his shoulder on the kitchen to unpack later, before we move to check out the other rooms. A washroom connects to the bedroom we venture into, complete with a privacy door that makes me smile. We will finally be in living quarters to each other and a bathing chamber with a washroom to share … that will be … eye-opening, I'm sure.

I try not to think too much on it as my eyes catch the size of the soft, inviting bed in front of me. I pull my bag off my back and tug the small potted plant from it, finally able to leave it in view in the corner without worry of who might find my plant baby.

I know exactly where Seb's mind has strayed to as his fingers trace up my tired back, stepping in close behind me.

"Should we try out the new bed?" he asks with a sly smile as I turn to face him. "Test out if it's softer than the compound ones and if they've promoted our sleeping arrangements?"

"Except you're not suggesting we sleep on it," I say with a half-smile as I glance at the bed over his shoulder.

"Oh, fuck no." He chuckles, slipping his hands to my waist and pulling my hips flush against his. "I have much more *vigorous* ideas in mind."

His fingers play with the ends of my armored bodice laces, testing out my reaction before committing to taking my body the way I normally love him doing. But my mind is swimming with too much anxiety for the smile to reach my eyes, and I know he can see it. I don't want to talk about it, but I also don't know how to hide the way my body tenses at what our new lodgings mean for the future.

"What's wrong?" Seb questions with furrowed brows.

"It's nothing ..."

"Clearly not the fucking case. What's wrong?" he asks again. I know he'll keep annoying me with the same question if I don't tell him.

"I'm just worried about our first patrol tonight."

"Which part?"

I sigh. "All of it. I'm a squad leader now. What happens tonight, good or bad, rests on me." The words have never felt heavier on my shoulders.

He stops fiddling with the laces on my bodice and wraps his arms around my hips in a half-hug. He leans his upper body back to keep his eyes attentive to my face as he speaks softly. "It's going to be great. I promise."

"You can't know that."

Seb sighs heavily as his eyes drop for a moment, composing his response in the silence before he finally lifts them. I see his own worry for the future written plainly on his face and it feels soothing to know I'm not the only one panicking.

"No, I can't. But I do know there is a reason you were made squad leader and it's not the banshee thing. Well, not *only* the banshee thing. Axton trusts you. You're quick on your feet, make sound decisions, and deserve the position."

"I guess, but even the most well-trained Reapers die in the field and that was back when we had a peace treaty. What chance does *our squad* have against all the creatures from the Dark Courts now loose, especially when we've had less than full training? We got the full new Reaper guide *today* and we could run into any one of the species tonight. It's not enough time to learn it all efficiently enough to save my squad."

"Axton didn't have a choice, and at least we have a guide now, which is more than we can say for those who have died in the service before us."

"I guess so," I reply, and force myself to take a deep breath. I need to focus on the positives. If I don't, I might not even make it to my first patrol.

"Why don't we take a look at the reports Axton gave us about the area we're patrolling and study the most likely culprits we could come across," he says with a smile that suggests things will be okay, and for a moment, I want to believe him. I let the half-smile tug at my lips.

"That logic is supposed to be job," I say quietly, watching as Seb moves until he stands behind me, my body facing the inviting soft plush of the mattress. His fingers dig into my shoulder muscles in a way that makes me groan in pleasure as the knots in my body surrender to his touch.

"Well maybe if you weren't so tight and wound-up, your brain would be able to find the logic. Let me help you relax enough to find that logic again, and then we can spend every minute studying that guide until patrol."

"Maybe just a little bit of ... relaxing."

"Well, I guess I better make sure that I work really *hard* to make sure your body fully relaxes then," he whispers in my ear as his knuckles dig deeper, working their way down my back. My spine responds, dismantling itself like it's given up holding its structure as my posture ripples and my breathy sigh moans from my lungs.

He prods my body, and I step forward, unable to fight the weight he's using to usher me. As my legs reach the end of the bed and my knees press against the mattress, his fingers disappear from my back. I want to whimper and tell him to keep going with his muscle magick, but silence greets me as he works quickly and undoes the laces of my armored corset. Abandoning the item of clothing the moment it's opened, he gets to work kneading my breasts like they hold as much tension as my shoulder, pulling a gasp from my lips.

Cries join the gasp as his fingers pinch my nipples between grinding movements and then move to pull my undershirt off my head until my bare chest is exposed. The warm air somehow tingles my skin as though I'm standing in the cold just for him. The warmth radiating from behind me has me leaning against his chest as he pinches and squeezes. One hand snakes up to grip my chin, turning my head to meet his lips over my shoulder, while the other works its way down the front of my stomach, touching lower, lower, lower. My body relaxes, working itself into a surrender that has my head forgetting anything outside the room besides our bodies embracing.

As his fingers work between my legs, I sink into him and let myself embrace the privacy of our home together. That just for this moment, it's ours and only ours to enjoy. Where no one can hear my screams as he pushes my body to release the built-up tension over and over until I no longer feel tense ...

Chapter Thirty-Seven
Fire & Darkness
Azariah

Seb and I arrive at the rendezvous start point for our squad, unsure of what to expect. I was a ball of anxiety on the walk over, hoping I wouldn't turn up to find the pavement littered with the bodies of my squad, surrounded by dark creatures. Thankfully, they are all standing around lazily, waiting impatiently.

Seraphina and Darian lean against the wall of a house nearby, her black hair shining under the dim streetlights. Darian towers over her in height and size but looks at her in a way that says it doesn't matter to him because her presence in his life is a dangerous poison he can't get enough of. The two of them have started up their own relationship and I couldn't be more thrilled for them.

Ivan and Vadik stand side by side in the middle of the road with their arms crossed, shifting weight from foot to foot almost in sync. The way they refuse to even glance at each other tells me that it might be a tense squad tonight if they are in a fight.

At my appearance, the group closes in. Seb joins them and Darian moves to stand by my side. I had labelled him as my second, mainly because he is the most qualified person to be the leader other than me, and because I feared the idea of making Seb my second and being accused of favoritism. His overpowering build stands beside me, at attention, as he waits for instructions with an approving small smile.

It's the kind of smile that says, *'you can do this'* and it feels nice to be supported by my team.

Taking a deep breath, I let my shoulders relax slightly as I pull them back into a stronger, better posture to address the group. "Okay, we know the route, but I'll lead regardless. I hope over the coming days you can dissect the new guide as much as possible. I understand this first night might be hard without the proper knowledge, but we can do this. We *have to* in order to keep our city and species safe. I'll lead the group, and we'll spread in pairs in case of an onslaught. Vadik and Seraphina, you pull up the rear, and Ivan, you help Darian watch the back of the pack. Everyone understand?"

Nods and agreements resound with no complaint, and I feel the tightness of worrying about my leadership start to ease. I shift forward and use my hands to signal that we are on the move. Seb lines up with me and we both pull our weapons out of our holsters to be at the ready in case of trouble.

I expected our route to be fraught with danger at every turn, and while the sounds of screams and roars filled the distant air, we encounter a relatively quiet patrol as we move around the human residences in the city. I'm hyper aware of smells as we walk, knowing it's a good indicator of oncoming threats. It just smells of the usual stone and freshwater.

We come close to the entrance to the Culling tunnels, and I fight the thought of breaking away from our planned travel to see what has become of the tunnels since they pulled the children out and housed them in the Reaper compound to train. But I know it isn't safe. Those tunnels could have easily been taken over by anything now that they are vacant, and we don't need to find out what.

The longer the patrol goes on and the further through the route we move, I feel myself relax. My shoulders sag slightly, and my breathing deepens. It isn't until my gut clenches tightly in warning that I ready myself and signal the others for weapons at the ready. I could have been wrong but something in my body tells me to be alert. The smell of thick charcoal assaults my nose. As the creature with dark fur moves out of the alley ahead of us, I know I haven't been paranoid.

It's huge — larger than any wolf shifter I've ever seen, measuring to my height. While it looks like a black wolf, the glowing red eyes tell me not to be deceived. It's eyes fix on me, sending a chill down my spine that seeps into my veins. My body wants to freeze up and hope that it moves on, but my training has prepared me for this. The reports of these creatures detail them as aggressive and ferocious with no hesitation.

I signal for the attack to begin, and Ivan fires off his bow and arrow in a quick flurry that remind me of how dangerous he can be. Shot after shot lands, lodging into its body, while the hellhound, as they've so aptly been named, grunts at the actions. It doesn't falter as it stalks toward our group.

Turning the dagger over in my hand, feeling the secure weight of it in my palm, I toss it with all my strength before I can freeze. It sails through the air and wedges into its eyeball with a satisfying squish. It roars, the sound vibrating my bones like I'm being shaken in an aggressive storm. Even when the sound stops, I'm not sure if I'm shaking in terror or still feeling the aftereffects of the noise. I push myself, trying to keep a handle on my body through all the adrenaline that races through my veins. I pull out a new combat knife from another sheath on my body.

And finally, the most dangerous part of the battle is upon us. The hellhound is close enough to try and swipe its claws and snap its teeth at us. We can't risk backing up further; most of our weapons are close range. I know that the moment we report back to Axton, I'm requesting more long-range weapons to keep my team safe.

The usefulness of long-range weapons doesn't seem to do as we hoped — only the dagger sticking out of one of its eyes seems to bother the creature. The group flanks out around the creature, sticking as close to the walls of the buildings without pressing themselves against it and not being able to move or dodge if needed. I stay in front of it with Seb at my right, his sword ready to swing when the opportunity presents itself.

The hellhound snaps its jaws at me, and I jump backward. Ivan uses his sword at the hind of the creature to swipe for its leg. I can tell the movement has the desired effect when black blood gushes out of the creature's leg, severing it. The hellhound falters.

I almost breathe a sigh of relief as it looks at the limb it's missing, howling in Ivan's direction with a blood-curdling note of pain. The sound curls something tight in my chest. I glance to the left, feeling eyes in the alleyway. I catch sight of a banshee standing there, watching the scene unfold. All I can do is try to scream over the roaring of the hellhound.

"Ivan, get out of there!" My vocal cords strain at the effort, and I break from position as the creature lunges for Ivan. I stab my knife as deep as it will go into the body of the hellhound, and once it is buried to the hilt, I pull down on it with all my body weight. The body of the creature tears open, black breaking from the wound that gapes as I pull further down. Blood splashing across my body and face. The heat of it and the metallic smell make my stomach roll uncomfortably and bile rise up in the back of my throat. It burns as I swallow it back down.

Crunch.

The sound stops my attack even as the one that follows is a pained roar that fades to a whine. I step back quickly from the body, letting the black blood pool on the pavement. The warmth of it seeps into my shoes and socks, and the charcoal smell only grows stronger as the puddles do.

My whole body shakes as I look at the creature sinking to the ground. Next to its head is the still body of Ivan, separated in two. Everything in me stills for a long moment that feels like it will never end.

All I feel is cold.

Red is splattered over Vadik and Sera where they stand on either side of him. All color seeps from their faces. I want to sink to the ground and give in to the horrified sorrow gripping my throat, but we are too exposed and I'm the leader. I must get the remainder of my team to safety.

The banshee stands wide-eyed, backing into the alleyway she stood in, trying to make her exit. This is the death she's been called to witness.

"Seb, make sure the creature dies," I order, trying to keep my voice clear and strong, even though it's scratchy from the scream earlier. "Darian, Sera, patrol is over. Get Vadik home."

Darian and Sera look up at me wide-eyed over the slumped body of the hellhound. As though the command is still taking time to reach their ears. Finally, they nod and move over to Vadik who is slumped to the ground next to Ivan, his face streaming tears as his mouth opens and cries soundlessly. The sound of Seb sliding his sword into multiple new spots of the hellhounds body fills the now-quiet street.

I speed my steps up as I move toward the alley.

"Hey, wait! Banshee!" I say as I turn and head into the alleyway. "I know you!"

She turns to me from her place halfway up the house she has begun scaling, watching me with wide eyes. She is scared.

I might know her, but she doesn't know me.

I know I'm taking a gamble. I know it could cost me everything I have worked for with my squad if any of them follow me. I have enough faith they are listening to my commands and not walking within earshot as I quickly reach up and undo the clasp of the necklace.

I feel the surge of power like a slap to the back of my head and know that my eyes are lighting up the dark alleyway with a green glow, just like hers. Her movements slow and eventually she drops down to the ground, her head tilting in curiosity.

"I'm like you," I whisper, knowing only she could hear me.

Chapter Thirty-Eight
THE STRANGER ON THE AIR
MORANA

The human banshee girl grounded to a halt as she reached the middle of the alley. Wide-eyed and breathing hard, she held the removed necklace in her hand. Despite the fact that her face was completely unfamiliar to Morana, their soul's seemed instinctive to feeling at peace around the other. Morana supposed it was probably the fact that the darkness of her curse recognized another with the same affliction.

All Morana had been trying to do tonight was her job, and now she was sure she was about to end up embroiled in someone else's mess. For the first time in a very long while, the fae banshee had been called to the scene of more than one death in a night and the emotional load had made her susceptible to not thinking clearly. She shouldn't have stopped for the human that called after her, but clearly, she hadn't been thinking straight.

Earlier that evening, Morana had watched the glowing translucent figures of the wraiths — mostly non-corporeal in form except for when they chose to be — go after a luprender in the center of Skull's Rest. It was the first time Morana had seen the creatures in action or witnessed them in person. Before that, she'd only ever heard of them in stories told by other children when she was a child. It had given her anxiety and fear at the idea that one day she would eventually turn into the corpse-looking figure that inhabited dead bodies and used them like clothing outfits, all because she was associated with death's curse. As she grew up, she had eventually realized they were entirely different creatures and there was no chance of her developing their abilities or grotesque visual. Somehow seeing them in action had brought all her panic to the surface like she was a child scared of her own powers again.

They attacked the luprender slowly, turning certain limbs solid in order to attack the shifter in his wolf form and then phasing back before they could get hit in return. The Spire became the wolf shifter's final resting place, bloodied and broken in ways the old predators of Skull's Rest had never been able to do to an Other.

The wraiths moved on to find their next victim, thankfully not spotting her hiding on a nearby roof. As Morana considered whether she should transport the body of the dead creature to Malachai, her soul tugged her again. It was insistent and vicious. The idea of watching another death, most likely at the hands of another dark creature, made her sick to her stomach. But her curse was adamant and there was no ability for her to refuse, so she walked along the rooftops in the direction of the Culling tunnels.

When the pull faded, she knew she was nearly at the scene of the next death. Dropping down carefully into an empty alley, she tiptoed out to the opening to watch the street nearby. A hellhound strode up the street toward her, it's eyes glancing to where she stood. Holding her breath, she darted her upper body back out of view before it could notice her and waited until she heard the movement of the Reaper squad and the hellhound's turning in response, before she popped her head back out to watch carefully.

None of those involved in what transpired next noticed her. She watched them work more efficiently and smarter than any of the previous Reapers she'd seen against a hellhound, and despite the death, Morana had been there to watch. They fared better than those she had seen before. For once, she watched the hellhound die, too. Then the girl with the unglowing green eyes had spotted her and Morana knew she had to get out of there.

Those involved in deaths usually didn't have great words to say about those unfortunate enough to have to witness it.

She hadn't been fast enough.

By the time the human had called after her, she felt herself slowing down. The tone of her voice didn't suggest anger, and something about the desperation in her tone made Morana prickle with curiosity. And finally, when she stopped scaling the wall and looking back, she saw the eyes change to a green glow and all thoughts of leaving dropped away.

A human banshee.

It was something Morana wasn't sure she'd heard of in decades, and even then, it was from a rare time before her birth when humans and witches had a lot more interactions in a world without the peace treaty. Now they were back to it again and it appeared the witches were finally back to cursing once again.

Morana approached the girl with silky black hair, the strands curled around her face and shoulders, pale skin and green glowing eyes with fascination, stopping a few steps from where she stood in the middle of the alleyway. Her human squad moved back to their homes, except for the one she had called Seb. He approached the end of the alley, keeping his distance from the women and waiting at the entrance as a guard, respecting her to do what she needed to.

"You're a human banshee," Morana couldn't help saying quietly in the human tongue at the sight of the glowing green eyes mere steps from her, looking back with a mirrored fascination she was sure was etched in her own face.

"I am. My name's Azariah."

"And yet you're a Reaper." Confused amusement leaked into her tone as she tilted her head at the human banshee, as though doing so would reveal it all to be some sort of trick of the light. Nothing changed and the eyes glowed back at her.

Azariah nodded. "I am."

"Why did you wish to speak to me?"

"I want answers."

"And you think I possess them?"

"I know you do," Azariah said confidently, her shoulders rolling back. Morana's stomach tightened in anticipation. She wasn't sure what answers she had or why this human she'd never met would assume she had them, but something about it all was unnerving in a way she struggled to place. "I had a death dream. I witnessed the death of your elven mate and the Reapers the night the Shadow Court was unleashed. And I saw you there, as well."

The reminder of what she'd lost that night made her mouth dry and eyes prickle with more unshed tears she didn't want to lose down her cheeks. Breaking eye contact and looking to the sky for a moment, she blinked her eyes clear, hoping the tears would disappear.nShe sighed into the relatively quiet night. "Then you know as much as I do about that."

"Not exactly. My dream ended when they died and you ... held your mate. I'm really sorry for your loss, but when the Reapers investigated later, *my blood* was splashed all over the bodies. I wasn't there. I don't know how it ended up there or why. I thought you might have the answers."

"Witches arrived afterward. How they *got* your blood, I don't know, but the massacre didn't open the portal to the Shadow Court, at least not fully. There were two bloodlines, human and elf, used in the sealing ritual and only those two would break it," Morana explained, not questioning why she was giving this information to a human Reaper when the peace treaty was destroyed beyond repair. Something about telling this one person felt ... *right*. "My Alva was one of the bloodlines used to seal it away, but there was a human one, too. It's part of why the peace treaty initially existed and kept humans involved. If I had to guess, your bloodline was probably the other one." Saying Alva's name made her voice crack and her heart ache.

"The other bloodline that sealed away the Shadow Court was *mine*?" Her eyes widened further than Morana thought possible. She held the necklace clasped in both hands in front of her stomach. The elven banshee nodded slowly, as if trying to process the events with the information she now had.

"It's the only thing that makes sense. The door wasn't open when I was mourning Alva. As I left, the witches arrived, and if your blood ended up there, that would be why." The fated connection between them was evident and explained why Morana's soul somehow felt comfortable around Azariah's. They recognized each other somehow and clearly, they were meant to meet at some point.

"I ..." Azariah breathed, looking down at the pavement. "I had no idea my bloodline was that special."

"Yeah, you humans rarely do. Comes with the territory of abandoning your children to raise each other," Morana said with a huff at the very thought. Morana knew she was an exception in the fae world and the lonely memory of growing up alone was one she couldn't imagine a parent voluntarily making for their child, and yet, humans seemed to do it as ritual.

Azariah's eyes snapped up to meet Morana's, narrowing as her thoughtful expression was replaced by lowered eyebrows and her lips thinned into a straight line. "It's the best way to ensure survival of the strongest. We *need* the strongest." Azariah's hands dropped to her side, clenching into fists. One held the necklace, the other still held the bloody weapon she'd used on the hellhound, shiny silver mixed metal coated in black blood.

For a flash of a second, Morana worried that Azariah might act on her training.

"I didn't mean to upset you," she said calmly, watching as Azariah's remaining squadmate, Seb, walked up beside her. When Azariah caught sight of him, her face softened out of its frown.

"It doesn't matter," Azariah said quietly to Morana. She didn't look at her as she spoke, instead faced her friend.

"Hey, you got your answers. We need to get back inside to avoid running across anything else without the squad," he spoke softly to Azariah. Almost ... lovingly. His facial similarity to the man that had stabbed her Alva was striking. A pain stabbed into Morana's heart at the sight of him next to Azariah, glancing over his shoulder. His presence unnerved her.

Azariah nodded carefully back at him and began to back away. "Thanks for the answers. It was nice to meet you ..." The human banshee waited for an introduction she realized she hadn't been given.

"Morana."

"Morana," Azariah echoed as she stepped backward toward the alley opening, her squadmate glancing out to check that the street was clear of danger ahead of her.

"Until we meet again, Azariah," Morana said softly, but loud enough for her to hear. She watched Azariah lift the necklace around her neck, securing it in place. The glow in the human's eyes faded to nothing and reduced her back to a non-glowing jade green color, making Morana wonder how many more secrets different species had been harboring in this growing conflict.

The two humans disappeared around the corner, leaving Morana alone to dissect what she had just encountered. Goosebumps danced over her skin, and she wasn't sure if it was because of the interactions fate had gifted her with tonight, or because she feared there was a much bigger reason at play than just the opening of one realm's prison cell.

Chapter Thirty-Nine
A New Fire's Crucible

Azariah

The streets of Skull's Rest felt oddly quiet as I followed behind Seb back to our house. Maybe it was that I was too consumed by how I'd finally met the banshee from my dreams and spoken to her, or maybe it had grown quieter in the stone streets around me.

But I knew I was too focused on Morana to care that much.

I knew I shouldn't be, but it was becoming increasingly hard to snap myself out of the spiraling thoughts in my mind, replaying our conversation. The revelation that my blood was the key to the Shadow Court release was hard to believe and yet it made an incredible amount of sense. It still didn't explain how blood that had been donated to a venue in Skull's Rest, that was owned by a couple of dragayastir, had ended up losing blood they deemed powerful to witches that had used it for a ritual.

How had they even known that I was the bloodline they were looking for? Should I be worried I have witches after me?

"Are you okay?" Seb asks, glancing over his shoulder, temporarily snapping me from my questions that can't be answered.

"Yes ... yes ..." I repeat, my stomach twisting as the half-lie slips from my lips. I know the internal war stealing my focus puts us in more danger.

I know that I shouldn't be doing this, but I can't stop. "Just absorbing what happened."

"The banshee or losing Ivan?" he asks as we continue walking. I catch up to walk beside him, no longer letting him move ahead of me in the dangerous streets. My empty stomach twists at the reminder, somehow feeling worse than I already do that my brain has focused on meeting someone from my dreams than the loss of our squadmate.

"Both," I say quickly, lying without a second thought. I can't admit to him that I'm such a horrible person that Ivan's death has already become a footnote by comparison to what I've learned from the banshee.

"Maybe wait until we're home to absorb it all. That way we can make sure we're safe."

I nod, rolling my shoulders back and lifting my chin. "Will do." I take a deep breath and lift my weapon as though we are about to meet our enemy on the battlefield. We move through the streets, so close to home I know I can keep my focus. I have to hold on a little longer and then I can spiral inside my underground sanctuary.

I finally notice alongside the quiet that has overtaken the streets of Skull's Rest, the lack of screaming and growling in the distance I've become accustomed to. A fog has settled in the streets, making the street-lights more useless than normal at lighting the paths ahead. As we turn one of the last corners toward our home, I spot movement in the thick white fog ahead. Grabbing Seb's wrist, just in case he hadn't seen it, I grip it and pull him toward the nearest alley, out of view of anything that might be waiting for us.

Peering out around the corner, I notice the darker shadows in the dimly lit fog, some moving, others very much stationery. As my eyes adjust, I realize exactly what is going on, surprised at how quickly I manage to make sense of the vision in the street. Bodies lay on the ground, unmoving. Some have no eye color left, their soul magick long gone from their bodies. Others bleed out, their orange glowing eyes lit up. Above them, walking through the bodies, picking them up and removing them, are glowing green-eyed fae. For what, I'm not sure.

I look at Seb where his face glances around the corner above me, his body pressed close to mine. He meets my gaze as he looks back at me.

I mouth my question, careful not to make any noise to avoid the Other hearing. "What do we do?"

"I don't know," Seb mouths back, making my stomach sink as I realize he's just as stuck for how we can get home safely and quickly as I am. The prospect of having to wait for them to leave is far too exposing, even in this small dark alley.

The smell of spiced smoke appears on the air, making the hair on my arms stand up. I feel the hard grip on my shoulders before I can register what is happening and I'm thrown backward into the alleyway.

Crack.

The impact of my head against the wall is blinding, and I can't help but cry out as it radiates through my skull. The second impact with the ground is only slowed by my quick instinct to put my hands out to soften the fall face-first. The scrapes on my hands burn.

How I am still awake?

Before I can question why the painful collision with the back of the alleyway didn't knock me out or kill me, I push myself off the ground. I don't want to think about the pain too much as doing so will only make me slow. I need to figure out what the hell just happened.

I peer into three sets of red glowing eyes, noting the fangs of three very hungry looking dragayastir standing between Seb and me.

Seb's eyes widen. He catches mine before we both focus on the massive problem at hand.

Brandishing my steel and silver knife, I push through the panic that threatens to seize my muscles. I will never be the victim I was in the alleyway of O Positive ever again, and Reaper training has helped provide me with the instinctual movements to push through.

Lunging for the closest dragayastir, I swipe my knife for its throat, not bothering with non-lethal attacks. It misses by a breadth of space, and I quickly pull my arm in to cover the gap I've left open for retaliation. I'm not quick enough though, and the male dragayastir with disheveled hair and a sadistic grin grips my wrist and pulls before I can get it away.

Stumbling forward, I work to get my feet under myself and use the weapon in my other hand to stab his thigh as I move within reach. I hear the roar behind me as the dragayastir presses in closer behind me, his chest flush against my back. A hand reaches around and holds my chin so tightly, I fear it might shatter. I hold the hilt of the knife tightly in his thigh and yank it out before stabbing into the flesh. Again.

And again.

And again.

With each shunk of the weapon slicing through its flesh, black blood coating my hand in warm waves, the dragayastir cries out. Each stab echoes in my mind like ping pong balls bouncing on tiled floors. My eyes lock with Seb, running toward me and crying out as he unleashes his anger on the two Others in his way. They are strong and we are outnumbered. Our training was designed for one-on-one or to work in a large squad, not this.

We're so fucked.

I continue to struggle and hope that my actions will eventually release me from my weakening position, but as the dragayastir seem to overpower Seb, I know I'm going to die.

Green eyes come into view at the opening of the alley. So unfortunately timed. Seb is knocked back into them and they seize the opportunity without a second thought. The two elves grab Seb's shoulders and body between them, using their strength to lift and carry him away.

"Noooo!" The guttural screech rips at my vocal cords like they will snap at any second. I struggle against the hand on my chin and the arm wrapped around my corset. It's no use but it doesn't stop me, hoping for one second that the dragayastir's grip will falter unexpectedly.

It doesn't.

"Azariah!" I hear Seb's guttural roar as he keeps fighting uselessly.

Pain stabs into the muscle between my neck and shoulder. Seconds later, black spots dance in my eyes. The screeched words turn breathy as the world falls out of focus and my eyes involuntarily roll back. The strength in my limbs seep away. I know my dragayastir attacker is holding me up, knees wobbling and warmth dribbling down my neck.

Ice floods my veins, cooling my heated body, bringing with it a sense of comfort I didn't know I needed at this moment. My eyelids struggle to stay open, tiredness overcoming my body, forcing me to feel the world around me.

No matter how much I want to fight, I can't anymore.

It's all over.

Chapter Forty
Earth's Alteration

Azariah

It's unnerving how awake and unhurt I feel when I open my eyes to green ones looking down at me. The memory of what I've seen catches up with me. I sit up and scramble backward, wild eyes darting around, unable to make sense of my surroundings.

"Hey, it's me!" the fae says quickly.

I move far enough away to see more of the world around me. My back meets the wall that had sent me dizzy not long before. The green eyes belong to Morana, the banshee I'd met before our attack, and the alleyway around me is completely empty, except for us. The dragayastir seem to have disappeared. All the pain and aching in my body has disappeared with it.

Surely I didn't imagine it. The attack was real, I was sure that it was, but as I look around and no fae or dragayastir evidence lies in sight, I wonder if perhaps it had been some weird waking dream I hadn't realized I'd experienced.

Where is Seb?

"What ... what happened?" I ask, hearing how fine my voice sounds despite the screaming and pain I thought I'd been through. No scratches in my throat, just uncertainty. I look down at my hands and chest as I lean against the wall in a sitting position, somewhat thankful to see the trails of blood down my chest already drying. Something *had* happened. I wasn't imagining it. And yet the relief is replaced quickly by a tightness that squeezes my stomach uncomfortably. My body is painless, and I feel better than I have in a long time despite the events of the evening.

"You and your squadmate were jumped by dragayastir and fae. You didn't stand a chance," Morana says slowly, watching the reaction on my face carefully.

"You saved us?" I hadn't remembered her appearing as the world faded to black, but I very easily could have missed the appearance of her presence.

"Well ... no," she says, her eyes dropping to the ground for a moment, the action speaking volumes.

"Where's Seb?" I ask, tone harsher than I expected.

"They took him. The fae, I mean. By the time I arrived, they'd disappeared and so had the dragayastir ..."

There's something she isn't telling me.

I reach up to where the trails of blood would have started, where the pain that had sent me unconscious originally came from, and my hand meets a wet pool between my neck and shoulder. When I pull it away and glance at my palm, I pray I'm not going to find exactly what I do. My hand is coated in dark scarlet red, still relatively fresh and smelling of rust. Being able to smell it so easily isn't something I'm accustomed to. The amount of blood is so severe that there is one question burning at the front of my brain, unable to be ignored.

"How am I alive if you didn't save me?"

Her eyes drop again and my stomach clenches in warning. "The dragayastir didn't kill you. They fed ... and ... well ..."

I want to shake the answer out of her and scream, but the way she glances up at me as though she knows I'm about to physically attack her makes me stop. Morana catches something on my face that make her eyes linger, and before I can find a way to avoid her touch, she reaches her finger out to my lip and brushes something from the corner of my mouth.

"What are you—" She pulls her finger back for me to see, and the sight of black blood on the tip of her finger makes my spine straighten with realization. "No."

"I'm sorry," she says, dropping her hand to her knee where she squats in a long drape dress in front of me, wiping the blood on her black dress.

I need to be sure that my worst fears are correct.

"No, no, *no* ..." I whisper as I pull a knife from the sheath on my hip and hold it up like a mirror to my face. The reflection is severely distorted but there is no hiding the thing I am looking for in the silver blade.

Red glowing eyes.

It doesn't matter that I still wear the necklace Ezekiel gifted me, this kind of magick can't be hidden.

Silence falls between us. Morana waits for me to digest my new reality.

I'm a *dragayastir*. No longer cursed but no longer human, either. Everything I've worked so hard to get is gone in a heartbeat, and I never saw it coming. My stomach rolls over like all the human food I've eaten in the last day is about to be thrown up all over the pavement. I lay my head back, feeling my neck complain as I stare at the dark night sky, hoping the fates could explain what is in store for me. Somehow, I expected to feel worse if I ever became an Other, not *better*. I feel strength in my body I've never had before, and a magick that I'm scared to touch. I feel *powerful* and it was never supposed to feel like this. The only problems I face now are the loneliness of losing all the humans in my life who wouldn't be able to look past this, and what to do with my life now.

"What the fuck do I do now?" My voice protrudes into the quiet that overtakes the night. I put the knife back in its sheath and wait for the banshee to give me answers. I can hear more things now — water dripping somewhere onto a metal pane, growling and breathing even further away than before, and other steps within several blocks. I should've noticed earlier, but clearly I'd been blinded by my focus on making sense of everything to care.

"I can't help you there, I'm sorry."

"Seb … he'll know what to do about this. He wouldn't leave me to this fate alone."

"He's not here."

"Then I'm going to get him back," I say, pushing myself up from my seated position, using the wall to help me. I don't need it; my whole body holds more strength than ever before in its limbs, but something about the way my world is shaken gives me a sense of normality pretending as though I need it. "You're going to help me. They're *your people* who took him."

"That's not a good idea," Morana says under her breath. She stands with me, keeping a little bit of distance between us every time I move. It doesn't go unnoticed. "For all you know, he's as good as dead."

"I don't give a shit whether you think he's dead or not. I'm not leaving him in the hands of some *pointy-eared pixies*." I'm done holding back my anger, and with my new strength, I don't care who hears it. I have more physical power than I've ever had in my life and I'm not about to waste it when there is a chance of saving the only person who might still care about the new version of me.

Morana holds up her hands, eyes narrowing in anger. "If you want my help, the *language* stops now."

I press my lips into a thin line, not regretting my anger but rethinking my word choice. "I'm sorry," I say, hoping it will help make her more inclined to help me. Dragayastir or not, I need her help. "Now will you please help me get him back?"

"Are you really sure you want to do this?"

"I'm as good as dead to my own kind. My—the Reapers won't take me in anymore. Not with the treaty gone. All I have is him," I say, something in my gut telling me that the truth is going to be the only way to get her help.

Her features shift from passive to surprise, my words resonating with her on a level I can't figure out. I thought it would've taken more time to convince her, but the slow nod she offers has my heart squeezing painfully.

"I know how that feels." The tightness in me eases just a little bit as I watch my new ally with curiosity. "I know where they've taken him, but we can't do this on our own. There's too many of them, so we're going to need a plan."

Taking a deep breath, I begin to lead the way back to my house, knowing no one will have taken the space away from me yet. "Follow me," I instruct. "I know somewhere we can plan privately."

Chapter Forty-One
CARVE IT IN THE EARTH

AZARIAH

I don't know why my gut tightens as I open the door of my home I share with Seb. Morana follows me inside, eyes darting around the space as if searching for danger. I lock and shut the door behind us, and the hallway lights up.

"Okay, we need a plan and probably some more weapons." I sigh, letting my steps audibly trudge down the stairs to the bedroom and bathroom. When I get to the bottom of the stairs and see the bed Seb and I have barely gotten to enjoy more than once, my heart squeezes uncomfortably.

Brushing aside the nagging thoughts that I might not get to see him again, because that will only put me in a depressed fetal position in the middle of the bed, I turn to glance at Morana as she reaches the base of the steps. Her eyes are wide as she looks around the room. The way she reveres the ceiling, like it might cave in at any second, makes me curious about what her home looks like.

I'd heard rumors about the fae lodgings but never witnessed them for myself. Something told me I'd be in awe if I did.

I busy my brain with trying to imagine what a house of fae looks like to avoid spiraling over the thought that would make me feel hopeless if I lingered on it too long. I will get Seb back, there is no other option. While Morana looks around the large bedroom and bathroom I call home, I get to work collecting weapons from my trunk. It isn't hard. Every arrow, sword, knife, and dagger is pulled from the case I packed them into earlier this afternoon while Seb had bathed. I lay them out on the bed, taking stock of all the weapons, knowing I'll take every single one of them to save Seb. It doesn't matter if I have new powers and strength, I will make sure I have every option at my disposal. And when I find him, he'll need his.

I cross the room quickly, opening the trunk on the other side of the bed with Seb's belongings. I know he'd forgive me for rifling through his things to get what we need when I save him, so I don't bother being tidy about it.

"Feel free to take whatever weapons suit your fancy off the bed for this mission. Just make sure it's returned afterward, if possible," I say to Morana. My head is buried in the depths of the packed case, pulling out swords and knives and placing them on the floor beside where I kneel.

"I don't need those," Morana says. The tone of her voice makes me turn my head for a moment. Her lip curls back in disgust as she looks over the sheer number of weapons on the bed. Her distaste of my old life reflects in her eyes as she glances over all the metal in front of her. I choose to ignore it for now — there is no point getting into an argument with the only person who can help me get Seb back now.

"And you want another person to help us?" I ask, trying to change the subject as I take a temporary break from collecting weapons.

"Preferably many someones," she retorts with a glimmer of a smile as she looks over at me instead of the weapons. "There are a lot of fae involved in this."

"They're really cleaning up after the Dark Courts messes then, aren't they?"

"Mmm ..." Her eyes trail to a place that seems to consume her thoughts. I see the tiredness and sadness that pulls down her face. My heart constricts at what she's lost. I can't imagine watching Seb be murdered right in front of me, and I hope I never have to.

"I'm sorry for your loss. I know I've said it before, but I really mean it. Jayden wasn't a good guy. On multiple occasions I've seen him doing some questionable things, but this was something I couldn't have imagined, or I would've told someone earlier."

"There are a lot of things that have been *odd* lately." She says it like there is more she hasn't told me, and I can't help questioning it just to see if she will trust me enough to tell me.

"Well, maybe they're connected somehow?" I suggest.

"I'm not sure. I've seen more anomalous activity from the witches of late than any other species when answering the call of death."

I raise a brow. "Witches? I thought they were extinct."

"They're definitely not. I wish that were the case. Instead, they're meeting with succubi and using rituals to speak to their leader from the Dark Court, who I'm sure is out and causing havoc now."

My body seizes tightly as everything stills. I could have sworn my heart skips a beat it's supposed to thump. "Did you say succubi?"

"Yes, why?" Her eyes meet mine, and whatever she sees on my face captures her attention. She refuses to look away as I swallow harshly.

"I saw Jayden with a succubus not long before the attack. He's always been *sexually orientated* so I didn't think much of it. I figured they'd come to an arrangement to trade sex for soul feeding, but ... what if Jayden was in on the attack, too?"

"That's a lot of ifs," Morana says slowly, digesting my theory. "But it's not out of the realm of possibility."

Silence falls between us the puzzle pieces start to click together. I feel uncomfortable in the stillness doing nothing.

I have to get Seb now, before anyone else conspires against me. I turn back to Seb's trunk and collect more weapons on the top of the case before burrowing down past the clothing in it, checking for any weapons that might have fallen down the sides. I reach the bottom, lifting the sweater Seb only pulled out for comfort when he needed the extra warmth. I consider curling up on the bed with it for a second, and thanks to my new sense of smell, I can already scent him in the air. I close my eyes for a minute, my face turned away from Morana as I take a deep breath.

As I work to shuffle it back where it had been in the trunk, I feel the weird shift in its fabric, like it has items tucked inside it. If it's something we can use as a weapon, then it needs to be added to the pile. I pull away the fabric.

Small bags of liquid and a wad of folded up letters falls out of the sweater, dropping into my lap. Looking down, the contents of my stomach drop just like the little bags and letters had.

Lifting one of the bags up to the light, to be sure I'm not imagining their scarlet red color, I exhale everything from my lungs. "What the fuck?"

"I'm guessing that's not something you know how to explain then?" Morana says as she moves closer to look at the bag of blood over my shoulder.

"I'm not sure why he'd have this. Whose blood is this?" I say as the smell of it engulfs my nose. It's earthy but also rusty, and the very presence of any of this is sending my mind reeling.

We all have our own secrets and weird things we like keeping private, but there is no way I can comprehend why he has bags of blood in his trunk.

Morana makes a noise that draws my eyes over my shoulder quickly. She shifts from one foot to another as she looks at the blood, her lips in a thin line like she is fighting to hold in her answer. Upon my intense glare, she decides it isn't worth hiding anymore.

"It's *your* blood. Human you. It's the same scent you had earlier tonight before you changed. It's the same smell that's been all over your shirt since I found you."

My fingers shake, the blood slurping in its casing. "Wait, *what*?" My voice comes out as a shaky whisper. "Why does he have my blood in bags …"

"You wondered how your blood ended up at the scene of the attack. This might be your answer," she says quietly. I don't dare look at her for fear I might rip her head off for even suggesting such a thing.

"No! He wouldn't do that. Seb isn't like his brother, he … cares about me." The words feel like rocks that are getting harder and harder to swallow. Every word uttered at Seb's defense has left conviction behind it. I can hear it.

"His brother?"

"The Reaper in the faerie ring attack who went after your soulmate was Seb's brother. But they aren't close. He told me so … and I could see the way they acted whenever they were together … I—I used to be close to Jayden, and I hated him for how he betrayed me. But Seb was determined

... to show me he wasn't like that. He's *not* like that. He ... fought to get me to let him in ... just like his brother did ... before he ..." My heart feels like it's exploding in my chest, blowing out my internal organs with it. I sift through thought after thought, scared of the conclusion I'm connecting them all to.

My hands drop to my lap as I keel over my stomach in my position on the floor and fight to keep the tears from my eyes.

I can't be this stupid again. Can I?

Morana stays silent, not responding to my words. I don't look up at her. My gaze trains itself on the blood bags and envelopes I hold in my lap, as though they'd disappear and prove me wrong. The paper is soft against my fingers in one hand and the clear bag of blood weighs in the other, bringing forth the pained tears. The hole in my chest only seems to grow and consume my entire body, threatening to kill me.

"He wouldn't do this to me. He wouldn't ..." I whisper to the air as though I can make it real, but the hopelessness in my voice only serves to make everything seem more pathetic.

I'm alone.

My life dream, the person I thought I lo — all gone. The future seems dark and uncertain, and one I don't want to explore. The only confirmation to finally prove to me this is the truth lies in the letters in my hand. I'm sure of it. I lift them from my lap, freeing the first one from the group and opening it up slowly, hoping every word in here will explain this to me and prove my suspicions wrong.

Seb,

I know I'm not going to be around in the Culling to keep you strong anymore, but I know you've got this. You and I will figure out how to get through what's coming, too. Until then, find attached the notes from my Crucible.

I'll see you soon with answers.

Jayden.

I flick open the next one, feeling my heart rate hitch to a painfully fast speed.

Seb,

I found the thing we've been searching for. Did you know the witches aren't actually extinct? The Reapers have been lying to us to keep us powerless and compliant.

Lucille, my new succubus girlfriend, introduced me to one today, and you will not believe how powerful they truly are. Definitely not extinct. I'm working on a way in for us to learn how we can have their sort of power, too.

I'll keep you updated.

Jayden.

My hands are shaking, making it hard to read the words that keep moving. I feel the warm streaks down my cheeks, and I press my lips together as I fight the noises that try to force their way up my throat.

Seb,

I know what we need to do to become some of the most powerful beings in Skull's Rest. We need to trade something. And they have something very particular in mind ...

Do you know Azariah Delstron? Green-eyed Reaper wannabe bitch? We need her blood. See it done and I'll keep you updated on next steps.

Jayden

The letters slip through my fingers as my eyes refuse to see anything except blurs and shapes. The little holes Jayden had left behind years ago in my psyche are now large gaping ones. Somewhere along the way, I'd let Seb take my whole heart and never noticed it was a robbery.

"May I?" Morana offers as her delicate fingers drift into view, offering to take the rest from me. I swallow harshly and nod, handing the entire pile over to her. I know I can't do it anymore. Maybe it will finally be the confirmation I need or maybe it will heal me and tell me what I've read so far is wrong.

The sound of rustling papers consumes the silence between us as I try to keep my breathing even. It feels like my throat is coated in glass with each inhale.

Morana finally speaks.

"They suspected your bloodline to be the one required for the ritual they wanted the witches to perform. I'm so sorry, Azariah. He never loved you."

Something inside me splinters at Morana's explanation and fire burns in my chest. Hot, alive, and angry. The only emotion I can stand to feel is rage.

Rage at what I fell for.

Rage that he could have just stolen my blood and left my heart alone.

Rage that everything I thought I knew is gone.

I have nothing left to lose.

And it's at the hands of Jayden, yet again, and his brother.

I stand with fire burning inside. I'll let anyone who stands against me burn.

I throw the bag full of blood against the far wall, watching as it explodes alongside my scream. It splashes and coats the tan colored paint, looking like a violent murder scene with no body. The wall cracks where the bag broke.

When the echoes of my rage-filled scream disappear, I straighten and look away from the mess I've left behind. "I know who can help us at the facility as backup. We won't need anyone else if he says yes," I say as I turn to Morana, letting the hole in my body be consumed by the raging fire that my new powers revel in. The new strength I feel waiting to be unleashed is intoxicating.

"You still want to go? After everything Seb did to betray you?" she questions.

I fight the urge to flinch as her words hit me like a physical blow.

"Yes," I say, not faltering as I confidently hold her gaze to show her just how serious I am. "Because I'm going to look him in the eye and kill him myself for what he's done."

Chapter Forty-Two
THE EARTH OF ANIMORA

AZARIAH

The gates in front of Animora Castle don't feel as imposing this time around. I walk along the bridge to the front gate, feeling taller than I ever have before as I barely glance around. The idea that I have somehow moved up the food chain with my change of species is oddly refreshing, and while the Shadow Court creatures could still kill me, the fact that I'm no longer the prey of every rogue Other in the city makes my steps a little more relaxed.

By the time I make it to the front gate with the guard in front of it, he already spotted me approaching and moves to let me through. Between my new red glowing irises and the visible pendant I used for entry last time, there is no surprise on the guard's face as he opens the gate and lets the guard inside the gate lead me inside.

"I'm here for an audience with Ezekiel," I say, voice clear, even though the guard has already begun to lead the way, letting the gate swing shut to lock behind us.

"Who may I say is calling?" the guard asks, not turning around as he continues to walk ahead of me.

"Azariah. He'll know who I am."

The entrance to the castle and subsequent rooms I'm led through are beautiful and elegant, no longer overwhelming the way they once had been. So much of my world has opened to me since the last time I was here — staring at the high ceilings, ornate pieces of furniture, and the rich dark colors. They're no longer a priority.

I stride behind the guard, catching up to his steps quickly. My heart doesn't stutter when I'm left alone in the library and the lock clicks across the door. I simply venture over to the wall of books on the far side of the room and let my eyes trace the spines as a means of distraction, determined not to take my anger out on any of the no-doubt precious books.

In the stillness, when there is only myself and the books to keep me company, the heat inside me bubbles as I'm reminded of Seb's betrayal. It's hard to forget and even harder to ignore. Ducking and weaving my way through the streets was enough to keep my brain away for a moment. But now the active awareness of looming danger has passed, and when I feel my body relax, my mind wanders to the pain and rage once again. It's consuming, heating my insides like I'm a boiling pot of water that can't be contained by a lid no matter how hard I try. The books are definitely too close for whenever I explode.

Thankfully, I hear the click of the door before any damage can be done. I freeze in place, my back turned to the door. I know from the slow, deliberate clicking of boots on the hardwood floor, and the way the back of my neck still prickles, that it's *him*.

"My Belladonnna, why are you here?" Ezekiel asks. His tone isn't accusatory or angry, merely soft and surprised by my presence. I don't blame him, considering how I left the last time I was here and denied any help. I hope he can look past that for what I'm about to request.

"I need your help." My voice comes out clear, but I make no effort to turn around, feeling the tightness in my stomach through the hot rage, scared to show him what I've become.

"Anything."

The quickness and willingness in his voice is what makes me turn, everything else but my surprise simmers away to nothing, as though that one word is like comforting ice-cold water to every emotion inside me.

When he sees the new red irises, shock opens his expression wide. "What happened?" he asks, stepping closer. He stops a few feet away, as though scared to rush me in my new state.

"I got jumped by a few rogue dragayastir on my way back from my first patrol. I was stupid enough to send my squad home while I spoke to a banshee about something and ... it was just Seb and I on the way home when we ran into them and a group of fae collecting bodies. I got stuck with the dragayastir and Seb was kidnapped by fae."

Ezekiel's jaw tense briefly and his eyes drop to the floor as though the object of tension is there. But as quickly as the tension appears, it's gone, replaced by a cool mask of calm as his eyes return to mine. "Do you remember who they were? I will punish those responsible for removing your choice." His eyes are like an inferno, mirroring the way I imagine mine must have looked when I discovered Seb's betrayal for the first time.

"I don't remember them. And it's my fault, really. I shouldn't have sent my squad away when it was unsafe to do so. Clearly I was not meant to be a Reaper." Despite the confidence in my voice, I only half-believe what I'm saying. I spent ages convincing myself it was the case, but I also know that a large part of my downfall is due to the recent sped-up training and early release into patrols before any of us were ready. I'm glad my whole squad hadn't been there — they might not have made it through either and that thought was one I struggle to even think on.

Ezekiel's lips press into a hard line, as though he is holding himself back from arguing. Mine are the same but for a whole different reason. Admitting my failures as a leader is also something I never thought I'd do so early.

"As your ally, I'm sorry I wasn't there to help," he finally says after leaving me to wonder if he'll fight me on my admission and make me talk on it more.

"Well, at least my curse is broken." I shrug, hoping we can move on quickly from how I've lost my dream and become one of the Other's.

"And what have you come to me for help with?"

"I need to break into a fae facility to find Seb," I say simply, hoping he won't dig into why and I can just get his help to do what needs to be done to sate the rage-filled heat inside me.

"I'm not sure that's possible. It would ruin any hope of future relations with the fae, and as the Animora Prince I can't, in good conscience, jeopardize peace like that."

"I have it on good authority that the owner of this facility will not *ever* be interested in peace," I say, thinking about what Morana had told me about the new King of the Fae's proposal to her as we formulated the plan. It is very clear he is more than happy to take advantage of recent events and has no inklings of ever letting the fae have peace with Others again, unless he is ruling over all of them.

"I can't do this to save your beloved, Belladonna. I'm sorry." Ezekiel moves closer until he is a mere step away. I glance up at him, wanting to ask how he can tell that Seb is my beloved, wondering if maybe he has still been keeping an eye on me when I hadn't realized. The question must have been written on my face because when he catches sight of my expression, he explains, "You don't think I can't smell his scent all over you? Exactly where his body has ... *lingered* against yours?"

Ezekiel's eyes trail along my body like he can see every place Seb's hands and mouth had stopped. I can't help the way my skin flushes under his gaze, as though I'm standing here wearing nothing but Seb's handprints. It's embarrassing, even more so knowing how foolish I was to let him touch my body the way he had, knowing what I do now.

Before I can stop it, my eyes heat with angry tears. I fight to blink them away before Ezekiel can spot them, but as his eyes return to mine, I know he has seen it. He waits, saying nothing, but his face opens as he realizes my struggle for words to speak about Seb.

"He's not my beloved," I try, my voice cracking on the last word. Ezekiel's eyebrows raise, but he continues to say nothing. "He made me think he was, but he ..." I ball my fists up as though I can funnel all my anger into my fingers. Running my tongue over my teeth behind closed lips, I hold back the words I don't want to say out loud. The angry tears well again as I break eye contact with Ezekiel and stare at the bookshelf over his shoulder, fighting the urge to punch the beautiful books.

"Azariah ..." Ezekiel whispers, bringing my focus back to him and away from the bookshelf. "I want you to know you can trust me with your secrets and tell me why you need my help."

A moment of silence passes. Then another.

It grows until it becomes a physical weight prodding me into admission, simply so I won't have to keep my mind spinning over thoughts of shame and anger at my own stupidity.

"He lied. He lured me into falling—" I'm unable to say it, hoping to find some other that could still convey how much of my anger is rooted in a pain I desperately need him to help me fix. "He made me think he cared but he stole my blood and used it to open the doorway to the Shadow Court. He's been working with the witches all along."

Ezekiel stays quiet for a moment, the muscles in his jaw and neck tensing as he digests what I said. "We will find him then," he says, resolutely.

He starts to move, turning to lead the way to somewhere we can perhaps formulate a plan or maybe he wants to head straight to the facility now.

Without thinking, I press a hand to the center of his chest and he stills beneath it. "I get to kill him though," I say, watching as understanding falls over his face.

He nods with an approving smile that makes shivers dance up my spine.

Chapter Forty-Three
The Air of War

Morana

The way Morana's stomach clenched with every step closer to the fae facility told her all she needed to know about what awaited her. As she led the way, her human banshee turned dragayastir acquaintance and Prince of the dragayastir followed quietly behind. She wasn't sure how a young girl who'd been a Reaper for such a short time had accumulated a powerful ally, but it was enough to make her confident in only having one person to assist them in their mission to find the ex-partner of Azariah's and kill him for his betrayal, not only to her, but to all of Skull's Rest. His struggle for power had meant he'd doomed all of the city to be subjected to the dangers of the Dark Courts. He was in league with a group that had been responsible for the death of Alva and unleashing a great evil upon the city that had taken so much from everyone to get it imprisoned the first time.

The closer the three of them got, the more silent and deliberate their steps were on the forest floor. The pace slowed, but they were able to dodge sticks, twigs, and anything else that might give away their position. As they neared the position of the facility, Morana could hear voices in the darkness ahead.

Ducking and weaving behind tree trunks, she led them closer, until the sight of the source made her still. Deep in the grove, exactly where King Malachai had said the building would be, was a giant metal monstrosity that looked out of place in fae woodland territory. In front of it stood the King himself, in whispered conversation with a witch Morana recognized.

Morana knew her place in this plan, even though they hadn't expected this to be waiting for them outside the facility. She looked back to where Azariah and Ezekiel's heads glanced out around the trunks of trees. She nodded to them without a word, letting them know in their silent, unspoken understanding that she had these enemies under control. With a nod back from each of them, she watched as they lifted the dark hoods that enveloped their black armored gear. Their red glowing irises were smothered by the darkness.

Turning back, Morana took a deep breath, feeling the weight of the bag that she carried across her body grow somehow heavier with every step out of the cover of the trees. The knowledge of what she was doing, even just to keep her cover, made it feel as though the weighted bag holding the evidence was going to drag her into the earth at any moment. The thought of what she was doing to keep the ruse made her sick to her stomach, but she had no other option.

Malachai spotted her as she moved into the light of the facility windows, clearing the treeline as she walked straight for the King and the witch. "Morana, what a surprise!" he said, his face breaking out into a smile that held no suspicion at all.

She worked to push her lips up in a mirroring expression, but she knew it didn't feel genuine. It couldn't, not when there was a dead body in her bag that she stole from its place of rest. Morana wasn't sure if the Unseelie fae required the same farewell ritual when they died, but if so, she had committed a disgusting act she wasn't sure she'd ever forgive herself for. She hoped she'd never have to find out the answer.

"I thought about your offer," Morana said clearly as she stopped a few steps from the two of them. They had turned to include her in their conversation. The witch beside her didn't smile, dark eyes narrowing as she pulled the hood back off her head, letting it drop to her shoulders and displaying white hair that looked as though it had lost all its color. Morana tried not to stare. Instead, she rested a hand on the bag at her hip, bringing Malachai's attention to the mound that sat securely held in it.

The changeling child had died before Morana found it, but she'd definitely used its death to her advantage when Azariah and her were formulating the plan. It had seemed like fate when they found the Unseelie fae child discarded in its human baby form outside the Culling tunnels to die. It had most likely died from starvation and probably discovered by the humans when they moved the children to the Reaper compound. There was no telling where the human child it had originally been swapped out with was now, but Morana held on to the thought of what it had stolen as she picked up its corpse and decided its fate was to gain her entry to the compound with King Malachai.

"Glad to see you've realized the good you can do for your own kind," Malachai commented as he looked between Morana and the witch. Morana wanted to argue with Malachai and tell him that he was not helping her kind at all, that he was ruining the peace they'd all enjoyed and thrived in, but knew that wasn't why she was here.

"Hi, I don't believe we've met," she said to the witch, extending her arm in greeting the way humans were accustomed to. "I'm Morana."

"A banshee helping out ... how *refreshing* ..." the witch responded, like the fae in question wasn't standing directly in front of her. "I'm Ravenna."

"Glad you two could meet," Malachai interrupts, looking between the two. "What did you bring us, Morana?"

The excitement in King Malachai's tone made Morana's stomach curl with disgust. Fighting not to show how true feelings on her face, she finally opened the bag, hoping the fates would forgive her as she showed off the corpse of the changeling child to the sadistic King who only cared about power.

All she could hope was Azariah and Ezekiel were quick and thorough in the facility before she had to sacrifice too much more of her soul for the sake of distraction ...

Chapter Forty-Four
HIDDEN IN THE EARTH
AZARIAH

Getting into the facility was surprisingly easy. If I hadn't known better, I would have thought this was a building to house nothing of consequence, but clearly the fae were too prideful to think they'd ever have anyone try to break in. The proof? It took me putting in my lock pick for a matter of seconds to get inside.

Honestly, with how wide-eyed Ezekiel had looked at me, I expected there to be a guard on the other side of the door waiting. Or maybe it was a surprise that the woman he'd been watching over for years was a lot more rebellious than he thought.

I didn't have time to ask.

Instead, I walk further into the facility, using my improved hearing to listen out for footsteps and other fae that might be lingering ahead. I hear screams, and for a facility that seems to be involved in the cause of destruction of Skull's Rest, it's surprisingly unmanned. I guess the King of the Fae isn't too open on sharing his dirty little experimental secrets to his kind, which I can only thank the fates means I'm able to dodge any other people with ease. I almost feel like it's too simple, but I try not to think on it for too long.

I'm not going to question my blessings.

I duck my head around a corridor before I turn into it, checking it's empty. At the first door, I pull out my lock picks again, glad I'm getting to test them out. Even though the Culling tunnels had been nearly doorless, it hadn't stopped me from learning how to get through locks on other buildings in Skull's Rest to test out my skills. I had to make sure that I was proficient for just this sort of occasion to arise.

We push inside to find a plain room loaded with papers on a desk and a cabinet that seems to house even more. Ezekiel follows me, saying nothing. He's there to assist me as needed. We slip inside the room, shutting and locking the door from the inside. It's dimly lit, the candle chandeliers that hang from the ceiling nearly burned out with how long they've been going, and it smells musty, like this room is always closed away from the rest for the building. Still, I know that I should collect intel while I'm here. Even if Seb's death is the main goal, I need to make sure that other options are checked out. It could save lives that have been endangered by him, and maybe reverse some of what has been done.

At least that's what I hope.

The notes and scribblings on various pieces of parchment are messy and disorganized, written in the fae native language. Ezekiel picks up pages and glances at them, but it becomes clear very quickly that he is getting nothing out of it. I, however, am feeling very cold, despite the warm air around me. My stomach clenches so tight, I'm afraid it might disappear.

"You can read this?" Ezekiel asks as he glances up, noticing the color draining from my face as the cold reaches my expression.

I nod quickly, swallowing the lump that's forming in the back of my throat. "I don't think we can leave all this information here in the hands of the King."

"And why's that?"

I glance up from the notes King Malachai has on species, ones that could only be retrieved by torturing live specimens and try to figure out how to describe all the horrors I'm reading about.

My mouth opens, but for a moment, it seems uselessly silent. "Judging by the witch outside with him, it's clear that not only was Seb working with the witches, but the King of the Fae was, too. On top of that, he's establishing weaknesses and capabilities of every race in Skull's Rest and, from what I can tell, researching weapons to kill them on a *massive* scale. This is nothing like the Reaper guides. This is calculated and so far from peaceful. I ... we can't let him keep this information. It will kill every non-fae if we do."

I've been scared before and shaking, but it's nothing compared to the dread that empties my bones of their marrow, like I'm being sucked dry by being in this place.

"What are you suggesting?" Ezekiel asks with furrowed brows.

"That once I find Seb and get the answers I need, we torch this place."

His widen. "There are *people* in here. Ones that could very well be innocent in all this. Victims. Researchers who don't know better."

"It's better than the torture they're experiencing now, I can tell you that," I say quickly, looking down at the notes in my hands that tell me I'm right. "And the researchers are far from innocent."

Chapter Forty-Five
The Fires of Rage

Azariah

The sight of Seb unrestrained and reclining on a long, cushioned seat makes me want to stab him where he stands.

After doors and doors opened to find more research, corpses used for experimentation, one or two researchers still around that had to be killed swiftly by Ezekiel to ensure they didn't alert anyone, and live subjects that looked worse off than anyone else I'd ever seen, we finally found Seb. He didn't look up at first as we entered the unlocked room, reading some parchment in front of him, unaware of the new company. When I purposely made my steps click on the stone floor and shut the door behind me, he didn't look worried to see me.

He should have been.

"Az, you came for me!" he says, eyes wide and a smile breaking out across his face. Something about his excitement and obliviousness makes my heart dance in my chest in anticipation of the moment I get to break it to him. The dark, murderous anger is ready to revel my own deception. It's only fair.

The ruse is up ... Well, not yet.

I want to see how far he will take this.

"Oh, God, I'm so sorry I wasn't there to help!" he continues, catching sight of my irises.

"Of course I came for you!" I gasp, ignoring his clear reference to the new color of my eyes and moving closer to him. Looking around at where he stands, pretending not to know or realize that he is *clearly* a guest of the fae and was never at risk of death or torture. "You're not … tied up?"

"Oh!" My new quick reflexes don't miss the way his eyes dart around as he fumbles for words. The old me would have bought it, but I know better now. "They didn't really think a *human* was much of a threat, and they made me a deal that if I complied with their … experiments that they'd spare tying me up."

"Experiments? That's horrible, Seb!" I step closer again, trying not to cringe as his hands touch me. One pulls me closer to him by my waist, and the other cups my cheek as his eyes meet mine.

"I'm so glad you're here."

The space in my chest where the warmth of my feelings should be is searingly hot. It's a miracle I don't burn from the inside out.

I can't take it any longer.

My eyes prickle with hot tears.

"So you can steal more of my blood?" I say, hearing the darkness take over my voice. I get an odd sense of satisfaction as I watch the realization take over his face and the happiness to see me slips away like it has been slapped off.

His hand drops away from my face and reaches for his weapon. With my new dragayastir speed, it seems like a crawling pace. I can act quicker than him. Hitting his wrist hard, I hear the clatter of the knife hit the ground as I shove him into the wall, my hand holding his throat in warning. All it would take would be to squeeze and I could watch the life drain out of him in minutes.

But I need answers and there is no way I'm not taking my time with his death.

"Why?"

His face hardens, making me realize that the person I knew is completely fake. The ruse is up, and the cruel and arrogant triumph written all over his face reminds me of Jayden in every way that makes me hot with rage.

I never knew him at all.

"Why what?" he asks, as though he doesn't know exactly what I'm talking about.

"You could have stolen my blood any other way. Why push so hard for me to trust you, to like you, to *move in* with you?"

"Oh, come on, you were begging me to. You wanted someone to break through your walls and prove you were worthy of love so badly that you almost made it too easy." The cruel smile pulling his lips up ever so slightly tightens the ends of my fingers, straining his voice. "Plus, my brother said the fuck was worth it."

I hear the low growl from Ezekiel standing watch at the door, but I keep my eyes forward.

Fear flits through Seb's eyes as he glances at Ezekiel over my shoulder, almost so fast that if I hadn't been paying attention, I would've missed it, but it all makes sense. He's goading me into killing him quick.

He's not fucking getting that mercy.

"Aww, bloodsucker, you want a taste too, don't you? Are you mad I got there first?"

I flex my hand against his throat, watching him intently as he returns his attention to me. The arrogant mask slips back over his features.

"Why make a deal with the witches? You know how untrustworthy they are. They trade their souls for power!" I say, hoping to get through to him to at least make him realize that doing deals with the witches was a mistake. It's evidently clear that he doesn't care about me, but his own self-preservation might make him think twice.

"And do you know how much power they really have? They could rule this whole city if they wanted to and they will." The confidence in his voice makes me sick. "And I'll be right there with them."

"That won't happen. They will be stopped, and you're not walking out of here."

He chuckles breathily as my hand grips tighter again, robbing him of some of his breath. "I think I chose the winning side."

My lips curl back as the saliva in my mouth sours. "And why is that?"

"Because you won't do what it takes." Something about the way he meets my gaze so steadily as he says it, a challenge to everything I've worked for my entire life, is the final straw. I have everything I need now. He never cared, and he never will. I made the mistake of trusting anyone in his family.

They are just as soulless as those they wanted to become.

"You want to bet on that?" I ask and press my closed fist against the middle point of his chest.

"I'd bet my life on it," he whispers, his smirk pulling up every time my lip twitches in disgust.

Just like everyone else who's underestimated me, it's his fatal mistake.

"You want to know a secret?" I whisper, my words clipped as I lean closer to him. "You are a speck of dust in the food chain. The witches were never going to give you what you wanted, and even if you found a way to get their power, you were always going to be weak."

He looks mildly amused by my words. But I see the way he stares, unblinking. He swallows hard, and his heartrate spikes. The burning in my chest is sated slightly by his fear.

Only slightly.

"Oh?" he breathes, inviting me to keep talking as he glances toward the door, hoping someone will come spare him.

"Because you underestimated what I will do to those who cross me."

I recoil my hand quickly and shove it with all my strength into his chest. It's surprisingly easy with my dragayastir brute force to punch through his ribs. I have to pull the punch before I continue into his spine and the wall. The inside of his chest is warm and wet. I don't care that it's swimming in his blood and internal organs — I know what I'm looking for.

His eyes widen as his last realization and pain let him know that my fist has securely gripped his heart. I feel it trying to pump in my hand, an organ he doesn't deserve to have. With all the heat and rage fueling me, I don't think twice as I rip it from his chest, watching the awareness fade as his eyes became unfocused and his mouth opens in silent agony.

Ezekiel says nothing behind me, but I feel the weight of his stare as I stand there and watch Seb's body crumple to the ground against the wall, blood smearing behind him.

"Time to burn this place to the ground," I say, gripping the heart of my last mistake.

I drop the bloody organ to the ground, relishing in the squelch of it landing at my feet. With a satisfied grin, I lick the blood off my fingertips as I exit, Seb's lifeless soul trailing after me.

So...what did you think?

If you enjoyed the story and want to see more in future, your feedback is INVALUABLE.

If you could take 5 minutes out of your day to leave a review on your preferred platform, it would be greatly appreciated.

CONTENT WARNING

This book contains mentions or depictions of:

Explicit language

Scenes of violence

Death

Reader discretion is advised.

ACKNOWLEDGEMENTS

The first thank you I have to make is to the amazing readers, like you, supporting my storytelling. You're amazing and every book sold makes my heart sing with so much happiness that I can't even describe it. Being an author is something I've dreamed of as a kid and seeing it out in the world and reading everyone's thoughts is one of the greatest feelings in the world.

There are so many people that have helped me on this journey—and continue to—and, in particular, this book.

The top of this list of thank you's is Ben. My real life book boyfriend. You have kept me accountable and happy, making sure I eat, sleep and take breaks from my hyperfixations. You've been a cheerleader for me (and sometimes even a chauffeur to events) and I can never express how much I appreciate it all. You are my true life book boyfriend I'm so thankful I found, and my authoring and life wouldn't be as good as it is without you.

Next, my incredible beta readers who helped me see what was missing from my story early on and cheered me on as I wrote ahead of them. Steph, Kerty and Sarah—you are all incredible women that have spared time out of your lives to support my work and give me your honest feedback. I can only hope the story is everything you wanted it to be to repay those efforts. Thank you!

My incredible new editor for this book—who will absolutely be back for many more—Chloe Higgins. Your comments, efficiency and communication have been an amazing help through this process and helped improve my writing for future books to come.

To my supportive friends and family who have made chasing my dreams much easier, I'll never be able to thank you enough but I hope I can show you through my actions and words. You have changed my world for the better.

About the Author

Harley Jane Rose is a force to be reckoned with. Or, at least, she's striving to be. Be it writing, reading, social media, dance, or craft, Harley is always striving to try anything life has to offer. Anyone who knows her will tell you she's someone who only ever gives 100%, and the amount of heart she puts into her stories is no exception.

She draws inspiration from every aspect of her life. Her travels, friends, lived experience and instinct are just a few of these sources drawn upon when sculpting new worlds and characters.

Harley Jane Rose's stories can be described as both psychological and heart-wrenching. Despite this, her worlds are full of fantasy, romance, hope, horror and much more.

You can find Harley on any of her social media profiles under the username: Harley Jane Rose.

www.ingramcontent.com/pod-product-compliance
Lightning Source LLC
Chambersburg PA
CBHW020259120726
47904CB00001B/261